Scribe Publications
LOVE AND THE PLATYPUS

Nicholas Drayson is a novelist and naturalist. His first novel, *Confessing a Murder*, was critically acclaimed in the UK and the US and short-listed for *The Age* Book of the Year. His essay 'Strictly for the Birds' won the 2003 inaugural international WildCare Tasmania Nature Writing Prize.

Born and raised in England he now lives in Australia, so instead of newts and sticklebacks in his pond he now has frogs and galaxias. He is consultant to the National Museum of Australia on platypus acquisitions.

Love and the Platypus

NICHOLAS DRAYSON

SCRIBE
Melbourne

Scribe Publications Pty Ltd
PO Box 523
Carlton North, Victoria, Australia 3054
Email: info@scribepub.com.au

First published by Scribe 2007
This edition published 2008

Copyright © Nicholas Drayson 2007

All rights reserved. Without limiting the rights under copyright reserved above, no part of this publication may be reproduced, stored in or introduced into a retrieval system, or transmitted, in any form or by any means (electronic, mechanical, photocopying, recording or otherwise) without the prior written permission of the publisher of this book.

Edited by Aviva Tuffield
Typeset in 11/15 pt Simoncini Garamond
Cover designed by Miriam Rosenbloom
Printed and bound in Australia by Griffin Press

National Library of Australia
Cataloguing-in-Publication data

Drayson, Nicholas.

Love and the platypus / author, Nicholas Drayson.

Carlton North, Vic. : Scribe Publications, 2008.

9781921215995 (pbk.)

Naturalists--Australia--Fiction.
Scientific expeditions--Australia--Fiction.
Platypus--Australia--Fiction.

A823.4

www.scribepublications.com.au

There is a land in distant seas
Full of all contrarieties.
There beasts have mallards' bills and legs,
Have spurs like cocks, like hens lay eggs.
There kangaroos go on two feet,
And yet few quadrupeds so fleet:
As for the trees, another wonder,
Leaves without upper side or under.
There birds construct them shady bowers,
Deck'd with bright feathers, shells, and flowers;
Others a hot-bed join to make,
To hatch the eggs which they forsake.
There missiles to far distance sent
Come whizzing back with force unspent.
The sun, when you to face him turn ye,
From right to left performs his journey.
The North winds scorch; but when the breeze is
Full from the South, why then it freezes.
There vice is virtue, virtue vice,
And all that's vile is voted nice.
Now of what lands can such strange tales
Be told? — Queensland and New South Wales.

Extract from *The Southlanders* by M. Fox (1860)

one

Of all the Mammalia yet known the water-mole seems the most extraordinary in its conformations. Future observation, made in its native regions will, it is hoped, make us fully acquainted with natural history of an animal which differs so widely from all other quadrupeds, and which verifies in so striking a manner the observation of Buffon; viz. That whatever was possible for Nature to produce has actually been produced.
George Shaw, *The Naturalists' Miscellany,* 1799

And what, thought William, should he do now? He sat on the edge of the wharf, its timbers already warmed by the sun, and turned his head towards the dusty track. Someone would be along soon, surely. His eyes were drawn back to the water of the river flowing brown beneath his feet. On the far bank tangled roots of mangrove trees clawed from the mud. What curious plants, with roots that seemed to go not down but up into the air. William stroked the unfamiliar roughness of his chin. An unseen bird sang from an unknown tree. A large wasp droned past.

It was as long as his little finger, its black body connected to a yellow abdomen by an impossibly long and slender waist. As it flew under the loading platform beside him he noticed that it appeared to be carrying something in its mouth. It landed on one of the posts that supported the platform, not two yards away. He could see its wings, now folded along its back, vibrating in short bursts — *dzz, dzz*. It stuck whatever was in its mouth to the post then flew away fast and straight towards the river. He realised that wasp had been carrying mud, and that it was building a nest.

William was immediately taken back to his Scottish childhood, when on a summer's morning he would wander up onto the hills behind the house and sit for hours among the heath, watching a delicate little potter wasp build her flask-shaped nest on a heather stem. Then spend further hours watching while she stocked the clay nest with small limp caterpillars for her young to feed on. This wasp, though ten times the size, must surely be an antipodean relative.

How long had he been in this strange country now — three, nearly four weeks? From a Cambridge spring to an Australian autumn (no, that was not true; there was surely no autumn here, only different gradations of summer). He looked out across the mangroves to where the sun was already climbing in the sky. His fingers wandered from chin via cheek to upper lip. A late monsoon storm had made the journey up the coast from Brisbane too rough to use a razor. What good was a moustache if its effect was lost among a sea of unshaven whiskers? He would be glad to get to the hotel and have a bath and a shave. If he got to the hotel. Once more he turned to look up the track.

The loading platform was about twelve feet long and six feet wide, built smack in the middle of the wharf. Massive trunks, unhewn, formed its legs. Rough-sawn planks its floor. Sun-bleached and cracked, both wharf and loading platform looked as if they had been there for decades, though the date carved deep on the rubbing strake — '1879' — told him that they were only four years old.

'Last one got washed away in the flood of '78,' the skipper had told him earlier that morning as they watched his equipment being unloaded.

There was no crane on the wharf. His crates, cases, trunks and boxes — all twenty-two of them — were piled up where the ship's derrick had dropped them. Now that the wasp had gone all was quiet. The river flowed fast but silent on the ebb tide. No wind stirred the leaves of the trees that lined its banks or raised dust from the ground. Nor were any human voices to be heard.

According to the gazetteer the wharf was some five miles from the main town of Bundaberg. William had long ago made his arrangements to be picked up — he had the letter of confirmation in his pocket. Not only that but the skipper made a point of sounding the steam whistle as they came up the river.

'That'll rouse 'em.'

He was beginning to fear the skipper's confidence misplaced. Standing up to take a watch from his trouser pocket, he looked again up the dusty track that led to the town. Nearly an hour and still no sign of anyone. He could always walk, but would it be safe to leave the luggage?

The wasp returned, another ball of mud in her jaws (he realised now it must be a female — only female wasps build nests). This nest was taking shape as a long, hollow cylinder as wide as his thumb, with clear rings as each new section of wet mud was added to the last. Already the air was warm enough to dry the mud before the wasp had returned with her next load. He wiped his brow. Yes, it was definitely warming up. But the thin shade offered by the vertical leaves of the tree growing beside the wharf — a gum tree? — was hardly worth moving for. He took off his hat, mopped his brow with a large, green silk handkerchief and sat back down.

There was a pattern in the wasp's visits. A long interval between two arrivals — five or six minutes, he timed it with his watch — was followed by a shorter one of two minutes, then a long one, then another short one. Why? He looked at the insect working away at its nest, then at the pile of boxes and crates beside him. He had not brought himself and all this equipment from the other side of the world to study insects, but surely there was no reason why he could not include a little old-fashioned nature study in his programme. The spirit of discovery — that was why he was here, was it not? Perhaps even this small creature had secrets to reveal. When next the wasp appeared he was on his feet; when she had finished her work he was ready.

The wasp headed towards the river, flying at about breast height. Hat in hand, William jumped from the back of the wharf and ran after her. The wasp flew fast but he was able to keep her in view and saw her drop down to water's edge. He arrived only a few seconds afterwards, panting for breath. The wasp had not landed on one of the extensive patches of mud that now lined the bank of the ebbing river but on a flat pebble at the water's edge. She took a few steps towards the water and bent forward. Her abdomen pulsed. The insect was clearly drinking. After less than a minute she stepped back from the water and took off into the air, heading back towards the wharf.

She flew slower this time, presumably weighed down by her load, and he was able to keep close behind her. About five yards from the wharf the wasp dropped down onto a patch of bare earth that looked like a dried-out puddle. And as he watched, she began to make her very own mud.

Out of the wasp's mouth emerged a small sphere of water, sparkling in the sun. The droplet slowly grew until it was hanging from her jaws like a dewdrop from a blade of grass. She lowered her head, letting the water be sucked into the parched earth, and began kneading the wetted soil with her jaws and forelegs. When she had formed the mud into a round ball the shape and size of a small pea she picked it up in her jaws and flew up to the wharf.

As William watched the insect add the fresh mud to its nest he reflected on what he had just seen. The wasp had not simply gathered its building material, it had *manufactured* it. How marvellous that this little insect, a creature with a brain probably no larger than the head of a pin, could engage in such a complex — such an apparently premeditated — action. No wonder that people saw nature as proof of God the Great Designer. But how much more wonderful, he thought, and he smiled as he thought it, had Mr Darwin shown nature to be.

His professor at Cambridge, the famous Frank Balfour, told of once visiting Charles Darwin at his home in Downe in Kent.

'It was,' he said, 'like meeting Moses wearing worsted.'

Both were now dead. But while Darwin had been an old man of seventy-three when he died, the dashing young Professor Frank Balfour had been killed in a climbing accident when he was only a few weeks past his thirtieth birthday. In different ways William still mourned them both. Yet even they would have agreed with the brutal fact: no death, no natural selection. That the size and shape and colour, that every action of this wasp — of every living thing upon the earth — had been crafted and honed not by some mythical Creator but by the one great force of natural selection, now that was wonder indeed.

The wasp finished moulding her ball of mud and flew off towards the river. No, not towards the river. She again dropped down onto the dried-up puddle. Another drop of water emerged from her mouth, another mud ball made. The wasp again picked it up and flew the few yards back to the platform to continue her nest building. Wonder upon wonder. The insect had stored enough water in her crop to make more than one ball of mud. And this explained the different timing between each visit. A long trip to the river, then a short trip to the mud works. How efficient, how — there was only one word that seemed to sum up what William had just seen — how beautiful.

He squinted up at the sun and again at his watch. Nearly two hours. It looked as though he might have to walk into town after all even if it did mean leaving all his stuff sitting there. But as he got to his feet he heard a sharp crack, then another crack accompanied by a distant human voice, shouting. A minute later another, louder crack, and this time he thought he could make out a few words. Words, but not their meanings. He looked up the track to see a long line of bullocks appearing round the bend, pulling an enormous wagon, and on the wagon a man. In his hand was a long whip.

'Haul up there, you carny scaff-raffs, haul up.' (That, at least, is what it surely sounded like.) The whip cracked again and the wagon pulled up just short of the wharf. Its driver climbed down and walked — or was that swayed? — over to where William was now standing beside his pile of luggage.

He spoke again, and William saw that the words he had been speaking had not only to squeeze past the short pipe clenched between jaws that appeared completely bereft of teeth, they then had to fight their way through a grizzled beard.

'I'm sorry …?'

The man took the pipe from his mouth. ''Arry Norton.'

'Ah yes,' said William, taking a letter from his pocket. 'Mr Norton.'

Now that the man had finally arrived William felt his patience dissolve. He had a strong inclination to make clear to this taciturn yokel his annoyance at being kept waiting for so long. But hang on — what was it his uncle Angas used to say about Englishmen? *Strange creatures, Sassernachs, like bairns and beasts. A kind word works better than a curse.* Perhaps Australians were like that, too.

The man grunted and began to walk slowly round the pile of crates and suitcases. Harry Norton was not a tall man, but wide and strong. He pushed at one of the two largest crates, eight feet square and a couple of feet thick, standing upright on the ground. His face creased into a frown.

'Larty duggers,' he said, looking round at William and still frowning.

'I did say in the letter, Mr Norton ...'

'Letter?' The man looked him in the face for a long second then grunted once more.

He walked over to one of the smaller boxes, leant over it and lifted. 'Humph.' He sniffed, letting the box back down. He looked at the large crates again, then towards the wagon. 'Right,' he said.

The bullock team was a mixed bunch of what William supposed to be shorthorns — not quite the thing for the Lord Mayor's carriage but no doubt satisfactory for their purpose.

As the man passed the lead animal it raised its head. The man thrust his own face towards it. 'Dush me, would you?' But he took hold of the animal's trace gently enough and led the team forwards until the side of the wagon was lined up beside the loading bay.

The bullock driver climbed back up onto the cart and pulled hard on the wooden lever beside the rough plank that served as seat. Worn timber brake blocks closed on the iron rims of the two back wheels. He went to the rear of the wagon, unhooked two wooden wedges tied to bits of well-frayed rope and kicked them into place beneath the offside wheel. Taking two buckets that had been hanging from other hooks at the back of the wagon, he walked down to river. The bullocks waited, snorting and farting, while he carried the buckets of brown water back and swung them onto the ground before each of the rear animals. They sniffed the water, then drank. Harry Norton turned, spat on his hands and clapped them together in preparation for work.

The wasp buzzed towards the loading platform. William saw that it was again carrying a ball of mud.

'You will be interested to know, I am sure, Mr Norton, that during the three hours I have been waiting on this dock' — he paused just long enough to let the words sink in — 'I have not been idle.'

The bullock driver looked up at him, unclasped his hands and gave a grunt, which could equally have been understood as expressing interest or the complete opposite. Taking it as the former, William proceeded to tell him about the marvellous events he had just been watching.

'So you see, don't you,' he finished, 'the *efficiency* of the whole operation. I mean, lots of birds build nests of mud — swallows and such-like — but they simply find a patch of mud near a river or a pond and use that. It would be much simpler for the wasp to do exactly the same thing, but it would be less efficient. By carrying only water and making the mud on site, as it were, the wasp ends up having to carry much less weight overall.'

Harry Norton had been looking at William during his whole oration without any noticeable change of expression. Now he turned his back on him, climbed onto the loading platform where William's things lay piled and tested another of the crates.

'Clever little bleener then, ain't it?' he said, not looking round. 'Think it could carry something for me?'

'Oh, here,' said William, 'let me help you.'

He scrambled onto the platform and took hold of one end of the crate that the man was about to lift. And immediately dropped it with a yelp of pain. His right hand flew to his mouth.

'Just a splinter,' he said, examining the injury.

The man took hold of his hand and, after a brief glance, dropped it. Another sniff. 'Thicker skin on a nun's tuddy. Best leave 'em to me.'

'Well, yes, all right — if you don't mind. I might just go and see if I can do something about this. I think I've got some forceps in my kit.'

William wandered over to one of the smaller suitcases, sucking at his wound. Though it hadn't gone deep, it was a very large splinter. He extracted a cloth bundle, unrolled it and withdrew a pair of fine forceps. Sitting down on a sack that the man had just thrown from the wagon onto the platform — judging from the feel of it, it seemed to be tightly stuffed with wool or something similar — he began digging away at his finger. Damn — he'd broken off the end of it. Now it would have to be a job for a scalpel.

As a small child, William had delighted in examining the contents of the pale wooden box that contained his father's medical kit. One drawer for scalpels and lancets, one for scissors and forceps, a third for needles and syringes. On the other side of the box were two deeper, shallow drawers whose fronts hinged down to reveal jars and bottles of powders and liquids, some blue glass, some clear. Each bore a label — *Sal. Vol., Antim., Sub. Corr., Ipec., Nux Vom.* But it was look don't touch, and William had always been an obedient child. Before he had entered Professor Frank Balfour's laboratory for his first class in vertebrate anatomy, William had never handled a scalpel in his life.

It was his fourth week at Cambridge, and he was sitting with thirty other eager young men on the benches of the new natural sciences room behind the Corn Exchange. The young professor let his gaze wander slowly along the rows of students, catching the eye of each in turn. From his breast pocket he took what appeared to be a steel pen. When he removed the cap they saw not a nib but a small, curved blade.

'Welcome, gentlemen,' said the professor. 'Today, I will be teaching one of the most valuable lessons that you will ever learn.'

He held up the scalpel.

'This is the instrument of our trade, gentlemen. This. Not the trap to catch with, not the lens to see with, nor the pen to write with. This is the anatomist's truest friend.'

All eyes fixed on the gleaming steel.

'Modest in appearance though she be, her powers are vast. She makes visible the invisible, she lets light into dark places. It is she above all who unlocks the secrets of the organism. Though she is made from the finest steel, from the strongest metal man can forge, yet she is a delicate thing. She will bend so far but no further. She passes joyfully through tough tendons but starts at the feel of bone. She does not faint at the sight of blood or other aqueous fluids but if too long immersed she will lose her desire to please us. You must treat her well, gentlemen, you must treat her kindly. Do so, and you will be well rewarded.'

No one spoke. The professor looked around the room, again holding each student's eyes in turn. The scalpel, though still held lightly between his fingers and thumb, now seemed to William suspended in air.

'Above all, gentlemen, you must keep her appetite sharp. You must keep her hungry. You must keep her honed to such keenness that she will cut through flesh as a swallow flies through air. She will pass through veins and arteries like a shark through water, she will sever sinew like a cleaver through a cucumber.'

He reached into one pocket of his jacket and took out a small rectangular box.

'Today, gentlemen, for your first and most important lesson, you are going to learn how to sharpen a scalpel. Gather round.'

The students formed an eager circle around the table where Frank Balfour had placed the box.

'The scalpel, you will note, is of carbon steel, manufactured by Herr Huppmann of Jensz. I am using castor oil, Bromley's Egyptian, No. 4. The stone is, of course, from Arkansas in the United States of America.'

The professor opened the box to reveal a smaller rectangle within, pale brown in colour.

'Gentlemen, the Arkansas stone.'

As the professor expounded on the matchless properties of this American whetstone for putting an edge on a blade, and why Egyptian castor oil is superior to any other for lubricating the stone, William found his eyes still riveted on the little steel blade. The professor showed how to grip the scalpel, how to apply the blade to the stone, what angle and pressure to use, what movements to make, and how to 'finish off' on the small piece of oiled horsehide that was glued to the back of the box — just two light wipes. They could test the blade for sharpness on thread or cloth, he told them, but never, ever, on paper.

'And now, gentlemen, shall I ask our friend if she is ready to begin her work?'

From another pocket he removed a large, green handkerchief, held it for a moment above the scalpel, then let it fall. As the silk square drifted down to settle over the professor's outstretched hand the students gasped to see, poking out from a small slit in its centre, an inch of bright steel.

Frank Balfour smiled. 'I think we have our answer. And that, gentlemen, concludes your first lesson.'

Harry Norton had thrown three more sacks over towards one of the large crates and arranged them casually with his foot. He grunted for William to move from the sack he was sitting on, still digging at his splinter. When he was satisfied with the positioning of all four he got behind the crate.

'Nothing ... fragile?' he said.

Before William had a chance to reply he heaved against the crate with his shoulder. It teetered, then toppled forward. But the sacks broke its fall just as he knew they would and it fell with a soft thump. Harry Norton jumped down onto the wharf and slid out three thick planks from somewhere under the wagon. He placed one end of each carefully into matching recesses at the edge of the wagon, resting the other ends on the loading platform. From the way he handled them they looked heavy.

'Tallow-wood,' he said. 'Best for this kind of work.' His face softened slightly. 'Best for dance floors, too.'

William tried to picture this squat, toothless bullock driver gliding over a dance floor. As if he could read his thoughts Harry Norton gave him a look that dared him to smile. William turned his attention back to his finger.

The bullock driver now took several ropes and pulleys that had been hanging from the front of the wagon and began threading and knotting. With two sets of blocks and tackle, with hawsers attached to stanchions and with much heaving and sweating, he began easing one of the heavy crates up the planks and onto the wagon. Once it was on board he picked up a crowbar and levered it slowly along until it was as far forward as it would go. After checking by eye that the crate was loaded centrally, he jumped down from the wagon and refilled the buckets, giving them to the next pair of bullocks up the line, then set to work on the other large crate.

William put down the scalpel. The incision should be deep enough by now to use the forceps. It was. As he held up the sliver of wood for closer inspection he heard the now familiar buzz. Mr Norton seemed to be getting on fine by himself with the loading. With finger once more in mouth, William turned his attention again to the wasp.

Her mud nest was now about three inches long and still open at one end. She flew away again, not south towards the river this time, but west. After about ten minutes she returned, bringing with her a long, green shape grasped between her jaws and hanging down backwards between her legs. A caterpillar. The wasp disappeared headfirst into the nest with her prey, emerging after a few seconds to fly off west again. A few minutes later she returned with another caterpillar, a little smaller than the first.

Over the next half hour William counted eight caterpillars of various sizes being taken into the nest. After the last one was carefully stowed he watched her reverse her abdomen into the hole at the top of the nest and he knew she must be laying her egg. Just like the little potter wasp of home, this wasp had laid in a food store for her young. Though the caterpillars appeared lifeless, the wasp's sting had only paralysed them. They would be living food for the young wasp grub to feast upon when it hatched from the egg. William put the scalpel and forceps back in their bundle and replaced them in the bag.

From that first lesson with Frank Balfour, William had come to delight in dissection. Physiology, histology, taxonomy and even embryology, none could compare to the anatomical revelations of scalpel, scissors and probe. The way this muscle attached to that bone, the way each bone articulated with its neighbour, the way the circulatory vessels and nerves wound into and round and through the whole. And the way the cold steel of the scalpel could take on the warmth of your hand and become part of your own body, your own mind.

But along with increasing enthusiasm came a small exasperation. At the end of his second year at Cambridge, when he had already been taken under Frank Balfour's wing as one of the most gifted and promising undergraduates that the Zoology Department had seen for many a year, he was still unable to reproduce the professor's trick with blade and handkerchief. The fact that no other student could do it was neither here nor there. Had not William bought scalpels from the finest surgical instrument-makers, the purest oil, the most expensive Arkansas stone? In desperation he built up enough courage to ask if he might use the professor's own scalpel and stone. Frank Balfour had handed them over with a wordless smile, and continued to smile as he watched his student apply oil to blade, blade to stone, then finish off on the horsehide. Without a word he reached into his pocket and passed William his handkerchief. When it came to rest over William's hand, the sharpened blade remained stubbornly hidden beneath.

Despite this failure to whet his scalpel's appetite to ultimate keenness, William took ever-increasing pleasure in the secrets it revealed. Who would have thought that the elongated finger bones of a bat could be recognised in the foot of a rhinoceros? The digestive system — mouth, stomach, liver, intestine — was the same whether in a mouse or a whale. There was an underlying unity to living things that only the blade could reveal, and William rejoiced in acquiring the anatomist's skills and practising them on anything from shrews and hedgehogs to tortoises and ptarmigan. And Professor Balfour was noted for providing his students with more exotic specimens. On one occasion a large crate had arrived at the laboratory containing folded within it a dead giraffe. The animal had choked to death in the London Zoo after swallowing a cricket ball hit into its enclosure from adjoining Regent's Park during a match between St John's Wood Grammar School and Merchant Taylors', and though the story made page three of *The Times* what impressed William most was to find out by dissection that the seven cervical vertebrae in the giraffe's neck, although greatly elongated, were no more in number than those of any other mammal. Most of the students' work, however, was on cats.

The use of dead cats as subjects for dissection had long been established at Cambridge University. Their procurement had also become a tradition. William soon learned that any self-respecting Cambridge undergraduate would no more buy a cat for dissection, or even breed one, than shoot a fox or sell his sister to a Chinaman. There was only one way to get a cat — yourself. Firearms, traps and poison were the usual methods. The well-aimed brickbat was favoured by the elite, though for the true sportsman only the bare-handed approach would do. The resulting scars were worn as proudly by Cambridge zoology undergraduates as those of any Prussian duellist.

The wasp headed back to the river. Two more mud balls were all it took for her to seal off the open end of her nest. Yes, thought William, how wonderful was nature, how perfect in all her parts. He looked over to where the bullock driver was now lifting the last of the smaller boxes bodily onto the cart. And this country, how fascinating a place.

two

We are favoured by the Literary and Philosophical Society of Newcastle upon Tyne, with the figures and descriptions of a very rare animal, sent to them from New South Wales, by James Hunter Esq., Governor of that settlement. It seems to be an animal *sui generis*; it appears to possess a threefold nature, that of a fish, a bird, and a quadruped, and is related to nothing that we have hitherto seen.

Thomas Bewick, *History of Quadrupeds*, 1800

It had been Frank Balfour that had first put the idea of going to Australia into William's head. One spring morning in 1882 the young professor strode into his Cambridge laboratory waving the *Daily Telegraph* in his hand (Frank Balfour seemed forever to be waving things, no matter whether they be made of paper or sharpened steel).

'Take a look at this, laddie.'

He threw the newspaper down on the bench where William had been preparing some microscope slides for that afternoon's lecture — one of his many tasks now that he was the professor's junior demonstrator.

'See?' he said, pointing to a headline. '"Giant Ape Thought to Be Missing Link." Who writes this stuff? Missing link — missing brain more like.'

William was about to say something — though he was never quite sure what to say when his professor was in one of these moods — but Frank Balfour was not finished.

'Missing links, living fossils: terms that do no more than admit our own ignorance. Just because it lives somewhere that *we* don't. Just because *we* haven't seen it before. But,' he said, perching himself on the bench beside William, 'on the other hand, there is *Ornithorhynchus anatinus*. The platypus, now there's a prize.'

He folded the paper and slapped his open palm. 'First of all — do the blighters lay eggs or don't they? Owen still says they don't, still says they're ovoviviparous and give birth to live young — but then Owen still says species don't evolve, doesn't he? Meanwhile the Frenchies insist that they do lay eggs, and as far as I've read most of the population of Australia seem to agree with 'em. But to find out who's right, that's only half the prize. If we could get our hands on the full embryological sequence — from ovum or egg or whatever it is, through to when they're weaned, say — what couldn't we discover, eh, William?'

What indeed? Ontogeny recapitulates phylogeny, just as Haeckel said. Did not even the human embryo have little gill slits at one stage, just like its fishy ancestor? Did it not have a tail? The development of the embryo: that was surely the key to the relationship between all living things. Again William opened his mouth to speak, again his professor forestalled him.

'Are they close to marsupials, are they close to reptiles? Are they an ancient lineage or a modern offshoot? I have a feeling, laddie,' said Frank Balfour, 'that the dear old platypus might be the key to solving more than one problem. I've half a mind to pop over to Australia myself to have a look.'

And perhaps the young professor would have popped over to Australia to have a look if five weeks later he had not fallen off that Swiss Alp on his annual climbing holiday. The following year, when William applied for and was awarded Cambridge University's inaugural Balfour Memorial Scholarship, what better way to spend the most-generous stipend than on a trip (no, an 'expedition') to Australia. Two hundred pounds a year for three years — that was nearly six times a demonstrator's annual salary. And money followed money. Doctor M. from Christ's College had conferred with his learned colleague Professor G. at Emanuel. Professor G., down in London for a meeting of the Royal Society, mentioned the subject to Professor H. Ten days later, after further communication and informal discussion, Doctor M. felt able to suggest to William, 'with some confidence', that a call on the discretionary funds of the society might be viewed with favour. William applied and was rewarded, though neither of them had expected the society's favour to amount to so generous a sum.

He looked at the pile of crates on the wharf beside him, mostly the result of a single visit to the Army and Navy Store in London. 'Tropical, temperate, or arctic, sir?' was the first question the man in the shop had asked him. Since William was not sure exactly where he would end up, they had decided it might be better to err on the safe side and cater for both tropical and temperate. The resulting collection of tents, fly-sheets, folding tables and chairs, beds, ropes, nets, pots, pans and other necessities would have equipped a ten-man expedition to find the source of the Orinoco via the North-West passage. William had even been persuaded into taking a collapsible armchair — indispensable, according to the shop assistant, for that after-dinner brandy and cigar, wherever you might end up. But more important than these were the six stout crates containing all the paraphernalia of the most up-to-date embryological laboratory. If William Hay Caldwell should fail to crack the platypus puzzle, it would not be for lack of money or equipment.

Harry Norton tied down the last of the boxes with expert knots and slid the tallow-wood planks back into place beneath the wagon. He tugged the chocks out from beneath the wheels and hung them up beside the ropes and buckets.

'You walking?' he said, pulling himself up onto the wagon and reaching for the whip with one hand while releasing the brake with the other.

As William climbed up onto the wagon he felt the wind of the lash passing inches from his ear.

''Nuff loundering, you gapy dummocks.' The stockwhip cracked again. ''Eave along there.'

The bullock team strained, the wagon creaked, the wheel rims began to turn. They were off.

'Bozy slatter-factries,' said Harry Norton (quietly though, under his breath). He turned to William. 'So. Gayndah, eh?'

'That's the idea. I've been told it's a good place to start.'

Harry Norton nodded towards the crates behind them. 'Mining, eh?'

'Mining? Oh no, no. No, platypuses actually. Water-moles.'

Harry Norton snorted sharply. He gave William a long sideways look then reached under his seat and extracted a bottle. Still looking straight ahead he removed his pipe from its almost permanent position, uncorked the bottle, took a long swig, recorked the bottle and replaced the pipe. It was clear that Harry Norton did not for a moment believe that anyone would come all the way to Queensland to study water-moles.

On his first trip by bullock wagon, two things in particular impressed William. First was the quantity of excrement continuously generated by twelve large ruminant mammals. The second was their speed of travel — or lack of it. Though the road — thickly lined with some kind of man-high grass — was as flat as a billiard table, the animals rolled along at the pace of a slow man walking (no wonder Harry Norton had taken so long to arrive). But there was no hurry. William looked around him at the dusty road, at the green grass, at the sun already sinking towards the horizon in a bright blaze of pink. The pink of what, though?

William's mind — more specifically the prosaic nature thereof — had been the despair of his good friend Charles Gilbert at Cambridge. Romanticism was in the air — even science was romantic. But the airy language of Brown or Byron, the more earthy words of Emerson and Thoreau (even among more empirically-minded Cambridge students, Henry David Thoreau had been all the rage in the late 1870s) were to William as strange sounds spoke in foreign tongues. There was no helping it. When William Caldwell saw a sunset it was a sunset — not dusk's rosy fingers still clinging to the western sky, nor the carmine shroud of eventide bidding day adieu. But since arriving in Australia, he noticed, a change had occurred. Whether it was the result of time or place or who knows what, he recently found his mind searching for ... analogies. That sky, now. Was it not exactly the colour of a fine, ripe salmon roe?

William well remembered his first sight of the delicate orange-pink eggs of a salmon. It had been on his first fishing trip with his uncle Angas, just after his parents died, and he must have been ten years old. Towards the end of the day he had hooked and managed to land a smallish hen fish. After it had been dispatched by the gillie, his uncle took from his tackle basket a sharp knife and a small silver spoon. Slipping the point of the knife into the salmon's vent, with one smooth push he slit open its belly. There, glistening among the guts, were the two long egg masses.

'Know what you're looking at here, Will?' said his uncle, lifting up a spoonful of the small translucent eggs. 'Scotch caviar.' And he slipped the spoon between his nephew's unwilling lips.

William closed his mouth, swallowed, and gave a weak smile.

'Not half as bad as you thought they'd be, eh?' His uncle laughed.

And they weren't. On what came to be an annual fishing trip with Uncle Angas, William often enjoyed a spoonful or two of Scotch caviar.

The sun disappeared. William was still not used to the way it seemed to travel anticlockwise through the sky in Australia, nor the suddenness with which night came in these latitudes (on the ship's captain's charts he had been surprised to see that Bundaberg was only two degrees south of the tropic of Capricorn). As he watched, the horizon seemed to go first dark then light again as the stars appeared — surely these southern stars were brighter than the stars of the north? And in the starlight appeared a building.

Despite the wagon's slow pace it seemed to leap out from the darkness, and it was enormous — a monolith of unpainted boards. Dwarfing even the building was a brick chimney, a hundred feet high.

'Is this Bundaberg?'

'Mill,' said Harry Norton.

'Mill?'

'Sugar mill.'

Of course, that grassy plant they had been passing: sugar cane.

Five minutes later the bullock driver spoke again. Nodding towards a slightly smaller building he said, ''Stillery' — and half a minute later, 'She's a rum town, Bundy.'

It took William a moment or two to notice Harry Norton looking at him from the corner of one eye, and a few moments more to realise that he had just made a joke. In what he took to be the spirit of things, William just sniffed. The bullock driver reached under the seat for the bottle, pulled the cork and passed the bottle to William. William took a mouthful and handed the bottle back.

'How far is it to the town?'

''Nother mile, maybe two,' said the bullock driver.

William looked up towards the stars. What colour, he wondered, would be the egg of a water-mole?

William had seen a picture of a platypus even before he had seen his first salmon. It was in Uncle Angas's library. There had been few books in William's own home — there was barely enough money for the medical texts his father needed for his work. William had been an only child. His father, sole physician to the small Fifeshire town of Lochgelly, was as stern and aloof as the God of the Old Testament. His mother was loving (William never doubted for a minute that he was loved) but at the same time distracted. 'Who is this child?' her expression seemed always to be asking. 'And what is he doing here?' But her brother Angas was different, both engaging and engaged. Yes, perhaps he was an idle man (who would not be compared to the ever-busy, ever-bustling, ever-*doing* doctor?). Perhaps he did spend too much time at the billiard table (and wager and lose much money). And perhaps he did not spend the income he derived from the family paper mill (a 'considerable income', according to the doctor) as wisely or as well as the good doctor himself would have, had it been his to spend. But Uncle Angas was a generous man. He gave money to his sister, and he gave time to his nephew. And William never had enough time for Uncle Angas, nor with his uncle's library in the big house at Morar. If Uncle Angas might not be an angel, he seemed to the young William at the very least one of the more senior saints. And the library was heaven.

How many books were on those shelves — a thousand, two thousand? And a large proportion of them picture books (grown-up picture books, of course) of birds, butterflies, beetles and shells. Huge books they were, heavy books, by writers with weighty names. John James Audubon, Henry Archibald Simon, the Lewins, father and son. All of John Gould's books were there, magnificent in colour and beauty. *British Birds*, *Birds of the Himalaya* and, most exciting of all, a complete collection of books on the birds and mammals of that faraway place, Australia. Bright parrots played among strange blossoms, soft-eyed kangaroos looked out on distant landscapes, the impossible emu 'on whose haunch eight men might dine' stared from the page in haughty splendour. And William could still see the platypus, eyes shining bright from the page, webbed feet spread, posing relaxed yet alert on the bank of some remote creek or billabong. And now here he was, perhaps heading for that same billabong, to discover more about the creature that was, according to Mr Gould, 'unquestionably the most singular and anomalous of all Australian mammals'.

Before leaving England he had been eager to find out as much as he could about the mysterious monotreme. Monotreme, now there was an interesting word in itself. From the Greek, apparently, for 'single hole', referring to the fact that in these mammals, and in these mammals only, the urinary tract, alimentary canal and reproductive tracts all ended in the one cloaca. The order contained two species, the platypus and the echidna, unalike in external form but sharing this peculiar anatomical feature — as well as certain peculiarities of skeletal structure otherwise found only in reptiles. And that strange duck-like bill, and the horny spurs on the hind legs of males that were hollow and connected to a poison gland. 'Singular and anomalous' — indeed.

It was Professor Moseley who had suggested to him that he should look up Sir Richard Owen before he left.

'Owen still knows more about platypuses than any man in England. A fine anatomist: show him a toe bone and he'll sketch out the whole animal, living or dead.'

Professor Sir Richard Owen — a legend in his own lifetime. Britain's foremost expert on anatomy, among whose many discoveries was that platypuses had milk glands and so must suckle their young. But it was Owen who maintained — and had gone on maintaining in the face of strong opposition from Monsieur Etienne Geoffroy Saint-Hilaire and Baron Georges Léopole Chrétien Frédéric Dagobert Cuvier of the mighty French school of zoology — that simply by looking at platypuses it was clear that they could not possibly lay eggs. The animals were warm-blooded, they had fur and they had milk glands; *ergo* they were mammals. And no matter what any Frenchman, or any pack of Frenchmen may say, mammals do not lay eggs.

'Don't believe everything he tells you,' Professor Moseley had warned him. 'I expect you know it was Owen who coined the word *dinosaur*, but I fear that as far as modern theory goes he is something of a dinosaur himself. Whatever you do, don't mention Darwin.'

But it was also Owen who had for many years lobbied the British parliament for a Natural History Museum in London. Now, this winter afternoon, William had come down to London by train and was on his way to the new museum in South Kensington to meet its first director, Sir Richard himself.

William knew that he was well prepared for the interview. Every word that Owen had ever written on the subject of platypuses, William had read. But he was not prepared for the man himself. Professor Sir Richard Owen was a long, lean giant of a man. His enormous head, with its deep set eyes and mane of white hair, seemed more suited to a fire-and-brimstone preacher than a man of science. Yet he was cordial enough to the young student when he greeted him outside his office at the head of the grand staircase.

'So, our first Balfour Scholar,' he said, taking William's hand in an enthusiastic greeting. 'A great honour, a great honour.'

It was unclear to William whether the honour was meant to be his or Sir Richard's, but as the famous man led him into the room William felt one huge paw curl round his shoulder in a manner almost avuncular.

'And off to Australia, I hear. A wonderful country — a wonderful continent. Careful though — look what happened to Darwin, eh?'

Sir Richard gave him a long-toothed grin. Could any man of science, especially one as knowledgeable as Sir Richard, deny not only the evidence of the fossil record but the simplicity — the beauty — of Darwin's theory? He recalled Professor Moseley's warning. He was not here to question; he was here to listen. In the mostly one-sided conversation that followed, William made replies that he hoped were of suitable deference, and as he was being ushered from the room after the meeting he had no doubt what was expected of him. He was not going to Australia to find whether platypuses laid eggs; he was going to confirm that they did not.

'Never mind what the Frenchies say.' Sir Richard gave another ivory smile. 'Eggs — strictly for the birds, eh?'

Outside two lamplighters were already turning up the gaslights against the late afternoon gloom. As William paused to watch them in their work he found strange questions forming in his mind. Here he was in London, at the centre not only of the British Empire but the whole empire of natural science. It had been a hundred years since the British had settled Australia, eighty years since the first specimen of the platypus had found its way back to England. Yet still great men were squabbling over where this little animal stood in the scheme of things, which rung it occupied on the *Scala Natura*, the great ladder of creation.

He turned back to look at the new museum, truly a temple to modern science. Modern science, metropolitan science — that was the way of the future. Shedding light where there was darkness, what more noble, more important work could there be? But it needed modern men. Sir Richard, though, had been generous with his time. William had in his pocket a letter of introduction to the director's very good friend in Sydney, Doctor George Bennett M.D., and in his hand a book by the very same Doctor Bennett, *Gatherings of a Naturalist in Australia*. 'You'll find out all you need to know about platypuses in there,' Sir Richard had told him. By the light of a street lamp William turned the volume over and opened it to the title page. He smiled to himself — my God, it was over twenty years old. Taking a moment to get his bearings, he slipped the book into his coat pocket and headed east along Gloucester Road towards the brighter lights of Knightsbridge.

Despite the creaking of the wagon wheels and the soft beat of the bullocks' feet on the dusty road, it sometimes felt as though they were not moving through the night at all. Only when he looked sideways and saw a low star pass behind the sugar cane, or caught a glint of light on the metal wheel rim, did William have any sense of motion. It had been like that on the ship coming out. Sometimes on a tropical night when he stood on the foredeck of the good ship *Jane Dark*, leaning over the rail and looking out towards the horizon, it was as if he had come from nowhere and was going nowhere. Starry night or cloudy, all was still — himself, the ship, and all around. He liked those nights.

The *Jane Dark* had departed Tilbury on 2 April 1883 on a late-afternoon tide. William boarded that morning, and found himself occupying a tidy cabin just aft of the main mast, well fitted out with desk and shelves — shelves soon filled with his books (including the one from Sir Richard but more importantly both of his uncle's sets of Gould: 'More use to you than me, Will. But bring 'em back, won't you?'). The Channel had been rough and the Bay of Biscay all he had feared. Only on rounding Cape Finisterre did the waves slacken enough for him to even think of getting out of his bunk, and the ship had cleared Gibraltar before he dared take a book down from the shelf. The first that came to hand was *Gatherings of a Naturalist* and despite himself he was soon entranced. The animals that George Bennett had seen on his own sea voyage fifty years before were those that William was seeing now. Flying fish, ferocious sharks and Portuguese men-o'-war trailing tentacles of pain. Once, off Malta, they saw a whale. And one memorable night they sailed out of the Red Sea into the Gulf with a trail of phosphorescence behind the ship a mile long, just as Bennett had described. But there was more rough weather in the Indian Ocean, and it was not until after they left Colombo that William came to Bennett's account of the platypus. The doctor described in charming detail both the appearance and habits of these enigmatic animals; how they made long underground burrows in the bank of a river where they rested during the day, only appearing at dusk; how they spent most of their time swimming and diving in water; that they appeared to eat small aquatic insects and shellfish. He described how he had tried to keep platypuses in captivity but the longest he had kept them alive was five weeks. He had also questioned local Aboriginal people about whether platypuses laid eggs, receiving 'no satisfactory answer'.

William turned to the *Mammals of Australia* by the ever-reliable John Gould (also, it seemed from the introduction, a friend of Doctor Bennett).

'It is true that Professor Owen has given an elaborate paper on the anatomy and physiology of the platypus in the *Transactions of the Zoological Society of London*, and that the same work contains Mr Bennett's interesting account; still I am persuaded that much more remains to be ascertained and made known respecting this extraordinary type among quadrupeds.'

There, Gould had as good as said it. Owen and Bennett didn't know what they were talking about. But by now William had already decided that when he arrived in Sydney, Doctor George Bennett was the first man he wanted to meet.

The bullocks plodded on. Could it really be only five miles from the wharf? It seemed to William they had been travelling for hours. He took out his watch but despite the brilliance of the stars all he could see was a faint disc. He looked up. There was still no moon. The Milky Way was a broad stripe from horizon to horizon, and was that Scorpio there, or was it Orion's Belt? But low to the left, there shone bright the Southern Cross.

The first time he had seen the cross was just after they had passed Malacca and were sailing — or steaming, for there was no wind — down the straits towards Singapore. One of the other sailors had shown him the new constellation low to the south, and thereafter each night it was the first he looked for. The five stars had become emblematic of his journey, of his quest. On his first night in Sydney — a city whose size and sophistication had surprised him — he had looked out for the kite-shaped constellation and had been comforted to see it shining through the bright lights and smoke of this new antipodean civilisation.

And not only were the stars by night different from home. So, he soon discovered, was the sky by day. It was so blue. On his third morning in Sydney he awoke in his hotel and looked out through the crack in the curtains. The sky was not yet the ridiculous azure of an Australian noon, but it was still a sight bluer than any sky he ever remembered seeing in Scotland or Cambridge. He turned his head towards the watch propped up on the table beside his bed — four minutes to seven — and smiled a contented smile. He had written to Doctor Bennett the day of his arrival and his letter had been answered promptly. They had an appointment that very day. But it was not until ten — still time to lie in bed a while. No matter how blue the skies, bed was bed. As William lay warm beneath sheet and blanket he could not help recalling again his old friend from Cambridge, Charles Gilbert.

As students together, then as fellow demonstrators for Professor Balfour, he and Charles (who even as a freshman was known for wearing blue socks and smoking Burma cheroots) had shared lodgings above the tobacconist's shop in Sydney Street, just over the road from Christ's. Charles had taken full advantage of the location of his lodgings to indulge in every form of tobacco, and of his position in the laboratory to experiment with intoxicants of other kinds. Ether, ethanol and associated hydrocarbons, nitrous oxide, cocaine and opiates of various sorts: all had found their way by inhalation, ingestion or injection into Charles Gilbert's blood and brain. At the end of a year of exhaustive trials he had declared to William that without any doubt at all, none of them 'absolutely not a single one of them, old man' gave more pleasure to a fellow, more sensual and mental bliss, than a pipe of good cavendish or lying of a morning in a warm bed dozing. William had not acquired a taste for tobacco, but as for lying in bed of a morning ...

He opened his eyes and looked again at his watch. Five past eight. Oh well, time to rise. He got out of bed and went to the window. Crossing the courtyard below he saw the house girl — Sally, he remembered her name was. As he opened the window she looked up.

'I don't suppose there's any chance of some hot water?'

In reply the girl smiled and nodded. 'I'll be right up.'

This was another difference about Australia. There was no 'sir' or 'madam' — or only occasionally so. Jack was as good as his master here, and William found it all rather unnerving. He was scarcely into his trousers before the maid appeared with a jug of hot water and put it down on the washstand.

'There you are.'

'Thank you, Sally. I'll be down in half an hour. Will that be too late for breakfast? A cup of coffee and some toast would be fine.'

'Leave it to me.'

Again, no 'sir'. William sighed and picked up soap and shaving brush. He did not think of himself as either vain or dilly-dallying, but he did like to take time over his morning toilet. He examined his moustache. It was, he had to admit as he lathered up his face, of pleasing shape but still a young man's moustache. To show it to best advantage required careful razor-work. He put down the brush, picked up the bone-handled razor and lifted it to his face. He wanted to look his best. For the interview, of course.

William had already discovered that Doctor George Bennett was a man of some importance in the colony of New South Wales. According to his own account, Doctor Bennett had first arrived in Sydney in 1829 as a twenty-five-year-old ship's surgeon. He had liked the place: it was the kind of place where a man could make a mark. He returned in 1832 to settle and in the fifty years since had consolidated his place in the colony as a medical man of wide repute, and as its foremost naturalist.

William had always been comfortable in the company of men, whatever their age or status. Against other men he could judge his own worth, and usually found it high (it was only with women — that strange species — that he found himself at all uneasy). At ten minutes to ten he was at the museum door. After introducing himself to the doorman he was escorted into the main hall and ushered through a door marked 'PRIVATE'. He found himself in what seemed to be an outer office where he was greeted by a young man seated at a desk whom he assumed to be Doctor Bennett's secretary. The young man stood, and after giving William a perfunctory handshake (which felt to William as though a small dead fish had been briefly slipped into his palm) sat down again.

'Seat,' he said. He picked up a pen and resumed whatever task he had been engaged in when William arrived.

'Caldwell. I have an appointment with Doctor Bennett,' said William, still standing. 'I forwarded a letter of introduction.'

'Yes,' said the young man, not looking up. 'Seat.'

William sat down and waited. After some five minutes during which not a word was spoken the young man got up from his desk, knocked softly on the door behind him, opened it and entered, closing the door behind him. Another few minutes elapsed, during which William, weary of sitting, stood up and began to examine his surroundings in detail.

The room, thought William, might have been an office in any of the provincial museums in Britain. It was large enough, he supposed, with a spacious high ceiling, plainly plastered — though nowhere near as grand as the one occupied by Professor Sir Richard Owen at the Natural History Museum in London. One tall window looked out onto a side street. The doors were solid, the walls were wainscotted all round with panelling or shelves. On the shelves Caldwell could make out bound volumes from various learned institutions. The journals of the Royal Society, the Linnaean Society of London and the Royal Zoological Society were well represented, as well as some more obscure publications. (William was not familiar with the *United Services Journal* nor the *Proceedings of the Asian Society*.) Another set of shelves was filled with medical journals — the *Medical Gazette*, *Medical and Physical Journal*, *Transactions of the Royal College of Surgeon*s. None of the books, he noted, seemed well used. He took down from one of the shelves near the door a volume of *Loudon's Magazine of Natural History* from 1832. As he was about to open it the young man emerged from the room beyond.

'Doctor Bennett will see you,' he said, looking not at William but at the book he was holding in his hand.

William replaced the book on the shelf, then watched as the young man reached towards it and pushed it into alignment with the other volumes. He assumed that he would now be introduced to the doctor. Instead, the young man began to check the other shelves for any other signs of interference. William stepped into the next room and shut the door behind him.

This room was larger than the first and had not one window but two. Before one of them sat a man at a desk. The light was behind him so that William could not make out his features much beyond a square head and a frizz of white hair.

'Doctor Bennett?' he said.

The man rose to his feet. He was more than a head shorter than William but that head sat large and solid on its truncated pedestal.

'Mr Caldwell,' he said, in a tone that William could decipher neither as friendly nor hostile. He picked up William's letter of introduction from the desk and glanced down at it. 'Another visitor from the old country, eh?'

William stood where he had entered the room, waiting to be invited in or asked to sit. Doctor Bennett carried the letter around to the front of his desk. He stopped there for a moment to stare at William, then dropped the letter back on the desk and stepped forward, so close that he was looking up at William, his chin jutting forward.

'And remind me,' he said, with a thin smile, 'what is it that brings you to Australia?'

'As you may have read in the letter, sir, it is the platypus. I hoped that I might —'

'Ah yes, of course, the platypus,' said Doctor Bennett. From a small table beside him he picked up a small stuffed animal. 'Our old friend *Ornithorhynchus*. And you thought that you might perhaps discover a platypus egg, am I right?'

'Well, I would certainly like to —'

'Have you read my own writing on the subject, Mr Caldwell?'

'Indeed I have, sir. And I think —'

'Yes, what do you think, Mr Caldwell? Do you perhaps think that a man who has devoted half a lifetime to researching the subject, who has travelled the length and breadth of the colony, who has questioned squatters and natives alike, might have something to say on the subject?'

'I am sure that —'

'Platypuses do not lay eggs, Mr Caldwell. If you choose not to take my word for it, perhaps you would like to read Sir Richard Owen's own opinions on the subject. But perhaps you know better than the foremost anatomist in England, a man whom I am honoured to call a friend?'

'I have indeed read Sir Richard's opinions, and I agree —'

'With the French perhaps, Mr Caldwell? Perhaps you agree with M'sieur Geoffroy? Perhaps you think that Sir Richard Owen' — he pronounced the name slowly and clearly — 'and I are wrong in thinking that platypuses are ovoviviparous. M'sieur Geoffroy thinks that they are oviparous, and is that what you think, Mr Caldwell, that they lay eggs?'

'I have read Sir Richard's papers, and I am —'

'Yes, you are what, Mr Caldwell?' said Doctor Bennett. 'What are you, exactly?'

William knew exactly what he was. He was tired of being interrupted and contradicted. He put out his hand. 'I am grateful to you for giving me so much of your valuable time, Doctor Bennett.'

The doctor looked down at William's hand, but did not take it. 'Sit down, sit down,' he said.

William paused, then sat in the chair that Doctor Bennett had indicated.

The doctor went back around the desk and sat down opposite him. He opened a box. 'Cigar? No? Well I'm sure you'll not mind if I do.'

The doctor lit a large havana. When he was satisfied it was burning well he continued. 'I may have been a bit short — excuse me. But it vexes me, Caldwell, it still vexes me. It's proof we need. After all these years, still one of the greatest puzzles in biology, and I know that until we can breed the damned things, or take photographs of them or something, then we won't have the proof.'

He inspected his cigar as if looking for some answer in its glowing end. Apparently finding none, he took another puff, blew the smoke towards the high ceiling and sighed deeply. 'When I came here, Caldwell — what is it now, over fifty years ago? — I was like you. Eager to make my mark, to show the old fogeys a thing or two about "modern" methods. I made my mark. One of the things I set myself to do was show that kangaroos do not, as many insisted, grow from their mothers' teats. Have you ever examined a young joey in the pouch? No? Well, at first they do look as though they are growing there, on the nipple. You can't pull them off without tearing the tissue. But I found the embryos in the uterus, just where they should have been. They pass from there down the vagina just like any other mammal, but it seems that once they get into the pouch and first get hold of the nipple, it swells inside their mouths. They can't let go even if they wanted to. And they're so small and undeveloped, it really does look as if they are growing there, and later bud off, like jellyfish or something. And still nobody — did you know this, Caldwell? — nobody has found out how they get from the birth canal to the pouch. Nobody has seen it. It's still a mystery.'

'I know your work on the subject, Doctor Bennett. It is still required reading in embryology.'

'Is it now, is it?' said the doctor, his features softening. 'But I suppose I'm the old fogey now, eh? And you've come to Australia to show me up — and Owen.'

'I prefer to think I've come to continue with the work you started, Doctor Bennett,' said William. 'I think I can say that no one has done more than you in investigating the mammals of Australia — but as you say, there are still mysteries to be solved.'

While Doctor Bennett sucked away at his cigar, William described his training in the latest embryological techniques. If he could only find enough platypus specimens during the breeding season he would be able to make microscope slides of a sequential series of embryos — unfertilised eggs, fertilised eggs, then at daily intervals until birth. Not only would this be the key to working out their relationship with other groups of animals, he would also be able to follow the path of egg and embryo through the female's reproductive system.

'You'll need a lot of specimens,' said Doctor Bennett. 'I doubt that you'll find them here. Thirty, forty years ago, maybe — but not these days. All shot out round here — for their fur, you know. You'll need to go further afield.'

'Where do you think I might find them then, Doctor?'

'Tasmania, perhaps. But there aren't any blackfellows there. You'll need blackfellows to help you, and they're almost as hard to find as platypuses these days. Same thing, I'm afraid. Shot out, or poisoned. Or killed off by white man's disease — smallpox, measles, syphilis.'

The doctor shook his head, and William realised for the first time that he had indeed noticed few (any?) Aborigines since arriving in Sydney.

'Is there anywhere else?'

Doctor Bennett took a thoughtful puff. 'It's a question of finding somewhere that's accessible but not overpopulated — by people I mean, white people, not platypuses. I expect you know that the animals have been found all along the east coast, almost up to Cape York.' He took another puff of his cigar. 'I know. We'll ask Herbert.'

Doctor Bennett shouted out the name and the young man who had first greeted William entered the room.

'You've met my son Herbert?'

The young man nodded to William. A surprised William nodded back. So this strange, young-old man was Doctor Bennett's son.

'We need platypuses, Herbert, and lots of them. Where do you think? Anywhere up north? Queensland?'

Herbert pondered. 'The Burnett,' he said, at last.

'The Burnett — where the deuce is that? A map, Herbert. Come, we need a map.'

Doctor Bennett cleared his desk of papers and writing stuff while his son went to a chest and pulled out a large map. He laid it on the desk.

'Yes? Well? Where is it then?' said his father.

Herbert Bennett pointed to a small indentation of the coast, just to the north of the big bulge where the coastline began sloping to the west.

'Here,' he said. He walked over to a shelf by the door and pulled down a gazetteer.

'The mouth of the Burnett River is near Bundaberg. The river itself rises in the Burnett Ranges one hundred and forty miles directly to the west, loops down to the south, passing through the towns of Mundubbera and Gayndah. It drains an area of approximately —'

'Yes, yes, thank you, Herbert. And plenty of platypuses, you say?'

'*Ornithorhynchus* abounds in its sometimes turbid waters.'

The Burnett River was beginning to sound to William like just the place.

Doctor Bennett went back to the map. 'Let's see now. Bundaberg itself is too close to the sea — still tidal there I should think. Strictly freshwater, your platypus.' He traced the river with his finger. 'Gin Gin, perhaps, or Gayndah. Yes, Gayndah, that looks as though it might fit the bill.' He looked up at his son.

'Gayndah, 224 miles north-west by north of Brisbane, situated on the Burnett River eight miles downstream from its confluence with the Bourne. Population: 430; principal industries: pastoralism and fruit growing; weekly coaches to Maryborough, Bundaberg and Mount Alice; three hotels; places of worship: Church of England, Methodist, Catholic —'

This time it was William's turn to interrupt. 'Thank you, Mr Bennett. Gayndah it is.'

The next hour was spent discussing how William might get there and what he might need for his work in the way of living and scientific equipment. The doctor advised he buy his things in Sydney.

'You never know what you'll find or won't find in Queensland. Tents, furniture, clothes, dry goods — if you haven't got them already, get them here. And books, what about books?'

William was able to assure Doctor Bennett that he had brought camping equipment from England and as many books on Australian natural history as he could lay his hands on.

'Ah yes, still easier to get a book about Australia in London than here in Sydney,' said the doctor. 'But it's getting better, it's getting better.'

He guided William back into the outer office and took down a large volume from the shelves.

'You've got this one, I suppose? It's by a friend of mine, don't you know.'

William read the title: *The Mammals of Australia* by John Gould.

'I do indeed have a set of Mr Gould's *Mammals*, and I remember reading in it that you and he were friends. I have his *Birds*, too.'

Doctor Bennett raised an eyebrow. 'Then you really are well equipped. There are still a few species in that book I haven't seen yet myself. You know, Caldwell, I've half a mind to join you. What do you say to that, eh, Herbert?'

Herbert Bennett, who had been looking with some dismay at the hole the doctor had just created in the carefully arranged row of books, turned towards them.

'Age?'

'Great God — I'm not in my grave yet.'

'Patients?'

'Ah yes, the patients.' The doctor shook his head. 'Never take up medicine, Caldwell, that's my advice. The patients. Well, maybe they'll all die soon, eh? — and then I'll be able to come up and see you. What are the chances of that, do you think?'

'Given enough time, Doctor Bennett. But perhaps you'll cure them all and then you will be able to come.'

The doctor chuckled. 'Aye, maybe I will. Anyway, good luck to you, Caldwell. I trust that whatever you discover you will not be disappointed. Oh. There's just one more thing I should tell you.'

William turned towards him.

'A friend of mine in Melbourne, a man at the museum there, told me a few weeks ago that there's a chap from Munich been nosing around — one of Haeckel's students apparently, so he'll know what he's doing. He's looking for platypuses, too. Menden or Mengen or something. But the breeding season'll be earlier up in Queensland. I'm sure you'll be all right.'

three

> The *Ornithorhynchus* inhabits the banks of the lakes, and is supposed to feed in the muddy places which surround them; but the particular kind of food on which it subsists is not known.
> Letter from Governor John Hunter to Sir Everard Home, 1801

By starlight the outskirts of Bundaberg appeared as a dark jumble of shacks and outhouses. Once over the bridge these gave way to more substantial buildings and Harry Norton stopped the bullock wagon outside one of the newest and grandest. Two storeys high with verandas all round, its paint still fresh enough to smell. A sign along the top veranda, lit by no less than four oil-lamps, identified it as the Melbourne Hotel.

'You'll be stopping here,' said Harry Norton. It was more a statement than a question.

'Yes, I've booked a room,' said William. 'But surely you'll stay here, too?'

'Me? Oh no, not me. It don't pay to stop now, not while I'm just loaded. Besides, travelling at night is easier on the beasts. The moon'll be up soon.' The bullock driver handed William down his travelling bag. 'You'll find me.'

Reaching underneath the seat for the bottle of rum he removed the cork and took a swig. He again offered it to William, who shook his head.

'You won't find better in there,' said Harry Norton, gesturing to the hotel. He took another long swig and threw the empty bottle to the ground. Wiping his lips with the back of one hand then the other, he took hold of the whip. 'Haaa, move along, you dropsy scallyrags.'

The whip cracked and the bullocks took the strain, leaving William alone outside the Melbourne Hotel.

After two minutes no one had come to take his bag. He picked it up himself and pushed through the main door into the lobby. The hotel bar seemed to be doing a fine trade — the door from the lobby was open and he could see, hear and smell men and beer and tobacco. He called out, 'Desk', with no result. On the side of the counter was a bell. When he rang it a round-faced man poked his head out from the bar. After looking William up and down he pulled his head back.

William heard the words, 'Maggie, desk', and a woman appeared through the same door, middle-aged and large. Large in size, large in the pattern of her dress. Wiping her hands on an apron she gave him a small smile, crossed the lobby without speaking and entered a door opposite marked 'OFFICE'. William heard bustling, then silence. There was a cough behind him.

'Now, sir, what can I do for you?'

The same woman had now appeared behind the reception counter.

'Oh,' he said, flustered. 'William Caldwell. I believe I have a reservation.'

'Caldwell, hmm ...' The woman opened a large ledger book and thumbed the pages. 'For tonight that'll be, will it?'

'I sent a letter, from Sydney.'

'Oh yes, yes. From Sydney — I remember now.'

She extracted a letter from a pigeonhole beside the counter. William recognised his own writing on the envelope.

'It only arrived yesterday so I haven't had time to read it yet.' She tore open the envelope, then appeared to search around for something. 'Oh dear, I don't seem to be able to find my glasses.' She looked up at him and smiled. 'Would you mind reading it to me?'

Taking the letter from her hand he read his own handwriting. 'Dear sir. Please reserve for me at your hotel a room for the night of Wednesday, April 16. I shall be arriving by regular steam packet and expect to be staying in Bundaberg for two days. Yours etc., W.H. Caldwell.'

'Ah,' said the woman, her smile collapsing. 'Well, I'm afraid there's a bit of a problem.'

Surely the hotel could not be full, but the woman looked serious enough.

'Yes, you see the problem is ...' she said, with clear concern. 'Well as you can see ...' She leant over the counter towards him. Then, looking first towards the door and then up the stairs, she continued in a quieter voice, 'The problem is that, um, well as you can see ... I'm not a Dear sir, I'm a Dear madam.'

She was leaning further over now and was looking William straight in the eyes. And could William stop those eyes falling onto her near and obvious bosom? And could he stop the equally involuntary and spectacular blush that immediately followed?

The woman's red-painted mouth exploded in a huge laugh, she took a gasp of breath and let out another laugh even louder than the first.

'Jacko,' she shouted, gasping again for breath.

The round face appeared from the bar, this time followed by a thin and wiry body.

'Jack, we have a guest. Show Mr Caldwell up to room three, there's a love.'

Jacko seemed to have enough fellow feeling to say nothing at all as he picked up William's bag and headed for the stairs. When he had shown him to his room and lit the lamps, he left. William sat down on the bed, straightened his back and took several deep breaths. In a mirror on the dresser opposite, he watched his redness slowly fade.

The trouble was not, he told himself, with the woman. The trouble was with women in general. He just couldn't get the hang of them.

After his mother died (of diphtheria, the same as his father) there had been few women in his life. No sisters, no cousins, certainly no sweethearts. Uncle Angas was married to Aunt Agnes, of course, and William was fond of his aunt, but — well, she was an aunt. When his uncle had sent him to school in England he found that the headmaster had so strong a belief in the polluting effects of the opposite sex that even the school nurse was a man (an ex-navy medical orderly whose administrations to some of the prettier pupils, while sometimes questionable, were at least thought safer than risking the boys to female hands). And afterwards, at university, William's companions had also been exclusively male.

The same had been true since coming to Australia. Apart from that maid — Sally, that was her name — at the hotel in Sydney, he had hardly spoken to a single woman since leaving London. And, he reminded himself with some relief, after he left this hotel and headed out into the countryside, perhaps he would not have to speak to another woman for weeks more, maybe months. With a grateful sigh he stripped off his shirt, poured some water from the jug and had a brief wash from the basin. When had he last eaten? He put on a clean shirt.

In the saloon he found Jacko and the landlady both busy behind a bar the length of which he had never seen the like in his life. It was thirty yards if it was an inch. Beer appeared to be the drink of choice among the clientele of the long bar at the Melbourne Hotel, with rum a very close second. And yes, all the customers were men. They were sitting or standing at the bar, apart from a small group around a billiard table in the far corner of the room. William was pleased to see the billiard table. If William Hay Caldwell had a weakness, it was billiards. It had been weeks now since he had had a game. He remembered with an inward smile his disappointment when he had found on boarding the *Jane Dark* that there was no billiard table in the saloon, and had taken some time to realise that perhaps the ocean waves might not be quite the place for a straight shot. Deck quoits had not proved a satisfactory substitute. Perhaps he would have a game later. Jacko caught his eye.

'What'll it be?' he asked, holding a glass beneath the tap of a beer barrel.

William nodded assent and went over to an empty table beside one of the windows. He had no sooner sat down than he heard the barman call his name and saw him holding out a glass over the bar. It appeared that there was no table service tonight. William went back to the bar and took the glass.

'And you'll be wanting some dinner, too, Mr Caldwell?' shouted the landlady from the other end of the bar.

Again William nodded and as he returned to his table he heard her calling through to the back of the hotel an order for 'one hot dinner'. No table service, and apparently no menu either. Things were certainly different up here. But the food was soon ready, and the landlady herself brought it to his table — a thick steak with gravy and mashed potato and a pale green vegetable that William could not identify.

'You get yourself outside of that, love,' she said. 'And there's more if you want it.'

The meat was delicious, and the potato; the green vegetable less so. William was turning over the limp slices with his fork, wondering what on earth they could be, when he heard a voice beside him.

'Not going to eat your chokoes, then?'

William looked up from his plate. He had noticed the man earlier, at the centre of a small group at the far end of the bar where he seemed to be keeping the crowd amused with some story. Now here he was standing by William's table, a tall man with a heavy black beard (judging by the rest of the men in the bar, beards seemed to be the fashion in this part of Australia). But a friendly enough smile showed through it, and in his hand the man held two glasses of beer.

'I noticed you'd finished your drink so I brought you another. Mind if I join you?'

'Please,' said William, 'and thank you.' He prodded the vegetable with his fork. 'What did you say these are called?'

The man put down the two glasses and sat himself at the table. 'Chokoes. You can grow them just about anywhere — though it's why you'd want to, that's what I've never been able to work out.'

William gave a wry smile. 'Perhaps I should have ordered the asparagus.'

The other man grinned. 'Don't worry, the beer'll wash 'em down. The name's Ben, by the way — Ben Fuller.' He half rose from his seat and held out a large hand.

William put down his knife and took it. 'William Caldwell.'

'Yes, Maggie told me your name. But she didn't tell me what you were doing here. Something to do with the mill, I suppose.'

'Well, no. I'm not actually staying in Bundaberg, not for long. I'm taking the coach to Gayndah in the morning.'

'Ah, mining, eh?' said the man. 'But coach? I'm not sure we'll be seeing a coach here, not for a while.' He leant forward over the table. 'Did you not hear about the bushrangers?'

Bushrangers? They were robbers, weren't they? A picture of another bearded face flashed into William's mind, a picture he had seen a couple of years before in the *Illustrated London News*: 'The notorious Victorian bushranger, Ned Kelly.' The face above the caption had looked, he could not help thinking, like a somewhat younger version of the face now before him.

'No. I didn't realise that there were bushrangers round here.'

'Nor did most people. Here, Jacko,' the man called out. 'Tell this cove what you told me about them bushrangers.'

The barman came over and explained that the mail coach had been held up not far out of town only the week before.

'Only one of them, though — did the whole job himself. Came as a bit of a surprise all round. Hasn't been a bushranger round these parts for near twenty years, not since the gold days.'

'Gold days?' said William.

'1864,' said the barman, 'the big strike up at Mount Alice.'

'You must excuse my ignorance,' said William. 'I have heard of the Victorian goldfields but ... Oh my goodness.' Another picture came suddenly into his mind, of his luggage and Harry Norton. 'Do you think they could still be about — I mean him, the bushranger? Only you see I sent some things on ahead, by wagon.'

Ben Fuller nodded. 'Ah yes, that'd be with Harry.' He leant back in his chair. 'He's right enough, is Harry Norton. As the poet once said:

What trouble has he for the ruin of lands,
Or the quarrels of temple and throne,

*So long as the whip that he holds in his hands,
And the team that he drives, are his own?*

But what did you say your stuff was?'

'Scientific equipment, mostly,' said William. 'I'm not a miner, I'm a scientist you see, a …' William hesitated. He thought of himself as a zoologist, an embryologist to be more precise. But perhaps he should use the more old-fashioned word. 'I'm a naturalist. I've come to study platypuses.'

The man threw back his head and laughed. 'Platypuses! Well, somebody's got to study platypuses, I suppose. Here Maggie, he says he's come all the way from the Old Dart to study our duckbills.'

The woman behind the bar snorted her now-familiar laugh. 'So, we've got a professor on our hands.'

'Now, Maggie, you keep your hands off him,' said Ben Fuller. Then turning to William, 'She always did like a book-learning man, did Maggie.'

This time it was the woman's turn to blush. 'Take no notice of him, Mr Caldwell,' she said, busying herself about the bar.

'And he reckons he's going to take the mail coach to Gayndah tomorrow. What do you think of that?'

'There won't be any coach to Gayndah tomorrow, love. Next Tuesday — maybe.'

'Oh dear,' said William. 'I told the driver — I told Mr Norton — that I'd catch him up tomorrow. He'll be expecting me.'

'Expecting you he may be, but whether he'll see you, that's the question.'

'Perhaps I can find a horse somewhere — it doesn't have to be anything special.'

Ben Fuller shook his head, leant back in his chair and looked William straight in the eyes. 'It's not a question of horses, special or not.'

'Oh, I've already seen the speed he travels,' said William. 'I'm sure it won't be difficult to catch up.'

'I'm not saying it'll be difficult.' Ben Fuller put his glass down on the table. 'Not difficult — impossible.'

'But …'

'No buts about it, Prof.' He leant forward again. 'Look, say we can find you a horse in the morning, and say by the time you're saddled up and ready to leave, Harry's already reached Gin Gin — that's about thirty miles from here. By the time you reach Gin Gin, is Harry going to be there? No. He'll have moved on. Doesn't matter how fast that horse of yours goes, Harry's moved on. So on you go from Gin Gin to where Harry is now — Ten Mile Creek, say. But by the time you've reached there, Harry's moved on again. On you go on that horse of yours, fast as you like. By the time you reach where Harry was, he isn't there any more, he's moved on a bit further. Seems to me you can keep that up all day, Prof, all week if you like. But every time you reach where Harry was, he'll have moved on. Well, you can see that, Prof, can't you — educated man like you? Any way you look at it, it's too late to catch up with Harry Norton. Unless, of course,' he added, emptying his glass and smacking his lips, 'he stops somewhere for a spell. I suppose if he stops somewhere you've got a chance.'

William paused, eyeing his companion. 'Yes. Well.' He gave a small frown. 'Let us forget about Mr Norton for a while. Let's just think about getting to Gayndah.'

'Well, that's different, that is, Prof. No problem getting to Gayndah, as long as you've got a horse.'

William looked over towards the empty billiard table. 'Do you by any chance play billiards?'

'I like a game. You mean you want to play now?'

'I believe there is nothing I would like more.'

'You're on.'

While William searched for the balls, Ben Fuller turned up the lamps over the table.

'There,' he said, adjusting a wick. 'Now the dog can see the bandicoot, eh, Prof?'

Though the baize was somewhat worn William could see that it was a good table — an Archer, all the way from England. Four half-inch slates and vulcanised cushions. Ben Fuller adjusted the lights for height, stilled their swinging and took a cue from the rack on the wall. William examined several of the others before choosing a dark cue, not too long and nicely weighted — it looked a little like sycamore, though he wondered if it were perhaps some local wood. He held it to his eye and looked along it. A slight bow, but not excessive.

'We toss a coin for break round here,' said Ben, taking a florin from his pocket. 'That suit you?'

'Where I come from,' said William, chalking the tip of his cue, 'we do exactly the same. Heads, I choose?'

Ben Fuller decided to take first break. He took the plain cue ball and placed it in the semicircle behind the baulk line, chalked the tip of his cue and lined up for the stroke.

His first shot was a good one, hitting the red at half ball and bringing both back down the table behind the baulk line. This meant that William would now have to go off a cushion to hit either of them. As he placed his own ball on the table and bent over to form his hand into a bridge he could hear the words of Uncle Angas.

Fingers well spread, Will — natural now, not too wide apart. Thumb up, that's it, nice and relaxed.

He settled his body, from feet through legs to hips and trunk.

Take your time, Will. There's no extra points for a hurried stroke.

The plain ball was just to his right, a good eight inches from the bottom cushion and ten from the side. The red ball was more or less over the bottom left pocket. It would have been the simplest of balls to pot directly but a devil to pot off the top cushion.

Never mind the pot, Will; it's early days. Play safe. Get a feel for the table.

William needed to get the red away from the bottom pocket and up to the top of the table.

Give your cue ball a good knock, now — a little low, just so it keeps its line.

William drew back his cue, practised the line of the shot three, four times, then hit his ball hard and just below centre. It whizzed up the table, bounced sweetly off the top cushion and back towards the bottom. He could see it was going to miss the red, but not by much. And he had put enough weight behind it that it bounced back off the bottom cushion, hitting the red on the rebound. Both balls rolled up the table, not quite as far as he would have liked but coming to a stop nice and close to the side cushions. He had indeed played safe.

His opponent nodded in appreciation of the shot and began studying the table.

'You know, I was thinking a bit more about that horse you'll be needing.'

William was concentrating on the game, thinking what he would do if it were now his turn. A long jenny off the red — to sink the cue ball in the top right pocket and bring the red out for a subsequent pot? A cannon perhaps, hitting the white first and bringing the cue ball back off the top cushion to collect the red (but then what?). Neither of them easy shots.

'I think I might be able to find you one. In fact, come to think of it, I know just where there might be one just right for you.'

Ben Fuller walked towards the left cushion and lined up on the red. He was going for the long jenny.

'Mind you,' he said, bending over the table, 'there's still that bushranger — no telling where he is now. You might want to think twice about going by yourself. And it's a bit of a way if you don't know these parts.'

It was already clear to William that his opponent was not an elegant player. Ben Fuller's stance was a little side-on, his back slightly bent so that he had to make an awkward curve with his neck to get his eye over the cue. But he was good. He hit his ball clean and with just enough check so that when it reached the top pocket after bouncing off the red it grabbed hold of the jaw and slipped neatly in. Three points. And he had knocked the red out to the centre of the table into perfect playing position.

'Fine shot,' said William. 'And I'm afraid I don't know these parts at all.'

'Wait a minute,' said Ben Fuller, straightening up. 'Gayndah, that's only about eighty, ninety miles — four days easy, there and back. I used to know the place. How about I come with you?'

'Why, I couldn't possibly impose.'

'Impose?' Ben Fuller lowered his voice. 'Now look, Prof, you won't tell Maggie this, will you? I've been here in Bundy a couple of days now and I'm starting to get a bit weary of the metropolitan life.

As the poet once said:
> *And I long in this city for woodland and grove,*
> *And the peace of wild forest home.*

I reckon you might be doing me a favour.'

William retrieved his opponent's ball and rolled it down the table. Ben Fuller caught it smoothly and placed it on the line for a half-ball shot onto the red and down the table for a cannon. His aim was true and the red followed his own ball up the table. All three balls were exactly where he wanted them.

'Oh, what was I thinking of — I should have been keeping score,' said William. 'Five points. Of course, if you were to come I would insist on paying you —'

'Pay me?' said Ben Fuller. 'Wouldn't think of it.'

He bent over the table and William was kept busy spotting the red and counting out his opponent's points until Ben Fuller had brought his break up to eighteen, then missed an ambitious screw back from the red for a cannon.

'Damn, missed the bugger.'

William hoped that his small, sharp intake of breath had not been heard. He had never quite been able to rid himself of his childhood indoctrination against 'scurrility', as his Aunt Agnes always described such language. Even though he was now twenty-four years old and twelve thousand miles from her hearing he still felt himself wince slightly at his opponent's utterance. But never mind that. The balls were nicely set up for him to make an equally large break. Ben Fuller put up his own score on the board and took a long pull from the glass of beer on the table beside him.

'But if you insist, I suppose we could call it a quid a day.'

'A pound? Is that with the horse?'

'Guide, horse and saddle,' said Ben Fuller.

If the amount seemed a little large, William did not feel in a position to quibble. He again held out his hand.

'It's a deal. Thank you, Mr Fuller, thank you indeed. Now I believe it is my break.'

Four reds and two cannons later William's score was standing at sixteen when he missed a difficult short jenny into the middle pocket.

The game already looked like being high scoring, with players evenly matched. A few of the men who had been talking at the bar drifted over to watch. Ben began chatting to some of them.

Keep your mind on the table, Will, not on the talk.

'You know, Prof, my friend Sam over here just reminded me' — Ben Fuller was holding his cue in both hands now, the heavy end cradled in one palm — 'we forgot to call the stake. What shall we say — a quid?'

It was a little late for that, thought William. Or was the man teasing him? You could not be sure with these Australians. 'Surely we should have agreed on a wager earlier.'

His opponent looked round to the men behind him and William saw his hands tighten on the cue.

He turned back to William. 'Gentleman's rules, eh?' Then, giving a sudden smile, he loosened his grip on the cue. It slid through his right hand to hit the floor with a thump. 'Fair enough. Though I tell you what — if you beat me it'll be my shout. A glass of Bundaberg's finest.'

'Only if you let me buy you one if I don't.'

Ben Fuller laughed. 'Good on you, Prof. But I reckon it might have to be a large one.'

The game continued well for both players.

At ninety-three to William and ninety-seven to Ben Fuller it was William's break. His ball was in hand after being potted by a slight mistake (miscue?) of his opponent's, which had left the other two balls close together over the top left pocket.

There can only be one winner, Will.

He placed his cue ball on the baulk line. A gentle cannon, a couple of easy reds, and the game was his.

Steady shot, not too hard, not too soft. A little bottom to keep it straight. And take your time.

It was a long way to the top cushion — a little backspin would indeed not go amiss. William drew back his cue and struck his ball hard and low. Too low. Much too low. The ball flew into the air, made one loud bounce and disappeared over the side of the table.

He had been in too much of a hurry, he hadn't practised the line; he'd done it all wrong.

No points for a hurried stroke, he once more heard his uncle say.

William stood up from the table. 'Foul shot, I'm afraid,' he said. 'Two points to you.' The other balls were in an awkward position for an easy score. 'And would you like the balls spotted?'

Ben Fuller accepted the option after a foul stroke of having the red ball put onto its spot, with William's ball on the middle spot and his own ball in hand. And he knew exactly where to place his own ball: a ball's width and a half from the left hand spot on the baulk line. To trickle his own ball off William's into the left top pocket was a simple half-ball, plain-ball shot away. Neither did he miss it. One hundred points. Game.

'Well done, Mr Fuller,' said William, offering his hand.

'Well done yourself, a fine game,' said Ben Fuller, taking it with a firm grip. 'And now — do you know what, Prof? I believe I feel a little thirsty.'

'A large rum for the winner, please, Jacko,' called William. 'In fact,' he said, looking round at the other men who were congratulating Ben Fuller on his win, 'drinks all round.'

Three drinks later William was still standing next to Ben Fuller at the bar surrounded by a dozen or so of the other customers, all with a glass in their hand.

'Yes, the Prof here's come to Queensland from — where did you say you come from, Prof? — from Cambridge University, to look at our water-moles.'

'Water-moles?' William heard one of the men say. 'Pull the other one, it's got bells on.'

'No, fair dinkum. You wouldn't be doubting the word of an educated man like the Prof here, would you?'

'Water-moles, my eye.' The man, another Ned Kelly double, gave a long look round the assembled company. 'Looking for gold, more like.' He jerked his chin towards William. 'You're not telling me he needs all that stuff to look for water-moles.'

The passing of the bullock wagon and its load had certainly not gone unnoticed.

'Pete,' said Ben Fuller. He put his glass down on the bar and gave that quick smile William had noticed before. 'Pete, my old mate. Are you suggesting that the Prof here isn't telling the truth? Are you saying that *I'm* not telling the truth?'

'Didn't say that, Ben. I just said you don't need a wagonload of stuff to look for water-moles. Ain't that right, boys?' He turned around, looking for support.

'But if I said water-moles, Pete, then water-moles it is. Everyone else seems to believe me. Wouldn't you say?'

Pete held his eye for a second, then dropped his gaze. 'Yes, Ben.'

'Sorry, Pete — what was that you said?'

'Yes, Ben. Yes, if you say so. Water-moles.'

'That's right, Pete, that's the way.' Ben Fuller turned to William, again with that quick smile. 'Always pays to be careful what you say round here, and when you say it, eh, Prof?'

He turned back to the other man. 'But you know, Pete,' he said, lifting his right hand from where he had quietly dropped it and clapping him on the shoulder, 'maybe you're not so wrong after all.' He picked up his glass and stared into it. 'I've been thinking. You all know how them water-moles root around in the mud for their food? I reckon that's what the Prof here's up to. He's going to catch those water-moles and train 'em to sieve around in the creeks for gold — am I right, Prof?'

There was an explosion of laughter. William smiled.

'There, you see, Prof? You can't fool a Queenslander. And now you know what, I reckon it must be Pete's shout.' Ben Fuller drained his glass. 'Right, Pete? That'll be a large one for me, and another one for the Professor here.'

As William accepted the brimming glass of rum he caught sight of the clock above the bar. It was past midnight. Though he had no coach to catch in the morning and should be able to sleep in, he felt suddenly tired.

'Well, if you'll excuse me, gentlemen, I'll bid you all good night.' He swallowed the rum from his glass. 'Thank you for the drink, er, Pete. And Mr Fuller — thank you again for the game, and the education.'

As he rose to go his hand came up to his chin, again feeling the unfamiliar whiskers. 'I forgot to ask. I'd like to have a shave in the morning — is there somewhere in town?'

Ben Fuller scratched his beard. 'Don't have much call for a barber myself, of course, but I believe there is one here. And as I recall, he shaves every man in Bundaberg who doesn't shave himself.'

'Thank you,' said William. 'He sounds like just the man I want.' He yawned.

'Of course the thing I never could work out,' said Ben Fuller, tossing back his own glass of rum, 'is who shaves the barber?' He smiled. 'Now I think I might turn in myself. Good night, Prof. Sleep well.'

four

An amphibious animal, of the mole species, had been lately found on the banks of a lake near the Hawkesbury. In size it was considerably larger than the land mole. The most extraordinary circumstance observed in its structure was its having, instead of the mouth of an animal, the upper and lower mandibles of a duck.

David Collins and George Bass, *An Account of the English Colony in New South Wales*, 1802

William was woken by daylight through the uncurtained window and the sound of horses and voices in the street outside. And a full bladder and a thick head. How much had he drunk last night? More than he was used to. He opened one eye. His watch, propped up on the washstand by a crumpled sock, said just past seven o'clock. He turned over. No, it was no good. He pulled back the covers and found a chamber pot in the usual place beneath the bed. Aaah. He flopped back into bed and pulled the blanket over his head, but the light and the noises made it impossible to get back to sleep. Lying on his back, he recalled the events of the day before. And especially his new acquaintance, Mr Ben Fuller.

A strange specimen. On the outside as rude and rough as any other man in the bar, yet with a poetical bent. But perhaps a man needed to be a little rude and rough out here. Played a damned good game of billiards, though. All that stuff about bushrangers — nonsense, of course. William was not quite so wet behind the ears as he perhaps appeared. Australians were notorious for trying to fool a 'new chum'. Did Ben Fuller and Jacko really think he would fall for that story?

He smiled, and once more his hand found its way to his chin. After breakfast he would go to that barber Ben Fuller had told him about, the one who — what did he say? — shaves every man in Bundaberg who doesn't shave himself. William thought about it. If the barber does shave then he — the barber — can't shave himself. But if he doesn't shave himself then he must shave himself. He shook his head. Damned silly thing, what was Ben Fuller talking about? Never mind, it would be good to have a guide and companion on the way to Gayndah, not to mention a horse. And he wouldn't be able to catch up with the bullock wagon, eh? Well just let Ben Fuller watch him.

William was wondering whether there might be a chance of a bath before breakfast when he heard a knock on the door. Jacko entered, carrying a large jug of hot water.

'Breakfast in twenty minutes,' he said as he emptied the steaming water into the wash bowl.

'Thank you, Jacko,' said William, taking a scoop of water and splashing it over his face. 'And I'd like a decent shave. Where will I find the barber?'

'Barber? Well, if I was you I'd try the end of Bourbon Street.'

'Thanks.' So much for Ben Fuller.

'And when you get to the end, just keep going.'

'Good, thanks.' William reached for a towel.

'Yes, keep going for about seventy miles.'

'Seventy miles?'

'Ain't no barber in Bundy. Maryborough, that'd be your nearest barber.'

And Jacko was out of the door before William could think to give him his order for breakfast.

After getting washed and dressed in something of a fluster, William found himself seated in the bar at the same table as last night, in front of a plate which seemed to contain the same meal — a large steak and a pile of pale green vegetables, chokoes as he now knew them to be. No, there was one difference: there was no mashed potato for breakfast. Beside his plate was a thick slice of bread, and instead of a glass of beer a cup of black tea.

Apart from himself, the bar was empty. Perhaps the others had already finished breakfast — or could it be that, despite the landlady's great show at examining the register last night, he was the only guest? The landlady herself was nowhere to be seen. William chewed the steak and sipped the tea, and found that chokoes were just about edible if you put enough salt and pepper on them.

Though there was no one else at breakfast the hotel seemed busy enough. Men passed in and out and much noise and shouting came both from the street and the back of the hotel, where he assumed the stables to be.

Having eaten as much steak as he could manage so early in the morning and almost reached the bottom of the large cup of tea, he left the table and found his way through the back of the reception hall to the courtyard. Jacko was helping two men unsaddle a pair of horses. The men appeared to be wearing uniforms, but were so covered in dust that any insignia were obliterated. Hats, beards, clothes and boots were all the same dull brown.

'Good morning again, Jacko,' he said. 'I was hoping I'd find that horse that Mr Fuller told me about last night.'

Jacko grinned. 'You won't find man nor horse here yet, Professor. These ain't them for sure.'

The two horses he was holding were as dusty as their riders, who, now that the horses were being seen to, began brushing themselves down with their hands. The action raised such a brown cloud that William was forced to step back.

'Ben Fuller had to leave early. He said to tell you he'll be back after lunch. 'Course,' Jacko continued, looking up at the sky, 'he didn't say which lunch.'

'Do you mean ...?'

'No, don't worry Professor, only joshing. If Ben Fuller says he'll be here, he'll be here.'

'Ben Fuller?' said one of the men, the taller of the two. 'It's a long time since I've seen my old mate Ben Fuller.'

'Then I dare say it's been a while since he's seen you,' said Jacko, as he led the two horses away towards a water trough.

The tall man grinned, then turned to William. 'So, a Professor, eh? Living here?'

A direct question, though spoken in a friendly enough manner. 'No,' replied William. 'I only arrived yesterday. And I'm leaving soon — as soon as I can find a horse, that is. My name's Caldwell, William Caldwell.'

The tall man exchanged a glance with his partner then put out a hand. 'Jim Perry — Constable Jim Perry.'

As William took the offered hand he could now make out on the man's shoulder badge the legend QCPS. 'And my friend, companion, associate and messmate, Sergeant Patrick O'Malley.'

The other man came forward and also shook William's hand. 'Queensland Colonial Police Service,' he said.

'You've been riding far?'

'Just up from Maryborough,' said the sergeant.

'And may I ask what brings you two gentlemen to Bundaberg?'

'You've not heard?' said the sergeant. 'We've come to catch a bushranger.'

It was true, then — there was a bushranger.

Sergeant O'Malley walked to the water trough. 'But first things first — I can't go around catching thieves and villains in this state. If you'll excuse me.'

And without waiting for a reply he stripped off his clothes and slid naked into the water. His action and the deep sigh that followed it was ignored by the two horses that were still drinking there. They were clearly used to him. So, apparently, was the constable.

'I think we might leave Pat to his bath. As for me, what I need right now is a cup of tea. Will you join me?'

'Why not?' said William.

'Right-ho. Lead on — Mr Caldwell, wasn't it? Thanks, Jacko.'

Jacko waved away the thanks and the two men went through into the hotel.

'It is true, then, Constable — about the bushranger?' said William, sitting down at the table he had just vacated.

The constable eyed him up. 'Well, I reckon that depends what you mean.'

'I heard the story last night, here at the hotel. As I say, I only arrived yesterday.'

'Yes, so you did,' said the constable, as the landlady brought out a pot of tea and two more large cups.

'I was told about it by Mr Fuller, in fact.'

'Ah yes, that'd be Ben Fuller.'

'Of course, you know him.'

'Oh, we knocked around together a bit a few years back,' said Constable Perry. 'I grew up here, see. But tell me, what's brought you here, if you don't mind me asking?' He poured tea into the two cups and looked up with a smile.

'I've come to Australia to study the animals. Platypuses, in particular. I'm a, er ... a naturalist, you see, and there are certain aspects of the breeding biology and development —'

'Oh, I get it,' said Constable Perry, leaning back in his chair. 'Mining, eh?'

'No, really. Platypuses. Whether they are oviparous ... whether they lay eggs.'

'You're telling me you brought half a ton of stuff all the way here to study platypuses?'

So this man already knew about his equipment, too. 'Well, I wasn't sure how much would be available here, you see.'

'All to find out if duckbills lay eggs.'

'Yes, among other things.'

'I don't know — some blokes. Won't believe a kangaroo hops till it lands on your bunion. 'Course the bloody things lay eggs, any bushman can tell you that.'

William was unfamiliar with the term. 'Bushman — is that the same as a bushranger?'

'No, no. Bushman: someone who lives in the bush — not a townie.'

'Ah yes, I see. And are you a bushman then, Constable? Have you seen platypus eggs?'

'Never seen them myself, but I'll bet Pat has.'

Sergeant O'Malley appeared, clad once again in his dusty uniform but no doubt a much cleaner man beneath it.

'Let's ask him. Hey, Pat, you'd have seen a water-mole's egg, wouldn't you?'

'I have. Why do you ask?' The sergeant drew up a chair but stayed standing as he poured himself some tea.

'Mr Caldwell here, he's a naturalist. He says he wants to find some. To show the bastards — sorry, people — back home.'

The older man smiled. 'Oh yes, I've seen them all right.' He took his seat at the table. 'And look, I do believe there's some coming now.'

The landlady emerged from the kitchen with two steaming plates each piled high with steak, sausages *and* two fried eggs.

William eyed the food. 'In that case,' he said, lifting his eyebrows and giving a long, straight-faced sigh, 'it looks as though I have come to the wrong place. You see, I was looking for eggs of the duckbill — not the chicken-bill.'

Sergeant O'Malley only just managed to swallow his mouthful of tea before his face cracked open.

'Oh, you'll do, Mr Caldwell, you'll do.' He laughed. 'Now, has Jim here given you the treatment? About the bushranger, I mean.'

'I have indeed, Pat,' said the constable. 'But I'm not sure Mr Caldwell here's going to be much use to us. He only arrived yesterday. Or at least, that's what he says …' He looked at William through narrowed eyes.

'Take no notice of him, Mr Caldwell,' said the sergeant, still chuckling, though now through a mouthful of sausage. 'Don't worry, we already know all about you.' He put down his knife and fork and swallowed. 'William Hay Caldwell, aged twenty-four. Arrived Sydney, 22 May 1884 on the *Jane Dark*. Arrived Brisbane June 5th left Brisbane on the 7th aboard the *SS Rockhampton*. Letters of introduction from the Governor of Queensland and the Chief Magistrate. Come to Australia for the scientific investigation of *Orno … Ornitho …*'

'*Ornithorhynchus anatinus*,' said William. 'Sergeant, I am most impressed.'

The sergeant bowed his head. 'It's our business to know things, Mr Caldwell. But I think we can rule you out as one of our suspects. No, it's another man we'll be looking for. And we'll find him, won't we, Jim? We'll find him.'

Constable Perry nodded.

'I am relieved to hear it, Sergeant O'Malley,' said William. 'But your words suggest that you are looking for only one man. Is it true that only one man robbed the coach?'

'That's what the driver says — it happened just the other side of Gin Gin. Old trick, dropped a tree across the road. The driver stops the coach and next thing he knows there's a rifle pointing at his head. Wore a mask, though the driver thought he could see a beard.' (Well, thought William, that rules out at least one per cent of the male population.) 'On foot, too, he reckoned — he didn't see a horse. But he wasn't going to argue with the gun. He's only got two passengers, government men, come from the mines at Mount Alice. The robber orders them all out of the coach, then throws the driver three ropes. Tells him to tie up the hands of the two passengers and throw the ends of the ropes up over the branch of a tree. The robber takes hold of them, pulls them tight so the poor blighters' arms are high above their heads and ties them to the trunk of the tree. Then he tells the driver to throw the other rope over another branch and make a slipknot. The driver has to put his hands in, wound round like, and the robber pulls that one tight too and ties it off. And away he goes with the strong box and four horses. Nice work, eh? It took them two hours to get free and another two to walk into Gin Gin.'

'But tell me, Sergeant, do you think it will be safe for me to ride to Gayndah.'

'Alone?'

'No, I have engaged a man here to accompany me. He seems to know these parts. I told your constable about him, he knows him. His name is Ben Fuller.'

The sergeant paused. 'Frankly, Mr Caldwell, my guess is that the villain is long gone now, or he'll be hiding away somewhere till things quieten down. This robbery came out of the blue as far as I can see. I think you'll be all right. Have you got a gun yourself?'

'Yes — but oh, I'm afraid my guns are all packed up in my boxes.

They've gone on ahead, in the wagon.'

The sergeant and constable exchanged a glance. 'They left yesterday?'

'Yes,' said William. 'Last night, with Harry Norton, he's the bullock driver. He said I'd be bound to overtake him before he got to Gayndah.'

'You — or someone else,' said the sergeant. 'What did you have in these boxes, besides the guns?'

'Well, everything really,' said William. 'I was advised that I should buy everything else I needed before I got here — tents, furniture, supplies and so on. And of course I brought a lot of scientific equipment with me from England.'

'Equipment?'

'Microscopes, slides, bottles, labels, preservatives, that kind of thing.'

'Any money?'

'I have my money with me.'

'Would Harry Norton have known what was in the boxes?'

'No. He didn't ask, I didn't tell him. He didn't seem curious.'

'Anybody else know?'

'I don't think so,' said William. 'I mentioned here last night that the wagon had gone on ahead, but I'm sure everybody already knew that — just as you seem to know all about me.'

'Like I said, it's our job to know,' said Sergeant O'Malley. 'But I confess I'm just a little worried about the boxes. What do you reckon, Jim?'

'They sound tempting,' said Constable Perry.

'As I said, my guess is that the villain is long gone. But it wouldn't hurt to ride out and check that everything is all right. Just to be on the safe side.'

'When? Should I come?' said William, then remembered he had no horse. 'I haven't got a mount yet, though. Mr Fuller is getting me one, but according to Jacko he won't be back until after lunch.'

The sergeant looked him up and down. 'I'm sure we can find you a nag, and another hand won't hurt.'

After Sergeant O'Malley and Constable Perry had finished their breakfast the constable went out to the stables to see about a horse.

'Useful having a local lad on a job like this,' said the sergeant, nodding towards the departing back of Jim Perry. 'People are more likely to talk.'

'Your constable mentioned he was born here,' said William.

'Born and raised in Bundaberg, family worked on the cane — lick him and he'll taste like sugar candy.'

'So tell me, Sergeant, how do you go about catching a bushranger?'

'Well, Mr Caldwell.' The sergeant helped himself to another cup of tea and leant back in his chair. 'I'll let you into a little secret — you might call it the Patrick O'Malley theory of the criminal mind. Twenty years I've been a policeman now, and I've made a few — shall we say — scientific observations. You'd understand. Now, it may come as a surprise to you to know that most thieves — most criminal thieves, that is — are not too bright. Clever maybe, but not bright. Of course there's thieves in every walk of life. The bright ones, they go off and become businessmen and lawyers and do their thieving legal. Police can't touch them. It's the others that we're left to deal with. And though a lot of thieves steal from need — it's the way they make their living, so to speak — there's always the other side to it. They steal for the fun of it, and the glory. And there's little fun or glory if you can't talk about it, if you can't skite a bit. Thieves always talk — to someone. Always. And that someone'll talk to someone else. So our job is to find that someone, or that someone else. And if we treat them nice enough we'll soon know what we need to know.'

'So you don't go round looking for clues, like detectives in a novel?'

'If I can get to where it happened soon enough, maybe. But I find that it's usually best to let the crime mature for a while — to ripen, if you see what I mean. Like I said, you've got to give them time to talk, give a chance for the word to start spreading. If there aren't people in this town now who know who robbed the coach, there soon will be. Then all I have to do is find 'em and, well, talk to 'em.'

Constable Perry appeared at the door. 'Jacko's found you a nag — she's no racer but she'll do for a day's trot.' He looked William up and down. 'Those togs'll be all right, I suppose, but you might need a hat.'

William went upstairs to fetch his things — as well as the hat he might as well take his bag, too. He found the other two men outside the stable getting ready their horses. Jacko was saddling a third horse, nearer to a pony in size.

'She may not look much, Professor,' he said, 'but she's got a busy foot.' He eyed William up and down before adjusting the stirrup straps. 'There, that should do you. And you'd better take this.' He hooked a canvas water bag onto the saddle and tied William's bag on behind.

The other two men made the final adjustments to their gear and mounted the horses. Jacko went into the stable, returning with two rifles that the policemen had left in his keeping.

'Have you used one of these?' said the sergeant.

William looked at the gun. An old Martini .303, just like the one his uncle had brought back from the Sudan, the one that he had learned to shoot with. He nodded.

'Then you take mine. I still have my revolver.' The sergeant unhooked the saddle holster and passed it across.

When William had fixed it to his own saddle Jacko handed him up the rifle.

'Fully loaded, safety catch on,' said Jacko. 'Good luck.'

William slipped the gun into its holster.

'Know where we're going, Jim?' said the sergeant.

The constable grinned. 'Follow me.'

The three men took the main road west out of town, Constable Perry leading at a trot. For the first ten miles or so the road was smooth and level, lined with fields of tall sugar cane that later gave way to open woodland. Homesteads and cottages got further apart, until by noon William noticed they had been riding an hour without seeing a single house or human figure.

There was no need for the constable to lead the way now; the road was clear enough for anyone to follow, even if the trail had not been well marked by cattle dung, not yet dried by the sun. William dropped behind the other two men, happy to have this opportunity to take in the sounds and smells of this new country without the distraction of conversation.

The scent of eucalyptus trees, the shape of their leaves and the way they hung down, the colour of their bark. Above the fast clip-clop of his horse's hooves shrill insect songs. Crickets, perhaps. Birds and other animals were more scarce. Once William saw what he thought might be an eagle circling high in the sky, and once the tail of a lizard — or was it a snake? — disappearing into the grass beside the road. But as they passed a bend in the river lined with tall gum trees a sudden cacophony of birds erupted into the air (like … like a thousand white petals tossed to the sky) and suddenly it was as if he could feel every leaf of every tree, every feather of every bird, every molecule in the air around him. And for the first time he really knew that he was on an adventure. He was an explorer — not of untrodden lands, perhaps, but of the mysteries of nature. He looked around him. The white birds still wheeled in the blue sky above, a dusty road stretched on ahead. With the wondrous tools of modern science, in service to its mighty empire, he would soon be baring secrets unknown from this unknown land. His whole life had been in preparation for this opportunity. He would not waste it.

They made good time, alternately walking and trotting the horses, until at about one o'clock they passed a single-storey house, then another and another and soon they were in a small village. William urged his horse forward and caught up with the others. Jacko had been right: she was a game little thing.

'Gin Gin,' said Constable Perry, pulling up at a crossroads in what William imagined must be the centre of the village. The constable nodded to the right hand fork in the road. 'A few miles down there on the Mount Alice road, that's where the coach was robbed. We'll stop here and maybe find out more about it, and when the wagon went through — about daybreak, I'd guess.'

Thin smoke from a chimney suggested that at least one of the homes was occupied and Jim Perry disappeared round the back of the small cottage. After some minutes he emerged from the front door followed by a boy. He looked about twelve years old, skinny, ginger-haired, bare-footed and freckled from nose to knees.

'The young fella here says that he heard a wagon go through just before seven.'

'It'll be at the creek by now,' said the boy. 'Ten Mile Creek. They always stop there for a bit of feed, the bullockies.'

'Well,' said the sergeant, 'sounds like everything might be all right then. I could do with a bite to eat myself. What do you say?'

'Would you believe the same thought had crossed my own mind, Pat?' said Jim Perry. As he spoke a young woman appeared from inside the house carrying a tray on which was an almost-whole loaf of bread, a joint of cold mutton, a knife and three plates. The constable beamed. The woman was followed by another boy, younger than the first but equally freckled and ginger-haired, carrying a large stone jug of milk in both arms.

'Help yourselves, gentlemen,' said the woman, setting out the food and milk on the veranda table. 'Bring the cups, please, Donald — and oh, could you find that chutney? Here, use the tray.'

The older boy went to fetch the things.

'I'm sorry,' said Jim Perry, 'what was I thinking of. Grace — Mrs Gordon — this is Sergeant O'Malley and Mr Caldwell. Gentlemen, Mrs Grace Gordon.'

William could not help but think Mrs Gordon a most handsome woman. Though dressed in a plain cotton dress with a white smock, the simplicity of her clothes only accentuated the quiet beauty of her face and the neatness of her figure. She did not have the fair skin and ginger hair of her sons (that must have come from their father). Her own skin was lightly tanned and her hair, now tied back in a loose bun at the back of her neck, was auburn rather than red.

'You are most welcome, Sergeant, Mr Caldwell.'

'And you are most kind, Mrs Gordon,' said William with a small bow.

'Indeed you are, Mrs Gordon, indeed you are,' said Pat O'Malley. He paused, looking first at the woman, then at his offsider. 'You'll excuse me asking, but are you by any chance previously acquainted with Constable Perry here?'

The woman smiled up at Jim Perry, and it was he who spoke.

'Didn't I mention? Me and Grace here was at school together. In Bundy. And Blue and me, we was mates.'

Seeing further explanation might be necessary, the woman added, 'Blue — David — was my husband.'

'Indeed he was,' said Jim, staring down into his cup of milk.

'He's dead, Sergeant,' she said, and realising that Jim Perry was not going to say anything more, she added, 'He was killed last year, in the mine.'

Jim Perry seemed to be feeling a little uncomfortable. Could it be that he had once felt — and perhaps still had — some feelings of affection for Grace Gordon?

'I'm sorry to hear that, Mrs Gordon,' said the sergeant, and William saw him turn to his constable and give a broad wink. The effect of this was to make Jim Perry choke on the milk he had just raised to his lips. The woman moved towards him to help. Grabbing the cloth in which the bread had been wrapped she began wiping the milk from his shirt. Pat O'Malley's grin became wider still. Perhaps it might be time to steer the conversation in another direction.

'Your children must be a great comfort to you, Mrs Gordon,' said William. 'There is a school here in Gin Gin?'

'Not at the moment, Mr Caldwell,' said the woman, wiping her hands on her smock and refilling Jim Perry's cup. 'I have been thinking of starting one myself, if I can save up a little money. My boys can both read and write — I taught them that myself — but there's other children in the village that can't. I think they should — do you not agree, Sergeant?'

Education was clearly a matter Sergeant O'Malley thought should not be taken lightly. 'Indeed I do, Mrs Gordon,' he said, his face now serious. 'In this modern age, it is hard to see how you can get along without an education.'

'And of course I hope it will provide me with some income.'

'The mine, where your husband worked,' said William. 'The mine company is of no help?'

'I'd like to see the day a mine owner takes to charity.' The woman spoke the words with some bitterness. 'The union has been a great support but I cannot go on relying on that for the rest of my life.'

'Nor would you, mother, if only you would let me work in the mine.'

The woman glared at her elder boy. 'Donald, we have spoken about this before. You will excuse my son, gentlemen.' She gave him another look even sterner than the first.

'Sorry, Ma.'

William looked more closely at the boy. He was small and skinny. His ears stuck out. His knees, below the legs of his short trousers, looked like knots in a rope. William could not imagine his being much use in a mine.

'How old are you, Donald?' he said.

'Fourteen,' said the boy, then glancing toward his mother, 'well, fourteen next January.'

'Another year of your mother's learning will be of more use to you than any job,' declared Sergeant O'Malley. 'Mark my words.'

'Thank you, Sergeant. I want no child of mine working down that mine.'

The boy looked up at her. 'It was good enough for fa —'

'It was good enough to *kill* your father.'

'I think you might listen to your mother, young Donald,' said Pat O'Malley. 'Why, was I not myself twelve years old when I left school — and look at me now.'

The boy seemed unsure how to take these words and Sergeant O'Malley, satisfied that his comment had ended the conversation, wrapped another piece of mutton in a thick slice of bread, tossed off his cup of milk and got to his feet.

'I think we should not waste any more of your time, Mrs Gordon. I thank you for your kindness to myself and my two friends — or should I say (and here the smile reappeared on his lips) to Jim Perry here and *his* two friends.'

Taking a large bite from his sandwich, he tipped his hat to the woman, shook hands with each of the boys and walked down the steps to where the three horses had been tied. No one seemed to be making any mention of payment for the lunch they had just enjoyed. William took a crown from his pocket and tucked it beneath the plate. He hoped the woman would not think of it as charity.

five

The peculiar characters of the *Ornithorhynchus* are:
— The male having a spur upon the two hind legs, close to the heel.
— The female having no nipples.
— The penis of the male being appropriated to the passage of semen; and its external orifice being subdivided into several openings, so as to scatter the semen over an extent of surface, while the urine passes by a separate canal into the rectum.
There is every reason to believe that this animal is ovoviviparous in its mode of generation.

   Sir Everard Home, 'A Description of the Anatomy of the *Ornithorhynchus paradoxus,*' *Philosophical Transactions of the Royal Society of London*, 1802

'So, what do you reckon, Jim?' said Sergeant O'Malley, glancing down at the road. 'Anyone else been by this morning?'

The signs of Harry Norton's bullocks, though now dried out by the hot sun, were still clearly visible as they headed out of town on the Gayndah road.

'Not as I can see. I asked young Donald if he'd heard anything. Sharp lad. He said he hadn't, but he reminded me about the back road round the town — that track on the right a couple of miles back. Cuts off a fair distance but it's too steep for wagons. Joins this road again about three miles before the river.'

Sure enough, half an hour later William saw on the right another track joining theirs. Jim Perry stopped and dismounted, crouching low over the dusty road.

'One horse, ahead of the wagon by the look of it.'

'How far ahead?' said Sergeant O'Malley.

'Difficult to say, but it must have come out of that side road before the wagon got here. In a bit of a hurry, too.'

William could see no signs of anything at all in the stony ground.

'What does it mean?' he said.

'Oh, probably nothing, probably just some local. But we'll find out soon enough. The wagon won't be far ahead now. We might just take it quietly, though.'

In silence the three men rode on, around a large hill then over a smaller one. William could still follow the trail of dung and occasionally he could see the tracks of the wagon wheels, but none of a horse. Jim Perry must have a keen eye. Just over the crest of the second hill the constable stopped them with a raised hand. Below, William could now see the river and the ford. And on the grassy flats twelve bullocks, released from their yokes, quietly feeding. Halfway into the river was the wagon. There was no sign of Harry Norton.

'We'll just stop here a minute under this wattle, eh?' said the sergeant, directing his horse into the shade of a small tree. He dropped silently from his saddle. Constable Perry and William did the same. 'There's no sense hurrying into these things.'

Holding their horses by the reins, the three men waited and watched.

'Are you seeing what I'm seeing, Jim,' said the sergeant at last.

'Looks quiet enough to me, but where's Harry?'

Save for the high trilling coming from the trees around (those insects again), all was indeed quiet. Quiet enough for William to hear the tearing and munching of the bullocks as they pulled up each mouthful of grass, quiet enough to hear the song of a small black and white bird that was dancing from one animal's back to another, its song amplified by the bowl of the valley. Quiet enough to hear a soft groan.

'Did you hear that?' murmured the sergeant. 'Where do you reckon it was coming from, Jim?'

The constable pointed towards the wagon and Sergeant O'Malley nodded.

'I think it might be time to take a little look down there. Why don't you two wait here?'

The sergeant gestured towards the rifle on Jim Perry's saddle. The constable slipped it from its holster and released the safety catch; William did the same with his. Sergeant O'Malley led his horse from the shade of the tree and began walking it down the hill. Another groan. The sergeant did not alter his pace. He continued walking towards where the wagon rested in the river, its wheels making small ripples in the current.

Blue sky, warm sun, cool water flowing through a shady valley with its trees and birds and insects and cattle grazing. It was as peaceful a picture as one could imagine, almost a painting. But something was wrong. William looked down at the gun in his hands, and back towards the river. He had shot deer before, and grouse, but he had never shot a …

A sudden shout from below interrupted his thoughts and he saw Jim Perry raise his rifle. Sergeant O'Malley had reached the wagon and was wading into the water. For a moment he disappeared behind the wagon and they could hear splashing, then they saw him again, struggling or pulling at something, and they could hear some indistinguishable words.

There was another groan and a splash and the sergeant stood up and called to them. 'I said you can come down now.'

William and Jim Perry got back onto their horses and trotted down the hill. They soon saw what Sergeant O'Malley had been wrestling with. He was pulling an apparently lifeless Harry Norton from the water. But as they came closer they found that as he was pulling, he was laughing.

'You can put those guns away,' he said, still chuckling. 'Here Jim, you take him. Come and have a look at this, Mr Caldwell.'

William followed the sergeant round to the front of the wagon. On the floor by the driver's seat was a large glass bottle, tipped over onto its side but still part full of a clear liquid.

'Would you recognise that?' said the sergeant.

Indeed William did, and he could now see that the lid of one of the boxes had been part opened.

Sergeant O'Malley picked up the bottle and smelled it. 'Not bad stuff,' he said, passing William the bottle. 'Powerful, too.'

'It's pure spirit,' said William. 'One hundred per cent ethanol.'

The sergeant took another sniff. 'And I thought a Scotchman like you'd be a whisky man.'

'It's not for drinking, Sergeant, it's for preserving specimens.'

Constable Perry had managed to drag the unconscious Harry to the edge of the water but it took the three of them to lift his dead weight clear and prop him up against a tree trunk. Throughout the operation the bullocky gave out a series of groans and half shouts. He was as drunk as a lord.

'How long do you think he'll be like this?' said William.

'Your guess is as good as mine,' said Sergeant O'Malley. 'But my guess is this wouldn't be the first time your man here's lips have touched hard liquor.'

'So what'll we do, Pat?' said Constable Perry.

The Sergeant looked William up and down, then over to Harry Norton slouched against the tree. 'It looks as though Mr Caldwell's stuff is safe enough — most of it anyway. I'm thinking you and me might head back into Gin Gin — we could get back there by sundown. I wouldn't mind having another chat with that friend of yours, Jim — maybe a few other people there, too. What about you, Mr Caldwell?'

William took a moment to consider his own options. Now he was here it might be better to stay with his equipment. It would take the bullock driver a while to sleep off the alcohol, but there were worse places to spend a few hours. Green grass, shady trees, cool rippling water. There were indeed worse places.

'I think if it's all right with you I'll stay with Mr Norton here. Perhaps you could take the horse back for me.'

'We can do that all right, can't we, Jim?'

The constable smiled his assent.

'But wait,' said William. 'I've just remembered. What about that other horse, the one that was ahead of the wagon?'

'You didn't notice?' said Jim Perry. 'It turned off the track just up the road there. Like I said, probably just a local.'

'In that case, I don't think I'll be needing this,' said William, unfastening the rifle and holster from his horse. 'Here you are, Sergeant. And may I say how very grateful I am to you — and to you, Constable Perry — for all your trouble.'

'No trouble at all, Mr Caldwell. I'm sure you'll be safe enough now. Harry here'll look after you, eh?' The sergeant strapped the rifle to his own saddle. 'And I hope all goes well with your water-moles.'

'I trust that your own investigations are equally successful, gentlemen. I cannot pretend to be sorry that we didn't come across the outlaw today, but I am sure that you will apprehend him before too long.'

'We'll catch him all right,' said the sergeant.

As Jim Perry handed down his bag William took three coins from his pocket. 'I fear I left the hotel without settling my bill. Perhaps you would pay the landlady for me — and Jacko, too, for the horse, you know.'

The constable took the money and after attaching a rope from his saddle to the bridle of William's horse as a leading rein, he swung himself up onto his own mount. With a wave, the two policemen set off back up the hill, leaving William to the peace of the riverbank.

Harry Norton was quiet now, apparently sleeping. The bullocks continued to graze on the deep grass. Insects still called from the trees. After all that excitement, perhaps William might have a rest himself. He found a spot beneath the shade of a tree a little distance from the snoring bullock driver, arranged his bag as a pillow and lay down. Within minutes he, too, was fast asleep.

The insects were still singing when William awoke though the sun was now just below the treetops. He felt drowsier than when he had fallen asleep. Harry Norton was snoring even more loudly now — perhaps that was what had woken him. The water looked cool and inviting. What he needed, he decided, was a refreshing bath.

Just below the ford the river deepened into a wide pool, though the water was clear enough to see the large round pebbles that covered its bed. He saw something move in the water and for a moment thought about crocodiles — but no, he was sure there were no crocodiles this far south. It was only a fish. He took off his clothes and waded in.

The current was slow and gentle and the water just right, cool but not cold. When he was waist-deep he sank down so that it reached up to his neck and ducked first his face under, then his whole head. Yes, this was what he needed. He put his head back and let his legs float up. As he drifted downstream the leaves of the trees dappled the sunlight, dragonflies darted around him, blue and red. A little grey bird leapt and pirouetted from a branch above, its tail spread out like a fan. And then suddenly he was scrambling from the water. Something had bitten him, something had bitten his buttock. He dashed for the bank — it might be following him. Grabbing the thin trunk of some tree he heaved himself clear, and as he turned to look behind him he saw a brown shape turn and swim away.

The thing swam back towards a ring of sand about ten feet away. The water was only a couple of feet deep there, and as it passed over the light sand he could see its outline clearly. It was a fish, about two feet long with broad head and tapered, unforked tail. He had been attacked by a fish? William twisted his neck and shoulders to look down at where he had been bitten. No mark was visible, no blood. It had been the shock rather than the pain that had so scared him.

The fish swam round the sand circle and appeared to pick something up in its mouth. It carried the object — William thought it might be a stone — to the centre of the ring and dropped it there. Then it returned to where it had picked up the stone and turning onto its side, flapped its tail to and fro, sweeping up the sand into the water. This had the effect of allowing any mud that had been mixed with the sand to float away, leaving the clean sand to sink back to the bed of the river. It also exposed another small stone, which again the fish picked up and dropped at the centre of the ring. Satisfied with its work, the fish rested on its pile of stones.

Another fish appeared from downstream, slightly larger but

similar in shape. It headed straight for the ring. As soon as it arrived there the first fish rose up from beneath it and both swam a tight circle over the pile of stones. They pirouetted in this way for a minute or two, the smaller fish sometimes nudging at the new arrival. Then the larger fish bent double around the head of the other, at the same time shaking itself. The two thus entwined sank down towards the pile of stones. Just before they touched them the larger fish untangled itself and swam off. The smaller fish stayed behind, swimming gently to and fro over the stones. Surely the two fish were mating. The ring of sand with its mound of stones must be their nest.

William again found himself thinking back to his childhood in Scotland, and to one Christmas in particular. It was some time before his parents died, so he can have been no more than nine years old. Uncle Angas had given him for a Christmas present a mysterious box and a book. He still remembered the book's dark red cover and the title embossed in gold: *The Aquarium* by the Reverend P.H. Gosse. And inside the box was indeed a real aquarium, glass on three sides, zinc at the back and bottom, puttied into a frame of welded iron. William devoured the book and marvelled at the little glass tank. He could hardly wait until the end of March when the small pond over the road from their home would thaw and he could start dipping for specimens to put into his wondrous glass-sided box. Among his first specimens, among the water plants and water insects and water snails, were five little fishes — five sticklebacks.

With the book to guide him, William watched as over the next few weeks two of the sticklebacks' bellies began to turn deep red. These, according to the Reverend Gosse, were the male fish and they were coming into their breeding colours. The two males fought frequently, the one chasing the other round and round the little tank, but each still found enough time to prepare a nest, a tunnelled bed-chamber of silken algae. Once its nest was complete each male took to hovering proudly outside, or swimming to and fro, to and fro.

The other three, duller fish were females and all were growing fat with eggs. William fed the fish — according to instructions —

on chopped liver and 'wurrums' (it was Uncle Angas's insistence that this was how the word should properly be spelt). The females were drawn to the males' displays as children to a circus parade. The closer a female came, the more frantic would be the display; the male darting back and forth, in and out of the weedy tunnel. And finally the female made her decision. Into the tunnel she went, closely followed by her attentive suitor. She laid her eggs and left in a trice. The male squirted his milt down onto them.

But then, horror of horrors. The female stickleback did not remain with her new husband. Off she swam, abandoning her mate and her soon-to-be children. And more horrors. The male continued to display outside his nest, and the next day a second fat female approached and watched and entered. Could she not see the other eggs already there? Did she not care? No, she laid her own eggs within the already occupied nest and the male shed more seed upon them.

The Reverend Gosse had certainly not described this scandalous behaviour in his book. Perhaps William had by chance caught some morally aberrant specimens — perhaps it was something to do with the size of the tank or the temperature of the water. But he suspected not. With a child's intuition he suspected that his sticklebacks were no different from any others of their kind living in any other pond or aquarium, perhaps no different from many other animals as well. The faithful spouse, the loving mother, the united family were perhaps not as universal — as natural — as Mr Gosse and William's own parents and teachers would have had him believe. This was a revelation to the young William Caldwell but one he knew instinctively was not the kind of thing to discuss with any adult — not even Uncle Angas.

Sitting on the bank of a Queensland river William felt a long way from that Scottish childhood. Even his Cambridge days seemed far away, as if the bright Australian sunshine was already bleaching his memories. Had he really spent a whole six years — a quarter of his life — studying and working at the university? It seemed so distant now, somehow unreal. He looked about him. There was nothing unreal about the fish in the creek, still patrolling its nest of sand. There was nothing unreal about the trees, or the feel of twigs beneath his bare feet, or the cool play of the breeze on his naked skin. He looked back upstream. There was certainly nothing unreal about the solid wooden wagon in the ford.

He stood up and wandered back along the bank. How on earth had Harry Norton known that there were bottles of spirit in that case? He checked the other cases but none appeared to have been tampered with. There was no doubt that they, or their contents, were worth money — though he doubted that a bullocky or a bushranger would have much use for a Coddington microscope or a Jaetz microtome, or the various bottles of fixatives and stains and other solvents that were packed away with them (thank goodness Harry Norton hadn't opened one of the bottles of methanol and drunk that — he might have blinded himself).

As William began pulling on his trousers he looked over to where the bullocky lay propped against the tree, still snoring, his stockwhip by his side. He stirred, and muttered in his sleep, his hand reaching for the whip. William hadn't noticed the stockwhip before. It was only when he took a pace towards it and saw it move that he realised that the long brown object was not a stockwhip at all. It was a snake, and the bullocky's fitful movements had disturbed it.

The snake's head was only inches from the outstretched hand of the sleeping bullocky. There was no time to wake him, there was no time to find a gun. Another movement and the snake might strike. Perhaps he could find a stick — yes, there was one, a good, straight, strong one. Not taking his eyes from the snake William bent down and picked up the stick, but before he could raise it the crack of a rifle bullet stung his ears. A cloud of dust spurted up beside the sleeping bullocky. The snake, as surprised as William, dashed for the water.

William turned to see a man on horseback. He was leading a second horse and for a moment William thought that Constable Perry had returned. But as the man trotted down the hill William could see that the horse he was leading was considerably larger than the one William had borrowed from the hotel. And his face was clean-shaven, and he wore no uniform. A wide-brimmed hat was low over his eyes. One hand held the reins, the other a rifle. He rode up to where William still stood half-dressed, stick in hand.

'Damn,' he said. 'Missed the bugger.'

six

The water-mole or duckbill is to be found throughout the colony. The female is oviparous, and lives in burrows in the ground, so that it is to be seen either on shore or in water.

Extract of a letter from Sir John Jamison, *Transactions of the Linnaean Society of London*, 1818

'What the blazes …?' said Harry Norton, scrambling to his feet.

One of the bullocks took off across the creek. With frightened bellows the others followed.

He turned to William. 'Can't a hardworking bloke have a kip without some clod-skulled gurnet shooting at him and scaring his beasts? Look what you've done.'

'It wasn't the Prof, Harry, it was me.'

William had only just recognised the new visitor as Ben Fuller. With his beard shaved off he looked a different man.

William pulled on his shirt and fastened his belt. 'Perhaps we should look at what *you've* done, Mr Norton,' he said, walking over to the wagon and returning with the half-empty bottle. 'And while you were, er … resting you were very nearly bitten by a snake. I think you owe Mr Fuller your thanks.'

'Yes, I reckon you owe me a beer, Harry,' said Ben Fuller, 'or something stronger. Mind you, if that snake had decided to bite you, I'm not sure which would have come off worse.'

'What do you mean?' said the bullocky, glaring at him, then at the bottle in William's hand. 'I was thirsty, I thought that stuff was water. Trying to poison a man like that.'

William looked towards the creek, flowing cool and clear, then back at Harry Norton.

'Bah!' said the bullock driver. 'Snake indeed. I can't see no furnickin' snake. And anyway, who's going to help me with my beasts?'

The beasts in question, having splashed their way across the ford, were now standing quietly on the other side. The water seemed to have had a calming effect and two or three of them were drinking at the bank.

'They look all right to me,' said Ben Fuller. 'And tell you what, I reckon I could do with a drink myself.'

He handed the reins of the two horses over to Harry and went down to the river, where he took off his hat and drank several handfuls of water, splashing more over his face and neck. William put the half-empty bottle of spirit back in its case and joined him.

'I must say, Mr Fuller, I'm very pleased to see you,' he said, 'though a little surprised. I didn't recognise you at first without your beard.'

Ben Fuller rubbed his cheeks and smiled. 'Not a bad job, eh? Had to do it myself, of course — couldn't seem to find a barber in Bundaberg anywhere. Looks like you didn't have much luck either.'

'He seems to be a hard man to find. I suppose Sergeant O'Malley told you what happened?'

Ben Fuller's eyes narrowed. 'Sergeant? I haven't seen any sergeant.'

'He left here not three hours ago, he and Constable Perry. They were heading back to Gin Gin. You didn't meet them on the road?'

'Three hours ago?' said Ben Fuller. Then after a moment's thought, he added, 'Oh, I see. They must have gone into town. I came round the back way. Must have just missed each other by a whisker.' He smiled again.

'Oh well,' said William. 'No matter. Now you're here I'm very pleased to see you. And I see you brought along that extra horse.'

Ben Fuller was riding a fine grey mare, but the horse he was leading was no less fine — another mare of about the same size but more dapple than grey. And she was wearing a saddle.

'I managed to get my business fixed up quicker than I expected. I thought I'd check up on Harry here, then go back and pick you up. Looks like I've saved myself a trip. You'll still be needing a hand, I suppose?'

William considered the matter. There was no reason he could not finish the journey on the wagon, but on the other hand there would still be some advantage in going on ahead to arrange things in Gayndah.

'Well, if you can still spare the time …'

'It's agreed then,' said Ben Fuller. He looked at the sun, now low in the trees. 'But I don't reckon we'll be doing much more riding today. This'll be as good a spot as any to spend the night:

A patch of sunshine here and there
Lay on a leaf-strewn water-pool
Whose tribute trickled down the rocks
In gurgling ripples, clear and cool.

What do you say?'

William agreed that it was indeed a fine spot and there seemed little point in riding further that day. If they made an early start tomorrow they would reach Gayndah by evening. Harry Norton was keen to move on.

'Better travelling at night,' said the bullocky, screwing up his eyes against the low sun. 'Cooler for the animals.'

'And for a sore head, eh, Harry?' said Ben Fuller.

He helped the grumbling bullock driver muster and yoke his beasts onto the wagon and within an hour they were ready to go. Harry climbed aboard and took hold of the whip.

'Get along there you clarty scumps,' he said, a little half-hearted but scowling with more than his usual malevolence. The bullocks took the strain and the wagon moved off out of the water and up the other side.

'Well if we're going to camp here we'd better get a fire going, eh, Prof?' said Ben Fuller. 'Here, catch.' He threw William a box of matches. 'I'll look after the horses.'

William looked around him. There seemed to be plenty of wood. As Ben Fuller unsaddled and hobbled the horses and let them loose onto the grass, he stacked a large heap of twigs and branches that he hoped would serve as a fire. By the time Ben Fuller had finished his work William had already used six matches trying to light his creation. Ben Fuller shook his head and took the matchbox from his hand. He made a small pile of twigs no thicker than straws and applied a light. The twigs flared. He added more and larger twigs until the fire was blazing.

'Haven't lit too many fires before, eh, Prof? Got the idea now?'

William nodded. He clearly had much to learn about living in the bush. Ben Fuller went down to the river and returned with several large stones, which he placed carefully round the fire.

'Do you reckon you could fill the billy?'

'Yes, of course,' said William. He went over to where the saddles lay on the ground, hoping that he would be able to deduce what a 'billy' was without having to ask. He decided on the one container he could see that might hold water — a fire-blackened tin pot — and filled it from the river.

'I'm afraid it'll only be tea and damper tonight,' said Ben Fuller, taking the billy from him and settling it over the flames.

'Tea and damper sounds capital,' said William. He was sure that he would discover soon enough what damper was.

The blazing fire gave a cheery feel to the camp and the billy was soon boiling. Ben Fuller threw in a small handful of leaves, stirred them with a stick and soon both men were sipping hot tea from a pannikin. The damper — a simple dough of flour and water as far as William could see — was cooking in the ashes.

'This is the life, eh, Prof? Like the poet said:
Here halting wearied, now the sun was set,
our travellers kindled for their first night's camp
The brisk and crackling fire, which also looked

> *A wilder creature that 'twas elsewhere wont*
> *Because of the surrounding savageness.*
> *And soon in cannikins the tea was made*
> *Fragrant and strong; long fresh-sliced rashers then*
> *Impaled on whittled skewers, were deftly broiled*
> *On the live embers, and, when done, transferred*
> *To quadrants from an ample damper cut,*
> *Their only trenchers.*

Sorry, there's no bacon tonight, Prof. But let's see what this damper looks like.' Ben pulled the dense loaf from the fire and brushed away the ashes. 'Here you go.'

He broke off a piece and handed it to William, who took a bite. Not bad really — a little solid, perhaps, but not bad at all.

That night William did not sleep well. His bones ached from the day's ride. The longer he laid on the ground the harder it seemed to get. His stomach rumbled and grumbled as it tried to digest the damper. Every time he felt himself drifting off some unexplained sound would startle him to wakefulness. But eventually he must have fallen asleep because he awoke well after dawn to the crackling of a fire and the smell of wood smoke. A bird was carolling from a nearby tree.

> *'Oh ye who are gifted with souls*
> *And delight in the music of birds.*

Awake at last, eh, Prof? I thought maybe that brown snake had bitten you in your sleep.'

Ben Fuller was squatting by the fire cooking something on some kind of grill. 'Help yourself to tea. This cobbler'll be ready in a tick.'

William sat up. The sun was almost over the hill. He got to his feet, stretched and walked over the fire. Between two loops that Ben Fuller had made from thin branches of some tree and woven between them a few similar twigs — forming what looked like a pair of primitive tennis racquets — was a fish, split open and gutted. Its head was missing but from its tapered tail William guessed it was one of the pair he had watched the previous day.

'Cobbler,' said Ben Fuller, turning it on the fire. 'Jewfish. Ugly buggers but they taste all right.'

'I think I saw one yesterday, making a nest in the river there.'

'Yes, that'll be the one. No more nests for this one though, eh? And she's about ready, so grab yourself a bit of damper.'

Ben Fuller took the fish from the fire, opened the makeshift grill and lifted off the bones in one. William broke off a piece of last night's damper and held it out. The fish tasted good, delicate and moist, and it certainly helped the damper go down. He poured out two pannikins of tea and the men ate their breakfast in a companionable silence.

Well before the sun was clear of the trees Ben Fuller had packed up their gear and they were on their way. Both the horses were in fine condition and they caught up with the wagon before noon. Harry Norton pulled up beside the road to share a billy of tea. William made a small show of inspecting the load — as far as he could see all the boxes were still intact — and in half an hour he and Ben Fuller were on their way.

It was another fine day, the sun shining bright in a clear blue sky.

'Keep this up and we'll be in Gayndah by nightfall easy,' said Ben Fuller.

They were riding mainly through forest — 'scrub', according to the local man — and again William was surprised at how seldom he saw or heard a bird in what otherwise appeared to be untouched country. But he did hear plenty of insects — 'locusts', apparently — and the noise they made more than made up for the lack of birdsong. Although William could not actually see one, they seemed to be calling from every tree.

A couple of hours after leaving Harry and the wagon behind, they came to a small stream.

'Time for another smoko, I reckon,' said Ben Fuller.

'Two-thirds of our journey at least is done
Old horse! Let us take a spell
In the shade from the glare of the noon-day sun
Thus far have we travelled well.

Wouldn't you say, Prof? Now, just give that horse of yours

enough rope to reach the water. That's the way. How about I'll do the billy this time? You fix the fire.'

William found some small twigs and soon had a fine blaze going. While he was getting more wood his eye was caught by a strange-looking creature on the trunk of a tree. As he approached it remained quite still, and it was only as he reached towards it that he realised it was dead. No, not dead exactly. It was the empty skin of some insect. Almost the size of his thumb, it clung to the bark of the tree with the claws of its four back legs while its front pair were slightly raised. They were strangely shaped, like the claws of a crab or a lobster. He unhooked the creature from the tree. It was as light as paper. He could see two protuberant eyes and a beak-like mouth tucked in underneath the thorax. There was a split down its back where the adult insect must have emerged. He had never seen anything like it.

'What've you got there, Prof?'

William brought it and the wood over to where Ben Fuller was arranging some stones round the fire.

'I don't know,' he said, holding it out.

'Oh, a locust skin. Don't you have them in England then?'

'No. At least, I've never seen one — nor in Scotland for that matter.'

'You're from Scotland, then, are you, Prof? My granny came from Scotland, you know. Let me see now — Inver-something or other I think it was.'

'Inver-something. Would that be Inverailort?'

'I don't think so. Something like that, though.'

'Inveraldie, perhaps?'

'No. No, I don't think that was it.'

'Inveralligin? Inverallochy?'

Ben Fuller shook his head.

William took a deep breath, perhaps the deepest breath he had taken since he was eight years old. 'Inveramsay, Inveran, Inveraray, Inverarish, Inverarity, Inverarnan, Inverasdale, Inveravon, Inverawe, Inverbeg, Inverbervie, Inverboyndie, Inverbroom, Invercannich, Invercassley, Inverchaolain, Inverchapel, Inverchoran, Invercoe, Inverdruie, Inverernan, Inveresk, Inveresragan, Inverey,

Inverfarigaig, Inverfolia, Invergarry, Invergelder, Invergeldie, Invergloy, Invergordon, Invergowrie, Inverguseran, Inverhadden, Inverharity, Inverie' — another breath — 'Inverinan, Inverinate, Inverkeilor, Inverkeithing, Inverkeithny, Inverkip, Inverkirkaig, Inverlael, Inverlaidnan, Inverlair, Inverlochlarig, Inverlochy, Invermay, Invermoriston, Invernaver, Inverneg, Inverness, Invernoaden, Inverquharity, Inverroy, Inversanda, Invershiel, Invershin, Invershore, Inversnaid, Inverugie, Inveruglas, Inveruglass, Inverurie' — last breath — 'or perhaps you were thinking of Kilmichael of Inverlussa?'

The expression on Ben Fuller's face was all that William might have desired.

'How the hell did you do that?'

'I'm surprised I could remember them,' said William, panting but amused. 'I haven't spoken that list out loud for fifteen years.'

'Well, stap me. Can every Scotchman do that, then?'

'Not as far as I know. It was my uncle. Very proud of Scotland, was Uncle Angas — still is, he's not dead yet. He made me learn them. No, that's not quite right. He said he'd give me a shilling if I did.'

'I reckon you earned your bloody shilling, Prof. And no doubt my dear old granny did come from one of those places you mentioned, but I'm blowed if I know which one.'

'Perhaps she came from Inverness — that's near where I grew up.'

'Well I reckon that's it then,' said Ben Fuller, putting three large pinches of tea in the billy. 'And I suppose that means we're cousins — what do you reckon?'

William laughed. 'Almost certainly.'

'Well if that's the case, I reckon you should call me Ben. Here, give me that.' He took the insect skin that William was still holding in his hand. 'You know, when I was a kid we used to make money out of these. There was this old Chinaman, he'd give us a penny a hundred. Used them for medicine, would you believe? I don't know what he did with them, but. Ground them up maybe, I don't know.'

'Where did you grow up, Ben?'

'Oh. Lots of places. We moved around a lot. Mostly up here in Queensland — Toowoomba, Rockhampton, Bundy for a while — but we had a couple of spells down Sydney way too. Itchy feet, had my dad.'

'Is he still alive, your father?'

'I don't know, and I can't say I care much. He shot through when I was twelve, when my mum died. What about yours?'

'Both my parents died when I was ten. There was an epidemic — diphtheria. My father was a doctor. He sent me away, to my uncle up near Inverness. He stayed on. And my mother.'

It was strange, when he thought about it, to lose both parents like that. But was it not even stranger that he felt nothing? Nothing then, nothing now. Had they really loved him, had he loved them? It was hard to separate reality from memory.

'Who took care of you after that, then?'

'My uncle, my mother's brother, Uncle Angas — the one who made me learn all those Invers. He and my Aunt Agnes, they didn't have any children of their own.'

'Blimey, we're a couple of sad stories then, aren't we? Here, come on, pass me your mug.'

As soon as he had finished his tea William went back down to the stream. Now he had got his eye in he could see the strange insect skins on every tree. 'Locusts,' Ben had called them — but locusts were a kind of grasshopper, weren't they? These looked like no grasshopper he had ever seen.

'Here, Prof, over here.'

Ben was holding a large green insect in his fingers. 'Greengrocer,' he said. 'We had names for all the different ones when I was a kid. Greengrocers, floury millers, black princes, double drummers. Double drummers, they were big 'uns. Twice this size. Only needed fifty of them skins for your penny.'

William took hold of the insect in his own fingers where it struggled, slowly. Though it looked similar in some ways to the empty shell he had found — the same triangular head and large bulbous eyes — it was not only its colour that had changed. This creature had wings. Magnificent wings, transparent but veined with a network of green threads. The effect reminded William of the leadlight windows of Uncle Angas's library at Morar. They were folded along each side of the insect's body but he could see through them to the abdomen beneath. Set into each side of the abdomen was a flat area, the size and shape of ... what? A baby's fingernail? He may never have seen a creature like this but he now knew what it must be. It was a cicada.

He released the insect onto his other hand, where it began crawling towards the tips of his fingers. It did not fly away, but settled itself and began to call — a loud but quite musical buzz that started from nothing but got louder and louder as it blended in with its neighbours. Another insect flew past, another 'greengrocer' by the size and colour of it. It circled close, then suddenly landed on his hand with a clatter of wings. William was so surprised by this unexpected manoeuvre and the feeling of being gripped by three pairs of insect feet that he shook his hand. Both insects fell, but before they reached the ground they spread their wings and zoomed back into the trees.

Fascinating. Was the second insect, he wondered, a rival of the first that had been about to do battle — or was it a member of the opposite sex which had been attracted by the song? He again tried to find one of the singing insects for himself. They were all around him — he could hear them — but find one he could not. It was impossible to tell just where each individual song was coming from. He listened carefully, turning his head this way and that. One must be singing from that small tree over there. He got to the tree and paused. He could still hear the sound but now it seemed to be coming from behind him. He turned and crept slowly back to where he had been a moment ago. No, he had been right the first time, it *was* coming from that small tree. And he was sure the insect hadn't flown off; he would have seen it if it had.

Ben Fuller had packed up the billy and was bringing the horses up from the stream. 'Looking for one of them locusts, are you?'

'Yes, but it's strange. Every time I get near one, the sound seems to be coming from somewhere else.'

'Come over here, Prof,' said Ben, an amused expression on his face. 'Now turn around.'

William felt something being plucked from the back of his shirt. He turned to see Ben Fuller holding in his fingers a large green cicada.

seven

In the *ornithorhynchi* the yolk-bags are formed in the ovaria; received into the oviducts, in which they acquire the albumen, and are impregnated afterwards; the foetus is aerated by the vagina, and hatched in the oviduct, after which the young provides for itself, the mother not giving suck.

Sir Everard Home, 'On the Ova of the different tribes of Opossum and *Ornithorhynchus*', *Philosophical Transactions of the Royal Society of London*, 1819

West of the hills the road dropped down once more into the valley of the Burnett River. Not only was it flatter here, it was drier. The trees, though still tall, were widely spaced. Coarse grass grew between them, dry and already turning brown. In the distance ahead William saw what looked like a cloud of dust.

'Yes,' said Ben. 'I seen 'em. Heard 'em, too.
Hark, the bells on distant cattle
Waft across the range,
Through the golden-tufted wattle
Music low and strange.
That'll be drovers, bringing a mob up from the Darling Downs.'
'A mob?'
'Cattle.'

'Where are they taking them?'

'Maryborough, I expect, or Bundy. They mostly go to Brisbane but if you bring them up and around here at this time of year you can put a bit of fat on them on the way. I've done a bit of droving myself in my time.'

'And what else have you done, Ben?'

Ben continued looking into the distance. 'Oh, a bit of this and, er ...'

'A bit of that?'

Ben turned to William and smiled. 'That's about it. Horses mostly, a bit of prospecting — and pearling once, up north.'

'Prospecting — gold, you mean?'

'Gold, silver, copper. Plenty of money there. Plenty of heartbreak, too.'

'So you've been a miner?'

Ben gave a horrified look. 'Mining? Digging holes in the ground? Not for me, thank you very much. No, no, that's a fool's game is mining.'

'What do you mean, then?'

'Prospecting, trading, speculating. You make a strike, and then you sell it. Or you buy a claim and look for someone else to buy it off you. That's the way to fill your pocket.'

'And the droving, is that a way to fill your pocket?'

'Ah, the droving.' Ben shook his head and looked again towards the cloud of dust down in the valley. 'No, that's the way to fill your soul. Like the poet says:

With a running fire of stockwhips and a fiery run of hoofs
Oh! the hardest day was never then too hard!'

He continued to stare off towards the cloud of dust. 'What about you, Prof? Ever drove cattle?'

William shook his head. 'We have led very different lives, Ben. Since I graduated from the university I have only had one job: in a laboratory, at the same university where I studied for three years, looking down a microscope all day. Cambridge is said to be a lovely city but for the six years I was there I sometimes think I hardly saw it. I seemed to live and work in that basement — in winter I wouldn't see the sun from one day to the next. It was dark when I went to work, dark again when I went home.' William looked around him at the wide valley and broad sky. 'I think part of me envies your freedom, and your experiences.'

'Yes, maybe you're right at that, Prof.' He turned to William. 'Look, we'll be meeting up with this mob soon, and the usual go is to stop for a bit of a yarn. Never know, might be some old mates. All right with you if I ride on ahead?'

'Of course.'

Twenty minutes later William caught up with him squatting beside a small campfire with three other men.

Ben stood up. 'You're just in time for a brew, Prof. And I want you to meet some friends. Charlie, Mac, Johnny — this is Mr William Caldwell as I was telling you about.'

A pannikin of tea and a piece of dusty damper were thrust into William's hands and he found himself being inspected by three pairs of inquisitive eyes. All three men were bearded, all wore hats (one of them so full of holes it was a wonder it held together) and all were covered from head to foot with the red-brown dust.

'I am delighted to meet you,' said William, raising his cup in greeting.

No one else raised theirs, but one of the men spoke.

'You're giving Ben here a bit of honest employment, I hear, Mr Caldwell.'

'That's right, Mr — er — Charlie. And may I say he has already proved his worth. Did you tell them about the snake, Ben?'

'Yes, we heard about that,' said the man. 'You'll have to look out for them round these parts, Mr Caldwell. Plenty of snakes round here, all sorts. But Ben tells us you're looking for water-moles.'

'That's right. I've been told Gayndah will be a good place to find them. Do you know the area?'

A discussion followed on the merits of Gayndah, and the Burnett River, and it was agreed that it would be as good a place as any to look for moles if moles were what you wanted. The talk turned to droving. More tea was poured and stories swapped about places that William had never heard of but liked the sound of — Wallumbilla, Goondiwindi, Waar Waar — and herds and flocks in thousands, tens of thousands.

'Do drovers move sheep, too?' said William.

'Used to,' said Charlie. 'Not any more, not round here. There was some fine runs round here, back in the old days. Then the speargrass came. Moved in from out west during the drought of '64, they say.'

'Ever seen speargrass, Prof?' said Ben.

'I've never even heard of it.'

Ben looked around him and plucked the head from a tall whiskery grass stem. To William it looked a little like barley.

Ben pulled out two seeds, still attached to their long, stiff hairs. 'Here you go.' He gave one to William, the other he put in the palm of his hand. 'Now watch this.' He spat on the seed.

William watched, and within seconds the seed began to writhe as the long hairs began to curl and twist.

'Like a drill,' he said. 'And got barbs on 'em, see?'

William inspected the seed he had been given. It ended in a sharp point armed with two short backward-facing bristles.

'They get into the wool, and then every time they get wet, or they dry out, they twist and they twist. With them barbs they can only go one way, deeper and deeper into the wool — then into the skin. Drives the animals mad.'

The seed continued its writhing, though there was little chance of it penetrating the scarred and calloused skin of the hand Ben Fuller was holding out.

'This, this little grass seed, means that you can't raise sheep here?'

'Can't raise them, can't run them through,' said Charlie. 'Cattle are all right. Speargrass don't stick to cattle like it does to sheep. A few years back we'd bring ten thousand sheep through here in a single mob, no trouble. Not no more.'

'Yes,' said Ben. 'Good times, eh, Charlie?'

'Some good and some not so good.' Charlie got to his feet. 'But we'd better get these beasts moving on. Good to see you, Ben. Nearly didn't recognise you without a beard. Good to meet you, Mr Caldwell.'

He held out his hand. The others stood up. The man with the perforated hat kicked dirt onto the fire while the other began packing up the billy and cups. Charlie untied the reins of William's horse.

'Nice animal,' he said. 'Where did you get her?' William nodded towards Ben. 'Won't ask where *you* got her, eh, Ben? Must have cost you something.'

'Nothing I couldn't afford. I know where there's a couple more like her if you're interested.'

'Not sure I could pay your prices, Ben.'

'Ah well, you get what you pay for, eh, Charlie?'

Charlie smiled and looked him in the eye. 'And you pay for what you get, eh, Ben?'

Charlie held the horse while William mounted then handed him up his reins. 'Let me know if you want any droving work, Ben. Good luck, Mr Caldwell. And watch out, won't you? For those snakes, I mean.'

Once they were out of sight of the drovers William looked over to see Ben Fuller loosely clutching the reins of his horse, his chin on his chest. He was surprised to see that Ben's body was being racked with what sounded like small sobs. William stared at him in puzzlement.

'Is there anything I can ...'

Ben Fuller lifted his head and William saw that he was not crying, he was laughing.

'Well,' said Ben, 'I never thought I'd see it.'

'See what?'

'Charlie, Charlie Boyd, droving cattle again. I never thought I'd live to see the day.'

'But I thought you and he were drovers together?'

'Yes, a while back. But now? Charlie Boyd? I'm surprised anyone'll let him near a beast.'

Seeing that William was still none the wiser, Ben explained. 'Look, Prof, I'd better come clean. Better you hear it from me than from someone else. Like I said, I've had plenty of jobs in my time, but I spent a bit of time inside a while back — guest of Her Majesty, if you understand my meaning. That's where me and Charlie met up.'

William was not sure what to say. Should he be impressed or horrified at the news that the man he was riding with had been in gaol? This was Australia after all — half the population had been sent out here as convicts, hadn't they? And as Ben said, it had all happened some years ago.

'What was he gaoled for?'

'That's the joke, see? Duffing, cattle duffing,' said Ben, and laughed again. Seeing that William still did not understand, he said: 'Stealing cattle.'

'Oh, I see. And you?'

Ben flashed him a dark look. Then his expression softened. 'You're a new chum, Prof, there's a lot you got to learn here. Take it from me, that's not a question you ask. But, I suppose there's no reason I shouldn't tell you — after all, it's not like I killed a man or nothing. Fraud, they called it. I was done for salting a mine.' And seeing William again shake his head, he said, 'Suppose you're trying to sell a mine — well, you want it to look its best, only natural, isn't it? So you might sort of "decorate" it.'

'With "decorations" brought in from somewhere else, you mean?'

'You've got the idea, Prof. And no one would have known, if a certain party hadn't found out and mentioned it. It was your mate Jim Perry, in fact. Used to be my mate, too, a few years back. But don't you worry. Like I said, that was a while ago now. I learned my lesson. As the poet says:

Could half the foolish things that might be told
Of each and all of us, be somehow rolled
Into a visible heap upon our track
The wisest — yea, a Solomon, alack!
Would look behind him — only to behold
A mountain of sheer folly at his back.'

He gave a rueful smile, then his face became serious.

'Oh yes, I learned my lesson well.' He looked over towards William. 'Still — funny about Charlie.'

'Funny?'

'Well, cattle duffing — that's a capital offence round here.'

'I'm not sure I understand.'

'You know, Prof, I'm not sure the judge understood it either.'

Ben Fuller reined in his horse. William stopped beside him.

'As I recall, the trial was on a Monday morning. Old Judge Barwick it was, so of course there's no doubt about the verdict — guilty as charged. The judge comes back after lunch and says to Charlie: "Well, my merry boy. You're found guilty by a jury of your peers and the law says you're going to be hanged. Now I don't like these things dragging on any more than you do, so we'll get it over quick, shall we?"

'"Suits me, Judge," says Charlie. "What say Friday at the latest?"

'"Right," says the judge. "And as I'm sure you know, noon is the usual time."

'"Good-oh," says Charlie.

'Now old Judge Barwick, he's known throughout Queensland as a hard man but a Christian man and a man who always keeps his word. So Charlie thinks a bit.

'"But there's one thing, Judge," says he. "If it's all right with you I'd rather not know the actual day I'm going to meet my maker. I don't mind dying — we've all got to die and it looks like my time's up — but I can't think of anything worse than knowing exactly when it's going to happen. I know it'll be one day this week, but how about I don't know which day until you tell me on the morning of the hanging?"

'"Fair enough," says the judge, "you have my word on it." Like I said, he was a hard man but a Christian man and he didn't want Charlie to suffer any more than he had to.

'"Thank you, Judge," says Charlie, "and good on you. 'Cause it looks like you'll have to let me go."

'"Let you go be buggered," says the judge.

'"Well, think about it, Judge," says Charlie. "You can't hang me on Friday. That's the last day you said, and if I'm still alive Thursday night I'll know for sure I'm going to be hanged at noon on Friday. That's against what you just promised me, so I think you'll have to agree that Friday's out."

'"Humph," says the judge.

'"That means Thursday's the last day you can hang me," says

Charlie. "But you can't hang me on Thursday because by Wednesday night there's only two days left — Thursday and Friday — and Friday's already out so the hanging'll *have* to be on Thursday and I'll know for sure on Wednesday night."

'"Hurrumph," says the judge.'

'I think,' said William, 'that I'm beginning to see where this is leading.'

'I thought you might, Prof, educated man like you. That left Tuesday and Wednesday. Says Charlie Boyd to the judge: "I won't know which day I'm going to die until you tell me on the morning of the hanging — that's what you promised, wasn't it, Judge? Now, Friday's out, and Thursday's out, and if I'm still alive Tuesday night I'll know for sure I'm going to be hanged at noon on Wednesday, so Wednesday's out, too. That leaves tomorrow. But you can't hang me tomorrow because I knows it for sure today."'

'And?' said William.

'Well, Prof, you just seen Charlie for yourself,' said Ben Fuller, urging on his horse with a dig of the heels and click of the tongue. 'Judge Barwick, though. I never did hear what happened to old Judge Barwick.'

An orange tree, its dark foliage and bright fruit incongruous against the more muted colours of the surrounding bush, gave the first sign they were reaching their destination. Looking for a house to which this tree might belong, William saw only a ruin of broken timber and rusty sheets of iron. As they rode further into town it was clear that Gayndah was a town past its best. Their weary horses clip-clopped down the single main street, past two boarded-up hotels, some run-down houses and an empty shop. In such a new country it seemed strange to find such desolation and decay. One building stood out. Freshly painted, the little cottage lay behind a flower-filled garden that still caught the last rays of afternoon sun. Each rose, marigold and snapdragon glowed as if lit from within. But it was an exception that only served to emphasise the general drabness of the town.

Ben pulled up his horse outside a building whose peeling sign labelled it as the Club Hotel, while another sign above the open door identified the licensee as William Henry Pike. The inn showed little sign of life. Tying their horses to the hitching rail the two men pushed open the door to find themselves the sole inhabitants of a large but somewhat decrepit bar room. Thick dust and cobwebs masked the windows, no lamps were lit to counter the gloom. Yet beneath the dust, polished timber and faded mirrors spoke of a grander past.

'Anyone here?' shouted Ben. 'Billy, are you there?'

A noise, apparently coming from beneath the floor, indicated that someone or something was about.

'He's in the cellar.' Ben walked across the room to an open side door and shouted through it. 'Billy, are you there?'

William heard the sound of heavy footsteps on stairs and a man appeared in the doorway carrying a crate of beer. He was bald and fat, and he dropped the crate onto the counter with a rattle and a grunt. 'Yes, I'm bloody here. Who's asking?'

'It's me, Billy,' said Ben. 'It's me, Ben Fuller.'

The man stepped back and peered at his face. 'Bloody hell so it is,' he said. 'Ben Fuller. I didn't recognise you. Jeez, I thought they'd strung you up years ago.'

'I thought they'd have strung you up, too, you bastard,' said Ben, slapping the publican on the shoulder. 'How are you going?'

'How does it look as though I'm bloody going? Going to hell via purgatory, that's where I'm going. That's where the whole bloody place is going.' He pulled a bottle from the crate, swung open the stopper and took a long pull. 'What in God's name are you doing here, Ben?' he said, wiping his mouth on the back of his hand. 'I thought you'd be pleased to see the back of this bloody place.'

'So you're glad to see me, eh, Billy?' said Ben. He coughed theatrically. 'Billy Pike, I'd like to introduce Mr William Caldwell.'

Billy Pike peered up at William as if he had only just noticed him. 'Happy to meet you, mate,' he said. He sounded anything but.

'Mr Caldwell here, he's come from England — sorry, Scotland — to look at water-moles.'

'Water-moles? Plenty of bloody water-moles round here — not much else.'

'I am delighted to hear it, Mr Pike,' said William.

'What do you want 'em for — fur? There's not much bloody fur on a water-mole.'

'No, no,' said Ben. 'Mr Caldwell is a scientist — that's right, isn't it, Prof? He's looking for their eggs.'

'And Mr Fuller — Ben here — has been kind enough to act as my guide.'

'I thought we might have a bit of a look around, you know, up the river,' said Ben.

'And you want to stay here?'

It seemed to be a concept the publican had not had to consider for some time.

'Just for a couple of nights maybe,' said Ben. 'To start with. While the professor here has a look around.'

Billy shrugged his shoulders. 'I can give you a bed, I suppose, and I can give you a bloody drink. I can't give you much else.'

'Well let's start with the drink, eh, Billy boy? I think I might start with a small glass of water.'

'Water? This is a bloody pub. Here.'

The landlord pulled two more bottles of beer from the case and opened them. Ben picked one up and raised it in salute. Billy picked up another and also took a swig. They both looked over at William.

'You would not by any chance have a glass, would you, Mr Pike?'

The landlord paused, then reached under the counter and pulled out a dusty glass. He peered into it, turned it upside down, and knocked it against the counter a couple of times before putting it down in front of William.

'Thank you,' said William. 'And when you're ready, would you be able to see to our horses?'

Billy Pike gave both the men a long hard look. He put down his bottle and left the room. William poured his beer into the glass and went to sit at the large table by the window. Ben joined him.

'I'm sure I saw a sign outside saying that this was a hotel.'

'Indeed it is, indeed it is,' said Ben. 'The finest hotel in Gayndah, in the old days.'

'So,' said William, 'you know the town, Ben?'

'I used to know it, back then. Did a bit of work around here.'

'Prospecting?'

Ben nodded. 'Used to be a big gold town, Gayndah — did I tell you that? I did all right here, for a while.'

Was this a reference to the unfortunate incident of the salted mine? William now knew better than to ask. 'So that's when you met Mr Pike.'

'Yes. Billy was here when I came. He was one of the first to make a claim, him and his mate, and he made enough out of it to buy a block of land and build this hotel. This was going to be his real goldmine. Doesn't look like it turned out that way.'

'And you?'

Ben was silent for a moment. 'Well, you could say I struck lucky. Found myself a bit of gold — just lying round on the ground, it was.'

'But not enough?'

'Enough at the time. Should have done something with it I suppose, but well — *Could half the foolish things that might be told*, eh, Prof?' Ben took a long mouthful of beer. 'Yes, used to be quite a place, did Gayndah. And this hotel, packed it was, every night.'

William surveyed around him. The room looked as though it had not been swept or dusted for years. Cobwebs draped not only the windows but even the lamp glasses (when had they last been lit?).

Billy Pike came back and dropped into his seat by the bar. 'I've put your horses round the bloody back, but you'll have to see to the saddles yourself. It's more than my bones'll bear.'

'That's all right, Billy, you leave 'em to me,' said Ben. He finished his beer, tilting back the bottle to reach the last drop. 'Any feed out there?'

'Might find some hay in the back stable.'

'And what about some tucker for me and the professor here?'

'You could have let me know you were bloody coming. Look, I'll go and ask Mary. She might have an egg or something.'

Billy Pike heaved himself to his feet and disappeared through the front door, while Ben headed for the back. William looked again around the empty room.

Now that his eyes were more accustomed to the gloom he

could read an advertisement on the wall extolling the qualities of Charles Heidseck's Finest Extra Quality Champagne. When had champagne last been drunk at the Club Hotel? A faded poster on the far wall announced that Miss Jenny Renn, 'Australia's brightest song-bird', was due to appear at the Club Hotel, Gayndah, on November 18th — which year, it didn't say. Perhaps he would have another beer, though it looked as though he might have to get it himself. He leant forward on the table to push himself up and as he did so felt the top give way slightly beneath his hands, as if the oilcloth was covering no more than loose boards. William lifted the cloth. Beneath it were indeed boards. And under the boards was another table, a billiard table.

There was still no sign of the landlord. William cleared the bottles from the table, rolled up the oilcloth and lifted the boards off one by one, resting them against the wall. Dust and dirt had fallen onto the faded green cloth. A jagged tear stretched from the baulk line almost to the centre, revealing the cracked slate beneath. Fastened to the side at the bottom end William found the maker's label: 'GEO. ATKINSON, WOLVERHAMPTON, ENGLAND.' How sad to see a good billiard table so neglected. He heard the back door opening and Billy Pike came in with an empty tray.

'A fine billiard table, Mr Pike.'

'Waste of bloody space, if you ask me,' said Billy Pike. He picked up William's empty glass. 'You finished with this?'

'I'd like another if you don't mind. But does nobody use the table?'

'Used to.'

'Perhaps if you had it repaired?'

'And who's going to bloody pay for that?' said the landlord.

William looked around the empty bar. 'Well, yes, you have a point, Mr Pike. You do have a point.'

All in all William spent a surprisingly comfortable first night at the Club Hotel. The kind neighbour had provided not only eggs but some chops for their dinner, and Billy Pike had found a few potatoes which he boiled up to serve with them. The bed had been neither too hard nor too soft, the sheets dusty but clean. True, William had a slight but now familiar sense of déjà vu when at breakfast he was again offered chops and eggs, and once again there seemed no time to shave, but when he and Ben rode off just before nine o'clock to explore further upriver the day was fine and so were William's spirits.

In the clean morning air the town did not seem quite as depressing as it had appeared when they had arrived the previous evening. As they rode back along the single street that formed the main thoroughfare of Gayndah, William tipped his hat to each of the few people they saw. Some smiled back. A grocer's shop, a telegraph office, a haberdasher's and a hardware store-cum-undertaker's seemed to be the only commercial premises. The bank, by far the grandest building in the town, was not only closed but closed up, and even the church looked unused. The two-storey house beside it — presumably the parsonage — was also empty. All the other houses in the town were single storey, including the one whose garden he had noticed the previous afternoon. Its kaleidoscope of orange marigolds and nasturtiums, red geraniums, blue wallflowers and tall hollyhocks of many colours made, thought William, a most pleasing display. In the corner of the veranda he noticed a girl — a young woman, perhaps. She was sitting on a chair in the sunshine, her dark hair tied back with a red ribbon, some knitting on her lap. William tipped his hat. She looked towards him but made no sign of acknowledgement.

'And which house did you live in when you were here, Ben?' said William, still looking at the girl as they rode on past.

Ben had his eyes on the road before them. 'Oh, don't ask me, Prof — like I said, it's been a while.'

William continued to look at the girl for as long as he could. He thought he saw another face through the side window of the house but when he looked again it was gone. He could only see the girl sitting, knitting.

Ben had suggested over breakfast that they explore the river upstream of the town for a suitable place to set up camp. In fact he might know just the spot. He had camped there himself and he was sure he would remember. William had already made up his mind not to stay in Gayndah. Apart from the quality of accommodation, he wanted to be close to the area where he would be collecting. When his tents and equipment arrived he would be self-sufficient as far as living arrangements went. A weekly trip into town for fresh supplies would be all that was needed.

The two men wandered along the riverbank for a couple of hours, through glades of trees and across the occasional small stream — no, he must get used to calling them creeks — running into the river. There were no fences and no sign that the land had been cleared. But despite this William did not have the feeling of being out in the wilds. The land may have been untouched, it did not seem untouchable.

Ben stopped his horse. 'This is it,' he said.

The place where they had halted was in relatively open woodland, raised well above the water. Ben looked around him. 'Yes, this is it for sure.'

How typical of an Australian, thought William — or of an Australian bushman like Ben Fuller. He could not remember a house from twenty years ago but he could remember a camp site. The river was fifty yards away, down a steep bank.

'Would it not be better to camp lower down, closer to the water?'

Ben shook his head. 'See that?' he said, pointing to some leaves and branches caught twelve feet up a paperbark tree growing near the bank. 'That's how high this river can rise, and it can happen just like that. I've seen it. It might be dry as dust here but if there's a storm up in the ranges the water'll come thundering down this valley like a tidal wave. Always best to camp up on a rise.'

William looked around again. Away from the riverbank the ground was flat for a hundred yards in each direction. The tall trees gave a pleasant shade. It seemed as good a spot as any. The two men dismounted and tied their horses to a bush.

'Coolabahs,' said Ben, noticing William looking up at the trees. He pointed over to the opposite bank. 'River red gums. You don't camp under red gums, not unless you want to wake up dead.'

'Why not?' said William. Was this some bush superstition?

'Widow-makers, red gums. Always dropping their branches.'

As if the trees had heard his words there was a snapping sound and a crash from across the river. William again thought how fortunate he had been to meet Ben Fuller.

'I see what you mean. And do you think there'll be platypuses in the river here?'

'Here as much as anywhere, I reckon.' Ben took off his hat and scratched his head. 'But look, Prof, you can come clean with me. You know I'm not one for blabbing. What are you after? Gold, silver? What's all that stuff you've got on that wagon really for?'

William laughed. 'Ben, I probably wouldn't know a lump of gold if I tripped over it. I assure you, my research is purely platypusical.'

'All right, Prof.' Ben Fuller shook his head and replaced the hat. 'If you say so. So, how are you going to get these water-moles? Shoot them?'

'I wouldn't want to take the chance of damaging them with gunfire. I've been told that it is quite a simple matter to dig them from their burrows.'

'Rather you than me. Sounds like you've got a bit of a job ahead of you.'

'I thought I might be able to hire some men — some boys, perhaps — from the town.'

'Well, no harm in trying.'

'Or some of the native people. An acquaintance in Sydney — Doctor Bennett — told me that he always used to employ the local natives.'

'Hah,' said Ben. 'You'll be lucky to get any of them to work. Like the poet said:

There's not the slightest danger, friend,
That you'll be asked to take the spade!
That game was tried and in the end
We hardly think the labour paid.

Anyway, you won't find too many niggers around here these days. Most of them cleared out twenty years back.'

William was shocked. This was 1884.

Ben Fuller saw the look on his face. 'Short for Negro. Like Ben's short for Benjamin. Nothing wrong with that, is there, Prof? I'll tell you what, you should hear some of the words they call us.'

His companion's choice of language was not William's only worry. Doctor Bennett had taken some care to emphasise the usefulness of employing native people. If there really were none round Gayndah, this was bad news. But perhaps some of the townspeople would assist.

After a midday meal of tea and damper (what William would already give for a piece of fresh fruit) he and Ben spent the afternoon surveying the new camp site. The tents would be best up on the high ground. A latrine could be dug in the sandy soil closer to the river. The two men rode up and down the river for a couple of miles in each direction. During his ride William kept an eye open for a platypus, though he had read that the animals seldom appeared in full daylight. Once he saw an animal swimming along the surface of the river and called out.

'Water rat,' said Ben.

Another time he heard a loud splash.

'Water dragon.'

Ben explained that a water dragon was a large lizard. 'If you want to see a water-mole you'll have to wait until it starts getting dark. But we don't want to be hanging around till then. I'll brew up a billy and then we ought to be getting back to town.'

eight

> Cookoogong a native, chief of the Boorah-Boorah tribe, says that it is a fact well known to them, that this animal lays two eggs, about the size, shape, and colour of those of a hen.
> Doctor Patrick Hill, 'Observations on *Ornithorhynchus*', *Transactions of the Linnaean Society of London*, 1822

Going by the number of empty bottles on the bar, Billy Pike was already on his ninth beer of the day by the time William and Ben Fuller arrived back at the Club Hotel. William's glass was standing ready. Before they had even come in through the front door the publican had lifted another couple of bottles from the crate on the table and opened them.

'Good on you, Billy,' said Ben Fuller. 'I'm as thirsty as a dingo in a drought.' He picked up one of the bottles and took a long pull. Clearly William was now such an accepted member of their drinking fraternity that he could pour his own beer.

'How did it go?' said Billy. 'Did you find a camp?'

'Just the spot,' said Ben. 'Down from the old blacks' camp. Anything been happening around here?'

'Let's see now.' The publican appeared to give the matter deep thought. 'Oh yes, I remember. About midday. Had to kick a bloody blowfly out of the bar for bloody buzzing.'

Ben Fuller laughed. 'And what have you found us for dinner?'

Before the landlord could answer they heard familiar sounds from the street outside, the plod of hooves and the creak of wooden wheels followed by a string of incomprehensible oaths.

William put down his glass and went outside to find Harry Norton climbing from the wagon. 'You made good time,' he said, looking at the boxes — as far as he could tell all seemed to be in order. 'We weren't expecting you until tomorrow.'

Harry fixed him with a dusty stare. 'Amazing how a thirst can hurry a man along.'

William took the hint. 'Perhaps you'd like a beer, Mr Norton. Why don't you come inside.'

Harry grunted and followed him into the hotel. Nodding to the others he took the open bottle that was offered to him and downed it in one.

Billy opened another. 'So,' said the publican, 'how's it going, Harry?'

The bullocky grunted again, took the second bottle and raised it to his lips.

'No more ... problems, then?' said Ben, and by the smile that he exchanged with Billy Pike, William knew that the publican had already been informed of the incident at the creek.

'I'm here, aren't I?'

'And I suppose you'll be wanting some bloody grub, too?' said the publican. Another grunt seemed to indicate affirmation. 'All right. I'll see what I can do.'

As Billy Pike disappeared into the back of the hotel to prepare dinner, the bullocky reached for his third bottle of beer.

'So, a nice quiet trip, Harry?' said Ben.

Harry eyed him up. 'I met those troopers again — well, one of them.'

'Troopers? The professor here told me they'd gone back to Bundaberg.'

'Seems like this one had heard something that made him change his mind. The young one, it was.'

'Ah, that would be Constable Perry,' said William. 'When did you meet him, Harry?'

'Yesterday — he was talking with them drovers. He said to tell you he had a couple of other people to see and he'd be here in Gayndah in the morning.'

'Did he say anything else?' said Ben.

'Yes,' said Harry looking hard at him. 'He told me to make sure I looked after the boxes.' He took another long swig of his beer. 'Now, who's going to help me unload them?'

'A few more miles to go yet, I'm afraid, Mr Norton,' said William. 'Mr Fuller and I have already found the place where I intend to establish a camp site. It's not far.' Harry looked up at him with a scowl. 'Of course, I realise that there will be an additional charge.'

'Better get those animals of yours fed and watered, eh, Harry? Want a hand?'

Ben followed the bullock driver out the back door. William, having nothing better to do, followed.

The bullock driver went to the back of the wagon to get the buckets. Ben Fuller found two more by the pump, filled them and put them down in front of the lead pair.

'Not like that, you loundering scullop,' said Harry Norton, reaching for the two full buckets. Too late. The other bullocks, scenting water, heaved forward, pushing the front pair over the buckets and tipping the water onto the dusty ground.

'Don't you know nothing? You got to start with the last pair, you always start with the last pair.'

As he put his own buckets down before the rearmost animals the back door swung open and Billy Pike appeared. 'Tucker's ready.'

The three men trooped back into the bar.

'Right, who's first?' The landlord put down a plate in front of William and soon reappeared with two more. 'A treat tonight, boys.'

Each plate contained a large fried steak, some damper and some slices of a familiar pale green vegetable. William picked up his knife and fork from the pile that Billy Pike had dumped on the table and prodded the choko with an unenthusiastic fork.

'Oh well,' said Ben. 'At least it'll keep the rot away, eh, Prof?'

'The rot?'

'The Barcoo rot.'

'Barcoo?'
'When we reach the dry channels away to the South
And reach the far plains we are journeying to,
We will cry, though our lips may be glued with the drouth,
Hip, hip, and hurrah for the pleasant Barcoo.
Scurvy.'

'Nasty thing, the rot,' said Harry Norton through a mouthful of sliced choko. 'Teeth falling out, throwing up all the time, sores everywhere.'

With a glance at the bullocky's toothless gums, William pushed some choko onto his fork.

'So, you going to be around tomorrow, Ben?' said Harry. 'I'll need a hand with this stuff.'

'No mate, I've got to be on my way.'

'Oh,' said William, surprised at the news. 'I had hoped you might be able to stay on for a few days, Ben.'

'Sorry, Prof, but four days I said, two days here and two days back. I've got business to attend to. In fact, I reckon I might follow Harry's lead and make a start tonight. The moon, she'll be up soon, eh, Harry?'

It was true that Ben Fuller had originally said that he could only spare four days, but already William had come to rely on his bush skills and enjoy his easy company. How would he cope by himself? *Could* he cope by himself?

'I must say that I'm sorry, too, Ben. And it has just occurred to me that I'll be needing a horse. Would you be willing to hire me the one I have been riding?'

'I don't know about that, Prof, I only just got her. Still, I don't know where else you'd get one round here. What do you reckon, Billy?'

The publican shook his head. 'You could try one of the stations, I suppose, but I wouldn't bet on your bloody chances.'

'I'd be happy to lend her to you, Prof, but there's no telling when I'll be back.'

'I'll buy her from you then. I'll give you a good price.' Once again William felt lost in the negotiation. 'What shall we say? Twenty pounds?'

'You wouldn't be wanting the saddle, then?'

'Thirty?'

'Done.'

'By the way,' said William, 'what's her name?'

'Do you know,' said Ben Fuller, 'I'm damned if I know it myself.'

The following morning there was much to do. Ben Fuller had indeed made a start the previous night as he said he would, but before Harry Norton could set off for the camp site William needed to buy some supplies in town. The proprietor of the general store was happy to supply the basic things he needed — flour, sugar, lamp oil and so on.

'Looks like you're going to be here a while,' he said as he weighed out two pounds of tea from the box on the counter. 'Looking for gold, eh?'

William once more explained that actually he was prospecting for platypuses. 'And I'll be needing some help. Would you know of anyone?'

'No one I can think of, I'm afraid, not round here.'

'I would of course be willing to pay — to pay well.'

'Sorry. It's not the money — well, you've seen for yourself. There just aren't any men around. Soon as they're old enough they're off to Gympie or Mount Alice, to the mines.'

'What about natives?'

'Blackfellows? Precious few blacks round here now. Anyway, they'll all be down in the Bunyas this time of year.'

The storekeeper explained that what local Aborigines there were — the 'Tibboora mob', he called them — moved south every year at this time to feast on the nuts of the bunya-bunya pines that grew in the hills.

'I'm sorry, mate, but looks like you're going to be out there by yourself. You sure you'll be needing all this tea?'

By the time he left the shop William was feeling decidedly despondent. But he cheered up when he saw a familiar horse tied up outside the hotel and found Constable Perry already talking to

Billy Pike at the bar. A third figure was sitting at the table by the window. William recognised the boy he had met at Gin Gin. What on earth was he doing here?

'Ah, there you are, Mr Caldwell,' said the constable. 'Good to see you again. And good to see that Harry arrived all right — and your stuff.'

'I'm pleased to see you, too, Constable. And yes, no further incidents. Mr Norton told us you were coming.' William gestured over towards the boy. 'But we didn't hear you were bringing company.'

'Ah yes, young Donald. Donald, you remember Mr Caldwell? Donald here has something for you.'

The boy stood up and approached the bar. He reached into the pocket of his trousers.

'You left this behind, Mr Caldwell.' In the palm of his hand was a silver crown. 'When you visited us. Mother and me thought it must have fallen from your pocket.'

'No, I ...' William began, then stopped. No, they both knew very well that the coin had not fallen from his pocket. His clumsy attempt at paying the boy's mother for her hospitality had misfired and now the best he could do was go along with the small charade. 'Thank you, Donald.'

But as he reached for the coin he had an inspiration. 'Now that you're here, though' — and why was he here, why hadn't he given the money to Constable Perry to return? — 'now you're here perhaps you might be able to help me. As I think I may have mentioned, I've been hoping to find someone to assist me with my scientific research. Do you know what a platypus is?'

'I know what they is and,' said the boy, drawing himself up to his full height, 'I know how to skin 'em.'

'A useful skill I'm sure. I was looking for someone to help me find platypuses, but they'd need to be willing to cook as well, and fetch and carry and all that sort of thing.'

'I can boil a billy good as the next man.'

'Then you might be the very person I need. There is just one problem of course. What about your mother? I think we'd have to clear any arrangement with her.'

The boy looked over towards the constable.

'I think I may speak for Grace — for Donald's mother,' said Jim Perry. 'With my approval, I'm sure she will be very happy with any arrangement the two of you may make.'

Of course. That was why the boy had come.

'In that case,' said William, 'shall we say five shillings a day?'

'That sounds a fair wage to me,' said Jim Perry, nodding his assent.

The boy grinned.

'Five shillings a day, then, all found. Paid weekly — and the first day's wage to be paid in advance.'

The boy looked with wonder at the coin still in his hand. It was quite possible, thought William, that this was the most money he had ever owned in his life.

'And your first job, Donald, will be to help Harry Norton load some groceries I've just bought onto the wagon. By the way, where is Mr Norton?'

'Mucking up my bloody yard, that's where he is.' Billy Pike nodded towards the back door.

When William took Donald outside they found the bullocky just finishing the lengthy business of yoking the twelve bullocks to the wagon, with his customary endearments. And Billy had not been wrong. The hotel yard was inches deep in hay and dung.

Harry Norton acknowledged William's presence with a grunt, and stared at the boy.

'I've brought along someone to help you, Mr Norton. Donald Gordon, meet Harry Norton.'

The bullocky looked the boy up and down. 'Help me do what? Move feather pillows?'

The boy's eyes narrowed, his lips tightened. Without a word he strode over to some sacks of feed that were waiting to be loaded onto the wagon. He pulled one up onto its end, put his two arms around it and heaved. With the sack just clear of the ground, he began staggering towards the wagon. He had almost reached it when Harry Norton stepped forward.

'Easy there, lad, easy there,' he said. 'Here, I'll give you a hand.'

Donald had no breath left to protest. Harry took hold of one end of the sack and together they swung it onto the wagon.

'All right, lad. You'll do.'

William was almost as impressed by the bullocky's effusive praise as with the boy's strength and gameness.

'Donald has agreed to be my new assistant, Mr Norton. I've asked him to help you load up some groceries from the store — they're all paid for — then you could start off for the camp site.'

The bullocky grunted his usual reply.

'Just keep heading west — I'll catch you up. Donald, you ride along with Mr Norton. Oh, but before you go, do you think you could saddle my horse?'

'Right-ho Professor. What's her name?'

William thought for a moment. 'I think I shall call her Belle.'

Back in the hotel bar Constable Perry and Billy Pike were still deep in conversation.

'You haven't told us yet what brings you to Gayndah, Constable — or was it just to bring young Donald along?'

Jim Perry smiled. 'I hope you didn't mind, Mr Caldwell, but we — his mother and I — did think you might need a hand. Then we met up with those drovers on the way and they told me that your friend from Bundaberg had turned up.'

'Ben Fuller? Yes, apparently you just missed each other at Gin Gin. But surely you saw him? He left last night — you must have passed each other on the road.'

'So Billy here tells me. But no, I didn't see him. Saw his tracks this morning, of course.'

'Oh well, easy to miss someone at night, I suppose. No doubt you'll meet up with him in Bundaberg, or Sergeant O'Malley will. How long will you be staying in Gayndah?'

'Well, I suppose that depends.'

'On what?'

'On what I hear, on what I find out.'

'As you can see, Constable, I'm about to head out of Gayndah myself. I don't suppose your investigations would allow you to join me?'

'Well, why not?' said the constable, after a short consideration. 'After all, I should inspect young Donald's place of work, should I not?'

'Capital. You will be most welcome.'

'But I've got a couple more people to see here first. I might join you a bit later, if that's all right.'

'Of course, but will you be able to find us?'

Jim Perry smiled. 'I think even you could follow the tracks of a bullock wagon by now, Mr Caldwell.'

After packing his own bag and paying Billy Pike for his board and lodging and a surprising number of bottles of beer, William went into the yard to find Belle saddled and tied up by the water trough. He checked straps and girths — the boy seemed to know what he was doing. There was no one on the veranda of the little cottage when he rode past — he couldn't help but look — and he soon caught up with the wagon. He slowed his horse to ride along beside it.

'Not far to go now, Mr Norton.'

As expected, there was no reply from the bullock driver.

'And thank you, Donald, for doing such a good job getting Belle ready.'

The boy grinned. 'She's a fine horse, Professor, though from the look of her she hasn't been ridden much lately. Did you get her here?'

William once more explained how he had acquired her. 'Where Ben Fuller got her from I must say I have no idea.' But, he thought to himself with a smile, no doubt Ben had made an adequate profit on the deal.

'Well you leave her to me, Prof. She's a beauty. I'll look after her.'

After crossing a dry creek bed they soon reached the turn-off from the road that led to the camp site. William walked his horse on ahead and was pleased (and not a little relieved) when he recognised before him the glade of coolabahs beside the river that Ben had shown him the previous day.

'Is this it, then?' said Harry.

'Yes,' said William. 'This is it.'

'You're sure?'

William laughed. 'I am sure Mr Norton. You can unload the wagon now.'

'So, where do you want it all?'

Donald had already sprung down from his seat and was standing between two of the larger trees.

'I reckon over here might be good, Professor. There's a bit of a rise. For drainage. Just in case it rains, you know.'

'Over there, please, Mr Norton,' said William, pointing towards Donald. Harry Norton moved the wagon forward a few feet and applied the brake. He got down and began to untie the bullocks from their traces. As each was let loose it made towards the river, first to drink, then to graze on the long grass.

'Should keep them happy for a while — doamy lurders,' said Harry, with what William thought was almost a note of fondness in his voice. 'They could do with a spell. Now let's see about this stuff.' He started to untie the ropes that held down the boxes.

Clearly it was now up to William to decide on the layout of his camp, and William had never laid out a camp in his life. He looked around him with what he hoped was a thoughtful but authoritative air.

'You'll be wanting your sleeping tent up over here, I suppose,' said Donald from beneath a big gum tree. 'Catch the morning sun?'

'That's it,' said William. 'Exactly.'

'And your store tent — over by this coolabah? It'll be in the shade and you'll want to keep it away from that ants' nest.'

William looked towards the large mound of compacted mud that Donald was pointing to.

'Just what I was thinking.'

'Now, your fireplace. Over here, out in the open — am I right?'

'Just a little to the left,' said William. 'No — your right. Yes, that's it.' This wasn't so difficult after all.

Harry Norton had already fixed his tallow-wood planks to the side of the wagon and with Donald's help began sliding the boxes down. William searched his suitcase for an inventory to tell him which objects were in which box. On consulting it, there appeared to be one minor difficulty: the tools needed to open the cases were packed inside one of them. Harry Norton solved the problem by levering its lid open with a hatchet procured from under the seat of the wagon, and by the time the sun was sinking into the red gums on the far side of the river two large tents had been erected and a kettle was boiling on the fire (a fire that William had insisted on making himself). Half of the boxes lay empty, while most of the others, the ones containing scientific equipment and supplies, were safely inside one of the tents. Only the two largest crates were still on the wagon, but unloading them could wait until morning.

Donald found an enamel teapot among the domestic paraphernalia and soon they were sitting around the fire, each on a comfortable camping stool (the collapsible armchair remained in its box — it just didn't seem right to be sitting beside a campfire in an armchair), each with a steaming mug in his hand.

'This is the life, eh, Professor?' said Donald. He took a mouthful of tea. 'Yes, it'll suit me all right.'

A gentle breeze rattled the leaves of the coolabahs, shafts of sunlight fanned through their trunks. As he took a sip of the bitter liquid, William couldn't help thinking that, yes, it rather suited him, too.

'You'll tell me when you're ready, Professor, won't you?' said Donald. 'They'll be out any time now.'

It took William a few seconds to understand what Donald was talking about. With the activity of the last few hours, and now the well-deserved rest, the reason for William coming to this place had almost gone from his mind. Platypuses. Here he was, camped at last beside the banks of the Burnett River, and somewhere down there were platypuses. William swallowed the last mouthful of tea and put down his empty mug.

'Donald — lead on.'

William had spent many an hour on riverbanks — Scottish riverbanks. After his parents had died Uncle Angas and Aunt Agnes had taken their duties as guardians seriously. No sooner were his parents laid to rest in their modest graves overlooking the Moray

Firth than William had been whisked northward in search of salmon. What better than the king of fish to keep a young mind from unhealthy grieving? After that, fishing became part of his life. Though his education was now to be entrusted to one of the better English schools (as befitted this young ward of a wealthy Scottish mill owner), Uncle Angas made a point of filling William's holidays with endless activities — Scottish activities. He soon knew every pool of the Deveron from Macduff to Newmill, and brought home many a fine fish. So the annual pattern was set. School holidays comprised fly fishing for lowland salmon in early summer, travelling up to the moors on the Glorious Twelfth for a week or so of grouse shooting, stalking highland deer in the autumn, and winters filled with endless parties — Scottish dancing parties.

The parties were arranged by his aunt. William loved his Aunt Agnes, and his aunt loved Scottish dancing. So he learned the steps — the polkas and reels, the schottisches and waltzes — as before he had memorised for his uncle the names of Scottish towns and villages. Though he sometimes found it hard to remember the precise difference between the Highland strip-the-willow and the simpler Shetland version of the dance, or which hand to offer his partner on the second round of a Coldstream Polka, it was above all the company he found a trial. Twirling and bowing, skipping and prancing in some grand hall with the young bloods of the district was never half as much fun for William as standing alone, thigh deep in icy water, watching for a Spey salmon rise to an early dun. And with the lordly beauty of a six-point stag in its mountain fastness, what preened and perfumed daughter of a local laird could compete? Out of doors was where William liked to be, and if there were no girls there — well, so much the simpler. So it was with mounting exhilaration that he now found himself creeping down to the banks of this remote Australian river in search of a small amphibious mammal with the beak of a duck and the fur of a mole that might turn out to be the most exciting quarry of his life.

Donald was heading towards a fringe of reeds that marked the edge of a wide pool. 'They're not hard to see, Professor,' he said, keeping his voice low, 'if you know what you're looking for. But they've got eyes like hawks and they can hear a twig snap at a hundred yards. All you've got to do is be still and be quiet.'

'What about scent?' whispered William, remembering his deer-stalking days. 'Shouldn't we try and approach them downwind?'

'Don't worry about that, Professor. Just still and quiet.'

The light of a setting sun lit up the pool in front of them. The bullocks had moved away from the river and were now dark shapes against the paler grey of the river flats. Small clouds of gnats danced over the sedges, a leaf stirred in the slightest of breezes; a kookaburra gave its evening call from the coolabahs, a call which was answered by another then another and another in a chorus of bush laughter. William heard a high whine and felt something soft land on his cheek. As he reached up to swat the mosquito he heard the whispered words of Uncle Angas.

Leave it, Will. There'll be time enough for scratching when the deer is dead.

No deerstalker could take note of biting blackflies, no matter how they tormented — nor a platypus hunter, mosquitoes. William dropped his hand.

'There,' whispered Donald, leaning towards him. 'Our left, near the far bank just in front of the log, resting on the surface.'

William followed his gaze. Against the orange of the setting sun on the water he saw a black shape, like a short piece of wood floating low. William raised his field glasses. In the low light the magnification showed no more detail but William thought he could see small ripples at one end.

'It's eating,' said Donald.

William remembered reading in Doctor Bennett's account how the platypus gathers its food underwater into pouches in its cheeks. The food is only chewed and swallowed after the animal has risen to the surface. The ripples must be coming from its beak then, grinding back and forth to reduce the small insects it had caught to a paste before swallowing them.

'Of course, it's really not like a duck's beak at all,' Doctor Bennett had told him in Sydney, picking up the stuffed platypus from his desk. 'On a specimen like this it's hard, all dried out. On a living animal it's quite different. It's fleshy, velvety.'

How William would like to see that wonderful beak. But all that he could see of the platypus in the pool in front of him was a low black hump. In another minute, with a ripple not a splash, it had disappeared.

'He'll be up again in a minute or so,' said Donald, speaking less softly now. 'But I'm afraid that's about all you'll see of him.'

'Will there be others?'

'There's usually only one to a pool. That's all I've ever seen anyway.'

'Surely in the mating season —?'

Donald raised a finger and he looked again towards the water. It took a few seconds to spot the platypus back on the surface, much nearer to them now, not ten yards away. This time he could distinguish the low flat structure at one end that must be the animal's beak, with a slight bump where the nostrils were. He almost expected to see a plume of vapour from them, like the spouting of the great whale that he had seen on his voyage to Australia. The platypus gave no such spectacle. It floated on the surface of the water, the ring of ripples from where it had silently broken the surface spreading and fading around it. William found himself grinning with delight.

'You know, Donald, that this is the first time I have ever seen a real live platypus.'

Too late he realised that he had forgotten to lower his voice. There was a small splash. The platypus had vanished.

'You'll have to be quieter than that, Professor. We won't see him again for a while.'

'I'm sorry, Donald, I quite forgot. But no matter — we have seen the beast. It exists. Perhaps now might be the time to think about some dinner?'

'Leave it to me, Professor.'

nine

I thought, and I said, that the new elements introduced into this controversy were not what they had been announced to be. It is true that a richly glandular apparatus had been discovered on each side of the abdomen of an *Ornithorhynchus*; but it was a little too hasty to decide and declare that it was a mammary gland. I examined the facts again in a specimen preserved in spirit which formed part of Baron Cuvier's collections; I saw a glandular structure, but simple. There were none of the characters which distinguish a milk gland. In my opinion, therefore, this creature is not a mammal. [Translation]

J.F. Meckel, 'Uber den Stachel und das Giftorgan des *Ornithorhynchus*,' *Deutches Archiv fur die Physiologie*, 1823

William was woken by the laughter of kookaburras — perhaps the same ones that had provided the evening chorus beside the river — and found himself smiling. He seemed to be doing a lot of that recently. Other birds were singing, too: unidentified warbles and whistles, the distant screech of what he imagined must be some kind of parrot. No need to get up quite yet.

How different this was from his past life. Everything — the birds, the trees, the people. True, the people here spoke English, but there was something indefinably different about even this, something uniquely Australian. Yet he could not help feeling at home. Or rather, it was as if he had come home.

His thoughts drifted back to Donald's dinner last night. Grilled chops, boiled cabbage and potatoes. Simple enough fare, but excellent. Even Harry Norton, not a man previously noted for culinary enthusiasm, had managed a grunt that was clearly an appreciative grunt. William could not but congratulate himself for finding a helper so young yet so capable, as he had last night congratulated the *chef de cuisine* in person for providing such a fine meal. Donald had been both pleased and embarrassed by the praise.

'Wait till you try my damper,' he said. 'I'll make some for breakfast. You'll see.'

Though William's recent experiences with Ben Fuller's damper made him somewhat wary of the offer, he declared that he would be looking forward to it. Now, judging from the whistle of kettle and clang of camp oven distracting his thoughts from the birdsong, he would not have much longer to wait. He threw back his blanket and emerged from the tent. 'Good morning to you, Donald. Would that be shaving water?'

'Ready when you are, Professor,' said the boy. His arms were floured to the elbows. 'Leave some for the tea if you can. I'm just making up the damper. Would you like a bit of bacon with it?'

A shave, a cup of hot tea and some bacon for breakfast was just what William wanted. 'Capital,' he said, and the word seemed pretty much to sum up how he felt.

What with the boat journey, the precipitous departure from Bundaberg, sleeping out on the way to Gayndah and the limited facilities of the Club Hotel, it had been — how long? Almost a week now? — since his face had seen a razor. Donald had already put out his mirror, a towel and an enamelled basin on a folding table. William unpacked his shaving gear and laid it out beside them. He stropped the razor, once, twice. How good it would feel to be smooth-cheeked and smooth-chinned again. Though, of course, he would be keeping the moustache.

The damper was as good as advertised — light and crumbly, halfway between bread and a fresh-baked scone — a far cry from the item of the same name that Ben Fuller had cooked for him. Spread with some of the tinned butter that William had brought from Sydney it made a fine accompaniment to the bacon. He breakfasted alone (neither the noise nor the delicious smell from the frying pan had roused Harry Norton, still wrapped in a blanket under his wagon, sound asleep and snoring), and was just wiping his plate with the last of Donald's superior product when he heard, then saw, a horseman approaching.

'Constable Perry — good morning. You had no difficulty tracking us down?'

'No need for tracks this morning, Mr Caldwell,' said the constable. 'With the smell of that bacon cooking I just followed my nose. Would there be any to spare for a hungry trooper, do you think?'

Donald put some more rashers in the pan for Jim Perry and the now-awake Harry Norton. He handed the constable a mug of tea.

'How did your business go yesterday?' said William.

'Oh, I managed to fill in a few details.'

'Are you any closer to finding your man?'

'Let's just say the police are still pursuing their enquiries and are confident of an early arrest — that's what they always say in the newspapers, isn't it?'

'I'm pleased to hear it,' said William, though he had been hoping for more specific information. 'I should know this, I'm sure, but how many horses did you say were stolen from the mail coach?'

'Four. Four's the usual number. Any reason you ask?'

'No. No reason.'

Jim Perry looked up from his mug. 'You wouldn't be wondering if that horse of yours might be one of them, I suppose?'

William said nothing. Since learning about Ben Fuller's criminal past, he had to admit that he had indeed been wondering over the exact extent of Ben's 'bit of this and bit of that'. But he had also learned not to ask.

'Well, not according to the descriptions we have,' continued the constable. 'Yours is a mare. According to my information, there were four geldings in harness when the coach was robbed, that's what we heard.'

William gave an inward sigh of relief. What had Ben told him? Mates should stick together. And that was just what he'd done.

'You know, Mr Caldwell, this is a fine spot you've found yourself.' Jim Perry looked around. 'Better than a hotel any day. And this breakfast.' He picked up the plate that Donald had put in front of him. 'I'm blowed if I can get my damper to look like that. You've got your mother's touch there, lad.'

Donald smiled but said nothing, busying himself with pouring more tea.

'You're right, Constable — Donald's cooking alone is worth the trip. And of course, you are welcome to stay as long as you like.'

'No, no, I'd better be starting back to Bundaberg soon. Just thought I'd drop by and see how you're going, both of you.'

Jim Perry looked around at the empty boxes. 'Mr Caldwell, I hope you won't mind me asking, but all this stuff — are you really just looking for water-moles?'

William laughed. 'Yes, I'm sure. You're not the first to ask me, though. I'll be studying monotremes in general, I suppose. But platypuses — water-moles — in particular.'

'Monotremes?'

'Platypuses and echidnas, you know.'

'Ah, you mean porcupines.'

'I believe the animal is sometimes so called, though unrelated to the true porcupines of the northern hemisphere.'

'Is our porcupine not true, then?'

'True enough in its own way. What I meant was … well, though the echidna superficially resembles the porcupine — the hedgehog, too, for that matter — it belongs in a completely different, shall we say, group of animals.'

'Right-ho, Mr Caldwell, if you say so. But it looks like you haven't even finished unpacking yet.' Jim Perry gestured to the two large cases still on the wagon. 'What are those you've got there?'

'Ah,' said William. 'Well as you've asked, perhaps it might be time to open them up.' He put down his plate and mug and got to his feet. 'First, we need somewhere flat and level. Let me see.'

Going over to the other side of the fire, he knelt down and with head on one side and one eye closed, surveyed the ground. He did the same in another spot a few yards away. 'I think this will do. Mr Norton, I would like the two cases over here, please.'

Harry Norton looked up from his seat by the fire. 'Oh yes, and how do you expect me to hump those rumplin' great things over there?'

'Having already seen one demonstration of your skill with ropes and planks, Mr Norton, I have every confidence in your abilities.'

'My instructions were to deliver seventeen cases from Bundaberg to Gayndah. It didn't say nothing about half-ton boxes full of — well, whatever it is they're full of.'

Bairns and beasts, William.

'Mr Norton, I cannot tell you how grateful I am to you for bringing my equipment to Gayndah,' said William, reaching into his pocket for some coins. 'You have more than earned your fee already. In fact I was hoping that you would accept a bonus payment for getting my things here so quickly. Should you consent to this further task, your payment will of course be increased commensurately.'

Twenty minutes later, with the help of Jim Perry and Donald and what must have been at least half his vocabulary of expletives, Harry Norton had eased the cases off the wagon and manoeuvred them exactly as William directed, end to end onto a piece of flat ground beside the store tent. The cases were well built and stencilled with the word 'TOP' on one side. It seemed that Harry Norton could read.

'Thank you, Mr Norton. Now, if I can just find the instructions and the necessary tools.'

After a couple of minutes he returned from the store tent with two shining steel braces, their handles of polished wood, each fitted with a flat screw-driving bit. 'You will see,' said William, consulting a small booklet that he had also brought from his tent, 'that the cases are not nailed together but screwed. Donald, would you be so kind?' He handed Donald one of the braces and read from the instruction sheet.

'"Ensuring that the two cases are first aligned as shown" — yes, that seems correct — "undo the screws of Crate 1 in numbered order."'

The position and number of each screw was indeed marked on the crate, which was itself clearly stencilled 'CRATE 1'. Donald removed them with little difficulty.

'"Ensuring that the side flap is fully extended, fold back the lid."'

The lid and side of the crate swung back on strong hinges to reveal a thick felt cloth.

'"Slide top and sides of crate off hinges. Remove cloth. Stow carefully."'

The top and sides of the crate were removed and leant up against a tree. The cloth was pulled back revealing beneath it what looked like a large mahogany tabletop, its surface polished and gleaming.

'"Repeat with Crate 2."'

An identical tabletop was revealed.

'"Lift off removable tabletops. Stow carefully."'

As Harry and Donald between them lifted one of the tabletops — it was surprisingly light — both they and Jim Perry gasped in surprise. Beneath was the green cloth of a billiard table — or rather, half a billiard table. Under the other tabletop was the second half.

'Bloody oath, Professor,' was all Donald could say.

'Strong language is the mark of a weak man, Donald,' said William, echoing his Aunt Agnes's frequently expressed thoughts on the subject, 'as I'm sure Constable Perry would agree. And Mr Norton, no doubt.'

Jim Perry smiled. The bullocky scowled.

'Is this really what I think it is?' said Jim Perry.

'Now, as I remember,' said William, 'comes the tricky part. They showed me how to do it at the shop. What we are looking for are the Main Lifting Screws.'

With further reference to the diagram the two screws were found halfway along each side of the half-tables, each covered by a swinging brass plate. From beneath the table, four heavy legs slowly unfolded. As it rose, they could see that the table's legs ran on brass wheels along steel rails built into the bottom of the crate. Though the mechanism was strongly made and well lubricated, it took a full five minutes of solid winding until a soft click indicated that the legs were locked into place.

'"Now repeat with Half Table No.2."'

'Right,' said the constable. 'And I do believe it is indeed what I thought it was.'

William took over the brace and bit from Donald and soon the two halves of the table were up, looking as though a full-sized billiard table had been cut clean across the middle with a razor blade through playing surface, cushions and edges — even the leather-coated steel rim of the centre pockets.

'It's a wonderful thing,' muttered Jim Perry to Donald (though loud enough for William to hear), 'but I'm damned if I can see how he'll catch a water-mole with it.'

William ignored the aside. About six inches separated the two halves of the table. The edge of the green baize on either side was tucked under a recessed brass strip, below which were eight equally spaced, brass-lined holes.

'So far so good, gentlemen. Now. "Withdraw the two Alignment Rods located toward the inner side of each half."'

'So tell me,' said Jim Perry, as he found the rods and began adjusting the two halves of the table so that they were level and parallel, 'what's so special about them — these monotremes of yours?'

'Well monotreme of course simply means "one hole", referring to the fact that unlike other mammals both males and females have only one orifice — the cloaca — which serves as anus, urethra and genital opening.' William turned his attention back to the table for a moment, confirming that the two halves were correctly aligned. 'And then of course the skeletal structure is also of particular interest.'

'Their bones, you mean?'

'The formation of the pectoral girdle, the presence of epipubic bones in the pelvis, both quite unlike any other mammal. And the reproductive system of the females is most unusual. Their uterus is divided into two distinct branches, similar to marsupials but not placental mammals.'

Again reading from the instructions, William searched for and found the Draw Bar Extender Screws.

'On the other hand female monotremes do not have the unique lateral vaginas of marsupials. Now, nearly there, I think.'

With just a little more winding, there beneath the gum trees in the middle of the Australian bush the two halves came together into a perfect, full-sized, twelve-foot billiard table.

William ran his hand over the surface where the two halves joined. Not a ridge, not a dip. He turned to Jim Perry.

'Not bad, eh? And all this is quite apart from the question of whether or not they lay eggs.'

'You know Mr Caldwell,' said Jim Perry. 'I've often wondered what they teach you fellows at university. I reckon now I know: how to locate and operate a Draw Bar Extender Screw.'

And William had to smile. 'I'm sure I would never have managed without your help, Constable. There's one last thing, though. It says here that the table must be levelled and "this is achieved by the use of the four spirit levels mounted into the sides of the table." I was wondering whether you might …?'

When the table had been made level to everyone's satisfaction William slid open a drawer in the end of the table and took out three balls. Another drawer in the side contained four cues. 'Right then, who's for a game?'

Harry Norton opened his mouth to speak. No sound came. He closed his mouth, slowly shook his head and walked away.

'What about you, Constable?'

'No, thank you, Mr Caldwell,' said Jim Perry. 'I'm afraid it's time for me to be going. But I tell you what.' He, too, was shaking his head. 'Pat O'Malley — he's not going to believe this.'

It had, of course, been Uncle Angas's idea. Eleven days before William was due to leave for Australia his uncle had summoned him to lunch at his London club. Lunch with Uncle Angas was something William always enjoyed and he had not been disappointed. After a lavish meal of woodcock ('Shot 'em myself on the bottom meadow'), salmon ('Pulled this little beauty out of Becky's Pool — you know, just below the weir') and roast venison ('Only a two pointer, but you know what they say — the fewer the points the less the chewing'), his uncle had told William that he had a surprise for him. They hailed a cab outside the club and William found himself heading out of the Adelphi and up Regent Street, then east along Oxford Street. After they crossed Tottenham Court Road William had but the vaguest idea where they were going (he was not a London man) until the cab eventually stopped at 4 St John's Square, Clerkenwell. A sign outside announced it as the premises of A.H. Churchman & Sons, Manufacturers and Sellers of Fine Billiard Tables.

'Here we are, Will,' said his uncle.

Telling the cabman to wait, they entered a small showroom to be greeted by Mr Alfred Churchman himself. On the floor were two crates.

'This is the item you ordered, Mr Macfarlane.'

'Good, good,' said his uncle. 'But as you know it's not for me, it's for my nephew here. Better show him how it all works, eh?'

So the crates were opened and William was given his first view and demonstration of the wonderful Churchman's Patented Portable Convertible Billiard Table.

'Swansea slate, three-sixteenth of an inch,' Mr Churchman explained. 'To keep down the weight you know. India-rubber cushions, of course. The frame is beechwood, steel-braced — guaranteed not to warp. That's how we can get away with having the slate so thin, you see. And of course, the table can be converted for dining.'

Mr Churchman signalled to an assistant and two polished lids were fitted over the billiard table. 'Mahogany. French-polished, but in normal use we recommend the use of an oilcloth. Crumbs, you know, sir — in the crack.'

'Thank you, Mr Churchman,' said William. 'This is really a most kind gift, Uncle. I look forward to many a fine game on my return.'

'On your return?' said his uncle. 'On your return be damned. Why do you think I got the thing? It's going with you.'

'We have arranged delivery as you instructed, Mr Macfarlane, to Mr Caldwell's ship at Tilbury. You may have every confidence, Mr Caldwell, sir. We have supplied these tables to customers in India, Jamaica, even the United States of America. I will send one of our men to make sure that it is properly stowed. I must say we are all very excited here: it will be our first table to go to Australia.'

'An early birthday present from your uncle, Will. Can't have you out there in the wilds without a decent billiard table.'

As he sat at the table on his fifth day at the camp, his open journal before him, William had to concede that Churchman's Patented Portable Convertible was already proving its use. Though he doubted that it would ever fulfil its secondary function as a family dining table (a dozen people could have sat comfortably around it), the large flat surface — now covered, as recommended, with an oilcloth — made an excellent general table, desk and bench. Donald had rigged a double canvas fly over it, which, though William had not seen a drop of rain since his arrival in Queensland, at least kept off falling leaves and provided welcome shade in the middle of the day. And each evening the table was cleared, the tops removed, the lamps lit, and William relaxed with an hour or so of billiard practice. He thought he might try to interest Donald in the game. A fine lad was young Donald, proving his worth more with every passing day.

The Burnett River was home to many other animals besides the platypus. Water rats could be seen swimming in the water or running along the banks at any time of day or night. William could now distinguish them at a glance. They floated higher in the water than platypuses and swam with a more direct and sinuous motion. And they seemed less shy, often coming close enough for William to see the white tip to the tail. The empty mussel shells that he often found on the riverbank were, Donald told him, a sure sign of water rats at work.

'See where their teeth have gnawed through the shell, Professor?'

It was always at just the right place to cut the muscle that held the two shells together.

William was surprised at the number of reptiles he saw along the river. Donald was able to confirm that Australian crocodiles were not to be found as far south as the Burnett, but he would often see goannas of impressive length around the water's edge and watch — or more usually hear — three-foot water dragons leap into the water from their sunbathing spot on an overhanging branch as soon as they saw him. And then there were the tortoises. He would see a few of them every day sunning themselves on stranded logs or rocks in the middle of the river.

William got into a morning routine. He would rise at daybreak and walk down to the river. A platypus, like as not the one that he had seen with Donald that first day, was bound to be there somewhere, swimming and diving, floating and feeding. Though William was getting better at staying still and quiet, he was sure it noticed him. But already the animal seemed to accept his presence. After about half an hour of busy activity it would retire to its favourite spot to groom itself — always the same place on the bank beneath an old beached log. It took a good fifteen minutes scratching and nuzzling and combing its fur, then slipped back into the water, swam straight over to the opposite bank and disappeared into its burrow for the day.

After breakfast William would resume his search along the banks of the river. Stopping by each likely pool he would check for the presence of his quarry. Donald had shown him the signs to look for — the runways that each animal made to its tunnel in the bank, and whether the entrance was dry or wet, indicating an animal within. The burrows were flat-bottomed with a low arched top. To William they looked too small even for a platypus's body, but Donald explained that as the animal entered the burrow, water was squeezed from its fur. As he went along the river he drew a map — not a cartographic masterpiece, he had to admit, but a serviceable enough effort — with every burrow marked on it. Each pool usually had more than one burrow — why, even Donald did not know — but there were only footprints around one of them.

William already knew from his reading that platypuses' back feet were webbed and equipped with wide claws, and that their front feet were like no other creature's. At first glance they looked like the back ones, broad and webbed with long, flat claws. But folded into the palm was a flap of skin that could be unfolded against the claws to make a kind of extension to the webbed foot. When the animal took to the water, it had two large front flippers of great utility. According to Doctor Bennett's observations, platypuses kept their back legs folded against the body and tail underwater, using only their front feet for swimming. William had yet to see a living platypus close enough to confirm this. After his morning exploration was done he would have a light lunch then read, or write in his journal. Or sometimes, he would do nothing at all.

The design of a platypus's foot, the shape of its tunnel, the wonder of a wasp building its nest. Could Darwin's theory really explain them all? *The Origin of Species by Natural Selection* had been published when William was one year old. When he was eleven and starting school (Shrewsbury, the school that his uncle had chosen for him, was the very one where Darwin himself had been taught) the great battles were long past. Evolution by natural selection was the orthodoxy, though still a fresh-enough orthodoxy to need proselytising and defending by a host of eager followers. Numbered among them had been William's teacher when he entered Lower Remove, Mr Edwin Harrison.

By the time William arrived in Mr Harrison's class he had already endured four years of Bible study and the first book Mr Harrison had made his pupils read made a deep impression on fifteen-year-old William. It was William Paley's 1802 treatise *Natural Theology: or, Evidences of the Existence and Attributes of the Deity, Collected from the Appearances of Nature.* He had it still.

> In crossing a heath, suppose I pitched my foot against a stone, and were asked how the stone came to be there; I might possibly answer, that, for any thing I knew to the contrary, it had lain there for ever. But suppose I had found a watch upon the ground, and it should be inquired how the watch happened to be in that place; I should hardly think the watch might have always been there. Yet why should not this answer serve for the watch as well as for the stone? For this reason, and for no other, viz. that, when we come to inspect the watch, we perceive (what we could not

discover in the stone) that its several parts are framed and put together for a purpose.

The inference is inevitable, that the watch must have had a maker: that there must have existed, at some time, and at some place or other, an artificer or artificers who formed it for the purpose which we find it actually to answer; who comprehended its construction, and designed its use.

And so with the natural world. Could the young William be in any doubt that the human eye with mechanisms for focusing light more delicate than the finest telescope, the wonderful structure of the inner ear with its tiny bones and membrane, were irrefutable proof of the existence of a 'divine watchmaker'? Even the hinges in the wings of a common earwig were 'as highly wrought as if the Creator had nothing else to finish'. Mr Harrison had shown them to the boys under a microscope. When an earwig pulls its delicate wings backwards, each folds up along a score of clever hinges into an area a fifth of its extended size and disappears beneath a wing case. Move the folded wing forward, and it unfolds and locks into position for flight, tissue-thin but self-braced and strong enough to pull the insect off the ground and through the air with the ease of any eagle flying. No professor of geometry, no master of Japanese paper-folding could even have imagined so beautiful a thing. If young William had ever had any doubts about the existence of God, he was now a firm believer.

The next book that Mr Harrison introduced to his students had been Thomas Robert Malthus's *Essay on the Principle of Population*. William was again impressed. Surely 'the constant tendency in all animated life to increase beyond the nourishment prepared for it' was self-evident? How could it be denied that human populations tended to increase geometrically? Despite war, famine and disease, did not the population of the world keep doubling and redoubling over the centuries? And was it not equally true that the supply of food was limited, or at best could only be increased arithmetically? The inevitable result of this is that humans end up competing for resources (how to reconcile this situation with the existence of a benevolent God was a question that Mr Harrison left unasked and unanswered). But while Malthus's arguments had caused William and a few of his friends some philosophical bewilderment they had had no time to solve the puzzle before Mr Harrison set them to reading the third preparatory volume of his didactic trilogy: Charles Lyell's 1827 text, *The Principles of Geology.*

How grand a book was this. From descriptions of modern physical processes to an explanation of the formation of the very earth itself over countless aeons of time, the author brought in examples from around the globe — earthquakes in the Mississippi, pitch lakes in Trinidad, volcanoes in Java — as well as describing and deciphering more local phenomena in Dorset and Essex and Orkney. Mr Harrison had combined the reading of Lyell's book with excursions into the countryside around Shrewsbury. Here, not three miles from the school, were layered siltstones that must have been lain down on the bed of some great sea, yet beneath them were basalts like the ones that had flowed from Vesuvius just ten years ago — had not Mr Harrison on his desk a piece of that very rock, gathered on a recent holiday to Italy? And over there was a fracture in the rocks, the sign of some ancient earthquake just like the one which last year had shaken the statue of Sir John Whittiker from the wall of Shrewsbury Cathedral and cracked eight gravestones in the churchyard. And look at the thickness of these rocks — miles thick, some of them. The processes of deposition and erosion, uplift and subsidence, must have been going on for millions upon millions of years. There was a relentless logic to Lyell's thesis that William could not deny, no matter if it did contradict the Biblical account of creation.

But even if the story of Genesis was not the literal truth, surely neither Lyell nor Malthus contradicted the God of William Paley? The existence of a Great Designer could no more be denied than could the existence of that lump of black basalt on Mr Harrison's desk. It was at this point that the teacher introduced his pupils to Charles Darwin. Lyell had already introduced the idea that fossils were the remains of creatures from a distant past. He had argued for change in organic life through time. He had discussed variation in domestic animals. Now Darwin put them all together into his great synthesis.

We see, do we not, variation within species? If we look hard at any two individuals of the same species we are bound to notice differences, no matter how slight. This is well known to breeders of domestic animals, who select an animal with the desirable trait to breed from. Through many breedings, selection of this kind — 'artificial' selection — eventually gives rise to new varieties. What happens to the animals that are not selected? They are not allowed to reproduce, and they die. Only the chosen survivors pass on their traits to their offspring. But what happens in the natural world? It is clear, as Malthus has shown us, that populations tend to increase beyond the ability of their food supply or other resources to sustain them. Eventually this will lead to competition for these resources. Which animals will succeed in this competition? If there was no difference between individuals the process would be random — but there *are* differences between individuals. Some are taller or shorter, some faster or slower. These differences mean that some individuals will be better adapted to the situation in which they find themselves. They will survive and breed, the others will not. Many of the survivors' offspring will inherit the advantageous traits and also tend to survive and breed. And so, through this process of 'natural' selection, a new variety will arise: given enough time, a new species will evolve. And Lyell has given us enough time, countless aeons of it.

William saw Paley's God, the Great Designer, vanish like a watch from beneath a conjuror's handkerchief. If young William Caldwell had been a believer in Paley before, he was now a devoted disciple of Mr Darwin. He was not slow to appreciate the implications of the theory. If no design, then no intent. We are on a journey without destination in a universe which, though set to inexorable rules, has no purpose. And we are part of that universe. Like balls on a cosmic billiard table, we bounce around in a game that has no beginning, no end, and no reason.

ten

Ornithorhynchus inhabits the marshes of New Holland. It makes among tufts of reeds bordering the water a nest composed of down and interlaced roots, in which it deposits two white eggs, smaller than those of ordinary fowls; it broods on them for a long time, hatches them like a bird, and only abandons them when threatened by a formidable enemy. [Translation]
    Anon., 'Sur les Habitudes de l'Ornithorhynque', *Annales des Science Naturelles*, 1827

The young William Caldwell had been mildly surprised to find that, like the death of his own parents, his conversion to Darwinism had been accompanied by neither sorrow, grief nor guilt. Without a God to create and sustain them, did the sun shine less brightly, the birds sing less sweetly? Were the marvels of the world around him in any way diminished? He had to answer that they were not. The slightly older William Caldwell who now sat beside a campfire at the end of his sixth day in the Australian bush, replete with yet another of Donald's fine dinners, had to agree. That the brilliant reds and oranges lighting up the western sky were simply due to diffraction of sunlight by atmospheric particles made them no less beautiful than they had been when they were the work of the Creator. The sunset — and a dinner of fried chops, cabbage and potatoes washed down with several mugs of strong black tea: what else could a man wish for? Well, perhaps the occasional glass of beer.

'I think I might go into town tomorrow,' said William, as Donald cleared away their plates in preparation for washing up. 'A few supplies, you know.'

'I'll do that, Professor. Leave it to me.'

'No, no. I could do with a change of scenery.'

Yes, he would enjoy being back in civilisation (the thought of considering Gayndah as civilisation brought an involuntary smile) and he could surely buy a case or two of beer from Mr Pike at the Club Hotel. Perhaps he could pick up a few fresh vegetables from the store — even some fruit. And where had Billy Pike got those eggs he had cooked for William that first night? From that girl in the little house with all the flowers perhaps. He might call in there on the way back.

When William passed by the cottage the following morning there was no sign of the girl on the veranda, but he found Billy Pike sitting on the bench outside the Club Hotel, bottle of beer in hand. According to William's pocket watch the time was five minutes to eleven. According to the evidence beside Billy's chair, he was already onto his third beer of the morning. The publican raised the bottle in salute.

'Good to see you, Mr Caldwell. Would you be wanting a drink?'

'Thank you, Mr Pike,' said William. 'That is exactly what I wanted. Would you be able to spare me a dozen or so? I'd like to take them with me.'

'A dozen? I'm awful bloody short, Mr Caldwell.'

Despite William's entreaty Billy Pike was adamant that he could spare two bottles at most — supplies were due soon but he needed to make sure he had enough on hand to serve to his other customers. William had yet to see another customer at the Club Hotel — certainly there was no sign of any that morning — but had to be content with the offer. After packing the beer into his saddlebag he went over to the general store where he was able to buy two cabbages and a pumpkin. Now, what else was it that he wanted? Ah yes, eggs. The storekeeper confirmed that he might be able to get some from Mary Brown. And yes, she lived in the cottage with the flowers. But, thought William, did he really need eggs? He had seen no sign of the girl earlier. Perhaps she was not at home, or if she was, perhaps she would have no eggs to spare.

As he remounted his horse William found himself thinking that he should have sent Donald after all. He was here to investigate the embryology of the Monotremata. He should not be spending valuable time collecting grocery supplies. And anyway, wasn't there something about too many eggs binding the bowels? By the time he reached the house with the flowers he had made up his mind. He would just ride on by. But he could not help his eyes straying towards the house as he passed, and once he did so he could not help seeing that the girl in the white dress was now sitting quietly in a chair on the veranda just as he had first seen her, her dark hair tied back with a red ribbon. It was only polite to say something.

'Good morning,' he said.

'Good morning,' said the girl.

William supposed that he should say something else in answer to this reply. And it would be impolite not to stop his horse.

'I couldn't help admiring your garden,' he said. 'I mean, of course, the flowers in your garden. Well, not just the flowers, the whole effect is what I'm really getting at, I think. I mean, I *know* that's what I'm getting at, that's what I really meant to say. Altogether — the whole thing — if you see what I mean.' (Where on earth had all those words come from?)

The girl smiled. 'Thank you,' she said. 'Could you tell me who I'm talking to? I don't think I recognise you.'

'No,' said William. 'Sorry — I didn't mean that I can't tell you who you're talking to. Of course, I can, it's me. I meant, no, you probably don't recognise me. We've never met. That's all I meant.'

The girl laughed. She had, William thought, rather a musical laugh.

'Then you will tell me your name?' she said.

'Didn't I? Oh no, I didn't, did I? I'm so sorry. My name is William, William Caldwell.'

'I'm very pleased to meet you, Mr Caldwell.'

There was a pause. Was he supposed to say something else?

'Now, would you like to know my name?' said the girl.

'Thank you, yes. I was just about to ask that very question.'

'Then I think you should ask it,' said the girl.

William cleared his throat. 'And whom do I have the pleasure of addressing?'

'My name is Ettie Brown.'

'I am delighted to make your acquaintance, Miss Brown.'

'Well, Mr Caldwell, now that we have been introduced, perhaps you would care to inspect the garden whose effect you so much admire. I would be so pleased if you would.'

During their conversation so far William had stayed in his saddle. The girl had remained seated on the veranda of the house. As he dismounted she stood, walked down the steps to the gate and opened it. William tied up Belle to the fence and entered the garden. The girl was tall — perhaps only a couple of inches below his own six feet. He took her offered hand and shook it.

'You are most kind, Miss Brown.'

'It is my pleasure, Mr Caldwell,' she said. 'Now tell me, what do you see?'

William looked around him. Some of the plants he could recognise, many he could not. 'Why, roses I think — yes, there are many roses. And woodbine, of course, and jonquils.'

'Do you not admire my stocks, Mr Caldwell. I am particularly proud of my stocks.'

'Forgive me, Miss Brown, my knowledge of flowers is somewhat limited. What colour are they?'

'You must forgive me, Mr Caldwell — I forget. I know them better by their scent.'

The girl turned away from him and took a few steps down the wide path. She dropped to her knees and leant over a large clump of white flowers.

'It is such a sweet scent, Mr Caldwell, one of my very favourites. Come, try it yourself, then tell me what colour they are.'

What colour? Could it be that the girl was blind?

'The flowers are white, Miss Brown, like your dress.'

'Ah yes, all my dresses are white, Mr Caldwell — or so I believe.'

She laughed again, and again William thought how lovely a sound it was — unforced, neither too high nor too low.

'Do you like my garden? I spend so much time here. A garden is one of the great pleasures of life, do you not think?'

William thought back to his own life so far. School and university had given him little time to learn to appreciate the pleasures of the garden. There had been a garden at his aunt and uncle's great house outside Inverness, of course, but William had taken little notice of the flowers in it. Of more interest to him was the animal life the garden contained — the toads and hedgehogs, the blackbirds and throstles.

'I must be honest, Miss Brown. I hardly know a daisy from a delphinium.'

'What have you been doing with your life, Mr Caldwell?' The girl stood and turned her face towards him. 'I hope you will forgive my boldness, but how old are you? No, don't tell me. Let me guess. I am usually right about these things, you know.'

Taking William's silence for assent, she continued, 'You do not sound like an old man, but not a young one either. I think that you are thirty years of age. Am I right?'

'Almost exactly,' said William. 'I am twenty-four.'

'Oh, I was not right at all. But tell me Mr Caldwell, do you not wonder how old I am?'

'I confess I do wonder, Miss Brown, but even such a stolid fellow as I knows how unwise it would be to guess aloud the age of a lady.'

The girl laughed again. 'So, you are a stolid fellow are you, Mr Caldwell — and I am a lady, am I? I am nineteen. There, does that surprise you?'

It did not surprise William. He would have guessed that this pretty girl — for William had already decided that her black hair, pale freckled skin and clear blue eyes made Ettie Brown at least a little pretty — was not yet twenty. Despite her physical maturity, somehow her playfulness was still more that of a child than a woman.

'Again, Miss Brown, I beg to decline a reply.'

It seemed time for a change of subject.

'But forgive me, I have not explained why I am here.'

'Oh, you are here to look for water-moles, Mr Caldwell. Everyone knows that.'

Of course; though the girl may be blind there was no reason why she would not be part of the circle of communication that was bound to exist in a small town like Gayndah. In a place such as this, anyone's business would soon be known to everyone.

'And if you wonder how I know,' continued the girl, 'it is because my sister told me.'

A sister? Ah yes, that must be Mary. 'Well, your sister is quite right.'

It was only then that William realised that he and the girl were being watched. Another figure, a shorter woman dressed in a long brown smock with a white apron, had slipped out of the house onto the veranda without him noticing. She was looking at him with dark brown eyes set deep in a dark brown face.

William had seen very few Aboriginal people in Australia. In Sydney he had noticed a few dark-skinned people in one of the parks (Hyde Park, was it?) and in Brisbane some of the labourers at the docks were black. There had been three dark-skinned sailors on the ship to Bundaberg, but the ship's master had told him they were not Aborigines but 'Islanders', from somewhere to the north. He had half expected to see more Aborigines here in the inland, but so far had seen none. But then the storekeeper had told him, hadn't he, that the local tribe was all away somewhere — eating nuts, was it?

The girl seemed to be aware of the woman on the veranda. 'Oh, Mary,' she said. 'This is Mr Caldwell, the gentleman you were telling me about.'

Another Mary?

The woman spoke. 'I'm very pleased to meet you, Mr Caldwell.'

She came down the steps of the veranda towards him. She was shorter than Ettie Brown — much shorter than William — but carried herself with a natural grace that William found disarming. She did not smile, though, as she shook his hand.

'And I am very pleased to meet you, Miss …?'

'Why, Mr Caldwell,' said Ettie Brown. 'This is my sister — Mary Brown. We live together. Mary helps me. I am blind, you see.'

'What Ettie means is that we help each other,' said the woman. 'But tell me, Mr Caldwell, what do you think of our garden?'

It took William a moment to reply. Sister? How could these two be sisters?

'I think it quite lovely, though as I was saying to Miss Brown — to Miss Ettie, to your sister — I am no expert on these things. But I noticed it when I first came into town and I am delighted to have this chance for a proper inspection. Do I take it that you are the gardener?'

'We both —'

'Do not listen to her, Mr Caldwell,' said the girl. 'Mary is much too modest. She is indeed the gardener, and the cook, and the housemaid, and the groom. Without Mary I don't know where I should be.'

The woman turned towards the girl with what was clear to William was a look of great affection.

'And without Ettie, I don't know where I would be, Mr Caldwell,' she said. 'Now tell me, Ettie dear, should we offer our guest some tea?'

While Mary prepared things inside the house, William sat down with Ettie Brown at a table on the veranda, still puzzling over this strange enigma. Two sisters, one white, one black? But Ettie was eager to hear more about what had brought him to Australia — 'our distant country' — and questioned him eagerly on his impressions so far. What did he think of Australians? Had he smelt a eucalyptus leaf? Did he not love the song of the magpie?

William wanted to ask questions of his own, to find out more about his hostesses. The woman, Mary Brown, was quite outside his previous experience — no, experience was the wrong word — his previous expectations of the native people of Australia. He remembered reading Thomas Malthus's description of Australian Aborigines, of 'strange and barbarous customs', of the complete subjugation of women in Aboriginal society. Mary Brown certainly seemed neither barbarous nor subjugated.

But somehow the conversation never turned towards the subject of Mary or Ettie Brown. When the elder sister brought out a tray with tea things and a plate of the most delicious biscuits (it seemed an age since he had drunk from a china cup or been offered milk with his tea) the three of them talked about platypuses and Queensland, and about Cambridge and sea voyages. The women found out that William was an orphan, that he had no brothers or sisters, that he preferred cold weather to hot. William delighted in both the conversation and the company, but after two hours and countless refills of his cup he had to admit he knew very little more about the pretty young white girl or her fascinating black companion. Two hours? William got to his feet.

'You must excuse me,' he said. 'I'm sure I have taken up quite enough of your time. And I did promise Donald — my assistant, you know — that I would be back by lunchtime.'

'It has been a great pleasure to meet you, Mr Caldwell,' said Mary Brown.

'A pleasure indeed,' said Ettie. 'Perhaps we could come and visit you at your camp.'

'Visit me? Visit us? You?' William heard himself splutter.

'Of course, if you think we might disturb your work —'

William almost choked trying to get the words out. 'No, Miss Ettie, no, please don't misunderstand me. Nothing would give me greater ... I would be ... We would be ... honoured.'

'Then shall we say tomorrow?'

It was only when William arrived back at his camp site that he realised he had completely forgotten about the eggs.

According to Doctor Bennett the platypus breeding season was now only a month away. Soon William would have to begin collecting. Male specimens would be of some interest — there was evidence that their testes grew at the onset of the mating season then shrank soon afterwards and it would be good to confirm this — but it was females that he needed to concentrate on. Comparing the platypus with other mammals of about the same size, gestation might take anywhere from four to eight weeks. If he could manage to get one specimen every two days — maybe one a day at the very earliest stages — he would have a complete-enough series to show the full embryonic development. But exactly how many specimens would he need?

It was this question that William was musing on the following morning as he walked his horse back along the river after his usual recce. On nearing the camp site he saw that he had visitors. Another horse and a gig were tied up beside the store tent, and he could hear the sound of Donald's laughter. He thought he heard the sound of a woman's voice.

'I was wondering where you'd got to, Professor,' said Donald, hurrying to take William's horse.

'And I was wondering too, Mr Caldwell.' Ettie Brown was rising to her feet from the chair on which she had been sitting beside the fire.

'Thank you, Donald,' said William. 'I must apologise, Miss Ettie. Please, don't stand.'

The girl sat down. In the chair next to her was Mary Brown, who had remained seated.

'I am very pleased to see you, too, Miss Brown,' said William. 'Had I known you were both coming I would have been back earlier.'

And, he thought, stroking his upper lip, I would have made sure I was properly shaved. It really wasn't quite fair on a man.

'Oh, we have not been here long, Mr Caldwell, and Donald has been looking after us very well,' said the girl, bowing her head in Donald's direction. 'He was just about to make us some tea.'

'Capital. May I join you?'

'Surely it is we that are joining you, Mr Caldwell,' said the elder sister.

'Perhaps you are right, Miss Brown,' said William with a small nod. 'But no matter, a cup of tea sounds like just the thing. I see you already have matters well in hand, Donald — you can leave Belle to me if you like. If you will excuse me, ladies, just for a moment.'

Donald handed the horse to William and went back to preparing the tea. He had the billy on the boil and the teapot and three mugs at the ready. While he went to find a fourth William tied up Belle next to the tent. Donald had already put out oats and water ready for her return. William unstrapped the saddle and lifted it onto the rough saddle tree that Donald had constructed from a branch lashed between two saplings.

'There, now I can sit down and join you. I must say it is a great pleasure to have some guests, eh, Donald? Donald has been proving a most willing helper, but I suspect he must get tired of my company at times.'

'Don't you listen to the Professor,' said Donald. 'I've told him I like it here. Always learning something new.'

'That goes for both of us, I'm sure.'

'And what have you been learning today, Mr Caldwell?' said the girl, taking a mug of tea from her sister's hands. It was marvellous the way Mary Brown looked after Ettie, so casual yet so careful. William had been almost spellbound the previous day by the sight of the blind girl's busy fingers fluttering over teacup and table, and he now watched them move softly but surely around hands and mug until they found the handle. The four of them sat around the fire drinking tea while William told them of his discoveries of that morning: two more platypus burrows.

'Whenever I find one I mark it with one of these.' He pulled from his pocket a strip of red flannel cloth. And quickly added, cursing himself, 'It's a piece of cloth. It's red.'

'Then it sounds as though all is going well, Mr Caldwell,' said the elder woman.

'I have to say that it is indeed going well, Miss Brown, though I'm not sure if it is going quite well enough. Perhaps Donald has told you that I have already located twenty-three burrows well within a day's ride of here — twenty-five now — but I fear that I will need more. And finding the burrows is one thing, obtaining the animals is another.'

'I'll be able to help you with that, Professor, don't you worry,' said Donald.

'Able and willing though you are, Donald, I am slightly concerned that our joint efforts will not bring the reward we require.'

As if she could read his mind, Mary Brown spoke again. 'You are perhaps thinking that you could do with some more help?'

'I dearly would like more help, Miss Brown, though I am told that I am unlikely to get it.'

'Perhaps you have not been asking the right people, Mr Caldwell.'

'I have asked in town but no one seems willing to assist — as I am sure you know, all the young men seem to go off and work in the mines almost as soon as they can lift a shovel. I really don't see what else I can do. I find myself in something of a quandary. But enough of my problems — what brings you here?'

'Why,' said Ettie, 'that most irresistible impetus — curiosity. I — Mary and I — wanted to see for ourselves this wonderful camp that you had told us about.'

William felt something inside him flinch. To use the word 'see' to mean 'experience' — which everyone does — seemed in this circumstance a painful irony, but one the girl seemed unaware of.

'I — Donald and I — will be delighted to show you everything, will we not, Donald?'

As soon as they had finished their tea, the tour began. The girl wanted to touch everything — every plate and frying pan, every jar and bottle and instrument. She found William's microscope particularly fascinating and asked him to describe it and what it was for. Though willing to do so, William was not sure if he was able.

'I hope you won't mind me asking this, Miss Ettie, but how long have you been … um …?'

'Blind? No, I don't mind you asking, Mr Caldwell. I have been blind since I was four.'

How, then, to explain a microscope? What words could he use to describe such things to one who has no experience of them? He had a sudden inspiration.

'Have you ever come across a magnifying glass, Miss Ettie?'

'No, I don't think so, Mr Caldwell. I know the words, of course, but not the object.'

He took a large glass from its box on the table and placed it in the girl's hands. They fluttered around it, feeling its shape and composition.

'As you can see' — there, now he was doing the same thing; best ignore it and continue on — 'it is a round piece of glass of a special shape, and with a handle. Please give me the glass and one of your hands.'

He took hold of the girl's hand and held it so that its palm was pointing towards the sun. He noticed pale brown marks, old scars of some kind, he supposed.

'Do you feel the warmth of the sun?'

'Yes, I can feel it with my hand, and on my face.'

'Good. Now I am going to hold the glass just a few inches from your hand, directly between your hand and the sun. Tell me what you feel.'

With great care William held the glass so that a large round image of the sun appeared on the girl's hand.

'Oh yes. I can feel it. It feels hot.'

'Exactly,' he said, taking the glass away. 'Even though I have put this glass between you and the source of heat, the heat not only passes through it but is concentrated. And it can be concentrated even more.'

Taking a sheet of paper from the desk, he held the lens so that the sun's image was reduced to a bright dot on the paper. A spiral of smoke arose from it.

'I am now holding the lens between the sun and a piece of paper.'

'And I can smell burning. Why, Mr Caldwell, you might have burned my hand.'

'I would never burn you, Miss Ettie, never.' (Is that what those scars were? Had the poor girl's hands once been burned?) 'But I hoped that you might understand that just as the lens concentrates heat, it also concentrates the light by which we see. The lens makes things look bigger, and a microscope is a kind of special lens for making very small things look bigger, to make them easier to see.'

'I think I understand now,' said the girl — though how much she understood, thought William, he would never know.

'Cleverly done, Mr Caldwell,' said Mary Brown. 'I congratulate you.'

'Have you yourself looked into a microscope, Miss Brown?'

'I have seen pictures of objects under a microscope, but no, I have never looked myself.'

'Then, what shall we show you?' William looked around him, and around the camp site. 'I know. Donald, fetch me an onion.'

Donald rummaged in the tucker box and pulled one out. William opened his pocket knife.

'I am sure you have peeled an onion, Miss Brown, and you know that between the thicker layers are even thinner layers, as thin as tissue paper. There, I have a small piece on the blade of my knife.'

William spread the piece of onion skin onto a glass slide, added a drop of water and covered it with a small glass slip. He placed the slide onto the platform of the microscope and adjusted its various knobs.

'Now, what do you see?'

Mary Brown bent over the microscope. 'Nothing. Oh yes. I see rows of what — pale bricks? But it is as if they are transparent, and I can see small things within each brick.'

'What you are seeing is cells, the building blocks that make all living things, and the organula within them.'

'I shall take your word for what you say, Mr Caldwell,' said the woman, still peering down the microscope. 'And how big are these cells?'

'The ones you are looking at? Perhaps each one a hundredth of a hundredth of an inch across. So think how many there must be in the whole onion, Miss Brown.'

'I shall think about it, though probably not for very long. But tell us, Mr Caldwell, why do you need a microscope to see a platypus?'

The question brought a smile to William's lips. 'I need to look at the very earliest stages of the embryo, of the baby platypus just as it begins its development, when it may consist of only a few cells not much bigger than the ones you have been looking at.'

Ettie Brown turned her face towards him, a small frown across her brow. 'And how do you obtain these cells, Mr Caldwell?'

'By simple dissection. If I can find enough platypus embryos at the right stage of development I will be able to make a sequence of slides showing growth and development. Then I will be able to compare this sequence to that of other mammals and so will learn much about the relationship of platypuses to them, and to other animals.'

The girl nodded.

'You know, it may surprise you, Mr Caldwell,' said her sister, 'but I don't think I have ever seen a platypus.'

'I regret that we do not have one to show you, Miss Brown. As I am sure you know, they only leave their burrows at dusk. I am afraid that a burrow is all we could show you at the moment.'

'I would like that,' said Mary Brown. 'Perhaps Donald could show me.'

'An excellent idea,' said her sister, smiling sweetly. 'And Mr Caldwell can stay here and explain to me exactly why it is necessary that so many creatures must die so that he may see how they live.'

By the time Donald and Mary Brown returned from the river William was feeling distinctly hot and flustered. The girl had really been most annoying. How could anyone doubt the advantages of science over superstition, of knowledge over ignorance? But the way she twisted his words, the way she went off on tangents to the main question, it was almost as if she didn't *want* to understand.

'I disapprove of killing for sport, Mr Caldwell,' had been her final words. 'And what is your science but the sport of intellectuals?'

Mary was also showing signs of exertion from her climb back up the riverbank.

'It was so easy to see, once Donald had shown me. He says he can tell where possums are, too, by the scratching on trees.'

'I am delighted, dear sister,' said the girl. She looked at William. 'And most envious.' She stood. 'But thank you so much for all your kind efforts, Mr Caldwell. And thank you especially, Donald. You have been most hospitable, and your damper is quite delicious.'

While Donald unhooked the nosebag from their horse, Mary Brown helped her sister into the gig.

'Oh, but before we go … Mary, perhaps you could get those things from the box.'

Mary Brown took a basket from the box under the seat and handed it to William with the smallest of smiles.

'We thought that you might like a change of diet, Mr Caldwell,' said Ettie. 'Goodbye.'

'Goodbye, Miss Brown, Miss Ettie. Please, come and visit me — us — again at any time. And thank you.'

With one hand William waved the two women goodbye. With the other he held tight the basket that contained, nestling on some straw inside, twelve brown and speckled eggs.

eleven

Mr Holmes, well known to most naturalists in London as a gatherer of natural history collections, has lived for some years in New Holland. One day while hunting on the banks of the Hawkesbury he saw very distinctly an *Ornithorhynchus* leave a sandbank and escape into the river. On examining the place where the animal had rested, Mr Holmes saw a hollow in the sand about nine inches in diameter, and in this open cavity were some twigs and the eggs in question. These eggs measure 13/8 inches in length, by a breadth of ¾ inch; the shell is thin, fragile, semi-transparent, and of a uniform flat white colour.
  Letter from Professor Robert E. Grant to Etienne Geoffroy St-Hilaire, 14 September 1829

William was sure he would have enjoyed the omelette that Donald cooked him for breakfast the following morning a lot more if only he could have stopped thinking about that girl. It was not the girl herself, of course — indeed not. It was what she said. Sport of intellectuals, indeed. The conversation had been going over and over in his head. The trouble was that he had not known which tack to take. Should he have tried to defend the killing of animals for sport (salmon and deer, for instance), or should he have tried to explain how the pursuit of scientific knowledge — the pursuit of knowledge *per se* — differed in almost every respect from the pursuit of game? In the end he had done neither, and had lost the thread of his argument completely, and it was really most aggravating. Sport of intellectuals. *She* was really most aggravating.

On the other hand he had to admit that he had enjoyed Ettie Brown's visit. It would be a shame if this difference of opinion meant that he would no longer see her, and her sister. So when he came up with his brilliant idea he exclaimed 'Hah!' — and he exclaimed 'Hah!' so loudly that Donald asked him whether something was wrong with the eggs.

'No, Donald, nothing wrong with the eggs. Eggs — capital. And nothing wrong, I think you will agree, with eating platypuses.'

The boy looked at him with surprise.

'Yesterday, Donald, Miss Ettie suggested that it was wrong to kill animals simply for scientific research. It's nonsense, of course, complete poppycock, but I'm sure that even she would agree that there is nothing wrong with killing animals for food.'

'You're going to eat platypuses?' The boy shook his head. 'Rather you than me, Professor. Have you ever tried one?'

'Not yet, Donald, no indeed, not yet. But I have no reason to doubt that they are anything other than toothsome in the extreme. In fact, I seem to remember Doctor Bennett has something to say on the subject.'

He fetched his *Gatherings of a Naturalist* from the small chest in his sleeping tent and began leafing through it.

'Let me see now — ah yes, here we are. "The *ornithorhynchus* has a peculiar fishy smell, more especially when wet." Oh dear, that doesn't sound too good, does it? Ah, this is it: "The Aborigines use these animals as food" — there, did you hear that, Donald? Just as I thought.'

'Does it say anything else, Professor?'

'Let me see now. "The Aborigines use these animals as food, but it is no particular recommendation of them to say they are eaten by the native Australian, as nothing in the shape of provender comes amiss to him, whether it be snakes, rats, frogs, grubs, or the more delicate opossum, bandicoot or flying squirrel." Oh.' William's shoulders drooped.

'Snake's all right, Professor, and there's nothing wrong with possum.'

'Then there you are,' said William, closing the book with a snap. 'I'm sure platypuses will be equally delicious.'

And so it was, when on the following Saturday he returned from his morning ride and once more saw the gig pulled up beside the camp site, he was able to greet the Misses Brown with the news that very soon platypuses would be forming the staple meat item in his diet — though he would still very much appreciate the occasional egg.

'I'm sure you will agree, Miss Ettie, that killing animals for food is acceptable. And should I be able to make further use of said animals in some scientific endeavour then so much the better.'

Ettie Brown turned her face towards him. 'You will eat every one that you kill?'

'I will.'

'Then I concede the argument to you, Mr Caldwell,' she said, with a single nod of her head, 'at least for the while. And I look forward to hearing how they taste.'

'I am sure that Mr Caldwell will tell us,' said her sister. 'And I'm sure he will be pleased to hear that the mail arrived yesterday.'

'Yes, we've brought you something. I — we — thought they might be important. Mary, where is the basket?'

'It is right beside you. Would you like me to get the things?'

'No, I shall.' Ettie reached inside.

'Don't show me, let me guess,' said William, pleased that the 'sport of intellectual' ordeal now seemed to be over. 'It's a letter. No? It's a newspaper.'

'Wrong,' said the girl. With a flourish, she pulled her hand from the basket. 'Two letters, *and* a newspaper.'

William smiled, and he somehow knew that she would know he was smiling. 'Miss Ettie, you fooled me utterly.' He took the things from her hand. 'Hmm, a Sydney paper too, and only ten days old. And let's see, one letter also from Sydney, and this other one looks like it's from home.'

'Who is it from?' said the girl, and dropped her eyes. 'I'm sorry, Mr Caldwell. It was rude of me to ask.'

'Do you mean, is it from my sweetheart?'

'I'm sure it is no business of mine.' But as the girl spoke she lifted her face towards him as though expecting an answer.

'Perhaps it is not, but I feel inclined to tell you all the same.' He paused, turning the letter over in his hands. 'Now, if it were from a sweetheart it would be addressed in a female hand, would it not? That flowing script, those little curls at the end of the words — yes, this certainly appears to be a female hand.'

The girl turned away again with what seemed to William was a small but unmistakeable toss of her head. He began to open the envelope.

'And any sweetheart of mine would always write on coloured paper, I think. Let us see. Ah yes, I think I would describe this paper as lavender. Not quite pink, not quite blue. Yes, definitely lavender.'

'Will the tea be ready soon, Donald?' said the girl.

'And I think, too, that my sweetheart would scent her letter to me — a little lavender, perhaps, to match the colour?' He lifted the letter to his nose and sniffed — loud and long. 'That's strange.' He sniffed again. 'Not lavender — what could it be?'

'Rosewater,' said the girl.

'So it is, so it is.'

Surely she could not smell the faint scent from there?

'Then it is as I suspected. The letter is most definitely from … my aunt. And I'm afraid the tea will be a few minutes yet — Donald has only just put the billy on.'

Why did he enjoy teasing this girl so? Was it to get his own back, for being frustrated in argument? How often would this poor blind girl living out here get letters addressed to her from foreign lands with foreign stamps? And if she did, she could not read them. Flowing script, lavender notepaper, rosewater — he felt suddenly ashamed.

'Never mind the letter,' he said, putting it down unread on top of the newspaper. 'May I tell you about the tortoise I saw this morning? It's very exciting — well, I think it's very exciting. But perhaps everybody knows about this, perhaps it isn't very exciting at all really, only —'

'Tell me about your tortoise, Mr Caldwell,' said the girl.

'Yes. Right. Well, as I'm sure you know, tortoises are reptiles so they lay eggs. What I should say is that they are reptiles *and* they lay eggs, because of course not all reptiles lay eggs — quite a few, lizards especially, give birth to live young. And some snakes, especially in colder climates for some reason. And of course lots of other animals lay eggs, birds, of course, and, well, fish and frogs and —'

'Mr Caldwell. The tortoise.'

'I'm sorry, yes, the tortoise. As I was saying, tortoises lay eggs, but as I'm sure you know they live in water, in the river here. Now as far as I know no reptile lays its eggs in water. Crocodiles, turtles, tortoises, they all live in water but they all come out of the water to lay their eggs. But they bury them — for safety, I suppose. I saw one doing it this very morning. It was really most interesting.'

'Come, let us sit down, Mr Caldwell. You must tell me all about it.'

William reached out to take the girl's hand and lead her to the chair but she had already turned and was walking towards it, hands outstretched. It occurred to William that he had never seen her use a stick. She soon found the chair she had used on her previous visit and sat herself. Her sister sat down beside her. William pulled out another chair and sat opposite.

'As I may have mentioned, the river is rather low at the moment, but though many rocks are exposed — and this is where I often see the tortoises sunning themselves during the day — there is very little in the way of mud or sandbanks, at least around this particular part. In short, there is nowhere for the tortoises to bury their eggs close to the river at all. But yesterday I was walking over on the far side, not half a mile from here, when I came across one of the animals. It must have been a furlong from the river at least and was toiling over some rather dry ground with such deliberation that it appeared not to notice me. I decided to follow it. It was heading away from the river, but soon stopped and rested in a very slight depression in the otherwise flat ground. As I watched it began to scratch away at the surface of the earth with its back legs.'

'It was digging its nest?' said the girl, and turned towards the fire. 'I think the water may be ready now, Donald.'

Donald had put the tea in the pot and was already reaching for the kettle. William saw Mary smile her secret smile as she watched Donald pour the water. He wished he knew what it meant. If women were a mystery, this native woman was mystery on mystery.

'It was *trying* to dig its nest,' he continued, 'but the ground was so hard that it wasn't getting very far, I'm afraid.'

'So you decided to help it?'

'Perhaps I would have, but let me tell you what happened next. It scratched away for quite a while, but as I said it wasn't making much impression, but then it stopped digging and turned around.'

'Right around?'

'So that it was facing the other way. So that its head was where its back legs were, where it had been digging. Then — and I saw this with my own eyes — it threw up some water onto the ground. You know, from its mouth. It must have had the water in its stomach and a good cupful poured out right where the animal had being trying to dig. Of course the water was just sucked into the ground. Then the tortoise turned round and started digging again and in no time at all it had dug out all the wetted soil.'

By now the girl was clearly interested. She scarcely noticed Mary take the cup of tea from Donald and put it down in front of her, but William again noted with what care Mary took her hand and touched it to the cup so that she might know where it was.

'Of course,' said William, 'the water hadn't soaked in very far, so when all the wet soil was gone the tortoise turned round and did the whole thing again. And then again, and again — it must have been carrying a good pint of water. Isn't that wonderful?'

'It is indeed wonderful,' said the girl. 'It is as if it knew, as if it knew how to …'

'Exactly.' William was grinning broadly. 'Exactly. And then it laid its eggs.'

'Does it hurt them, to lay their eggs?'

'No, I don't think so,' said William, puzzled. 'The eggs seem to pass through the cloaca easily enough. They are not large, you know — much smaller than a hen's egg. But why do you ask?'

'So is it only human females for whom childbirth is painful?'

'I think that perhaps it is.'

'I'm sorry, I interrupted you,' said the girl. 'Tell me what happened next.'

'There's one more interesting thing. When the tortoise had finished digging its hole — I suppose it must have taken nearly an hour — as I say, it laid its eggs. There were thirteen of them — six first, which it covered with a layer of the damp soil, then another seven on top. Then it scraped more soil back over them and sort of smoothed it off with its shell. And then it stood right over the nest, raised itself as high as it could go on its four legs, and dropped down onto the loose soil — thump.'

'It was making the soil hard again.'

'Yes, it did this several times. And I must say, if you went back there now you wouldn't know there was a nest there at all.'

The girl sipped at her tea. 'No, I dare say I wouldn't.' Looking up from her cup, she said, 'I like you telling about what you have seen, Mr Caldwell. Thank you. I hope you will do it more often.'

William had feared that he might have been boring his companion. He was delighted with her response. She might even like to hear about the wasp he had seen on the wharf at Bundaberg.

'Tell me, Mr Caldwell,' said the girl. 'Do you believe in God?'

'In God?' A small feeling told William that this was going to be the start of another of those exasperating conversations.

'Yes, God — the creator of the universe and all it contains. You know, that sort of God.'

'Well I, erm, I ...'

'Oh, come, Mr Caldwell. Surely you have considered the question? You have just described to me the most wonderful example of animal action — of animal foresight. Is that or is that not proof of the existence of a wise creator? It is a simple enough question. If not, how do you explain it?'

William was almost thankful the girl could not see the waves of panic passing over his face. 'Have you seen my billiard table?' he said, with sudden inspiration.

'No. Have you lost it?'

'No, no, I didn't mean ... I thought you might like to ... I'd like to show you ...'

'Did God make your billiard table, Mr Caldwell?'

'Well, no. It's a Churchman actually. I just thought that you …'

The girl sighed. 'Mr Caldwell, I would love to meet your billiard table.' The corners of her mouth lifted into a smile. 'How did you guess?'

'And I would like Donald to show me how to find a possum,' said Mary Brown, also with a smile.

'I saw the marks of one this morning,' said Donald. 'On that tree just over there.'

The table was still uncovered from the previous night. William guided the girl towards the middle, let her hand down onto its edge and, as her fingers touched it, released the hand.

'Billiards,' she said. 'I'm sure I have heard of it. It is some sort of game, is it not?'

She felt along the wooden rail, first with her right hand, then with her left. Her fingers crept over the felted cushion and down onto the smooth baize. Flattening out her palms she passed them from side to side as far as they would stretch then, leaning over, reached forward. Her hands skimmed the playing surface. With all fingers again resting on the edge of the table she brought her two hands together to the middle pocket with its rim of thick, soft leather and the cotton net beneath. For a few seconds her fingers felt in and out and around it, then again moved outwards along the table's edge. To William it seemed as though the fingers were at once under her complete control and at the same time independent of her — two scouting parties sent out to reconnoitre and report back what they had seen.

When the girl had reached as far as she could with her right hand she took a couple of sideways steps, brought up her left hand to meet her right and again reached along as far as she could to the right until she felt the corner pocket. Again the digital exploring party went to work. The girl stepped sideways, rounded the corner of the table and began to work her way along the top of the table in the same manner. This was all done in complete silence, though her face was tilted upwards and William noticed again the small smile that sometimes lifted the corners of her lips. He realised that she was measuring the table. She slipped around the next corner, worked her way along the opposite side, round to the bottom of the table and back to where she had started from.

'I see,' she said, and once again William winced at the artlessness of her language.

He reached into one of the carefully crafted drawers to take out the two white balls and the red.

'The game is played with three balls,' he said, placing one of them in her hand. If he rolled one of the other balls hard across the table she might at least hear it hitting the cushions. With a flick of the wrist he sent the red ball up towards the top corner. It bounced off three cushions and returned to his hand. The girl said nothing.

'They are all the same size as the one you are holding. Two are white and one is red. The balls are hit across the table with cues.'

'Cues?'

'Long, thin sticks.'

'Long, thin sticks. Ah. And please explain how you play the game.'

'Well, to start with the red ball is placed on a spot marker, a small piece of dark cloth glued to the table. Then —'

'Where is it, this marker?'

'It is near the top end, to your left, in the centre of the table.'

The girl frowned slightly, but then gave a small nod.

'Towards the bottom of the table — that is to say the end of the table to your right — there are three more spots in — how shall I put it? — horizontal alignment.'

Again the girl frowned. 'I am sure you put it well, Mr Caldwell, but if you were to show me I think I would have a better idea. Is that possible?'

William doubted that it was. This had been a foolish idea. Really, what could be of such interest to a blind person about the arrangement of spots on a billiard table? Nevertheless, the girl had asked and he felt obliged to show her.

'If I can help you to the bottom end of the table,' began William, but as he spoke the girl was already moving. She centred herself exactly where he would have placed her. 'Right, now about a foot from the edge of the table a line has been inked onto the cloth.'

Her right hand moved forward; her fingers stopped no more than an inch beyond the line.

'Am I close?'

'Perhaps if I were to guide your hand,' said William. Taking her silence as assent he reached over and gently lifted her hand, putting the index finger down on the centre spot. As soon as he released it both her hands started skimming over the spot marker, across the table, back to the cushion. They soon found the other two spot markers.

'Ah yes. I can feel them. And what are these for?'

'They are to mark the area in which your ball may be placed. I should have explained that each player — there are two players — has his own ball. They are the white balls, but one is marked with a black spot.' He looked down at the ball left in his own hand. It was unmarked. 'The one in your hand is the spot — that is to say, the ball with the spot.'

The busy fingers turned the ball, feeling its surface until one forefinger was moving to and fro across the small indented mark.

'And this — area?'

'Is a semicircle.'

Again the girl nodded.

'It is defined by a radius drawn between the central spot and either of the outer spots, and extends towards the bottom of the table.'

'Like a D on its back.'

'Exactly,' said William, surprised by the girl's understanding of what to him were purely visual concepts. 'Like a large D on its back. The first player may place his ball anywhere within the D, and from there try to hit the red ball and score points. Points are scored by hitting the red ball into any pocket, or sinking your own ball into any pocket off the red.'

'Is this what you think life is like, Mr Caldwell?'

'I'm sorry, Miss Ettie, I don't quite understand.'

'Oh, nothing. And then what?'

William, flustered now, continued. 'If the red ball is potted, it is replaced on its spot at the top of the table. If you pot your own ball you start again by placing it within the D.'

'Resurrection, Mr Caldwell?'

'But,' he went on, ignoring the question, 'you may not play backwards from the baulk line.'

'I must remember that,' said the girl. 'It sounds important. I must not play backwards from the baulk line.'

Was she teasing him? She was surely teasing him.

'If no score is made, the opponent places his — or her — own ball within the D and tries to score. Now that there are three balls on the table the opportunities for scoring are of course increased.'

'Of course,' said the girl.

William cleared his throat. 'The player may now score by making a winning or losing hazard with the opponent's ball as well as the red ball, or may score by hitting both of the other balls in the same shot, which is called a cannon.'

'Both balls? How interesting. And I don't believe you have mentioned hazards before, Mr Caldwell. Certainly not on the billiard table.'

'I apologise, Miss Ettie. A winning hazard is sinking any ball other than your own into a pocket, a losing hazard is sinking your own ball off one of the other balls.'

'But win or lose, you still score?'

'Yes, you still score.'

'How very interesting. Show me.'

William again hesitated slightly.

'Please show me, Mr Caldwell.'

It appeared as though he must. 'Well,' said William, 'first I must "spot the red", as we say.'

'Allow me,' said the girl, holding out her hand.

Oh, why not? William put the ball into her outstretched hand. She put it into a pocket of her skirt and walked to the end of the table, her right hand trailing along the table's edge. When she felt the top pocket she stopped, turned to her left and took two more short paces.

'Am I close, Mr Caldwell?' she said.

William nodded his head in some amazement, and on realising that this silent gesture had gone unnoticed, stammered out, 'Oh yes, yes.'

The girl again leant over the table, this time stretching her arms wide so that she was touching the edge of each pocket with fingertips. She shuffled her feet slightly, then stood upright. As she did so her hands were drawn together along the edge of the table until they met at the centre of the top cushion.

'And is this spot the same distance from the edge?'

'No,' said William. 'Eight inches, no more.'

Keeping her thumbs on the cushion, the girl spread her fingers towards the middle of the table, brought thumbs up to forefingers and again opened her hands slightly. Her forefingers were touching the red spot. With one finger still on the spot she reached into her pocket with the other hand and placed the red ball in its proper position. She stood up and took a step back from the table.

'Let the play begin, Mr Caldwell.'

William became aware of a strange feeling in his chest. It was a tightness, as if there were at once something constricting his breath and something not quite right with his heart.

'Er, yes,' he said. 'Just one moment.'

There was no doubt about it; he was feeling decidedly odd. Blinking hard, he looked around him. It was a typical Australian scene — gum trees silhouetted against blue sky, the reddish brown earth dotted with smaller shrubs and dried grass. The sun was well up, washing the colour from leaves and soil. It was a scene he had grown used to by now, yet it all looked somehow different. He looked towards the girl. Nothing about her had changed. She was standing beside the table in her white dress, her face still just a little upturned though shaded by the broad brim of her hat. Her pale blue eyes looked straight towards him, the small half-smile still played about her lips, an expectant smile now. Still he felt that tightness in his chest. A touch of fever, perhaps? He stood up straight, relaxed his shoulders and took in two deep breaths. Much better. Another two. Yes, that was very much better. Reaching down to open the drawer that contained the cues, he selected one of them and slid it from its place.

'What are you doing, Mr Caldwell?'

'I'm sorry, Miss Ettie, I should have told you. I've just picked up the cue.'

'Ah yes, the long, thin stick. Please, go ahead.'

'Right,' said William. 'My break, as they say.'

He lined up his shot, rehearsed the line of the shot a couple of times, then made the classic break of hitting the red ball hard enough so that both it and his own cue ball ended up close to the bottom cushion.

'Good shot, Mr Caldwell. Both balls in baulk.'

How on earth did she know that?

'How on earth did you know that?'

'Know what?'

'How did you know that both balls were behind the baulk line?'

'I heard them.' She pointed at the table in front of William. 'That one, which I suppose must be the red ball, bounced off the cushion there at the end, then bounced off this side cushion and it must have stopped just there.' She was pointing at the red ball. 'Your white ball hit the top cushion, then the other side cushion, then the bottom cushion. Now it's there.'

William was amazed to see her finger indicate the position of the white ball, a couple of inches from the bottom cushion. Impossible. But the alternative? No, no — equally impossible. Oh dear, this was too much. As he felt his growing discomfort turning to panic he heard another female voice.

'Ettie, have you been teasing Mr Caldwell?'

Mary Brown had returned with Donald.

'Sister dear, how could you think such a thing?' said the girl. 'Mr Caldwell has been most thorough in his instruction, and if I —'

'I think I understand,' said Mary Brown, giving her sister a stern look. 'Mr Caldwell, I fear that Ettie has not been quite honest with you.'

'Do you mean that she isn't …?'

'I mean that contrary to the impression she may have given you, this is not the first time my sister has — shall we say — "encountered" a billiard table.'

'I am not sure I understand you, Miss Brown.'

Mary Brown again looked at her sister. 'We have known of occasions before when your jokes have had unintended consequences, have we not, sister dear? Will you tell Mr Caldwell, or shall I?'

Ettie Brown had turned her back on them both and appeared to be gazing at the sky.

'I believe you have visited the Club Hotel, Mr Caldwell?' said Mary Brown. 'You may have seen the billiard table there?'

William nodded.

'I will not go into the whole story now, but when my sister was a child — when we *both* were children — she spent much time at the hotel. It was there that she first learned about the game of billiards, and she developed an unusual skill. You have just seen it, Mr Caldwell. Visitors sometimes thought there was trickery involved — perhaps you thought yourself that some trickery was involved, Mr Caldwell. There was more than one difficult moment over the years. But no. My sister can indeed hear the balls as they move.'

'Now that you have quite spoiled my fun, sister dear, I think I would like to leave.'

Though Ettie Brown may have been put out, William was feeling nothing but relief. So, that was the explanation.

'If it is any consolation to you, Miss Ettie, knowing the story behind your remarkable ability only makes me doubly impressed. I bow to you.'

William bowed low, knowing that somehow the girl would be aware of his action — perhaps she could even hear it. The girl gathered up her skirt in a gesture as theatrical as it was feminine and climbed into the gig.

'Oh, Mr Caldwell, I nearly forgot,' she said as she seated herself and her sister took the reins.

'Yes, Miss Ettie.'

'Is it true?' She turned towards him with an innocent smile. 'Mary has told me that you are trying to grow a moustache. Is it really true?'

twelve

> From the peculiarity of its generative organs, and from its being considered as the connecting link between birds and quadrupeds, the platypus has lately excited considerable interest; yet it even now remains a matter of doubt, whether it is oviparous or viviparous. A gentleman residing near the River Hunter has assured me that he once dissected a female within which several eggs were discovered of different degrees of maturity.
> John Henderson, *Observations on the Colonies of New South Wales and Van Diemen's Land*, 1832

The rhododendrons at Morar House, Aunt Agnes wrote, had been something of a disappointment this year, and she had already had to 'talk to' the new parlour maid. But at least Uncle Angas had not had a recurrence of the gout despite his ignoring his doctor's orders about you-know-what. The letter continued with more domestic news and by the time William put it back into its envelope he was smiling again. Yet how far away it all seemed. In distance and in time.

The second letter was from Doctor Bennett in Sydney and contained information about the movements of his German rival. Through his Melbourne friend, the doctor had learned that Herr Richard von Mengden had decided on Tasmania as the best field for platypus research. 'In which case,' wrote the doctor, 'you will have a head start. The animals will not start to breed there until October at the earliest.'

'Most satisfactory,' said William, as he folded up the letter. 'Most satisfactory.'

'Good news, Professor?'

William told him about Herr von Mengden.

'As dispassionate scientists, Donald, I know we should welcome the presence of as many researchers as possible into our own field of study. But I have to confess that as a Cambridge man, and as a Scot, I find myself somewhat elated to think that I may still beat this German fellow to the truth.'

With each passing day the Australian bush was becoming more familiar, and with this familiarity came a certain appreciation of detail that before had been lacking. What had been just bush or scrub or forest now began to separate itself into its component parts. From subtle differences in bark and foliage, and with Donald's help, William could now distinguish red gum from white gum from blue gum, and tell at a glance a bloodwood from an ironbark, a blackbutt from a coolabah. And so with the birds.

Though he had noticed few when he had first arrived, now he saw them everywhere. It occurred to him that rather than the actual number of birds having increased, it was his faculties of observation that had improved. The birds had been there all the time, it was just that he had been unable to see them. Now not only could he distinguish a cockatoo from a corella by sight, he could even distinguish between their raucous calls. And he took pleasure not only in identifying the birds but in observing their actions. To begin with, both currawongs and magpies had simply seemed to him large black-and-white birds. Now he saw differences not only in their plumage and song but in the way they moved. Magpies flew with a sense of purpose — you could hear their wing-beats from twenty yards away. Currawongs on the wing seemed so relaxed it was a wonder they did not fall from the sky.

There was another pied bird about the same size as the other two but this one only showed its white feathers when it flew. Wandering round on the ground — always in a group with others of its kind — it appeared completely black. According to John Gould's *Birds of Australia* this was a 'white-winged corcorax'; according to Donald, it was a chough. Though the bird bore only a passing resemblance to the red-legged, red-beaked choughs of Scottish cliffs, William preferred Donald's term.

He was coming to know these birds well. Almost every day he saw a gang of them swaggering somewhere in the forest, sifting through the fallen leaves with tosses of their curved black bills. It was difficult to see what they ate — worms and insects, he assumed. They could be noisy and quarrelsome at times. For no apparent reason one would suddenly utter a loud cry and make a rush at another. The second bird would usually run or flutter away, but sometimes it would stand its ground and the two would squawk and hiss at each other. Such was their preoccupation at these times that William found he could approach to within a few yards of them, close enough to see that during this display their eyes bulged a most devilish red. It was most peculiar. When they were not engaged in these aggressive antics their eyes appeared almost black, though still with a thin rim of red. Magpies' eyes, on the other hand, were orange, and currawongs', yellow.

William took great pleasure in his new knowledge. With the help of Donald and Mr Gould he had taken to writing down the name of each new bird at the back of his diary. It was surprising how many there were; he had already seen twelve species of parrots alone and, despite some difficulty with the smaller birds, had identified over forty species altogether. But enjoy them as he might, he had not come to Queensland to look at birds. *Ornithorhynchus anatinus* was his true quarry, and he still needed to locate as many burrows as he could before the breeding season began.

William usually went alone on his platypus excursions. Each day he explored a little further, though there was little chance of getting lost; to get back to the camp site he simply had to follow the river. When he found an occupied burrow he would tie one of his strips of red flannel cloth on whatever vegetation was to hand, with another higher up the bank so as to be easily spotted from a distance. This morning had been particularly successful. He had followed the river upstream to where it curved almost right around the small hill to the south of his camp site. Three new burrows, and according to his watch not yet eleven o'clock. He slipped the watch back into his pocket. This platypus hunting gave a man quite an appetite. He could save time getting home by taking a short cut around the other side of the hill.

Away from the river the more open country made for easier riding. After about twenty minutes, when he judged that he had reached the camp-site side of the hill, he turned to the left. In five minutes he would be sitting by the fire with a cold chop in one hand and a hot cup of tea in the other.

Five minutes later, though, it was not the camp that appeared in front of him, but a large tea-tree thicket. These dense stands of small trees, growing near the river in what had once been billabongs but had long ago filled in, were common enough. William already knew from experience that there was no point in trying to push your way through them, you just went around them — they were never very big. Reasoning that turning left again would mean going back towards the hill, he turned to the right. And he was quite correct. The thicket soon gave way to more of the open woodland that dominated the local landscape. If he turned a little to the left now he would soon be home — and even if he missed the camp he would meet the river. After fifteen minutes, he had reached neither. After thirty minutes, he was still riding through the same, featureless woodland. After an hour, he knew he was lost.

Damn, damn, damn and blast. Damn it.

The last words were spoken out loud. He shook his head, reaching down to pat Belle's neck. 'I wasn't speaking to you, old girl. It's my own fault, my own fault entirely.'

He'd read about things like this. In the Australian forest or out in the desert, on horseback or on foot. Once a man lost his bearings in the bush, that was it. He looked around again at the unending trees. Much good it was being able to tell a coolabah from an ironbark if you didn't know where you were. There were no landmarks. He'd read that sometimes a lost man just headed off in completely the wrong direction, into the wilds, never to be seen again. Or thought he was heading in a straight line but meandered in crooked loops and circles — often within a few hundred unknowing yards of his camp or a homestead. Weeks or months later the body might be found, an empty water bottle beside it, perhaps a scribbled note. He must have read or heard about this kind of thing a dozen times, and still he'd done it. The sky was overcast; bright clouds, but no sun. He never took a compass with him — well, why bother, when you knew you could always follow the river back to the camp? Damn, damn, damn and blast. He felt a small panic rise up from his stomach. Lost in the bush. What was he to do?

But wait. He hadn't been riding long. All he needed to do was retrace his steps. He dismounted and examined the ground where Belle had just been walking. Dried leaves and twigs, no footprints. Once more he looked around him. Just trees.

Of course — trees! He couldn't see the hill from here, but if he climbed a tree … He looked around again. That white gum over there, that looked like the tallest, and it had a branch that he might just be able to reach.

But just a minute, what was it Ben Fuller had said about 'widow-makers'. Was it red gums or was it white gums, the ones whose branches suddenly broke off without warning, smashing down on anything — or anyone — beneath? He walked Belle over towards the tree. He would just have to take a chance.

The lowest branch was just out of reach but perhaps if he stood on Belle. Arranging her just where he wanted her, he climbed onto the saddle. Yes, now he could reach it easily, and there was another just above it for the next handhold. Hah! This was easy. He had almost forgotten what fun climbing trees could be. With more branches providing equally convenient steps he soon reached the top of the tree and looked around him. Ah, there was the hill (its relative closeness suggested that he had not been following a straight course after all). Where he was in relation to the camp site, he could not be sure. He could not see smoke. No matter. He would be more careful now. He would head back towards the hill, if necessary climbing more trees to check directions. Nothing would go wrong this time. Except that when he got back down to the bottom branch of the tree and dropped to the ground, Belle was nowhere to be seen.

He hadn't tied her up. Why hadn't he tied her up? Because he was a — the words that William used to berate himself would have mortified his aunt. He called, he whistled. He stood very still and listened. Nothing. Belle was gone. Once again that feeling of panic rising up from his stomach. What should he do? Steady now. Think. There are two alternatives; try to follow the horse or try to get back to the hill. Oh, why was he such a fool, such a ... But no, this was no time for weakness, William — of language or of spirit. Belle was gone. He would simply have to walk.

Two hours and two tree-climbs later he reached a tea-tree thicket — it must surely be the same one he had encountered before. It would save time if he could squeeze his way through — it wouldn't be difficult without a horse. He felt the beginnings of thirst; he needed to get to the river. But no, better safe than sorry. He would walk around it.

And when he reached the end of it, there, through the trees, he could see the hill. He was almost sure the river must be not far away on the right, but, again, better to take the safest option. He would climb to the top of the hill. From there he would be sure to see which was the best way to go. After forty minutes' climbing, a large jumble of boulders appeared on the ridge ahead with clear sky beyond and he soon found himself on the rocky outcrop that marked the summit. At that moment the sun came out and he knew he was safe.

The view itself was almost worth the climb. Lightly timbered woodland stretched out around him as far as the eye could see. A line of darker vegetation showed the path of the river; in a few places he could see through it to sunlight glinting on water. He realised now that the tea-tree thicket he had twice been forced to skirt was much further to the west than he had imagined. He must have been going way off direction. Even further to the west was a low line of hills that must be the Burnett Range, the source of the river below. Only far to the east could he detect any sign of the settler's axe, where cleared patches indicated the outskirts of Gayndah. He breathed a long sigh. It was all right, he knew where he was now. And he could afford to take a rest. He lay back against one of the rocks and closed his eyes, and he remembered a hill climbed long ago.

It had been on one of Mr Harrison's geological excursions.

One summer morning teacher and class had taken the train from Shrewsbury to Church Stretton then walked up Long Mynd, Mr Harrison pointing out the rocks along the way. Here, sediments from an ancient sea bed; there, layers of ash and lava; and over there the famous Church Stretton Fault — running across the landscape like a crack in a china bowl. From the top of the hill they could see for miles and miles; they could see Wales. Now, standing on the top of the hill in the Australian bush, the memory of that day brought a warm smile to William's lips. How his old teacher would have loved to be here, deciphering the landscape, identifying the rocks. What were these boulders he was standing among now — sedimentary limestone, perhaps? He got up and turned over one of the smaller rocks. No, from its colours and crystalline texture it must be igneous. He was pleased he remembered.

All around, endless forest met endless sky. The leaves of a small gum tree, its roots delving into a crack between two of the larger rocks, rustled in a waft of breeze. It was peaceful here. He lay back against the rock and stared up through the leaves of the tree, smelling the faint perfume of its leaves. At school the nurse would put oil of eucalyptus onto the boys' handkerchiefs when they had a cold. What was its function, he wondered, in the leaf itself? Why do some trees have leaves that contained these aromatic oils, and others not? Perhaps it provided some sort of defence against being eaten, perhaps it made the leaves unpalatable. But no, look at these leaves up there. They are ragged and torn — something has been eating them. What eats gum leaves — possums, koalas? Ah, caterpillars. Twenty or thirty of the little creatures were wrapped around one of the thin outer branches, all in the same orientation and overlapping each other like tiles on a roof. So, the eucalyptus oil doesn't seem to be much good as a deterrent against them.

But what strange caterpillars — black, slightly hairy, and all bunched together like that. They were about two inches long and unlike ordinary butterfly or moth caterpillars, with large round heads, three pairs of quite prominent legs with sharp claws that gripped the bark and at the end of the abdomen a single pair of sucker-like legs. He had read of caterpillars that have irritating hairs, but the sparse bristles on these insects could surely not be harmful.

William pushed himself up off the rock and reached towards them. When his fingers were only inches away from plucking one from the tree, the whole mass of caterpillars reared up as one. As they did so each exuded a drop of greenish liquid from its mouth. In reflex William pulled back his hand, but as he did so it brushed against the bunch of insects, leaving a streak of the green liquid on his little finger — and a strong smell of eucalyptus oil in the air. He rubbed at the liquid with his other hand. It was thick and slightly sticky. He smelt it. Yes, that familiar smell from his schooldays — oil of eucalyptus.

The caterpillars had quietened down now and were again lying motionless on the twig. William had no idea what they were but was delighted with his discovery. The green liquid must surely be *their* defence, probably against being eaten by birds. Though eucalyptus oil might have first evolved to be of some use to the tree against being eaten, it was now being used by creatures that had evolved the capability to eat it. Ah — evolution! Change, adaptation, a never-ending competition for survival. Yes, how Mr Harrison would have loved to be here.

The sun was so warm, the sounds of the wind in the trees so seductive. How good it would be to lie back, close your eyes and maybe even take a little nap. No, he must head home. Though for some reason his hunger and thirst seemed to have abated, Donald might be worried. William sat up and looked around.

And then he noticed something he hadn't noticed before. Those rocks over there, the pile of flat sheets lying against the larger rock, surely they could not be natural? He got up and walked towards them, then around them. There was no doubt about it. They were not scattered, they were arranged. Human hands must have piled them up to form this hollow cairn. But whose hands, and why? A small gap between the rocks and the boulder allowed him to peer inside. The space within seemed to be filled with a jumble of sticks. No, not sticks. Bones.

He began to lift one of the rocks away, but then stopped. Something told him that this place should not be disturbed. But by more peering and squinting he was able to assure himself that the little cave was almost full of bones. And they were human bones. He could see three skulls at least and there might be more behind them. Two of the skulls could only have belonged to children. The other, the larger one, had a small round hole just above the right temple.

For some minutes William stood silently, thinking. Then taking a bearing on the river, he headed off down the hill. As he looked back at the little cairn he noticed something he hadn't seen before. Tucked beneath one of the rocks was a small bunch of white flowers — stocks, jonquils and woodbine.

When he reached camp some three hours later he was greeted by the sight of a very peaceful-looking Belle and an almost distraught Donald.

'I didn't know whether to go into town to get help or what, Professor. First you're late back, and then Belle here appears without you. I didn't know if you'd been thrown, or fallen in the river, or what had happened.'

'Fear not, Donald. I'm pleased to say that I have sustained no injuries except to my bushman's pride.'

He proceeded to tell Donald how he had got lost, and how he'd forgotten to tie up Belle when he'd climbed the tree. Whatever had made him leave the rocks on the hill undisturbed made him decide not to mention that discovery to Donald. It would be better to wait until he had made further investigations. But he did tell him about the strange caterpillars he had seen on the gum tree.

'Spitfires,' said Donald, handing him a welcome cup of tea.

'A most suitable name. They must be the larvae of some kind of insect, I suppose. Do you know what they'll turn into?'

'It's a wasp — well, a kind of a wasp, but they don't sting. We get them at home every year, in the yard. Some people are scared of them, say they'll poison you, but they're harmless enough. When they're big enough they climb down from the tree and bury themselves in the ground. Just a few inches down. Then they make a kind of case …'

'A cocoon?' said William.

'Yes, I suppose so. Sort of papery, and all of them together, like a wasps' nest.'

'And then they hatch out into a kind of wasp, eh?'

'That's right, after a few months. Dark they are, shiny. Sort of blue, with orange wings.'

William regretted that his knowledge of entomology was insufficient for him to identify the insects. The books he had brought from England were all on vertebrates — he had not thought to bring along books on invertebrates. Donald soon found other bunches of these 'spitfires' on a small sapling close to the camp and over the following days William was able to make some interesting observations. There were about seventy of them altogether. They did not feed during the day, but if he went out with a lantern at night he would find that the bunch had broken up and spread out over the tree, each caterpillar munching away at its own leaf. By the morning they would be back together again. Despite their being clearly visible, William never once saw a bird attack them. His guess about the eucalyptus oil defence could well have been right.

For several days William kept a more or less close eye on the creatures. All day they rested and all night they fed, indeed they ate so much that after six days the sapling on which they were living had scarcely a leaf on it. Then one morning they were gone. Had some creature come and eaten them in the night, some animal that enjoyed a eucalyptus relish? Had they climbed down the tree and buried themselves, as Donald had described? He searched the ground with care but could see no sign of them, and was almost resigned to leaving the whole matter as a mystery when he saw them again. The caterpillars were moving en masse up another gum tree, a much larger tree some five yards from the now-bare sapling. Though their progress was slow they had already climbed eight feet.

Later that same day Donald showed William another kind of interesting insect.

'These ones,' he said, pointing to the mass of black and green striped grubs, 'they eat gum leaves, too. But they turn into beetles — almond beetles, I call them.'

After some searching he managed to find a couple of the adult insects, green and shaped like ladybirds but larger, as big as a farthing. He showed William some of their eggs, pale pink and laid in a neat rosette around a leaf stem, and more of the young larvae, smaller and flatter than the spitfires but with the same apparent liking for each other's company.

'Now, go on, Professor, give them a poke.'

William stroked his finger over the little huddle of insects. Like the spitfires they squirmed, though raising not their heads but their tails. On his finger he saw not a green smear but a trace of clear liquid. He raised it to his nose and sniffed. There was no mistaking the smell. Not eucalyptus but almonds — bitter almonds.

'See what I mean?' said Donald.

'How very curious.'

William went over to the tent and rummaged among his equipment. 'Let's see now — hydrogen peroxide, some filter paper. That should do it.'

He tore off a small piece of filter paper and brushed it over the little insects. Using a rubber-tipped pipette, he took a drop of the clear liquid from the reagent bottle and let it seep onto the paper. A brown stain appeared.

'As I suspected. Donald, your harmless-looking little beetles are defending themselves with one of the most deadly poisons known to man.'

'What's that then, Professor?'

'Prussic acid — otherwise known as cyanide.'

So occupied had the two of them been with their chemical investigations that they had not heard the sound of a distant horse and gig approaching. Though William had been half expecting another visit from the Misses Brown he was nonetheless startled to hear a voice.

'And what is today's discovery, Mr Caldwell?'

He was, he told himself, both 'surprised and delighted' to see the sisters (it was a phrase Uncle Angas often used — Uncle Angas would express himself to be both *surprised and delighted* at William's exam results, or at a salmon his nephew had landed, or to receive the single cigar that William had saved up for and given him for a Christmas present). He described the almond beetles, and on Mary

Brown's insistence once again demonstrated the chemical test for cyanide.

'Do not be afraid to smell it, Miss Brown. I assure you that there is no danger — it is just a trace.'

Ettie Brown also leant over to sniff the little insects. 'I wonder, Mr Caldwell, what Mr Darwin would have to say to this.'

'You know his work?'

'We have read his *Origin of Species* — most compelling, I thought — and what was the other one, Mary?'

'The *Descent of Man*, perhaps,' said William.

'That was it. Another fine book, though rather an odd choice of title, do you not think?'

'The ambiguity was indeed unfortunate. But I am pleased to hear that you enjoyed them.'

'The *Origin*, in particular. It was well written and it made sense — in fact it had all three virtues necessary to any good book.'

'The third?'

'Do you not remember the final sentence, Mr Caldwell?'

The girl closed her eyes. '"There is grandeur in this view of life, with its several powers, having been originally breathed into a few forms or into one; and that, whilst this planet has gone cycling on according to the fixed law of gravity, from so simple a beginning endless forms most beautiful and most wonderful have been, and are being, evolved."'

She turned towards him, eyes now open and eyebrows lifted. 'The third virtue, Mr Caldwell? Why, a happy ending of course.'

'And what else have you been discovering, Mr Caldwell?' said Mary Brown.

William started. Surely she couldn't know about ...? No, impossible.

'Oh, just some spitfires — more little insects. Perhaps you are familiar with them?'

He began telling them about the caterpillars he had seen and their eucalyptus oil defences. But not where he had first seen them. Tomorrow he was due to go into town for supplies. Billy Pike might know something about the bones on the hill.

William found the publican in his usual place on the hotel veranda and was greeted with the now-familiar invitation.

'Thank you, Mr Pike, I think I will,' he was surprised to hear himself reply.

Were his standards degenerating, or was it simply that he was relaxing into local ways? Billy Pike went into the bar. There was the sound of splashing water and he reappeared with William's glass.

'Been having any more ... visitors?' he said, handing over the glass and reaching for a bottle from the crate beside him. William suspected that the publican already knew the answer.

'The Misses Brown came to see me — us — yesterday. They have taken an interest in my work, you know.'

'Your work, eh?' said Billy Pike. Then after a pause, 'So, how's it been going? Catching any of them bloody water-moles?'

'I haven't tried catching them yet. I'm on a kind of reconnaissance at the moment, finding out a little about the animals, where they live, how many there are, that kind of thing. And I must say young Donald Gordon is proving quite a boon as an assistant.'

'And chaperone, eh, Mr Caldwell?'

William's blush meant that Billy Pike could not avoid seeing his confusion. 'Ah, don't you worry, Mr Caldwell. There's nothing going to happen to Ettie that I'll worry about. A bloody gent like you? And it'll be Mary who's the chaperone.'

'Indeed yes, Mr Pike. And you are right, of course, Ettie Brown is a most attractive young lady, and of an age where she should be chaperoned.'

Now the subject of the two women had been raised, perhaps this might be the time to find out a little more about them.

'You are fond of her yourself, Mr Pike?'

'Fond of her? I should bloody well say I am. Ettie, she's like a daughter to me.'

With a sudden insight, William said, 'Is it you, then, that looks after them?'

Billy Pike gave him a sideways look. 'I keeps an eye on them. Always have.'

'That is most generous of you, Mr Pike.'

'Generous be blowed.'

The publican took a long swig of beer. It now looked as though he was the one feeling flustered. He took another mouthful, draining the bottle.

'Look here, Mr Caldwell, you may as bloody well hear the story from me as anyone.'

He reached for another beer and gestured for William to sit. 'Young Ettie, her dad and me, we was mates, see? Chummed up in Ballarat in, oh, '52 it must have been. We didn't find much down there — a bit o' bloody 'luvial, that's all. Then we hears about the strike up here and we comes up and stakes a claim together. We did all right up here, better than most — Gantry Creek, heard of it? Even had our very own battery mill. Well, we was doing all right and we both liked it round here so we thought we'd settle. It's a nice piece of country, Mr Caldwell. You've seen it for yourself. I'd always had a bit of an idea of opening a pub, and Joe, well he was happy to keep on running the mine. Course, no sooner had we opened than he marries the bloody barmaid.'

Billy Pike's face broke into a grin and he slapped his thigh, but then his face became serious again. 'Well, you know what happened then.'

'No, Mr Pike, I'm afraid I don't.'

'You don't? Jesus, I thought everyone bloody knew.'

He took another pull from his bottle of beer. 'Well, Joe, he was killed, see? In the robbery, terrible it was. And soon after that, Lizzy had a daughter — that's Ettie, of course. No, no, I know what you're thinking — she was his all right, spitting image. Pretty little thing she was — still is, of course — and bright as a button. Lizzy stayed on here, and she still helped out at the bar when I needed it and little Ettie used to come in here and play. It was almost as if she were my own. Then ... well, Lizzy, she went mad, see? First it was her eyes — she used to ask me to turn up the lights, even in the middle of the day. Then she started forgetting things — I mean really forgetting things, like the name of her own daughter. At the end, well, I don't know where she bloody was but she wasn't here.'

'The end?'

'She died, Mr Caldwell. Maybe it was a broken heart, maybe ... well, who knows.'

'So you adopted her — Ettie, I mean?'

'Bloody pub's no place to bring up a little girl,' said Billy Pike with an emphatic shake of his head. 'Parson Bentham and his missus, they took her in just like they'd taken in Mary.' William remembered the disused church and the empty house beside it. 'They were good people. 'Course I still kept an eye on her.'

'You still "looked after" her?'

'Look, it ain't my money, Mr Caldwell. Joe and me, everything was fifty-fifty. It's as much hers as mine.' Billy Pike gave a short laugh. 'Bloody parson didn't have any money — bloody parsons don't, do they?'

'Was Ettie blind then?'

'No, that happened later, when she was just near turned five. She took a fever — measles they reckoned. I done all I could for her. The doctor here — there was a doctor here then, as well as a preacher — he said there wasn't anything he could do.' The publican shook his head. 'But by golly she's a game little soul. She may be bloody blind but she's twice most I've met.'

'She is indeed a remarkable person. But what about Mary?'

'Mary? Well, she was another little orphan, wasn't she? Parson Bentham, he didn't care nothing about the colour of your skin. Like I said, when she lost her family he took her in — that was before Ettie, of course. Him and his missus, they taught them both reading and writing and everything. They grew up together, Ettie and Mary. Thick as thieves they were — still are. And Mary's been her eyes for her — when she needs them, that is.'

A sudden light went on in William's head. 'The billiard table. The billiard table in the bar there.'

Billy Pike chuckled. 'Ah yes, Mary told me. I'm surprised Ettie can still do it. She used to play on that table all the time, soon as she could reach it — the parson didn't mind her coming in here, as long as she did her lessons too. Oh, she was a cute one. She used to love tricking the customers. I sometimes used to think she learned to do it so as she could pretend she wasn't really blind.'

The publican shook his head, still smiling at the recollection. 'I even caught her trying to bet on it a couple of times. Would you bloody believe it? Gave her a walloping — 'course, hurt me more than it did her.'

'I thank you for telling me all this, Mr Pike.'

'Best I tell you than you hear it from someone else. You know what it's like round here.'

'I can imagine.'

'So you be careful, won't you, Mr Caldwell?'

'Careful? How do you mean?'

Billy Pike gave him so transparent a grin that even as William was packing away the single bottle of beer ('Sorry, Mr Caldwell, all I can spare') the burning in his cheeks made him quite forget to ask about the bones on the hill.

William had a few more supplies to pick up before he left town, and as he led his horse from the hotel over towards the store he had much to think over. If Ettie's father had died, how had he died, and why had her mother stayed on in Gayndah? And Mary Brown — how had she lost her parents? And when? Despite Billy Pike's revelations, there were many questions still unanswered. And those bones on the hill, could they have anything to do with all this?

'Black Hill,' said the storekeeper when William finished describing the place. 'Black's Hill some people call it.'

'What happened?'

'I only know what I've heard. It was quite a few years back, before I came here. There had been some trouble with the local blackfellows — I don't know why. Like I say, it was before my time. One day some of them came into town and attacked a house here — miner, he was. Took some gold and killed the man, raped the woman, so they say. Someone saw what happened and raised the alarm. They found the whole tribe down by the river.'

Would that have been, William wondered, near his own camp site?

'When the blacks saw all these men riding towards them with guns they ran off up the hill. I suppose they thought they'd be safer on the high ground. The men climbed up the hill after them and surrounded them at the top.'

The storekeeper looked William in the face, unsure whether he should go on.'

'And they killed them all?' said William.

'A spear's no match for a Lee Enfield. All bar one little girl, so they say.'

'But there were other children, I saw children's bones.'

The storekeeper looked down at the paper bag he was filling with tea. 'Like I said, it was before my time. I'm only telling you what I heard.'

William was not sure which was the more appalling tale, the man being killed and the woman attacked, or the massacre of the Aborigines. Was this what was meant by survival of the fittest? Was this the true face of Australia? He suddenly felt very far from home. The storekeeper could tell William little more about Black Hill. He did not know about the bones, who had hidden them or when or why. He wasn't sure when the events had happened, only that it was 'a few years back', before he'd arrived in Gayndah.

'The couple, though, the ones that were attacked. They were Ettie Brown's parents?'

The storekeeper nodded.

'And the one that survived, the Aboriginal child. Mary Brown?'

The storekeeper nodded again, and folded the bag closed.

thirteen

> During the spring of 1831, being detached in the interior of New South Wales, I was at some pains to discover the truths of the generally accepted belief, namely, that the female Platypus lays eggs and suckles its young. No eggs were found in a perfect state, but pieces of a substance resembling egg-shell were picked out of the debris of the nest.
>
> Letter from the Hon. Lauderdale Maule, 39th Regiment, to Doctor Weatherhead, 1832

William decided not to call in on the Misses Brown this time. He didn't want to talk to them — to be face to face with them — not just yet. Neither, he thought, as he turned his horse towards the dusty road that led out of Gayndah, did he think he would mention anything of what he had just heard to Donald.

The road back to the camp site kept close to the riverbank for the first mile or so, then turned away to cross a small creek bed well upstream of its junction with the main river. There had been no water in the creek since his first arrival. Its gently sloping banks and sandy bed were easy going even for a well-laden bullock wagon. But as Belle reached the top of the far bank she stopped dead and William only just managed to prevent himself from tumbling forward over the saddle. As he levered his way back into his seat he saw what had caused Belle's sudden arrest. Writhing on the road not ten yards away was a large brown snake.

Since Harry Norton's close encounter on the way to Gayndah, William had looked out for snakes but seen few. Usually it was just a scaly tail disappearing into the grass, though on one occasion Donald had spotted and pointed out to him a beautifully patterned python curled high up in a tree.

'Carpet snake — lovely, ain't she? You don't want to believe all them stories you hear about snakes, Professor,' he'd said. 'Shy beasts, are snakes.'

The one that was now rolling about in the middle of the road was by no means shy. If it had noticed man and horse it was paying them no attention. It continued to turn and twist and kick up dust.

But just a minute ... William stared and frowned. Yes, he could definitely see a leg — more than one. A snake with legs? He stared harder, and now realised that what he was looking at was not a snake at all but two large lizards, and they seemed to be fighting.

In the part of Scotland where he grew up the total reptilian fauna had consisted of one species of snake (the adder) and one species of lizard (the lizard). Adders seldom reached a foot long and the lizards were insignificant creatures, scarcely bigger than a newt. Though the scaly creatures before him now were no giants, each must have been well over a foot long and they were solid, thickset animals. Leaving Belle tied to a tree, William crept towards them.

The two opponents seemed well matched. They were clearly the same species and about the same size and weight, but they were a most unusual shape. Rather than having the tapering tails of most lizards, these had fat blunt tails almost the size and shape of their heads, and were covered with large scales almost like a pine cone. One had the other's forearm in its mouth, and no matter how much its adversary wriggled and squirmed and twisted and turned it wasn't about to let go. Despite their enthusiasm, neither animal appeared to be hurting the other — certainly no blood was being spilt. As far as William could see their mouths were toothless, and their short legs were armed with only puny claws. There seemed little risk in watching them — even, thought William, in perhaps picking them up.

He straddled the warring reptiles, crouched low and positioned his hands above them. Then he swooped, grabbing each one just behind the neck. They were surprised enough to let go their grip on each other and William was able to lift them apart. While he stood up, holding the two combatants at arm's length, both hissed, opened their mouths and stuck out their large flat tongues. William particularly noticed the tongues. They were coloured a bright, cornflower blue.

The reason these wonderful lizards had been engaged in their wrestling match soon became apparent. Though at first they had seemed almost identical, as William turned first one, then the other, around in his hands he saw poking out under some scales beneath the tail of the second were two small pink appendages. And he recalled that many reptiles are blessed with not one but two intromittent organs. He could be reasonably sure that this one was a male. So presumably the other was a female, and what he had thought was aggression was no more than a bit of lizard love-play. He put the two reptiles down beside the road, climbed back on Belle and set off again for the camp.

Though William had decided not to mention anything to Donald about the bones, nor of what he had heard in town, he was eager to tell him about the lizards.

'Ah yes, sleepy lizards, we call them,' said Donald. 'But bloody, er ... blimey, Professor, I never heard of — well — that kind of thing, though.'

Donald said no more, but from the way he fussed a little more than usual over Belle and exclaimed a little too eagerly over each item he unpacked from the bags that William had brought from the store, it was clear that he had something on his mind.

'It'll be full moon tonight, Professor,' he said at last, as he poured the tea into its caddy.

William could not remember ever being as aware of the phases of the moon as since he had arrived in Queensland. It was mainly, he had decided, because of the clear Australian skies. If there was a moon here he could always see it — unlike the fugitive moon of

Britain's cloudy skies.

'Yes,' he said, 'so it will, Donald, so it will.'

'Well, I was wondering — all right if I do a bit of moonlighting tonight?'

William looked at him. 'I'm afraid, Donald, that until you tell me what moonlighting is, I cannot answer that question either yes or no.'

'Moonlighting, for possums.' And seeing that William was no closer to understanding him, the boy said, 'Possums, they come out at night.'

William well knew that possums came out at night. On only his second night at camp he had been woken from his sleep by a noise so scary that he had lain rigid in his bed for an hour hardly daring to breathe lest whatever bloodthirsty beast was without should hear him. He had stayed like that until he judged the creature distant enough for him to risk creeping out of bed to rouse Donald, who had woken up enough to assure him that the terrifying hisses and grunts were made by a harmless animal no larger than a tomcat and promptly gone back to sleep. But still William was often woken in the night by the caterwauling of a nearby possum.

'Do you mean you want to hunt them?'

'Yes, shoot them, by moonlight. I was wondering if I might be able to borrow one of your guns.'

The possibility of a better night's sleep was not unattractive.

'On one condition,' said William. 'That you take me with you.'

As the two of them sat round the fire that night after dinner, Donald explained the principles behind the noble sport of moonlighting.

'Possums, they're not shy, and they're not too clever. As long as they're up a tree they think they're safe. They can see you all right and hear you, but they won't run away. They'll just sit there on their branch looking down at you. 'Course, you can't see them mostly, but you can hear them. That's why you need the moon. You hear one up a tree, and you get the moon behind the tree, then you move around, looking along the branches with the moon behind them — see what I mean? Soon enough you'll spot a bump on the branch that's the possum. That's what you line up on. 'Course it's better if you've got a dog to find them in the first place, to show you the tree. But don't you worry, Professor — I'm nearly as good as a dog.' The white of Donald's smile shone bright in the moonlight.

William had already prepared the guns. According to Donald, rifles were the thing — it was amazing how many pellets a possum could take from a shotgun and still hang on. William had chosen his Harding Express. He equipped Donald with a .22 rim fire Webley.

'Have you got a bit of chalk, Professor?'

William found him a piece of white chalk and Donald showed him how to mark the front sight with it.

'Makes it easier to see, in the dark.'

At nine o'clock the moon had risen enough to be useful and the two of them picked up their guns and crept out into the forest.

Donald seemed to know where he was heading and William followed along the almost-invisible track. They had been going no more than five minutes when Donald halted.

'Did you hear that?' he said in a low voice.

William had heard nothing, his whole attention being focused on keeping up with his companion. Now, though, he heard a sound, away to his left. The familiar hiss and grunt of a possum, maybe a hundred yards off and high up.

'Follow me,' said Donald, and crept forward. This was, William realised, the first time he had been beyond the light of the campfire or lanterns at night.

The moon was well up now and shining brightly. Though they had had to leave the track, the forest floor was quite open and now that his eyes were adjusted to the darkness William found he could pick his way round the bushes and tall tufts of grass with ease, though in the clear night air the moonlight made shadows seem darker than darkness itself. The possum was still calling ahead of them.

'It's in that tree there,' said Donald, in a whisper now. Moonlight glinted off his hand, his finger pointing to a large gum tree — a white gum judging by the bark — now only twenty yards away. Without another word Donald crept forward, past the gleaming trunk of the tree and into the shadows on the other side. At a suitable distance he looked up at the branches above and began quartering back and forward, getting gradually further and further from the tree. William could see his face lit full by the moonlight. Donald was enjoying this.

The boy stopped, moving his head back and forth, then up and down.

'I've got him,' he said, not looking at William but still fixing his gaze towards the moon. 'Come over here, Professor, come and stand here. This is the best way to do it.'

William went to stand beside him. Still not looking round, Donald said, 'Now you just put your face right next to mine — that's it, closer.' Their cheeks were lightly touching. 'Look up at the moon. Now I'll move this way just a bit and you move, too. There, do you see him?'

William could indeed see on the branch that crossed the face of the moon a lump — a lump with a tail hanging below it.

'Do you want to take him or shall I?' whispered Donald, his face not touching William's now but still only inches away.

'Your shot, Donald,' said William.

Donald moved back into position, raised his rifle, sighted and fired. A second after the bang there was a thump, and more thumps as some bush wallaby or kangaroo, scared by the noise, thudded away. Donald hurried forward.

'We got him, Professor. We got him all right.'

William went towards where Donald was bending over the dead animal, its fur shining in the moonlight. Shining brighter was dark blood matting the fur on its head.

'Fine shot, Donald. What now, take him back to camp?'

Donald stood up and looked around. The light of the campfire could still be seen away through the trees. 'May as well.'

Donald found his way to the track and they were soon back at the camp.

'I haven't asked you yet what we do with the thing,' said William, taking a seat by the fire. 'Are we going to eat it?'

'By oath we will,' said Donald, throwing some wood onto the flames. 'Nothing finer. But it's the skin you really want. Feel that.'

He lifted the dead animal by the tail and held it up in front of

William. The fur was thick and soft. William could feel the warmth of the animal's body beneath it.

'I see what you mean. And what will you do with it?'

'Well I was thinking I might try to make a rug for my mam, if that's all right with you, Professor.'

'It's yours,' said William.

Donald held out the possum at arm's length. 'A shilling you can get for one of these skins if it's a good one. And I reckon this is a good one all right — worth a bob of anyone's money. In fact I'll skin it now if that's all right. Before it stiffens up.'

William watched with interest as by the light of the fire Donald tied a piece of thick cord to the animal's tail and strung it from a low branch. He took a folding knife from his pocket and a round pebble. After wiping the blade twice over the stone he lifted the fur from the base of the possum's tail and cut through the skin all around it. He did the same around each foot. Starting again at the base of the tail he ran the point of the knife under the skin and sliced down towards the belly, keeping the blade of the knife just under the skin. The skin gaped but Donald was careful not to slice through the abdomen. It was a long straight cut, right down to the animal's chin.

'Now, let's see what we can do with that.'

Donald put his knife down on the table beside him, spat on his hands and rubbed them. He pulled open the skin on either side of the belly, then with one hand pulling and one hand easing the skin free from inside, worked his way up towards the tail, first one side, then the other. He turned the possum round on its cord, reached over either side of the tail and grasping the two pieces of skin pulled down, rolled his knuckles over the animal's back as it came away. Three strong jerks and the whole skin was hanging down over the possum's head. He picked up his knife again and with a few strokes of the blade cut through the skin round the neck. The pelt swung free in his hand. The whole operation could have taken no more than two minutes.

'Bravo,' said William. 'I swear I could do no better with my Swiss scalpel.'

Donald grinned and rolled up the skin on the table. 'I'll clean it tomorrow. And it'll be fried possum for breakfast. Nothing better. So, are you ready to try for another?'

William picked up his rifle. 'Lead on.'

The next morning two skinned possums hung on a branch outside the store tent and another, pulled and jointed, lay sizzling in the frying pan. The hunters had spotted the second possum not far from where Donald had shot the first, and this time it was William's turn. His first shot whipped through the leaves at least two feet above its head but the possum, rather than making a run for it, just crouched lower on the branch. William's second shot smashed clean through the branch which crashed to the ground, possum and all. Before the animal could gather its wits Donald had knocked it on the head with his rifle butt.

'Fancy shooting, Professor.'

'Thank you, Donald. Your shot next, I believe.'

They had found the third possum down by the river and Donald had to wade in almost to his waist to get a sighting on it against the moon. But he brought it down with a single shot and it was this one, smaller than the other two and so — Donald hoped — younger and more tender, that was in the frying pan. While it was cooking Donald began mixing the dough for damper.

From his tent William watched him take a generous pinch of white powder from a bag on the table and add it to the flour already in the bowl. Ah — the mystery ingredient (baking soda, no doubt). To this mixture he added water and stirred it round with his hand. With the damper in the ashes, the possum in the pan and water in the billy, Donald went over to where he had already pinned out one of the skins onto a rough board and began scraping away at the inner surface with a large knife. There was no hurry, breakfast would be a while yet.

William lay back on his bed, luxuriating in that special morning feeling. Outside he could hear kookaburras calling and magpies singing, the occasional snap of branches being broken and fed into the fire. In the trees above not a leaf rustled, not a twig stirred — but there was another sound, very faint. It was a rustling, rushing sound. It was coming from the river. He threw back the blanket and pulled on his trousers and shirt. Where were his boots?

When he at last stumbled to the edge of the riverbank he saw that the water had risen a foot overnight. But how? The ground was dry all round, there had been no rain at the camp site. He recalled Ben Fuller's words. It must have been raining in the hills.

'Have you seen the river, Donald?'

'Yes, I noticed it's up a bit,' said the boy, lifting the camp oven from the fire. The smell of fresh damper mingled with that of fried possum. Clearly Donald was not worried about the river.

'Well, I reckon it's ready now, Professor. Are you?'

William relaxed. 'I should say I am. Let the feast begin, eh, Donald?'

When Ettie and Mary Brown arrived at the camp site at just after ten o'clock they found William bending over one of the skinned possums, his dissecting instruments laid out on the table before him. He had already opened the abdomen and laid out the viscera. He was now examining the reproductive organs. Donald was also hard at work. He had pinned out a second skin fur side down on a board and was busy scraping away at it with his knife.

'Miss Ettie, Miss Brown,' said William, holding out bloody hands. 'You must forgive me. We weren't expecting you. Donald, Donald, some water, please ... in the basin ... quick now.'

Donald dropped his knife and rushed to fill the washbasin. William plunged in his hands, took hold of the soap, dropped it on the ground, picked it up and hurriedly soaped his hands. The soap once again jumped from his grasp, and as William went to catch it his foot knocked against one of the legs of the trestle table on which stood the bowl. The table collapsed and the bowl thudded to the ground, splashing the water all over his trousers.

William, hands outstretched on either side, looked downwards. He looked up at the two women. Mary Brown was laughing, and despite being unable to see what had just happened, Ettie Brown was laughing, too.

'Oh, please forgive me, Mr Caldwell,' said Ettie Brown, trying to keep her face straight but failing. 'Has something terrible happened? Mary, you must not laugh so.'

Mary Brown, her dark eyes still almost hidden, could only shake her head.

'No, no, you must forgive me, Miss Ettie,' said William, his face by now the colour of a ripe cherry. 'What a clumsy oaf I am. Would you excuse me? I'm sure that Donald will be pleased to make you a cup of tea.'

Donald was already trying to put the table back together. He picked up the bowl and the soap and washed his own hands, then went to fill the billy. The two women got down from the gig and took their usual seats by the fire. From his tent William could still hear the occasional suppressed giggle.

When he was dressed (clean trousers — and a clean shirt, too; why not?) he opened the flaps of his tent to find Mary Brown examining the half-dissected possum.

'Mr Caldwell has a possum here with its insides laid out on the table,' she was saying. She looked towards him as he approached. 'Trying to divine the future, no doubt.'

'Augury, Mr Caldwell?' said Ettie Brown. 'Or science?'

'Science, I assure you, Miss Ettie. As it happens I was examining the reproductive system of the animal. It is very different from what I'm used to.'

'Indeed?'

Did he detect amusement still in her voice?

'Describe it to me, Mr Caldwell.'

William hesitated. From his days as a demonstrator in Professor Balfour's laboratory he was well used to describing vertebrate anatomy, but the descriptions were always an adjunct to the dissection itself, or at the very least to diagrams. How many times had Frank Balfour said to him, 'Tell them and they listen, show them and they understand'? But how could he refuse Ettie Brown's request without seeming rude or, even worse, condescending?

'I confess I find it difficult to know where to start, Miss Ettie.'

'Mr Caldwell, I realise that sometimes men have strange ideas about women's knowledge of their own bodies. Let me assure you I am quite familiar with the structure of the female anatomy. I know the position of my own ovaries and womb, and all their associated organs, and I know their functions. I assume this is what you meant when you talked of what you are used to?'

William felt his face again start to redden. 'Forgive me, Miss Ettie, I was not thinking of human anatomy. I was actually thinking about all the cats and rats that I have dissected in student lessons.'

'Oh yes. Yes, naturally. I was of course also referring to the anatomy of the higher mammals in general.'

It was Ettie Brown's turn to blush (and how very charming it made her look, thought William).

'"Higher" mammals — do you not think it a strange term, Mr Caldwell? It always makes me think of giraffes. So, tell me, what are the differences between the reproductive system of the possum and a, er ...'

'A giraffe?' said William. 'I would be delighted.'

As he described and explained the structure of the female possum's reproductive anatomy he found Ettie Brown to be a knowledgeable and receptive listener. The parson's wife had indeed been a fine teacher.

'So there are — if I understand you, and if I may use one of your fine words, Mr Caldwell — *analogous* parts in both systems. It is just that in one they are more or less developed than in the other.'

'Exactly so, Miss Ettie, exactly. The arrangement may be slightly different but the basic structure is the same. And it is of course all related to the size of the foetus on parturition — at birth, that is.'

'So the womb — the uterus as you call it — is more developed in the giraffe, as that is where the baby giraffe develops. In the possum the uterus is smaller, as the baby makes most of its growth within the pouch.'

'I could not have put it more succinctly.'

'And what more is there to know, Mr Caldwell? What is your further interest in the possum?'

'Well,' said William, 'it is quite true that I now know the gross anatomy. I have identified the organs, I know something about their structure. But there is still much to find out about what happens at the smaller scale. How does the embryo develop? What is the cellular structure of the membranes surrounding it? That kind of thing.'

'So that is where your microscope will come into use,' said the girl. 'And this is also the kind of thing you wish to discover about our water-moles?'

'Yes — the reproductive system, the development of the embryo, and of course, whether they lay eggs.'

'They lay eggs, Mr Caldwell.'

It was Mary Brown who had spoken.

'I believe there is still some doubt over the matter, Miss Brown. No egg has ever been found, and according to the great Baron Cuvier, and to M'sieur Geoffroy Saint-Hilaire —'

'Mr Caldwell, they lay eggs.'

The words were said with such quiet authority that had the great Sir Richard Owen heard them even he might have considered re-examining his opinions on the matter. And William realised with sudden conviction that he had been a fool. Could he — could anyone? — really imagine that this woman's people, people who had been here for countless generations, would not know everything there was to know about the land they lived in? And yet …

'Perhaps what I should have said, Miss Brown, is that I wish to discover an egg.'

Mary Brown nodded in acceptance of his statement. 'And I see another thing you need to discover, Mr Caldwell, is how to cook a possum.'

The contents of the frying pan were still on the table from breakfast. A couple of strips of meat had been torn from the joints, but otherwise they were almost intact. Delicious though the meat had looked and smelled, Donald's fried possum had not been a gastronomic success.

'Ah yes,' said William. 'I have to say we found possum a trifle tough. We think it must have been rather an old animal.'

'Old or young, Mr Caldwell, you'll not make a meal of a possum in a frying pan. I can see you — or Donald, perhaps — need some cooking lessons.'

'It was cooked for an hour at least, wouldn't you say, Donald.'

'Yes, both sides.'

Mary Brown smiled. 'There is only way to cook a possum. Would you like me to show you?'

'We would be honoured, Miss Brown.'

'Very well.' She looked around her. 'I shall need a spade and a large machete.'

'You shall have them.'

Having collected these alarming pieces of culinary equipment from the store tent, Donald began, under Mary Brown's instruction, to dig a shallow trench beside the fire.

While he was thus engaged, William finished his dissection of his possum's reproductive system and popped the ovaries into a jar of formalin. He wrote out a label, explaining to Ettie Brown that the liquid he had put the organs in would fix them so that they would be easier to section later. He then had to explain that 'fixing' meant preserving and hardening them, and that he would later section them into thin slices with the microtome which he could examine under the microscope.

Mary Brown, having finished directing Donald in the construction of the trench, came over and pointed to the possum on the dissection board. 'Shall we cook that one?'

'Why not?' said William.

'More wood on the fire, then, please,' said Mary Brown to Donald. 'Now, come with me.'

She picked up the machete and headed towards the river. Donald followed.

'I noticed this morning that the river was up a little,' said William to Ettie, 'though Donald assures me that it is unlikely to rise more.' Then half to himself, 'I wonder what the platypuses do when the river floods?'

'I imagine that a flood to a platypus is no more than a high wind to a bird,' said Ettie Brown. 'I dare say they find shelter, or ride it out.'

'Yes, I suppose they must. Well I know they must, but still I wonder how.'

'You are a curious man, Mr Caldwell.' The girl laughed. 'I meant, of course, a man who is curious. No — I mean that you are a man of much curiosity. Oh, you know what I mean.'

'And I think that you are a curious woman, perhaps, Miss Ettie.'

Ettie Brown looked at William. Her laughter had stopped but a smile was still on her lips. And her eyes — her eyes seemed to look right into him. He knew that she could not see, yet it seemed ...

'Am I, Mr Caldwell? Am I indeed?'

Their conversation was interrupted by the sight of a large, green object approaching the camp site, followed by Donald. The green object gave a shake, and a tumble of vegetation revealed that it had been Mary Brown laden high with branches and rushes. Donald was also carrying a heavy load, not of vegetation but stones — flat, round stones from the river.

'Now, Donald,' said Mary Brown, 'we need a good fire in that pit.'

She started pulling flaming sticks from the camp fire and laying them in the trench that Donald had dug beside it. The two of them took all the half-burned wood they could from the fire and piled more firewood on top, then the stones.

'We'll let that burn down for a while. Is there any tea?'

There was not. Donald filled the billy and put it on to boil.

'Is the river still up?' said William.

'Still up,' said Donald, 'but not rising.'

'I doubt if you have much to fear up here,' said Mary Brown. 'Probably just a thunderstorm up in the hills.'

'Do you think it'll get any higher? How can you tell about these things?'

'You can't, Mr Caldwell. Perhaps it will and perhaps it won't.'

She looked towards the western sky. 'But I can see no clouds over towards the hills. Chances are it will be down by morning.'

By the time they had drunk their tea the fire in the pit had almost burnt down and Mary Brown began the next phase of the possum-cooking operation. First she laid some of the small green branches she had brought on the embers. These she covered with a thick layer of cut reeds.

'Now, Donald, would you care to put the possum in the oven?'

Donald laid the possum on top of the vegetation.

'And have you any potatoes? Ah, good. We'll put them on just so. And no need to waste these,' said Mary Brown, spearing the pieces of cooked possum from the frying pan with a fork. She arranged them beside the uncooked possum and covered all with an even thicker layer of reeds.

'Now we must put the lid on. Go ahead, please, Donald.'

Donald picked up the spade and carefully covered the reeds with the soil that he had previously removed. It looked, when he had finished, as though someone had made a small grave next to the camp fire.

'At what time do you eat dinner, Mr Caldwell?' said Mary.

'Six o'clock, as a rule.'

'I think you will find your dinner just ready by then.'

'And we should be on our way home to prepare our own dinner, I think, Mary,' said Ettie Brown.

At six o'clock by William's watch Donald shovelled away the now-sunken lid of the earth oven. The rushes had been steamed by the heat into a flat sheet. They were too hot to handle — Donald had to use the spade to peel them away, releasing a cloud of fragrant smells. William found his mouth watering. There was not long to wait before a large plate of possum and potatoes was put before him on the table. The meat fell from the bone, and when he put some in his mouth it had a subtle herbal taste — from the green branches, he supposed. The potatoes were floury and tender.

'Not bad, eh, Professor?'

'Not bad at all, Donald. And if I may say so, your technique of frying the meat first was a stroke of culinary genius. The plain possum is delicious, but the pre-fried is superb. I'm sure it is quite the best meal I have had in Australia.'

'Aw, bloody oath, Professor.'

And while the sun set behind the river red gums and the kookaburras began their evening chorus, William once again took it upon himself to explain to Donald the desirability of moderating his language. But they both had second helpings.

fourteen

The *Ornithorhynchus paradoxus*, called also platypus, duckbill, or water-mole, is one of the most singular animals in existence. Some believe it to be oviparous, while others say it is viviparous; there are, also, not a few persons who affirm that the creature is both oviparous and mammiferous, laying its eggs and hatching them, and afterwards suckling its young. The natives declare they are oviparous, and it must be confessed I was once shown the remnants of an egg laid by one, or rather they were said to have been so, which, notwithstanding I doubted strongly, suspecting rather that they were once the egg of some bird or reptile. That it suckles its young will admit of little doubt, as the milk may be expressed from the lacteal glands through the skin of the animal: there are no nipples.

Lieutenant William Henry Breton RN, *Excursions in New South Wales, Western Australia and Van Diemen's Land*, 1833

Mary Brown had been right about cooking possums. She was right about the river, too. When William went down the next morning for his usual inspection it was back to its old level. His platypuses would have no high winds to battle today. The cool clear water, the gnats dancing over a tuft of reeds, a flash of blue across the far bank that could only be a kingfisher. He might almost be in Scotland.

Just there, Will, just below where those two rocks channel the water into the pool. That's the place to cast.

With its fast-running riffles, deep pools and wide banks the Burnett seemed almost perfect for salmon fishing. Perfect, but for one thing: there were no salmon in it. There were no salmon anywhere in Australia as far as William knew, none in the whole of the southern hemisphere. Though he had found this out before setting out from England, still he had packed his fishing gear — just in case.

He found the rod in the store tent still in its cloth bag, wound round with hessian. It was a fine two-piece greenheart, cork-handled, eleven feet long. He unwrapped it and fitted the pieces together. The ferrules, well greased, mated smoothly. It felt as good as ever in his hand.

'Is that a fishing rod?' said Donald, looking up from the possum skin he was scraping.

'It most certainly is. A salmon rod. Here, try it.' He passed over the rod.

'By oath, it's heavy.'

'You need something heavy for a big salmon.'

Donald looked surprised. 'I've always used a hand-line myself, Professor.'

Now it was William's turn to look puzzled. Donald must surely be jesting, but he was not wearing the grin that usually signalled one of his jokes.

'I said salmon, Donald, not gammon.'

'Oh, there's plenty of salmon here,' said Donald. 'I don't like them much myself. Taste of mud, I reckon. They eat mud, some people say.'

'Your Queensland salmon, then, must be a very different fish to the one that I know. If there is finer eating than a Spey salmon, I have yet to try it.'

Deep in his heart William was not convinced of the truth of this bold statement. Salmon — whether from the Spey, the Deveron or Billingsgate Market — were fine food every now and then. But each year, by the end of his annual summer fishing expeditions with Uncle Angas, William found himself in some sympathy with the apocryphal London apprentices who had it written into their articles that they should eat salmon no more than once a week. Every day of every fishing trip his uncle insisted on eating salmon cold for breakfast and hot for supper (not to mention the frequent samples of 'Scotch caviar'). After four weeks of such fare William would be longing for a chop, a steak, or just a humble sausage. At other times, though, national pride overwhelmed culinary experience and he would declare that there was no better food than Scottish salmon or even (God forgive him) a fine, fat Arbroath haggis.

'But I suppose there's no reason you can't catch one of ours on this,' said Donald, waggling the rod. 'Are you going to have a try?'

'Why not? — if I can find my reel. Ah yes, here it is. Now, dry fly or wet, do you think?'

Again Donald looked puzzled. 'I don't think our salmon eat flies, Professor. Like I said, they eat mud. But you catch them on weed.'

'Weed?' said William. (*Weed?* he heard Uncle Angas say.)

'Waterweed. You wrap a bit of weed round the hook and float it down to them. Come on, I think I'd better show you.'

Though it was clear that Donald was not accustomed to the sophistication of lightweight reels, greased and tapered silk lines and gut traces, between the two of them he and William managed to devise a tackle that would enable a baited hook to float into one of the pools where Donald was reasonably sure there would be a fish.

The weed that he insisted was the only bait for the Burnett River salmon was the green filamentous algae that grew on the rocks. William pulled a piece off and wrapped it round the shank of the bare hook. Standing on the downstream side of a sandbank that projected into the river, he cast into the water. As he paid out the line, the hook and weed sank from sight.

'That's the way, Professor,' said Donald. 'I couldn't have done it sweeter myself.'

William paid out more line. When he judged that the baited hook had reached the end of the pool he wound it back and recast, a little further towards the middle this time. Again he watched the hook and weed sink below the surface, again he paid out more line. When twenty yards had been let off the reel, he again started to wind it back. He had wound in no more than ten yards when he felt a dead resistance on the line. It was not a fish — there was no movement. It was a snag. Holding the reel checked, he raised the heavy rod. The rod tip bowed. He raised it again, further this time. It was no good, it was not going to come free.

'Got one, eh, Professor?'

'I'm afraid all I have caught is a rock, or a log or something. Look, it's stuck fast.'

But as he spoke the line began to move. Slow at first, then faster and faster, they watched the line cutting through the water towards the far bank. William once more heard his uncle's voice.

Give him his head, Will, give him his head. Now gently, pull him round.

He kept the rod tip raised and let out a little line, still keeping the pressure up. The line suddenly went slack. Had he lost the fish, or had it changed direction?

Tight line, Will. Tight line!

He reeled in fast. Again the rod tip bent. It was still on and heading towards him, and he had to reel hard to match the speed of his retrieval to the speed of the fish. At any moment it would be at the bank, and he hadn't even brought a net. But he had reckoned without Donald Gordon. As a heavy swirl indicated that the fish was almost at the shore, his young assistant leapt into the water. There was much splashing and thrashing and when Donald eventually stood up he had his arms around one of the largest and strangest fish William had ever seen.

It was four feet long and almost cylindrical, tapering away to a pointed tail. It had a blunt head and enormous scales. Donald hauled it out of the pool onto the bank.

'It's a salmon all right,' he said, 'and by oath it's a big one.' He dropped the fish onto the ground where it lay quite still.

William could now see that the fish had four fins. Strange fins they were, too, more like flippers — they reminded him of the wings on a penguin. Its head was smooth and slightly flattened with two small eyes, and its mouth turned up at the corners in a sad smile. The fish flapped its fins in a half-hearted way, and then it grunted.

William had caught many a salmon and trout in British rivers. From the deck of the ship on his voyage to Australia he had caught flying fish and bonito, and one of the sailors had even harpooned a shark and pulled it thrashing aboard. He had seen live eels in fishmongers' shops; in Cambridge he had seen Japanese carp taking bread from people's hands in the pond at the botanical gardens. But he had never heard a fish grunt. The fish gave a wriggle and a flap and grunted again — this time a longer sound, perhaps between a grunt and a snore.

'Don't you mind him, Professor. They always do that. They can breathe, see — breathe out of water.'

And suddenly William realised the true identity of the Burnett River 'salmon'. Of course, this strange creature at his feet must be the wonderful Australian lungfish. Here on the muddy bank before him was the so-called 'missing link' between fish and reptiles, between aquatic vertebrates and terrestrial ones. According to some, this ungainly animal might even resemble our own ancestor.

The lungfish gave another grunt, almost a groan this time.

'I hope you're hungry, Professor,' said Donald. 'How much do you think he weighs?'

The largest fish that William had ever caught, in Hunter's Pool on the River Deveron on July 2nd in 1877, weighed twenty-six pounds, fifteen ounces. The numbers and location were etched on William's memory because Uncle Angas had insisted on having the salmon stuffed and mounted, and for many years it had looked down at William from his study wall above a label which declared in proud gold letters the details of its capture. Just by looking at it William could see that this lungfish weighed more than any salmon he had ever caught or ever seen.

'I think we might have a fifty pounder here, Donald,' he said. 'I hope you're hungry, too. But you say that they don't eat well?'

'Like I said, all right if you like eating mud. Still, I expect Mary'll know how to cook it up nice.'

'Perhaps she will,' said William, 'but science comes first. I am most keen to dissect it. If it is as different on the inside from the salmon I am used to as it is on the outside, who knows what we may find?'

The fish grunted again and flapped its tail. Though William had not brought a net with him on his fishing expedition he had had the foresight to bring along another important tool. He felt in his pocket and pulled it out.

'Blimey, Professor. What's that?' said Donald.

'It's a priest, for killing fish. Here.'

He handed the little club to Donald. It was short but well weighted, ending in a solid lump of lead so heavy that Donald almost dropped it.

'I've never seen anything like that before,' Donald said as he handed it back. 'Handy little thing.'

'Very handy,' said William. 'No fisherman should be without one.'

With that he straddled the fish on the ground and brought the priest down smartly between its eyes. The enormous fish tipped onto its side and was still.

Death seemed to add weight to the body. The fish that Donald had wrested single-handed from the water he could now hardly lift. He grasped it by its gills, he tried lifting it with both arms under its body, but it flopped and slopped and slipped from his grasp. It was only when William found a stout broken branch to pass through both the fish's gills that he and Donald were able to carry it back to the camp site, though still its tail was dragging along the ground.

William unrolled his kit. Where to begin such an ambitious task? He picked out the largest scalpel, feeling the now familiar tingling in his fingertips whenever he started a new dissection.

'The first thing we need to do, Donald, is put a good edge on this.'

Donald watched mesmerised as William went through the process of sharpening the scalpel on the stone, then testing it on the piece of cotton rag he kept for the purpose. The gleaming blade passed through the cloth as if through smoke.

'Strewth, Professor.'

Inserting the point of the scalpel into the fish's anal aperture, he began slitting along the belly, past the fleshy pelvic and pectoral fins (they really were most unusual, quite unlike those of a normal fish) all the way up to the lower jaw. Entrails slid out onto the table.

'Now, let's see what we can see, eh, Donald? First, I think we might see what our friend here has had for breakfast. Could you bring me a bowl? The washbasin will do.'

William manoeuvred the bowl under the floppy grey sack that was the animal's stomach. With forceps in one hand and scalpel in the other, he made a horizontal incision about five inches from where the stomach narrowed to join the intestine. The contents poured out into the basin.

'I think we need some water in the bowl,' he said. Donald went to fetch some.

With the bowl half full of water it was easier to separate the different elements of the stomach contents.

'Well, we certainly have some weed here,' said William, poking the lumpy green-brown stuff around with a forefinger. 'I'm not sure what these little black things are. Oh, and look.' He teased away at a larger lump that revealed itself to have four legs. 'A frog, wouldn't you say? These little black things, then, I think they might be tadpoles. What do you think?'

William looked round to find that his assistant had turned slightly pale. Skinning a possum was clearly one thing, a thorough analysis of the stomach contents of a lungfish another.

'I think I might make some tea — all right, Professor?'

Donald retreated to the camp fire, but such was William's excitement as he continued his investigation that he could not help calling him back to show him the latest point of interest: the bony structure of the fins, the brain, and especially the single lung.

'See here how there's no separate windpipe? The lung opens directly into the ventral side of oesophagus, just right of the median line and — what? — six inches below the pharynx? I must make a sketch. And as far as I can see there's no diaphragm, and no muscles round the lung either. So the animal must breath by swallowing air rather than expanding its thoracic cavity. You know, like a frog.'

William's enthusiasm was so infectious that soon Donald had overcome his queasiness and was as fascinated as William, especially by the lung.

'A surprisingly complex organ, wouldn't you say, Donald? Well vascularised, as one would expect. Let's open it up.'

With small strokes of the scalpel he cut his way through the outer wall of the lung. 'Hmmm. Well, as you can see, the interior seems to comprise a single hollow chamber lined all around with this spongy material — presumably corresponding with the mammalian trachea or bronchus and the alveoli. You know, I think it would be very interesting to compare the microscopical structure of this lung with that of a mammal. A possum, say, or a giraffe.'

William cut the lung away and dropped it into a glass jar. Which fixative should he use — formalin? Yes, that would harden it up and make it easier to stain later if needed. He went back to the dissection.

'Now, let's see. A three-chambered heart — quite fish-like — but with a large inferior vena cava. And two quite separate parts to the liver, one ovoid, one elongate — almost as if the animal had two livers, wouldn't you say?'

'I've never seen nothing like it.'

'I thought you'd caught a few salmon, Donald?'

'Not the salmon, Professor — that knife of yours.' Donald nodded at the scalpel in William's hand. 'I wouldn't mind one of them for skinning possums.'

Two hours and five cups of tea later, eighteen jars of various sizes stood on the table, each containing a pickled specimen of one organ or another. The fish had been beheaded and eviscerated and its four fins removed. It looked as though it had, in fact, been prepared for cooking. And now William was faced with a slight problem. What was he to do, in the middle of the bush, with forty pounds of fresh — but according to Donald, inedible — fish (and, oh dear, what would Ettie Brown say?).

His culinary and philosophical musings were interrupted by a call. It sounded like a human voice, and seemed to be coming from somewhere towards the river.

'Professor, look. Look over there.'

William looked to where Donald was pointing. On the far bank of the river were a group of people, ten or twelve, and even at that distance he could see that they were Aboriginal. One of the figures, standing apart from the rest, again called out some indistinguishable words. He waved. William put down his tools and hurried down to the riverbank, waving his own arm in what he hoped would be seen as a gesture of welcome.

'Come, come,' he shouted.

The man began wading, then swimming, across the river and was soon standing before William, water running down his bare black skin, a big white smile across his face.

He spoke to William again in words as mellifluous as they were incomprehensible. He pointed to the water. Something about 'dinderi' and then something about 'meri'.

'Donald, have you any idea what this chap's talking about?'

Donald did not, but with many signs and drawings in the sand they managed to work out that a 'dinderi' was a platypus and that the man's name was Daraga. Daraga had come to help William find dinderi. He had brought his family with him. They would also help.

To William this sounded like the answer to his prayers. How they had found out about him he could not imagine, but never mind that now.

'Tea for our guests, please, Donald,' he said.

The man called for his family to come across, and together they made their way up the riverbank to the camp site.

William had never seen so much sugar put into single cups of tea. Nor had he ever seen so many Australian natives. Nor had he ever seen a naked female body. The group did not seem to be one family in the sense of a couple and their children. Daraga, with a few grey hairs in his beard, seemed to be the oldest, but the two other men in the group did not seem young enough to be his sons. Brothers, perhaps? The oldest woman in the group might have been forty — William found it hard to tell her age — then five other women and girls of all ages down to no more than two, and two boys of about ten. Apart from string belts around the waists of the older members of the group, they were all stark naked (and considering that he had never seen a woman naked he thought he coped rather well). Cups were shared by all and when both teapot and sugar bowl were empty, Daraga made William understand that he and his family would be camping by the river a little downstream. He would visit William again the following day.

As he spoke William noticed his eyes stray to the row of glass jars, then to the lungfish, still on the table. With a sudden flash of inspiration William walked over to it, put two hands beneath it and lifted. He held the huge fish out towards the Aboriginal man. Daraga nodded solemnly. He heaved the lungfish onto his shoulder, shook William by the hand and headed back towards the river.

That night William fell asleep to the sounds of singing and clapping drifting up from the Aborigines' camp site almost a mile away. Perhaps lungfish didn't taste quite as bad as Donald feared.

The dawn birdcalls woke him, and the sound of Donald bustling about his morning tasks. Things were looking up. With the help of Daraga and his family there should be no difficulty now in getting those specimens. Yes, things were definitely looking up. A black and white willie wagtail churred from a nearby tree, the resident family of kookaburras chuckled their morning refrain from down near the river. From closer to his tent came again that familiar three-note whistle of a ... of a what, exactly?

He had heard it before. It must surely be some kind of bird, but he could never see it. Donald had been of no help. Wonderful though he was at spotting birds, he seemed to have no ear for their calls. 'Poop, peep-peep' — there it was again. It seemed to be calling from just outside his tent. William pushed back his blankets, slipped out of bed and gently pulled aside the tent flap. Not three feet away, perched on the branch of a wattle bush was a tiny bird with short beak and short tail. 'Poop, peep-peep.' He could see its tiny throat vibrate with each note. It was quite the most beautiful bird he had ever seen.

It was not a garish bird. No extravagant plumes and tassels adorned its body, no gaudy colours flared from wings or breast. It was mainly patterned a simple black and white and grey: black head with a scattering of white spots on the crown and a bold white eyebrow, dappled grey on neck and back, and more black with white spots on wings and tail. Contrasted against this was a bright orange throat, and an orange and red rump. But somehow these elements came together in such perfection that William felt a lump rising in his throat. The little bird gave one more three-note call then darted away. What could it have been?

Unmusical though he was, Donald had no doubt from the description William gave.

'Oh, that's a diamond bird. Now you mention it, I suppose they do make that kind of sound.'

Together they looked through Gould's *Birds of Australia* and eventually found it, not under the name Donald gave it but under 'Spotted Pardalote'.

'An ungainly label for so elegant a bird, would you not say, Donald? And if I remember my Latin, *pardalotus* means 'spotted'. So, it seems I have spotted a spotted spotted bird.'

Donald smiled. 'I've seen 'em nesting, Professor. In little holes, little tunnels.'

'Yes, Mr Gould mentions that, too. And here, look: "The Diamond Bird of the colonists; native name *Weedupwee*." I think I much prefer either of those to so clumsy a scientific name.'

William heard the bird again, calling from a high tree. 'Poop, peep-peep. Wee dup-wee.' He closed the book. He hoped that he would see the bird again.

Daraga appeared at the camp site just as William was finishing his breakfast. Accompanying him were the two younger men, each carrying a spear and a long, slender club (the African word *knobkerrie* came into William's mind) tucked into the string belt round his waist. But one of the men was carrying something else as well: an animal, small and limp. William took it, gazing down with wonder. A platypus.

'Tea, Donald, tea for our guests.'

While Donald stoked the fire and filled the billy, William inspected the wonderful creature now at last in his hands. He could see why the animal was known as a water-mole. The fur was not long, but thick and dense, alike in feel to the fur of the little burrowing moles of Britain that were usually only seen nailed along country fences wherever the mole catcher had been at work. It was coloured a rich brown above, the colour getting paler around the flanks towards a silvery grey belly. The under surface of its tail was almost bare, but what was particularly intriguing was its beak. Although like a duck's bill in shape, it was covered in soft skin like damp shammy leather. On the upper surface it was the colour of slate, with two nostril openings about three quarters of the way down and with front and sides that curved over so that the lower jaw fitted snugly between them. Where the beak joined the animal's face the soft skin extended back as a kind of flap or collar, reaching almost to the eyes, now closed in death.

William pulled open an eyelid with thumb and forefinger and saw the bright black button of an eye. Just behind the eye, in the same crease of skin, was the ear opening. The animal could close eyes and ears in the same action. He forced open the platypus's beak. The animal had no teeth, but on the upper jaw two parallel ridges ran the length of the bill, neither tooth nor bone but hard to the touch. The lower jaw was equipped on each side with similar ridges, so that when the jaws were brought together they would be like two scissor blades. On each side extending inward from its margin was a parallel row of transverse ridges. These must be what the animal used for grinding or straining its food.

While Donald began handing round cups of tea, William was able to turn his attention to the animal's feet. The legs were short, tucked well into the body. The front feet were bare and leathery, the five toes were curled up and showing rounded, flattened claws. Indeed, William wondered whether he should not call them fingers and fingernails, so much did the platypus's foot resemble a human hand, and it appeared to be holding something. He uncurled the fingers. As he did so a flap of skin extended out from the animal's hand. It reached well beyond the fingernails, forming a broad paddle, a paddle which could be folded away when out of use. He stretched out one of the back feet. It was also webbed but without the extendable membrane. Its claws were rounder and sharper, slightly curved.

William could hardly wait to get out his dissection kit. He felt in his pocket and took out a silver florin which he gave with due ceremony to the man who had brought him the platypus. The man passed it to Daraga, who after carefully inspecting it offered it back to William.

'Meri,' he said, looking over William's shoulder. That word again.

William couldn't help turning round to look down the track that led into town. Surely he didn't mean Mary? Mary Brown? William opened the lid of his writing case and put the coin inside.

'I will make sure it is kept safe,' he said. 'Now, can I offer you some more tea?'

William pointed to the cups and the three men accepted his offer with nods and grins. While Donald filled the billy again, William took stock of his visitors. They were finely built men, perhaps a little shorter than his own height. Though their arms and torsos were strong muscled, their legs were surprisingly thin. All had well-rounded bellies — no doubt the result of last night's feasting. William took a cup of tea from Donald and handed it to Daraga.

'Meri,' said the man, looking again over William's shoulder. At the sound of hooves William himself turned. A familiar gig was appearing round the bend and had soon pulled up beside the camp.

'Good morning, Mr Caldwell.'

Mary Brown climbed down from the gig, leaving her sister on the seat. The three Aboriginal men stood quite still, then one of them spoke to her. She replied in the same language, then stepped forward and embraced each of them in turn. If they had been silent before, they now made up for it. As they laughed and chatted William saw them looking towards him, then towards Ettie Brown who was still seated up on the gig. One of the men said something to her, and to William's wonder Ettie Brown also replied in their strange musical language. At her answer they broke out into a new stream of conversation.

'So, Mr Caldwell,' said Mary Brown, turning at last towards him. 'I see you have met our family.'

fifteen

The duckbills (*Ornithorhynchus*) long excited the scepticism and astonishment of naturalists; who beheld in these creatures the perfect bill of a duck, engrafted, as it were, on the body of a mole-like quadruped. It was first made known to the world by our countryman, Doctor Shaw, who clearly demonstrated it was no fictitious deception. The foot of the male is armed with a spur, through which passes a poisonous liquor, rendering the animal dangerous. It has lately been clearly proved that these duck-moles not only lay eggs, but suckle their young
   William Swainson, *An Encyclopaedia of Geography: Comprising a Complete Description of the Earth*, 1834

'Miss Brown, Miss Ettie, how good to see you. It seems as though I have no need to introduce you to our guests — perhaps the reverse would be more appropriate.'

'You look so surprised, Mr Caldwell,' said Mary Brown. 'I hope I have done nothing rash — but you did mention that you needed some assistants.'

It was Mary Brown, then, who was responsible for these people's arrival. 'On the contrary, Miss Brown, but …'

Ettie Brown spoke. 'Donald, would you be able to provide us, perhaps, with some tea?'

That was what was needed, more tea. Donald set to filling the billy and stoking the fire. Mary Brown led her sister down from the gig to a seat and herself sat down. The three Aboriginal men stayed standing. William gestured towards the man to whom he had first spoken the previous day.

'Miss Brown, Miss Ettie, am I correct in understanding that, er, he ...'

'His name is Daraga, Mr Caldwell.'

'Thank you, Miss Brown. Yes, we managed to establish that. Did you ask Daraga and his family to come here especially to help me look for platypuses — for "dinderi"?'

'Very good, Mr Caldwell. Yes, that is indeed why they have come.'

William decided to leave for now the question of how Mary Brown had managed to contact Daraga. That could wait. But she had called them 'her family'. Had not the storekeeper assured him that all Mary Brown's family had been massacred on Black Hill?

'In that case, Miss Brown, I would be most grateful if you could help me as translator. I tried yesterday to come to an arrangement with Daraga but I'm not sure if we understood each other.'

'Certainly.'

With the help of his new interpreter William was able to confirm that the Aborigines would indeed be willing to help him find his platypuses. And they agreed on payment: a shilling for each male platypus and two shillings for each female. William took a silver crown from his pocket and held it up.

'And five shillings for any female with eggs.'

On hearing Mary Brown's translation Daraga looked puzzled. He spoke to his companions. They shook their heads. William felt his heart sink. Had Mary Brown been wrong? If these people had never seen a platypus egg, what chance did he have of finding one? Daraga spoke a few rapid words.

'My brother asks, why do you want eggs?' said Mary Brown. 'You can't eat the eggs.'

The man held up his finger and thumb half an inch apart.

'He says, too small.'

William almost laughed out loud. 'I don't want to eat them.

Please tell your brother that I just want to see them, to show them to my friends in England.'

The look Daraga gave him on hearing the translation suggested the Aborigine was not totally convinced. He spoke again to Mary Brown.

'My brother agrees to your terms. But he wonders whether they could take payment in sugar and flour. It is of more use than tokens — money.'

William was pleased to accede to this request and the deal was struck with a solemn handshake.

'There is one more thing, Mr Caldwell,' said Mary. 'I expect you know that the sale of alcohol to my people is forbidden by law in Queensland. I happen to know from past experience that my brothers are very fond of liquor. I would be very grateful, though — and I think my sisters would be, too — if you would not give them any.'

'I will certainly do as you ask.'

'And now, Mr Caldwell, I suspect that you yourself have some questions. Am I right?'

William nodded.

'You are wondering, perhaps, how these men are my brothers, when Ettie is my sister.'

'Mr Pike has already told me something of your past, but I confess I am puzzled.'

Mary Brown moved her gaze to the fire and began again to speak. 'You know that I, too, am an orphan?'

'I heard about the massacre, Miss Brown.'

The woman looked up at him, and nodded. 'It is a sad tale, is it not?'

'Sad?' said William. He looked Mary Brown in the face, then Ettie. 'It is a tragedy. It is a tragedy and it is a sin. Do you know how many people — how many of your family — were killed?'

'I know exactly, Mr Caldwell. Seventeen people were killed.'

'You were the only one left?'

'Yes, Mr Caldwell. I was the only one left.'

'But how did you survive — afterwards, I mean?'

'I wandered in the bush, for many days. I knew something

about where to find food and what to eat, but not enough. I was only a little child. One day I wandered into town — into Gayndah — hungry and tired and the parson's wife found me and took me in.'

As she looked towards Ettie Brown her face softened. 'And then later, she took Ettie, and I had a sister.'

'This explains much,' said William. 'I am sure that you will not be surprised, Miss Ettie, that I have been curious as to how you two … how the two of you … how you could have a sister who is …'

'Black, Mr Caldwell?' Ettie gave a small smile. 'So, Mary is still black, is she?'

William felt foolish. Of course, what did skin colour matter to a blind person? There was surely a lesson here. But there were still more things that he wanted to know and if he didn't ask now he never would.

And so he told the two women about his discovery on the hill. As he spoke Mary Brown translated to Daraga and his companions. William thought it important to mention that he had not moved the stones and was pleased to see both Mary and Daraga give a small nod when he did so.

'Yes, Mr Caldwell,' said Mary Brown, 'it is as I am sure you have suspected. The bones, they are my family.'

'And it was you who …?'

'I went back there, many years later, back to where my family had been killed. I gathered up all their bones I could find, and I made a place for them. I am pleased you did not disturb them.'

'There is one more thing I should like to know,' said William. 'You have said that all your family were killed, and yet you say that these men are your brothers.'

Mary Brown smiled. 'In your language, we are … of the same tribe. My immediate family was killed, but I was not forgotten, not abandoned. Daraga and his family live in the next valley, but they soon found out. I have never lost contact with my tribe.'

'But you preferred to stay in Gayndah, with the parson?'

'It was my duty to stay, Mr Caldwell. It was my duty to stay here. There was no one else to look after the land.'

Ettie Brown stood up. 'It is my land too, Mr Caldwell. Just as

Mary is my sister, I am hers. And I am sister to her brothers, and niece to her uncles and aunts, and aunty to her nieces and nephews. And her place is my place.'

The flowers, the flowers on the hill.

Mary Brown turned to the Aboriginal men and began speaking to them again in their own language. She then turned to William. 'If you will excuse us, Mr Caldwell, we shall now go and greet the rest of our relations. No doubt you are eager to start preparing your first specimen.'

The dead platypus that the men had brought still lay on the table where William had put it.

'So, you already have tonight's dinner, Mr Caldwell,' said Ettie Brown, after Mary had led her back to the gig. She felt beneath the seat and removed a small basket. 'Good. In that case I'm sure we will find someone else to appreciate these eggs.'

William lay the platypus belly-up on the dissecting board and pinned it down with stout, wooden-handled skewers through the lower part of each leg. The absence of spurs on its hind legs suggested that it was a female. He unrolled his dissection kit. Here it was, the moment he had been waiting for. He held out his hands in front of him. Quite steady, despite the fluttering in his chest. Straight scissors to start with, and a Number 4 scalpel. But first, he must give the blade its edge. He opened the wooden box that contained his Arkansas stone and wiped it over with a cotton rag. After removing the cork from the oil can and applying one drop to each side of the blade and one to the stone, he began moving the blade in the familiar slow circle, bending his hand so that the whole length of the blade was drawn across the stone, from tip to heel. First one side, then the other. The gentlest of pressure. Then a quick strop both sides on the horsehide. Ready.

With scalpel in right hand and forceps in the other, he lifted the loose skin just above the vent. The familiar feel of blade slicing through fur and skin. William smiled. He picked up the scissors and made one long vertical incision, through the skin but keeping clear of underlying tissue, then two horizontal ones top and bottom. The skin was more firmly attached to the subcutaneous muscle than was usual for a mammal of this size, but the scalpel — and William's dissecting skills — made short work of separating them. He pinned back the skin.

'Neat work, Professor.'

Donald had finished clearing up the tea things and wandered over to watch.

'Thank you, Donald. Now, let's see what else we can find.'

He again picked up the scalpel and forceps and with three unhurried strokes opened the abdomen. 'Nothing too unusual about the alimentary tract, so I might just pull that over to the side. We'll see what it's been feeding on later. It's the reproductive system we're really looking for. Ah, what's this?'

William pointed out a thick tube extending upwards from the vent and dividing into two branches. 'Yes, here we are. You can see quite clearly the urogenital sinus, with the cloaca down here, and the colon emptying into it here. And just above it, the bladder with the two ureters coming from the kidneys. So above that, just where it's branching here, these must be the paired uteruses.'

'You've lost me, Professor. The what?'

'Well, in placental mammals — like us — this uterus would be where the foetus develops, where the baby lives. In the platypus, though … well …'

'You mean that's where you might find the eggs?'

'Exactly. And look here — only one of the ovaries seems to be functional, just like in birds. Fascinating.'

The arrival of Mary Brown's 'family' signalled the beginning of a new phase for William. It seemed that all the members of the newly arrived group were keen to be part of the enterprise and for the first few days William would be woken at dawn not only by the laughter of kookaburras but of children. Three or four of them would appear at the camp every morning, and every move William made seemed of the greatest interest. They would watch him dress, then stand giggling around the bush table that served as his washstand while he shaved (his moustache, he decided, was looking almost luxuriant now). This part of the daily entertainment over, the children would each accept a cup of tea from Donald then lead William away to where the older members of their family were already digging the riverbanks for platypuses.

For the first few days he joined them in the hunt. He was amazed just how quick his new helpers were at finding burrows — they found many that he had missed — and accurate in knowing which were occupied. Their only tools were the simple pointed sticks that they carried with them everywhere. On finding an occupied burrow one of them would reach in as far as an arm would go, then signal to the others where to dig down. When the burrow had been opened up from above, the arm would again be stuck in and another hole dug further along. Though the burrows might extend tens of feet from the entrance they never ran very deep (somehow the animals must know how far they were from the surface of the ground, though it was a mystery how they did so) and it seldom took the hunters more than half an hour to reach the end chamber. The platypus would be captured and killed with a knock on the head and handed over to William, who took it back to the camp for dissection. Payment would be made. The day's work done, the Aborigines would return to their own camp.

As the supply of platypuses near the camp dried up and the hunters had to range further, William would wait for them at camp. After Donald had paid them in sugar and flour, he would watch as William sharpened his scalpel for the day's dissections.

Males were more common than females.

'In males, what we are looking for here is any sign of increase in size of the testicles,' said William, as he opened up another specimen.

'You mean they get bigger as they get older, Professor?'

'Not exactly. According to Doctor Bennett's observations, the testes of adult males grow just before the mating season, then go back to their original size afterwards. Up to a ten-fold increase in weight, apparently.'

'That doesn't sound too comfortable.'

William laughed. 'No, I dare say it isn't. Just as well they are testicond — which is, of course, why we are doing this dissection.'

'Testicond?'

'Yes, with testes inside the abdominal cavity, rather than in a scrotum. Like birds, and reptiles. Some placental mammals are, too, I seem to remember. Elephants, and shrews, for example.'

'I'm not sure what a shrew is, Professor, but I can see why it might be useful for an elephant.'

William laughed again. He pushed aside the intestines to reveal beneath them the kidneys and, just above them, the two testes, small and white.

'There. What size would you say those were?'

'Not much bigger than a soup bean.'

'Hmm. I don't think this one is ready to mate yet. Of course, what we don't know is how old they have to be to breed — either the males or the females.'

'How do you know how old they are anyway?'

'Another mystery, I'm afraid, Donald. How old are they when they breed? How do they mate? How long do they live for? We're still just scratching at the surface. But if we can prove whether or not they lay eggs — then that'll be something, eh?'

Yet over the past days, with more and more dead platypuses being brought in to be dissected, and more and more pickled pairs of male or female reproductive organs being added daily to the jars, a small, insistent voice within had been asking if that something was really enough. What was he doing here, said the voice. What was the purpose of all this?

In Cambridge it had all seemed straightforward. Had he not trained as a scientist with a famous professor in one of the foremost educational institutions in the land — no, in the world? The job of the scientist was to go out into that world, to seek and explain. Now here he was in Australia, doing just those things. It had been his destiny; more than that, his duty. But now things seemed to be changing. Or could it be that he was changing? He looked around him — the dead platypus pinned out on the dissecting board, the jars, the microscope. What was it the girl had said — sport of intellectuals? If all this was really necessary — for what was it necessary? For whom? William sighed. Oh dear. Damn the girl and damn her questions. If only Frank Balfour were here.

But if William was having small difficulties about dissecting the daily specimens, he and Donald were having great difficulties in consuming them. No doubt platypus, properly cooked, was a fine food — if only he and Donald could find the proper way to cook them. Fried, boiled, baked or roasted, the meat still seemed to have a strange musty-fishy-gamey — no, platypussy — taste.

'Pigeons,' said Donald one evening as he was clearing away the dinner things.

Though William could neither see nor hear a pigeon, he grasped exactly what Donald was talking about.

'Wongs are best — white as chicken,' said Donald, 'but browns and squatters, they're fine if you can get them.'

William knew he had given his word (and knew that according to Uncle Angas a Scotchman's word was worth seven Sassenachs'), but after six straight nights of platypus for dinner even the idea of a change of menu was a relief. He had already seen several kinds of pigeons during his wanderings, usually towards dusk when they came down the river to drink. There were the large grey and white wonga pigeons, the smaller brown pigeons, and the little squatters that flew up from the ground a few feet in front of him when he was on horseback — he had never seen one when he was on foot. What Uncle Angas would have said to the idea of him shooting pigeons he could not imagine. No, that was not true — he could imagine it too well.

God made grouse for gentlemen, Will. God made pigeons for farmers.

It had been Uncle Angas who first taught William to shoot, initially with an old breech loader — it being his uncle's idea that having to load every shot by hand (charge, wadding, shot and cap) would make him a more careful shooter — then with the old Martini. He was now equipped with a somewhat more sophisticated piece, a double-barrelled breach-loading Holland & Holland shotgun, one of a pair that his uncle had given him on the occasion of his twenty-first birthday. William had pondered hard on the wisdom of bringing such fine and expensive things to the rude antipodes. Might he not do better to leave them safe behind for his return? It was Uncle Angas who had insisted he bring them.

A gun in its case is a gun gone to waste.

So the very next morning, with a 12-bore Dutchman under his arm and a handful of Mr Eley's finest 'Gas-Tight' cartridges in his pocket, William strolled out along the track from camp in search of Australian pigeons. Uncle Angas need never know.

Once out of sight of the camp he slipped two cartridges into the breach of the gun and closed it — a bird might appear at any moment. While it was true that William had never shot a pigeon in his life, he had noticed often enough the effect on the birds of seeing a man with a gun. An evening stroll in the garden before dinner with nothing more dangerous in your hand than a cigar, and wood pigeons and turtledoves would be cooing in every tree. Leave the house with a gun under your arm and every bird within half a mile would be on the wing and showing you its tail feathers. As he left the track he clicked on the safety catch (*Always remember, Will: walking on, standing off*) and picked his way between the sparse tufts of grass and sedge.

He walked slowly and quietly, listening out for the distinctive calls of his quarry. Blue wrens twittered in a tangled sedge, a diamond bird called from a tree; but no woops or coos or oooms that could be recognised as pigeon calls. Something rustled on the ground behind a bush — a lizard, perhaps, or a chough, tossing up the leaf litter in its search for food. He caught a movement from the corner of his eye, up in the sky. A heron, neck tucked in, flying high towards the river. In Britain there was just one kind of heron — 'the heron'. Here he had noticed several species but could not yet tell them all by name. He could still hear the rustling behind the bush, almost as if some bird was flapping its wings among dead leaves. Perhaps he should go and investigate.

He had read of American Indians whose moccasined feet made no sound as they crept through the forest, with not a leaf disturbed, not a twig snapped. Many a leaf was disturbed and many a twig snapped beneath William's booted feet as he made his way towards the source of the noise, but whatever was making it took no notice. The flapping, rustling sound continued. It was coming from just behind a thick bush, an acacia of some kind judging by the curly green seed-pods hanging from its branches. He peered round it.

Iridescent green-brown patches on both wings immediately identified the bird as a bronzewing pigeon. It was lying belly-down on the ground, flapping its wings among the dried leaves. The reason it was on the ground was that another, larger bird was standing on its back. This bird William did not at first recognise — it was certainly no pigeon. Its back was turned towards him but he could see long, pale yellow legs, dark grey back, and a small head. It bent down and pulled at some feathers on the pigeon's back with its beak. The pigeon flapped its wings, powerless. It was being plucked alive by what William now realised was some kind of hawk.

The hawk had been so engrossed in its work that it had not noticed his approach, but now for some reason it straightened up, beak full of feathers. It turned its head towards where he stood beside the bush, not five yards away. He could now see that the bird's throat and upper breast were faintly barred, brown and dirty white. Its eyes, hooded beneath dark brows, glowed a fierce, unblinking yellow. It stared at him for several long seconds, then with a flap of its wings and a twist of its tail took off and flew silently away through the forest. The pigeon, released of its captor, fluttered up onto the branch of a nearby tree. It almost certainly did not hear the click of a safety catch being disengaged, nor the crack of the gunshot that ended its life. Neither, hoped William as he reached down for the plump little bird, had Uncle Angas.

According to Donald, the other bird was a chicken-hawk. According to Mr Gould, it was almost certainly the young of the Brown Goshawk. According to Mary Brown, when she and her sister paid them one of their irregular but welcome visits later that very afternoon, it was a 'jekiwiri' — but Donald was right about it being a young one.

'An adult would have killed the pigeon first, broken its neck with one twist of its beak.'

Not that the pigeon would have survived long anyway. A quick autopsy on the bird had revealed heavy internal haemorrhaging. The goshawk's sharp claws had gone deep.

'I hope it cooks well, Mr Caldwell,' said Ettie Brown, a small amused smile on her lips. 'Did you shoot no more?'

'Believe me, Miss Ettie, I tried, but my English gun seems to scare away Australian birds before I even get within range.'

Ettie Brown smiled again, but said nothing.

'The river's still down, I see,' said Mary Brown.

'It is as you told us, Miss Brown,' said William, 'though still I confess I was a little concerned. Having seen the flood mark I would not like to be here when the waters really rise.'

'I think you will be safe enough here, Mr Caldwell. It will need more than a storm up in the hills to flood this camp site.'

'Then let us hope for fine weather. It is a lovely afternoon, is it not?' And with sudden inspiration, 'Do you know, from where I come we should say this would be just the afternoon for a picnic.'

'Oh yes, let's,' said Ettie Brown. 'A picnic! Mary, could you fetch the basket? You must see what we have brought you, Mr Caldwell.'

Mary Brown put a basket down in front of her sister. The girl's hands flitted lightly over it before reaching inside to reveal, wrapped in a cloth which her nimble fingers soon removed, a smaller basket full of what looked like cakes. No, they were scones.

'Why, Miss Brown,' said William. 'You surely know the way to a Scotchman's heart.'

The girl reached into the basket again and pulled out a glass jar, its paper lid tied with a neat string bow.

'And jam, too? You spoil us.'

'Yes, perhaps we do. It is apricot jam, you know.'

'Bottled sunshine,' said William. 'Donald, we are going on a picnic. What say we go down to the river? Could you organise that?'

'Leave it to me, Professor,' said the boy and began folding up one of the chairs.

'No, no, Donald. A picnic calls for a picnic rug.'

Donald hesitated for a moment before lifting one of the horse rugs from the saddle tree.

'Will this do, Professor?'

'Capital. Miss Brown, Miss Ettie, would you care to join us?'

When an arm was required for Ettie Brown it had always been her sister who had provided it. William was therefore surprised (and delighted) when the blind girl asked for his arm to help her down to the river.

'Please take care, Miss Ettie. The path is clear, but the slope is steep in places.'

While Mary stayed to help Donald pack the picnic things, William led Ettie Brown towards the river. He watched her feet feel their way with each step, felt her hand lightly touch his arm, always ready to grip harder if she should need to. He kept a slow pace, trying hard to make it seem as if he always walked at this speed, while in truth concerned that his charge would slip or trip. When they had made it safely to the riverbank she thanked him.

'It is my pleasure, Miss Ettie.' Then, he said, 'How did you come to be, er …?'

'Blind, Mr Caldwell?' The girl looked at him. She always looked him straight in the eyes when he spoke to her but he knew that if he moved his head her eyes would not move (whenever this accidentally happened it seemed as though he was betraying her).

'When I was four I was very sick — measles, they said. It was soon after my mother died. Then came the headaches — bad headaches, really bad, Mr Caldwell. I wanted to die. I would shut my eyes and pray for them to go away, pray for hours. One day they went away. I opened my eyes. I could not see.' The girl looked down. 'My prayers had been answered, had they not?'

'Was there no doctor? No one to look after you?'

'There was a doctor in Gayndah. He came. He had been drinking rum — I could smell it. He said that there was nothing that could be done.'

'Did he say what had caused your blindness? Did he know?'

'He said that it was something to do with the headaches, that it was something in my head, not in my eyes. He said that my eyes were all right, that it was my mind that was not seeing. I'm not sure that was a good thing to say.'

'Why not? I can see that it might be the case. Sight is a product of both eyes and brain.'

The girl seemed to stare out across the river. 'No doubt what you say is true, Mr Caldwell. It was not a good thing to say because … because I tried to see, Mr Caldwell, I tried. If it was something in my brain, in my mind, then perhaps if I tried hard enough … I thought that perhaps I could not see because I wasn't trying hard enough. I thought that perhaps it was all my fault.'

'I see,' said William. 'And I agree with you, Miss Ettie. It was not a good thing to say. Thank you for explaining it to me.'

'And now I have made you sad. It was a long time ago now. I am quite used to being blind, you know.'

What could he say? He looked towards her, at her gently smiling lips, her downcast eyes, the pale face framed with dark hair, at the slender hand still resting on his arm.

'Miss Ettie,' he said. 'Miss Ettie, I have something to tell you, something important.' He paused, and took a deep breath.

The girl turned her eyes again towards his face.

'I thought I should tell you, Miss Ettie.' He took another breath. 'I thought I should tell you that platypuses, Miss Ettie, platypuses are quite, quite delicious.'

The others arrived and Donald spread the rug and lit a small fire. While he returned to the camp site to fetch more things, the two women arranged themselves on the rug — Mary Brown with an almost regal elegance, Ettie Brown with a slightly hesitant but still confident charm.

William looked past them to where a large white bird was wading through the shallow water on the opposite bank. It had black legs and a long black beak, which it was sweeping through the water in a scything motion. When it lifted its beak from the water William could see that it was flattened and rounded at the end. It was a spoonbill.

'You must tell us how your work is progressing, Mr Caldwell,' said Mary Brown.

'Extremely well,' said William, looking away from the spoonbill, 'thanks to my new helpers. They are bringing me quite enough material.'

'I think Mr Caldwell means, Mary, that they are killing enough platypuses,' said Ettie Brown.

Oh dear. William was not in the mood for another argument. The spoonbill on the opposite bank continued its search for food and he noticed that it was now being followed fifty yards behind by a second, identical bird.

'At the moment it is the males that are of the most interest to me. They are just coming into breeding condition.'

'And how do you tell a male platypus from a female?'

Donald, who had now returned with plates and cups, was happy to provide the answer. 'By the spur.'

'Exactly so,' said William. 'The male has a large spur on the inside of each hind leg.'

'And once you cut them open you can tell easy,' said Donald. 'The Professor's showed me.'

Should William mention that the males were testicond? He decided no. Better to let Donald continue the platypus disquisition. Ettie Brown did not seem to enjoy interrupting him as much as she did William. Were giraffes testicond, too? He couldn't remember.

The spoonbills were closer now. How, he wondered, do you tell a male from a female spoonbill? The birds on the opposite bank seemed identical, though he assumed they were male and female. One of them picked something out of the water, a small forked twig. It started to play with it, picking it up and dropping it. Then it opened its wings and flew up to a high branch of river red gum, the twig still in its beak.

'Mr Caldwell?'

William turned. Had Ettie Brown said something?

'I'm sorry. I was distracted.'

'By what?'

'Oh, just a bird — or two birds, rather.'

'Then you do agree with me. That the living animal is of more interest than the dead one. Life is a wonderful thing, is it not, Mr Caldwell? Whether it is the life of a platypus or a bird or an insect — or our own lives. I am very fond of life — are you not, Mr Caldwell? Please pass me a scone, Donald.'

The second spoonbill stopped feeding and looked around. It spotted its mate in the tree and flew up to land on the branch beside it. As Donald began a detailed explanation to the Misses Brown of the internal anatomy of a female platypus, the second spoonbill took hold of the twig the first was carrying. There was a brief tug-of-war before the original owner let go. The second spoonbill raised its body and released a stream of white excrement from beneath its tail. As it did so the twig dropped from its beak to the ground. But the two birds seemed to have forgotten about the twig. They leant towards each other. The first bird raised its beak to the sky while the second bird flapped its way onto a higher branch. But not for long. Within seconds it had jumped down onto the first bird's back and with much flapping and tottering and tail twisting and beak entwining, the two birds mated. Thus reproduction, thought William. Thus natural selection. Thus evolution.

'I said I hope you'll have another, Mr Caldwell.'

Ettie Brown's voice was again interrupting his thoughts.

'Oh indeed. We have one every evening. As I said before, quite delicious.'

'No, not a platypus, Mr Caldwell. A scone.'

sixteen

It was maintained very lately by Geoffrey St Hilaire, whose opinion on all subjects of Natural History has great influence, that the Platypus was *oviparous*. Too credulous in believing persons unqualified to offer an opinion on such a subject, it is easily to be understood that the French could cite many instances where eggs have been found, it is said, in the nest of the Platypus.

Mr Owen, however, (who has paid particular attention to this subject) points most distinctly to its identity with mammiferous animals generally. The description, also, which is given by the Aborigines, of the habits of the Platypus, is quite distinct; and leaves no doubt, connected with other circumstances, of the fact that these animals are *not* oviparous, but born alive.

Anon., 'Remarks on the Natural History of Some of the Australasiatic Animals: Part 3,' *The Van Diemen's Land Monthly Magazine*, 1835

'I wonder, would netting them work?'

William was sitting beside the fire, perusing the inventory from the Army and Navy Stores that had been packed along with his camping equipment.

'Salmon, you mean?'

'Well, no, I was thinking about platypuses actually, Donald — it might be quicker than digging for them. According to this, there's a net in the stores somewhere. Have you come across it?'

'I think I know where to find it, Professor. I'll have a look, shall I?'

A minute later Donald emerged from the store tent with a large calico sack. William untied the cord then held the bottom of the sack while Donald pulled at the rolled-up net. When it had been opened out they could see that it was made of brown cotton twine, and was about twenty yards long and ten feet deep with a three-inch mesh.

'What do you think, then, Professor?'

William wriggled his hand through the mesh. 'No, too big for platypuses, I'm afraid. Doctor Bennett says in his book that they can get through holes much smaller than this. I suppose it would be all right for beach seining, or dragging a river or something like that. Don't know why I brought it really, except the chap at the shop told me I might need one. It *might* do for lungfish, I suppose — if we ever wanted to catch another. No, put it back in the tent, would you, Donald?'

He looked towards the river. Daraga should be here soon with the day's catch. And there he was with his two companions, loping towards them with that long stride, spear in one hand, platypus in the other. By the time they arrived Donald had just finished rolling up the net. Daraga handed over the specimen to William — it was another male — and immediately went over to where Donald was now trying to force the net back into its bag. He began talking to the other men. He turned to William and spoke again, pointing to the net.

'I'm afraid I've no idea what they're talking about, Donald, but I think they'd like to see it. Could you unroll it again? Sorry.'

With the net once more stretched out on the ground, the three men squatted down beside it, lifting and pulling. More discussion, with much vigorous nodding of heads. Daraga got to his feet. He first pointed down the river, then linked his two hands to make a flapping bird. William looked at him blankly. Daraga pointed again to the net, and quacked. William smiled.

'Do you know, Donald, I think I am at last beginning to

understand a little of their language. I think Daraga wants to use the net to catch ducks.'

It seemed to William only polite that he should reply to his Aboriginal friend. He pointed first to the net and then down the river, cleared his throat and — in finest lowland Scottish — quacked back.

With more smiles and signs it was established that the men would return later that afternoon with the rest of the family. But before leaving, Daraga picked up a stick and drew a shape on the ground. He made as if to pick it up and waved the imaginary object two or three times in the air, as if to throw it. Again William understood exactly what he meant. It was a boomerang.

The venue chosen for the duck-hunt was a long lagoon or billabong beside the river, some two miles downstream. William knew the place and knew that it often had ducks on it. And that they were shy ducks — he had never managed to get anywhere near gun-range of them. But the fact that there was no bird within gun-range — or boomerang-range — did not seem to worry the Aborigines. They were happy and busy breaking off branches from the tea-trees that formed thickets on either side of the billabong. These they pushed into the ground to form a rough fence extending from the thickets right into the water, leaving a gap of only about twenty yards. With the aid of ropes that they had also purloined from William's store tent, they fixed the net across the gap. William shook his head. It would be a fine trap for ducks — if only ducks didn't fly. Oh well, platypus for dinner again.

During the construction of the duck trap there had been much shouting and chattering and laughing. Now, as Daraga made his last inspection, the participants became quieter. Apparently satisfied, he spoke a few words, the sign for women and children to depart — in two parties, one along each side of the billabong. Daraga came over to where William had been sitting for the first part of the procedure. Pointing to the thicket, he made him understand he should hide himself there.

Through the thin trunks William could see all the way down to the billabong. And after about half an hour what he saw was ducks, dozens of them, slowly swimming towards him. Soon voices could be heard, too — distant hisses and whistles. Those whistles: he was sure he had heard the sound before. The ducks swam closer, the sounds grew louder. Still no human figures could be seen; the women and children must be close now but were hidden behind the tea-trees. Nor, when he looked towards the net, could he see Daraga and the other men. They had somehow melted into the thicket. The ducks were now no more than sixty yards away. There must have been a hundred of them, of three of four different kinds. Clearly nervous, they bunched together in the middle of the water. More invisible hisses and whistles — yes, now he remembered, the short rising notes and long descending whistle of a kitehawk. The ducks were milling round, not wanting to swim back towards the strange threatening sound, yet seeming to sense that something was amiss in front. But all they had to do was take to the wing. The net was only ten feet high, lower where it sagged in the middle. They could easily fly over it.

With a crash and a whoop, the women and children burst through the tea-trees. With splashing of feet and clattering of wings the birds rose from the water as a single body and rocketed towards the end of the billabong. At the same moment the men appeared from their hiding places, boomerangs at the ready. The curved missiles leapt from their hands as if alive, but they were not directed into the mass of flying birds. They were sent spinning into the air just above the flock. And thirty-two black ducks, seven wood ducks and three green teal went smashing into the net above the billabong.

'It was wonderful to see.' William prodded the nearest of four sizzling ducks — plucked, drawn and spatchcocked — that now lay cooking on a grill above the fireplace. 'And quite brilliant. As far as I can work out, the sound of the kite scares them and keeps them on the water — keeps them from flying off. Then when the hunters decide it's time to put them up, they surprise them from behind. The ducks see there's a way out through the gap, but don't see the net until it's almost too late. But then suddenly there are boomerangs flying just overhead — perhaps the ducks think they are some kind of hawk, too — so they stay low. Bang, right into the net.'

William poked at another of the ducks with a long fork. 'Brilliant, quite brilliant.'

'Wish I'd been there.'

'Yes, I should have taken you along, Donald. To be honest I didn't think they had much chance, but by jove — forty-two. Not bad for an afternoon's work.' He gave a third duck a prod. 'Five minutes and I think they'll be ready.'

Daraga had seemed quite upset when William would take only four of the ducks, and had insisted on him taking another gift. William reached beside the chair and picked it up. The curve of the grain showed that the boomerang had been fashioned from a bent branch of a heavy dark timber — Donald thought it might be blackwood. The carving was clever but not meticulous. It was undecorated. The unique properties of its flight seemed due to a small area of more steeply angled edge at each end. So far neither he nor Donald had had the least success in throwing it. Daraga had demonstrated how to hold it and the angle to throw it — just off vertical then launched slightly upwards — but when either of them tried it the damned thing kept cartwheeling to the ground. Daraga showed them again. As the boomerang spun from his hand, its trajectory flattened and it began to turn in a wide circle. It landed not two yards from his feet.

William was determined to master the thing. He tried again, and again, and Donald had another go. They might just as well have been throwing a stick. William thought about his own methods of hunting, of his guns and bullets and shot. Compared to using a boomerang there was little skill involved. Point gun, squeeze trigger. The real work was in the manufacture of the firearm and the ammunition. Yet these people had both invented and made this weapon, and knew all the subtleties of throwing it. And they had observed the behaviour not only of their quarry but its predators. If this was savagery, thought William, pulling a nicely cooked drumstick from one of the ducks on the fire, it was a most sophisticated savagery.

Uncle Angas would often note how surprisingly little meat there was on a duck. He might also have been surprised how much a diet of platypus whets the appetite for other flesh. William and Donald had no difficulty in polishing off two ducks apiece and retired to bed full and satisfied. When William woke sharp in the middle of the night, the taste of roast duck still lingered in his mouth. Something (someone?) had woken him. The camp site was in darkness. No human voice or animal cry had disturbed him. No wind stirred the trees, no night creature rustled the undergrowth. Yet if someone had shaken him by the shoulder or called out his name he could not have been more awake. He lay on his bed, looking up at the moon shadows on the canvas of his tent. Nothing. But something, something was not right. He rose from his bed and stepped outside the tent. He listened. Now he knew. He had heard it before. It was the river.

Pulling on his boots, he walked towards where the moon, now well down in the west, shone bright on the water. Bright enough for him to see that the river was up again, and running fast. The moon vanished behind a cloud but before it had gone completely he saw that the cloud was part of an inky band stretching right across the western sky. He hurried back towards camp and had just reached the store tent where Donald was sleeping when the first peal of thunder echoed from the hills. Donald was out of bed in a wink.

'Coming this way, do you reckon, Professor? Don't worry, I'll make sure Belle's all right. Then I'll check the tents and stuff. You leave 'em to me.'

The fire had died down, though in the moonlight William could still make out the white shapes of well-picked duck bones. He managed to light two lanterns — already the wind was too strong for candles — and took one over to where Donald was checking the straps and knots on Belle's halter. She whinnied and pulled at the rope. He could see the white of her eyes. He left one lamp with Donald and holding the other before him, headed over to where his equipment from yesterday's dissection was still spread out on the oilskin of the billiard table. Though the table was well protected beneath the generous fly, the stuff would be safer in the store tent. He had just finished rolling up his scalpels and forceps when he heard the first drops fall on the canvas above him.

From the first fat drop it was only seconds until water was

falling solid from the sky. It was rain as he had never known. There was no possibility of keeping himself dry. He ferried his boxes and jars to the store tent, shielding them from the downpour as best he could with his body. Donald was already there and took each item as he handed it in. The noise of the rain was tremendous, smashing down on leaves, on ground, on canvas. It drowned out speech — even shouting was useless. William had left his own lamp on the table rather than carrying it with him, but soon it didn't matter. The whole camp site was lit up by flash after flash of lightning. The accompanying thunder shook the earth. For the first time since he had arrived in Australia, William was afraid. When he got back to the tent with his final load he saw that Donald was scared too. The boy was sitting in the middle of the tent on a folding stool, his face pale. William found a blanket and pulled up another stool. There was no point in trying to get back to his bed. He sat down beside Donald and put his arm across his shoulders, pulling the blanket around them both. And so they sat until the dawn.

As daylight came the rain began to ease and the thunder rolled away. When at last William poked his head through the tent flaps he saw that it had in fact stopped raining, though water still dripped from sodden trees. A lone kookaburra called. It seemed a miracle that any bird was calling. How could any unprotected creature have survived such a night? But the first kookaburra was answered by another, and from a nearby bush came the twittering of a wren.

Another miracle was that all the tents were still standing. That such flimsy structures of pole and canvas and cord could have survived such a battering was a fine testament to the Army and Navy Stores, and to Donald's skill in erecting them. Belle was still tied up to her tree. All in all, the camp site did not seem to have suffered too badly. But the river — the river was unrecognisable.

From where he stood on the rise, William looked out on not a river but a lake. A single vast sheet of water spread out as far as he could see. Punctuated by trees with water ten feet up their trunks, it flowed more slowly now. It was quieter, too.

'Bloody oath.'

William turned to see Donald standing beside him and for once he had to agree — bloody oath, indeed. They both looked out over the flooded landscape.

'But we made it through, eh, Professor?'

'Yes, Donald, we made it.'

They had made it through, but what about the platypuses?

Apart from their own camp site (thank goodness Ben Fuller had known to choose it well) the nearest dry land was Black Hill, two miles away. It also was surrounded by water, but a thin column of smoke told them that Daraga and his family were not only safe, they had somehow already managed to make a fire. William looked back at the camp site. No smoke was rising from their own fireplace.

'Don't you worry, Professor,' said Donald, as if reading his thoughts. 'I always keep a bit of dry wood in the tent. We'll soon have a billy going.'

He was as good as his word. Not fifteen minutes later William found himself on a chair by the riverbank, dressed in a dry change of clothes and with a cup of hot tea in hand.

Sunlight broke through clouds already clearing to the east. Brown water was swirling past his feet, carrying with it everything from stalks of grass to the whole trees, roots and all. A raft of matted wool resolved itself into two sheep, dead and already beginning to swell. William watched them float downstream until he could see them no more. He wondered idly how long would they take to reach the wharf at Bundaberg — if the wharf was still there. How many other creatures had suffered the same fate? And what chance for a little water-mole?

Close to the bank, the branches of a flooded she-oak were sieving a selection of smaller material from the passing flood. A broken branch nosed its way into the foliage. Only when he saw something on it move did William realise that it was carrying a passenger, a small lizard of some kind which managed to scramble onto one of the branches — just in time. The other end of the branch, still pulled by the current, wheeled in a slow half-circle and it drifted away on its watery journey to who knows where.

William now saw that the tree was crowded with other survivors from the flood. Insects — beetles, mostly — crawled this way and that, searching in vain for a way down to dry land. A small brown mouse clung with all four feet to the outermost tip of a twig, shivering. The lizard set out to explore its new refuge, first along the branch, then another, then onto a dead stick that had been caught up in the feathery leaves with other detritus from the flood. The stick was straight and about four feet long. Tied to its end, almost obscured by small detritus from the flood, was a strip of red flannel cloth.

The next day he began packing. Donald had tried to persuade him against it — 'They won't *all* be gone, Professor. There'll still be a few of them left somewhere' — but by the second day, when the floodwaters had begun to recede from the land and they could see what had happened to the river itself, even Donald had to agree. It was unrecognisable. Where once had been sandbanks, now were deep pools; where once platypuses frolicked dawn and dusk, now were sheets of thick brown mud. At a bend a mile downstream the river had carved itself a completely new path, coarse sand and broken trees now filling the old channel. Even to a creature as at home in the water as a platypus, thought William, this flood had been much more than a high wind to a bird. Even an eagle, Miss Ettie, cannot survive a hurricane.

He had made up his mind. As soon as the road was passable he would go into town to make the arrangements. Donald pointed out that it might be some time yet until a bullock cart could get through.

'I'll stay and look after your stuff, though, if that's what you want.'

William looked again at the river. He was not sure what he wanted. It was strange: though part of him was devastated, another part was relieved to be unburdened of his task. He looked over to the tents and the tables, at the boxes packed but not yet closed. I'm sorry, Professor Moseley, for all that money wasted. And I'm sorry, Miss Ettie, for all those platypuses killed. There was nothing for him to do here. There was nothing for him to do in Gayndah. Perhaps it would be best to head back to Sydney — but what would he do there? It was too late to make a new start. He could wait until next year, he supposed, at some other river. But by then the Tasmanian platypuses would have yielded their secrets to Herr what's-his-name. Ah well, thought William, with a last look at the ruined river, good luck to him.

He walked slowly back to the camp site and pulled back the oilcloth from the Churchman Patented Portable Convertible billiard table. He lifted off the mahogany lids. No water seemed to have got in. The green of the baize glowed bright as ever; the spots and lines stood out neat and clear. He took the three balls from their drawer, spotted the red and selected a cue from the second drawer. He placed the plain white ball on the line and dummied the stroke once, twice, then hit it hard. The ball sped up the table, connecting with the red just where he had aimed. Both balls rolled down to rest almost touching the bottom cushion. It was a fine break; his opponent would have a difficult shot. But, thought William, who was his opponent now? He put down the cue and rubbed his chin, then his cheek. There seemed little point in shaving.

As he turned away from the table he saw Donald approaching, holding something on the palm of his hand.

'What do you reckon this is, Professor?'

It looked like a strand of horsehair, so dark as to be almost black, coiled in untidy loops on the palm of his hand.

'I found it on the ground, just behind the tent there. You watch.'

As William looked down, the hair began to move. Slowly, the loops slid over each other, uncoiling and recoiling. Could this thing be alive? He took it from Donald's palm and put it on his own. It felt stiff and dry, but didn't stop its slow writhing. He lifted it with his other hand and with gentle fingers began to straighten it. Uncoiled, it was all of a foot in length. As soon as he put it back on the palm of his hand, it began slowly to coil up again. A name came into his head, from studies long ago and half a world away.

'I'm pretty sure it's a nematomorph. I remember reading about them. Otherwise known as a Gordian worm — like the knot, you know.' He put it back onto Donald's hand. 'Have you finished packing the specimens?'

'What knot would that be, Professor?'

'Oh, Hercules, wasn't it? No, Alexander, Alexander the Great. This chap Gordius — I can't remember exactly who he was — had tied his oxcart to a pillar or something, and said that whoever untied the knot would rule Asia. Along comes Alexander and he untied the knot all right — with his sword. Anyway, the specimens — did you say you had —'

'But that's not fair. That's not untying it.'

'No, I've always thought it was a bit of a cheat, but there you are.'

William looked down again at the small creature in Donald's hand.

'But this little fellow here — and I seem to remember that you can tell the sexes apart by looking at their tails — ah yes, see? — bilobed, so it must be a male. This little fellow here must have just hatched out.'

'From an egg, you mean?'

'No. From some insect or other. They're parasites of insects, I believe.'

Donald took a step back and held his hand out further. 'Parasites! I don't want to touch no parasites.'

'I don't think it can harm us, Donald. They grow coiled up inside some insect, you see, then somehow they make the insect find some water and out they pop. I suppose the insect dies, but the nematomorphs find themselves a mate and lay their eggs, and the larvae hatch out and find themselves another insect, and around it all goes again. Amazing, really. And amazing that something that's so long can be so thin, or something that's so thin can be so long, or ... well, you know what I mean. I suppose the rain must have brought him out.'

When they both began looking they found several more on the ground round the camp site.

'Perhaps it's a sign, eh, Donald? If I can't have platypuses, perhaps I'll make my name studying nematomorphs.' He smiled and again rubbed his chin. 'But do you know, I think I need a shave.

How are we off for hot water?'

'Coming right up, Professor.'

William stripped off his shirt and picked up brush and soap from the table where Donald had already laid out his shaving kit. He lathered his face, stropped the razor the usual two times up and down, lifted up his chin and, pulling down on the skin of his neck, began the first upward stroke. He had finished shaving his neck and was about to start on his left cheek when he heard a noise behind him. It sounded, he thought, like a giggle. He turned round. Three small children were looking up at him in round-eyed wonder, trying in vain to hide white smiles with brown hands. Behind them was Daraga. In one of his hands was a spear. In the other, a platypus.

seventeen

The various contradictory accounts that have been given on the authority of aborigines (who may be supposed, from their so often seeking these animals for food, to be able to state their habits correctly) as to the animal laying eggs and hatching them induced me to take some pains to find out the cause of the error. The Yas natives at first asserted that the animals lay eggs, but shortly afterwards contradicted themselves. On the whole we may infer that no dependence can be placed on native accounts, but that naturalists must seek for information in their own investigations.

George Bennett, 'Notes on the Natural History and Habits of the *Ornithorhynchus paradoxus*, Blum.', *Transactions of the Zoological Society of London*, 1835

Judging by the sharpness of the spurs on its back legs, William deduced that the specimen was a young male. He put down his razor and reached for his dissection kit. With three deft strokes he had opened up the abdomen. There beneath the intestine were the two testicles, white and wet. They were the largest he had yet seen, the size of sparrows' eggs. Clear indication that the mating season would soon be starting.

'I'll need a Number 2 jar, Donald, and some formalin. Think you can find them?'

'I'll find them all right, Professor.'

Of course, he knew it was still hopeless. One male specimen wasn't going to prove anything. But for a few minutes at least he found himself caught up once more in the joy of dissection and the excitement of science, and it felt good.

'Well, there we are, Donald,' he said as he screwed tight the lid of the jar and held it up in front of the baffled Daraga. 'One more souvenir of our visit to the Burnett River.'

'By the looks of things, Professor,' said the boy, 'I think we might have more than one.'

William turned to see four more figures approaching, one of them on horseback. Mary Brown sprang down from the saddle and spoke a few words to her Aboriginal companions. They stepped forward. One held out another platypus.

'What?' said William. 'But how? I mean, I thought …'

'You thought what, Mr Caldwell? You surely didn't think a platypus would let a little flood bother it, did you?'

William stood there, silent, his mouth still half open.

'As I suspected,' said Mary Brown. 'Mr Caldwell, platypuses have been in Australia a lot longer than you have. I think we can assume that they are used to the country by now.'

'But the floods — the river. How did you find them?'

'Oh, my brother tells me it's easy now. With most of their old burrows washed out they're all busy making new ones. New diggings are easy to spot.'

Mary Brown explained that she had come as soon as she could, both to see Daraga and his family and to make sure William and Donald had weathered the storm. The track was still too wet for the gig so she had ridden over.

'Ettie says she is sorry she couldn't send you any eggs, but since the storm the hens have been quite off the lay.'

'Thank you. Thank you very much, Miss Brown. It's very kind of your sister to think of … us.'

Mary Brown acknowledged his thanks with a nod and a smile. 'I'm sure she will be happy to know that you are well, and still being provided with plenty of fresh meat.'

It was William's turn to smile. 'Your sister, is she well?'

'I'm afraid her headaches have been causing her much pain, perhaps more than I know. She does not complain.'

'If there's anything I can do.'

'If there is anything you can do, Mr Caldwell, I shall not hesitate to ask.' She climbed back onto her horse. 'Oh, and Mr Caldwell ...'

'Yes?'

'You must forgive us, we have been most impolite. We seem to have interrupted your shaving.'

William was suddenly aware of the white lather that still covered half his face. Oh well. At least it would conceal most of the blush that even now was spreading up his neck towards his cheeks.

It was well known in Britain — in Scotland, in particular — that total immersion in water was something to be avoided. Here in Australia it was different. After so much dissecting over the last few days William felt in need of a good bath. He stepped out of his clothes and waded into the river, enjoying the tickling, tingling feeling as the water crept up his legs, his groin, his stomach. He bent his legs to let the water come up to his chin. Ah, that felt good.

It was surprising just how quickly the river had recovered. Four days after the storm — two days after Mary Brown and Daraga's visit — it had been down to its normal level. Now, a week later, it was running as clear as before.

He lay on his stomach in the cool water and let his legs float out behind him. His fingers reached down to the stony bed of the pool. Long straps of waterweed wafted in the current. Small bold fish, no larger than the sticklebacks of his Scottish childhood, nibbled at his fingers (perhaps at some traces of flesh left over from the last dissection). The fish, now finished with him, began darting round in the water, snapping up tiny trifles of this or that. They seemed especially keen on little white specks that were rising up from the waterweed.

Some of the specks evaded the predatory pack and broke through to the surface, where they floated and drifted like so many small snowflakes. He noticed something else breaking the surface of the water, long stems arising from the base of the waterweed. At the end of each stem was a swelling that, as though waxed, seemed to repel the water to sit in a little dimple of its own making. He watched as one of the floating specks slid down the edge of one of the dimples and stuck fast to the end of the swelling.

He pulled himself into a sitting position. All around him he could now see the surface of the water spotted with dimples from the long stems just breaking the water, and hundreds upon hundreds of the little white specks. He watched another string of them emerge from the waterweed and float up to the surface. Where were they coming from? When he parted the fronds of weed he could see nothing. He took hold of the leaves where he thought the specks must be coming from and pulled. The roots gave way easily and he lifted the plant from the water.

The white specks had indeed been coming from the water plant. Tucked away between the bases of two of the leaves was a small sac, a purse you might almost call it, shaped something like the flame of a candle. Through its translucent walls he could see a mass of the little white specks — pollen grains or something similar. The swellings on the end of the long stems that broke the surface of the water then, they must be the female flowers. He pulled up more of the plants. Though he was no botanist, he soon managed to work out the whole amazing sequence of fertilisation and seed development.

The female flowers began as little buds right down near the base of the plant. As their stems grew long enough for them to reach the surface they gradually expanded. The flowers were simple in structure. They had no petals, just a long, green ovary topped by a water-repellent, three-lobed pistil. This sat at the centre of its dimple in the surface of the water until one of the white specks of pollen drifted close enough to tumble in. As soon as the flower had been thus fertilised the ovary began to swell and the long stem started to coil up like a spring. This caused the flower — or seed pod as it was fast becoming — to be pulled back beneath the water. When the seeds were ripe the underwater pod split open and the seeds floated away. All stages of this process seemed to be going on at the same time. Wind pollination and insect pollination he knew. He had never heard of water pollination before.

'Is that you, Mr Caldwell?'

William had been so engrossed in his botanical investigation that he hadn't heard the gig arrive. Here were the two sisters standing on the riverbank, not twenty feet away. Mary Brown spoke again.

'What are you doing?'

'Oh, just, um, well I'm, er, I was just having a bit of a dip and I found this plant here.' William held up a piece of the waterweed. 'It's very interesting, you know, very interesting indeed.'

'Good. Donald wants to know if you're ready for lunch.'

'Well, yes, I'm quite peckish actually.'

William eyed the pile of clothes by the edge of the water. Mary Brown saw it, too.

'I'll go and tell him,' she said and turned towards the camp site, leaving her sister alone on the riverbank.

'And what is so interesting about your plant, Mr Caldwell?' said Ettie Brown.

'Oh, er, pollination, you know, um, that kind of thing.'

Why was it always like this? He had lectured to classes of a hundred or more, had had easy conversations with great and famous men, yet in the presence of this one woman he felt like a stammering dolt.

'I would like to know more, Mr Caldwell. Please tell me. And I would also like it if we could conduct our conversation a little closer. Is it safe for me to walk forward?'

The girl took a tentative step. Another and her foot would be in the water.

'Miss Ettie. Please stay right where you are.'

William half rose from the water, then sat down with a splash.

'Mr Caldwell, are you all right?'

'Yes, yes, fine, I'm fine. It's just that …'

William could feel his face turning red. This was ridiculous; the girl was blind, she could see nothing.

'Mr Caldwell, are you undressed?'

William sighed. His blush deepened, and spread. 'Yes, I am actually.'

'Why goodness, Mr Caldwell.'

'Miss Ettie, would you please step back a few paces? I assure you that it is quite safe.'

The girl stepped back.

'Now, would you be kind enough to turn around?'

The girl appeared to consider his request for a moment.

'Very well, Mr Caldwell, if that is what you want.' She put out her arms and pirouetted once, a full turn. 'There,' she said, facing again towards him. 'Like that, Mr Caldwell?'

'Miss Ettie, would you be so kind as to turn around half a turn?'

'Half a turn? Oh yes, I see. I am so sorry, Mr Caldwell.'

The girl turned so that her back was towards him. 'Like this?'

'Like that. Thank you, Miss Ettie.'

William emerged from the water at a stoop and made a run for his clothes. In his rush to pull dry trousers onto wet legs the first one stuck. He took three hops, lost his balance and scrunched down onto the gravel.

'Are you sure you're all right, Mr Caldwell?' said the girl, the solicitous tone of her voice sounding to William's ears a trifle too earnest.

He managed to push one leg into his trousers, then the other. 'I am fine, thank you, Miss Ettie,' he said, getting to his feet and pulling up his trousers. 'Never better.' He managed to wriggle his damp body into the dry shirt, fastened his belt and grabbed his boots and socks in one hand. 'Now, I believe your sister said something about lunch.'

'She did, Mr Caldwell. And I believe that you said something about "feeling quite peckish".'

William took up a position beside the girl. 'Shall we?' he said.

The girl put her hand on his arm, and as the two of them together walked back to the camp site (William manfully attempting to ignore the stab of each sharp twig and stone on his naked feet) he told her what he had just witnessed.

'Donald has been telling me about his family,' said Mary Brown as Ettie and William arrived. 'It seems that he is an orphan, just like us.'

'No,' said Donald, 'my mum's alive.'

'Half an orphan then,' said Ettie. 'And Mr Caldwell — a full orphan if ever I met one — has been telling me about sex.'

She was doing it again, and once again William was unable to control that familiar pink feeling creeping up his neck to his cheeks. With the excuse of finding clean socks, he headed towards his tent.

'Your mother must miss having you at home, Donald,' said Mary Brown. 'But that reminds me, we have a letter for you, have we not Ettie?'

Ettie fetched two envelopes from a pocket in her skirt. 'There is a letter for you too, Mr Caldwell,' she called out. 'They arrived on Tuesday. I must apologise that we have taken so long to deliver them.'

Socked and booted, William rejoined them.

'No rosewater this time, Mr Caldwell.' Ettie Brown smiled sweetly as she handed him the envelope. 'No doubt this letter is from a different aunt. Now, Mary dear, I still have a slight headache. Do you mind if we don't stay for lunch. I really would like to go home.'

Donald's letter was indeed from his mother.

'And is she missing you?' said William.

'Doesn't say. Constable Perry's been back though — twice, she says.'

No doubt pursuing further enquiries, thought William, smiling to himself. What would Sergeant O'Malley have to say about that?

'Perhaps you should take a short holiday, Donald, go home for a few days. It must be nearly two months you've been here now. You deserve a break.'

Donald looked horrified. 'I couldn't leave you here, Professor. Not now the work's really starting. Couldn't think of it, leaving you to look after yourself.'

William had to admit that life would be a lot harder without Donald to run the camp, especially now that it looked as though the breeding season was about to begin.

'Well, let me know if you change your mind. I'm sure we could work something out.'

He opened his own letter. As Ettie Brown had guessed, it was not from his aunt. It was another from Doctor George Bennett. To William's surprise it informed him that Doctor Bennett and his son Herbert were planning a trip to Queensland. There was a fossil site in the Darling Downs that was of some interest to the doctor, and if he had time they planned to continue on to Gayndah. If so, they would arrive early in August. He looked forward to learning firsthand of William's progress.

And, thought William the following day, lazing once more in the cool waters of the river after another afternoon of anatomical investigation, exactly what was his progress? Platypus breeding season was approaching, that he knew. He had already confirmed an increase in size of the males' testes — just as Doctor Bennett had observed. This must surely be a prelude to mating, and so to reproduction. The next few weeks would be crucial.

The recent change in his own fortunes — first one way, then the other — seemed somehow to have bolstered his scientific resolve, sport of intellectuals or no. If he could get enough specimens — and he had no reason to doubt Daraga's confidence that he would — he might soon have the proof he needed. And have it before Herr von Mengden. But right now ... Right now he would continue to enjoy the delicious feeling of lying back in the cool water gazing up at the sky, or drifting with the stream watching the world go by. For sheer bliss, he decided, it almost rivalled dozing in a warm bed.

The river was a surprisingly good place from which to observe animals. A man on foot would send birds and beasts scurrying for cover. That same man immersed in the water with only his head showing would be ignored. William looked around him. An azure kingfisher clutched its branch above a pool, staring down; long, green water dragons basked on the bank; a pair of spoonbills, doubtless the same pair he had seen before, scythed the shallows with their strange, flattened beaks. While his attention was momentarily fastened on a bright blue damselfly that had just landed on a twig floating only inches from his nose, he heard a scraping sound coming from the far bank. He paddled slowly towards it. The noise was loud enough to suggest that whatever was making it must be of considerable size. It seemed to be digging. He could not only hear loud scratching and rustling but see showers of twigs and leaves being thrown up into the air. The riverbank at this point was lined with tea-trees and just high enough to hide whatever it was that was creating this commotion. William crept naked from the water on hands and knees.

Behind the screen of tea-trees was a large mound of dead leaves. Another shower of sticks and leaves was thrown up from behind it. A head appeared above the mound, then ducked down again. There was no doubt that it was a bird's head — he distinctly saw a beak — but it was an odd-looking bird. The head was almost bare of feathers and bright red. A very odd bird.

The head appeared again, this time from the right-hand side of the mound and was soon followed by the rest of the bird. Not only was its head and neck bright red, the neck ended in a kind of ruff that was an equally bright yellow. Next to these the bird's body was a disappointment. It was the size of a large chicken, with feathers a uniform dull black. The tail provided some interest, being fan-shaped and flattened sideways like a stern rudder. The bird's legs, presumably the tools with which it had been so vigorously rearranging the forest floor, were long and bare and the same pale brown as the leaves it had been tossing around.

Either the bird didn't notice William or it ignored him. It strode around the front of the mound to the other side and, facing away from the mound, gathered up a footful of leaves and threw them out behind it. The throw was well judged. The leaves arched up and landed neatly on the top of the mound.

What curious bird was this? thought William. What could it be doing? Both John Gould and Doctor Bennett had described the wonderful lyrebird of Australia, which scratches together a small mound as stage for its matchless song. This was no lyrebird — it didn't have that spectacular tail — but it must surely be related. And it must be building a stage for its courtship. Perhaps if he waited it would sing.

William waited. The bird continued to circle its mound, adding the occasional footful of leaves. Then it began to call. Standing by the edge of the mound it pushed forwards its neck, opened its beak very slightly and let forth a deep boom. This was very different from the magnificent mimicry of the lyrebird he had read about. It reminded him more of a bittern. Another bird appeared, about the same size as the first but with not quite such flamboyant colouring. It climbed up the mound and began to dig a hole, almost as big as its body. For a minute or two it lay on top of the hole with wings outstretched, then stood up, kicked a footful or two of the mound material back into the hole and ran off into the scrub.

What was going on? Was this some kind of display, some ritual competition? The first bird climbed up the mound and thrust its head down the hole. It climbed down and began tossing up leaves from the base of the mound, again with surprising accuracy, until the hole was filled. The bird craned its neck forward and let out another single, mournful boom, then wandered away, scratching and pecking, scratching and pecking, into the scrub and out of sight.

How would he describe to Ettie Brown the sight he had just seen? If he said that the bird was a little like a chicken, she would surely understand that. He imagined the girl's hands holding a white hen, her fingers touching soft feathers and comb, scaly legs, sharp claws. But the sound. She would know what a chicken sounded like, of course, but would she ever have heard a bittern? No matter, he was sure he could do a passable imitation. Thoughts of Ettie Brown were interrupted by another sound, again a rustling of dry leaves but a much softer one than that made by the birds. It stopped, and started again. He saw the trembling of leaves where something was passing between two tufts of sedge, but the something was low to the ground and still hidden from view. A snake? William was suddenly aware of his own undress. He felt as naked as Adam. A head appeared from the cover, a pointed scaly head. Through a tiny slit at the front of its mouth emerged a long forked tongue. William stayed as still as a statue. The head turned this way and that, the tongue flicked out and in. It moved forward. A long neck, then two splayed legs. It was not a snake, it was an enormous lizard.

He could see all of it now, the low-slung body, back legs and long tapering tail. What was it that Donald called them — iguanas? No, goannas. This one must be all of six feet long. It walked across the clearing and, without pause, up the side of the mound. It stopped where the bird had only recently been filling in the hole, flicked its tongue in and out once, twice. Then it began to dig. The leaves and twigs were easy work for strong claws and within a minute the goanna's head had already disappeared into the hole. It paused there a moment, then began to pull its body backwards out of the hole. As its head emerged William could see that in its mouth it was holding a large, white egg.

The goanna turned and with the same slow, determined pace descended the mound. The egg was quite a size, bigger than a hen's egg. Would it eat the egg, swallow it whole? The lizard stopped at the base of the mound and jerked its head a few times, rearranging the position of the egg between its jaws. Then like a dog shaking a rat it thumped the egg down onto the ground. The first blow was enough. The egg cracked and crumpled in its jaws and with another jerk of its head the goanna tossed the whole thing down its throat, shell and all. William was close enough to see some of the content of the egg dribbling from its mouth. The goanna wiped clumsily at its jaw with a forefoot. It walked round to the other side of the mound and began to climb. With no apparent hesitation, it began to dig another hole.

The mystery of the mound was solved, but other puzzles now presented themselves. If the mound was in fact a gigantic nest, why were the eggs buried inside it? Did the bird, or birds, sit on them and only cover them up when absent? Could so enormous a structure have been made by one bird by itself, or was it the product of some kind of cooperation? More observation might solve the riddles but if William wanted to remain here longer he must first make himself a little more comfortable — his legs were already aching from the awkward position he had been frozen in. The goanna already had its head well down into its new excavation. It would not notice if William stretched a limb or two.

He pushed himself up into a squatting position and was about to stand when the bird appeared again, running across the clearing towards the mound. The big lizard looked up from its digging just in time to see a squawking grunting flurry of feathers coming straight at its head. Despite its size the goanna almost leapt clear into the air. It turned and ran pell-mell for the scrub, its four feet kicking up a shower of dead leaves at every step. The bird stopped squawking, shook its feathers and looked all around. It stuck its head down into the hole where the goanna had just been digging. Seemingly satisfied, it began refilling the hole. William got down onto his hands and knees and crept backwards away from the nest towards the river.

Donald was able to inform William that what he had seen was a brush turkey. 'They taste good, good as chicken.'

The ever-reliable Mr Gould was able to inform him that what he had seen was *Talegalla lathami*. William read the description aloud.

> It has often been asserted, that Australia abounds in anomalies, and in no instance is the truth of this assertion more fully exemplified than in the history of this very singular bird. The most remarkable circumstance connected with the economy of this species is the fact of its eggs not being incubated in the manner of other birds.

Not even distantly related to the lyrebird, it was one of three birds to be found in Australia which incubate their eggs not with the heat of their own bodies, but by creating an enormous hot bed. Mr Gould described how the male bird builds a mound into which the female lays her eggs. The eggs are kept warm by heat from the decomposing vegetation, the male covering and uncovering them to regulate the temperature.

> As a moth emerges from a chrysalis, dries its wings and flies away, so the youthful Talegalla, when it leaves the egg, is sufficiently perfect to be able to act independently and procure its own food. This we know from personal observation of the bird in a state of captivity; several old birds having constructed mounds, in which their eggs have been deposited and their young developed, in the gardens of the Zoological Society in the Regent's Park.

'Where's that, Professor?' said Donald.

'In London, though I think there is a zoological garden in Australia — in Melbourne, I believe.'

'Don't suppose I'll see it then.'

Which seemed to William a final statement for one so young.

The boy was all for borrowing William's gun and shooting the bird, and it was while William was explaining to him about closed seasons and why, no matter how good eating a brush turkey might be it would be both unsporting and unwise to shoot the poor creature on its nest, that he noticed a horseman coming down the track.

eighteen

The naturalist Lesson has described the platypus, in his *Manuel de Mammalogie*, as a bird without wings; and Geoffrey has committed a still greater blunder, in describing the egg of some birds as that of the *Ornithorhynchus*. Its many analogies have strengthened the opinions pronounced by these great men; and, notwithstanding the reasonings of Cuvier and other anatomists, the greater number still hold it to be oviparous.

Edmund C. Hobson, 'Observations on the Blood of the *Ornithorhynchus paradoxus*,' *Tasmanian Journal of Natural Science*, 1842

'So, how's business, Prof?'

'Why, Mr Fuller — Ben.' William put down the book. 'And with your beard again I see. Donald, take Mr Fuller's horse, would you?'

Not only was Ben Fuller once more wearing a full beard, but he was riding a large black gelding not the grey horse of last time. William gestured to the rows of bottles and jars inside the store tent.

'As you can see, business is very well. If you'd asked me a week or two ago it might have been a different story, but right now I'd say my work is progressing pretty much according to plan.'

'Yes, I heard about the flood. But you're finding plenty of water-moles?'

'I'm pleased to say I am — with the help of my Aboriginal friends. I don't suppose you heard that I have some more helpers now.'

'Oh, I heard all right. I stopped over at the pub last night — Billy told me what had been going on. Hey, careful there, boy.'

Donald had been leading Ben Fuller's gelding over to where William's horse Belle was tied up, enjoying her usual lunch of oats. The large horse had shied as it neared Belle and pulled the reins from Donald's hand. He was now trying to grab hold of them again but the horse was tossing its head, keeping them from his grasp. Ben Fuller strode over and grabbed the reins.

'Don't you know how to hold a horse?'

It seemed to William that the trouble had hardly been Donald's fault. 'That's quite a spirited beast you have there.'

Ben Fuller tugged down on the reins. He smiled suddenly. 'Yours if you want to swap.'

'Oh no, thank you. Belle suits me well enough. Anyway, it's good to see you. You must tell me what brings you back up here, and what you have been doing since I last saw you.'

'Oh, a bit of this and a bit of that. But I'm just back from droving — can't you tell?'

As well as having grown back his beard, Ben Fuller was indeed looking a little more suntanned than when William had last seen him. He pulled up a chair beside the fire.

'Yes, I met up with Charlie Boyd again — you'll remember Charlie, eh, Prof? He had a mob to bring up from the Condamine, so I says right-ho. Paid off at Bundaberg last week. I thought I'd come up here and see how you were getting on.'

It was then that Ben Fuller spotted the billiard table, still uncovered from the last night's practice. He got up and walked towards it, then round it. He looked underneath it.

'Billy told me about this, but I said I wouldn't believe it till I'd seen it with my own eyes.' He ran his fingers over the cloth. 'So that's what old Harry had on the wagon — besides the grog.'

The memory of the drunken bullock driver brought a smile to

William's lips.

'Preserving spirits, Ben. Would you care for a game?' he said.

'Wouldn't I!' said Ben Fuller.

'A game it is, then.'

With Ben looking on in obvious admiration, William took the cues and balls from their drawers.

'By crikey, Prof, she's a sweet-looking table. You might have to give me a start, but. I'd say you've been getting in a bit more practice than me lately.'

'Well, what say I give you the same start you gave me on our last game?'

'Fair enough,' said Ben, with a laugh. 'Evens it is. So — toss for break, shall we?'

Ben Fuller went to flip the coin, but stopped. 'Wait on,' he said.

He took another florin from his pocket and put them both heads up on the table, just touching.

'Tell you what, Prof: if you can answer me this, you get to chose. Suppose I hold one of these coins still and then roll the other one around it, making sure that it doesn't slip, and they're kept touching at all times. How many times do you think the moving coin will have turned around after it's been right around the one I'm holding?'

William thought about it hard, trying to picture the moving coin in his head.

'It would have to be once,' he said. He watched as Ben Fuller carefully rolled the second coin round the first.

'Looks like I choose then, eh, Prof?' Ben chose to break.

After half an hour's play the first game was evenly matched, but this time it was William who, with the scores at 93 to 96, potted two reds and his opponent's white to win.

'Good on you, Professor,' said Donald, who had been called away from his possum skins to act as umpire and marker. 'I knew you'd win.'

'It was a close run thing, Donald. I'm glad I didn't have any money on it.'

'Not as glad as I am.' Ben Fuller gestured at Donald. 'Does the boy play?'

'He's coming along.'

In truth it had become clear to William that Donald — fine naturalist, steward and general factotum though he was — would never be a billiard player. Despite William's several attempts to try to teach him, the boy seemed to have no intrinsic ability to picture in his head where the balls would go, let alone the ability to hit them straight. And he showed little desire to perfect these skills. He would much rather be skinning possums, thought William — though he felt disinclined to mention this to Ben Fuller.

'Well now, Prof, it looks like I owe you a beer.' Ben Fuller put down his cue and went over to his horse. 'And it just so happens I picked up a couple of bottles at the hotel.'

He took two bottles of beer from his saddlebag, opened them both and passed one to William.

'What about some glasses, eh, Donny-boy?'

Donald produced two glasses and put them down beside William. William filled them both and raised one of them. 'Your health,' he said. 'I'm surprised you managed to get Mr Pike to part with this. I'm sure he told me he was down to his last case.'

'You don't want to believe everything Billy Pike tells you, Prof. He's a Queenslander, you know.'

'A Queenslander — how do you mean?'

'All Queenslanders are liars — didn't you know that?'

'But you, you're a Queenslander, aren't you, Ben?'

Another of Ben's little conundrums?

'Why, Prof, I never thought of that,' he said, eyes wide with innocent surprise. 'You're right. And if I'm a Queenslander, and I'm lying about Billy Pike lying, well — you don't know where you are, do you?' His face broke into a wide smile. 'Trust an educated man like you to spot that, Prof.'

The beer tasted good, and as the glasses were emptied and filled again Ben told stories about his latest trip. Of mustering cattle out on the wide plains beyond the Expedition Range, of branding and break-outs and the wild scrub-bull that had given so much trouble before he stalked it and shot it. Two days it had taken him.

'He was a tough bastard. Not big — scrubbies are never big — but strong, and smart with it. In daylight you couldn't get near enough to take a shot, then at night he'd come sniffing round the herd and in the morning six of your cows gone and a couple of young bulls raked half open. Horns like the bloody devil, and he knew how to use them.'

'So how did you get him?'

Ben grinned. 'Any beasts around here?'

William shook his head. 'Not as far as I know.'

'It should be safe then.' Ben took a deep breath, cupped his hands round his mouth and let out a high quavering roar.

'Ah,' said William, 'the challenge of another bull.'

'Jesus, Prof, don't you know nothin'? That's a cow in heat, not a flamin' bull.' He grinned again. 'Irresistible — though I says it m'self what shouldn't. 'Course, you have to be downwind. Sniff of a man and your scrub-bull won't come within cooee — cow or no cow. Here, have another beer.'

He took another bottle from his saddlebag. Billy Pike must have got some new supplies in.

After dinner another bottle of beer was produced, then another, and more stories from Ben were followed by the recitation of a long ballad about somewhere called 'The Paroo' — the amount of beer he drank seemed to have no effect on his ability to remember the words.

'You know, Prof, I've been wondering if now you're so busy, maybe you could do with another hand for a while.' Ben drained his glass. 'I told Charlie I'd shift another mob with him but it'll be a week or three till he's knocked down his cheque.'

William looked round to where Donald had retired to his own end of the camp site. The boy had finished tanning his last possum skin and was now in the process of sewing them together. He was really all the help William needed at the moment; nor could William forget the difference between the damper that Donald cooked and the ones Ben Fuller had made. On the other hand, here might be the opportunity for Donald to take that holiday.

'That's very kind, Ben. I'll give it some thought.'

'You do that, Prof. But you haven't told me yet about these niggers — sorry, Abos — of yours. Didn't think there were any around here any more. Where did you find 'em?'

William told him about the arrival of Daraga and his family and how useful they were proving. He didn't mention the role that Mary and Ettie Brown had played. He didn't mention them at all.

'Of course, the number of platypuses is tending to dwindle now that most of the local supply has been exhausted,' said William. 'And it's now that I really need them — females, especially.'

'Don't we all, Prof,' said Ben, chuckling at his own joke. 'Do you pay them, the blacks?'

'Oh yes. Flour and sugar and so forth.'

'What about grog?'

'I'm told it's illegal to sell alcohol to Aborigines.'

William could have said that Mary Brown had expressly asked him not to supply any alcohol to her family, but once again he chose not to mention the two sisters.

'So it is, so it is. Best to keep them away from the stuff.' Ben Fuller poured himself some more beer. 'They can't handle it, see — not like a white man.'

'I wouldn't know about that, Ben, but they seem happy enough with their flour and their sugar. And of course they seem to find so many things to eat in the bush around — roots and berries and so forth. Sometimes I think they might live better than us.'

Ben took a look around. 'It looks to me as if you've got things set up pretty sweet around here yourself. I don't know many blokes who'd be sitting around right now enjoying a beer after a game of billiards and some tucker, being waited on hand and foot.' Ben Fuller raised his glass.

'Yes, I suppose when you look at it like that ...'

'It's the only way to look at it, Prof. Now, what about another game of billiards on that fancy table of yours, eh? Your break, I believe.'

The next morning Donald's damper was as light and delicious as ever, the bacon fragrant and crisp. After he cleared away the plates the boy declared his intention to take the holiday that William had so long been offering him.

'It's my mam's birthday next week, see, and I'd like to take her the rug.'

He had been working away at his possum skins for weeks now. After stretching and cleaning each skin he had tanned it with wattle bark and softened it using what he assured William was the very best method — rubbing in the mashed brains of the animal itself. The technique seemed to have been successful. Now that Donald had stitched the skins together William had to admit that they made a handsome rug.

'How long do you think you might be gone, Donald?'

'I was reckoning on two weeks, if that's all right with you, Prof — was that about how long Mr Fuller said he'd be staying?'

Donald must have overheard Ben's offer of help. Could it be that he was put out by the older man's presence? No matter. Clearly he had thought it all through, and yes, two weeks would be plenty of time for him to get home and back. No doubt William and Ben would be able to shift for themselves well enough without him.

'That'll be fine, Donald. But how will you get home? I'm afraid I can't lend you Belle; I'll be needing her.'

'Walk.'

It would take the boy at least three days to walk to Gin Gin. And carrying that heavy rug? On the other hand …

'Look, it's Friday today. What say I take you into Gayndah right now to meet the mail coach?'

'Don't you worry about me, Professor. I'm used to walking.'

'Look at it this way, Donald. What it costs for the fare you'll save in shoe leather. No, *I'll* save — I'm sure our contract said something about an allowance for work clothes. Besides, think what your mother's beautiful rug will look like after three days on that dusty road.'

He suspected it was this last argument that eventually persuaded Donald to accept his offer. 'Right, we'd better be going then. I think the coach leaves at about eleven.'

Ben Fuller stood up. 'I noticed last night your Belle was looking a bit lame, Prof — front right foot. Why don't you take my nag? He's built better for two anyway. I'll take a look at the foot while you're gone — probably just a stone.'

'Why thank you, Ben, I will. Donald, saddle up Mr Fuller's horse, would you?'

'And when I've finished with that, I might wander over and see what our dark-skinned companions are up to.'

'I'm afraid they might not understand you, Ben. None of them speaks English.'

'Oh, I know a few words of their lingo. I'll be right. So you take your time, Prof — and see if you can bring back a beer or two, would you?'

William and Donald arrived in Gayndah to find Billy Pike sitting in his usual place on the hotel veranda. In his hand, the usual bottle of beer. They dismounted and Donald untied his swag and another carefully wrapped bundle — after much persuasion he had agreed to borrow a sheet to keep the dust off the possum-skin rug.

'I've brought you a customer for the coach, Mr Pike,' said William.

'And changed bloody horses, I see.'

As Donald tied the black gelding to the rail, William was surprised to see Mary Brown appear from the door of the hotel. She, too, had a bottle in her hand.

'Good afternoon, Miss Brown. I trust you are well.'

'I'm well enough, thank you, Mr Caldwell.'

'And your sister?'

'My sister is unfortunately not so well.'

William expressed his sorrow at the news.

'It is just the usual thing — her headaches, you know. I was just visiting Mr Pike here to get something for her — a little brandy sometimes seems to help.'

'If I can be of any use,' said William, 'my own medicine chest is at your disposal.'

'Thank you again, Mr Caldwell. We shall certainly take up your offer if we need to. Now, please excuse me, I should get back.'

As Billy Pike returned he lifted a bottle of beer from the crate beside him and offered it to William.

'No thank you, Mr Pike.' William sat down beside him. 'Mr Pike, do you think there is anything else we can do for her — Miss Ettie, I mean?'

'Ah, those bloody headaches of hers. She says it isn't anything serious. I don't know.' Billy Pike shook his head and raised his bottle to his lips.

'Please let me know if you think of anything, Mr Pike. But here comes the coach. Are you expecting any passengers?'

Billy Pike turned to look down the street. 'Bloody hope not — almost down to my last beer. But if you'll excuse me, Mr Caldwell. I suppose I'd better give the driver a hand.'

By the time the publican had put down his bottle and heaved himself to his feet the coach was pulling up outside the hotel. No passengers alighted, but mailbags were exchanged and the driver began unhitching the horses. Donald appeared from the back of the hotel and helped Billy bring out fresh ones from the stables. William paid the driver Donald's fare. Just as the last horse was harnessed Donald climbed aboard and took the seat beside the driver. He held the rug, still wrapped up in its sheet, on his lap.

'I look forward to seeing you today fortnight,' said William. 'Please give my regards to your mother. It's a fine present you're taking her.'

'I will, Professor.'

With a shout from the driver and a clatter of hooves the mail coach departed, leaving William and Billy Pike alone on the hotel veranda.

'I should be getting along myself, Mr Pike. I have some stores to pick up and I realise supplies are tight — but would you be able to spare me ...?'

'Ben Fuller still out at your place?'

'Yes, he said he could stay for a few days. I'll be glad of his company while Donald's away.'

Billy Pike gave a deep sigh. 'So, I suppose that'll be two bloody bottles you're wanting.'

William left Gayndah with saddlebags bulging. Not with bottles of beer — Billy Pike had been adamant in allowing him only the two — but with extra supplies of flour and sugar he had picked up at the store to pay his Aboriginal helpers. Now that they were again bringing in an animal a day his original supplies were almost exhausted.

No one was waiting at the camp site when he arrived. Though Belle was there, tied up where he had left her, there was no sign of Ben Fuller — out with Daraga and his family no doubt. He felt a small loneliness. The camp site seemed doubly empty without Donald's cheery presence. Breakfast things lay on the table where they had been left that morning, a small curl of smoke drifted up from the ashes of the fire. Well, he should hardly expect a grown man like Ben Fuller to do domestic chores. There was nothing for it, he would have to tidy things up himself.

First, the washing up. No, first the water for the washing up. No, first the fire for the water for the washing up — oh dear, this really was quite complicated. Last night, what with beer and billiards, he and Ben had stayed up late. The woodpile was well down. He looked around. It seemed that all the dead wood within a hundred yards had already been burned. Perhaps back along the track would be a good place to start looking for more — at least then there would be a clear path to drag it along rather than through the bush.

There seemed little shortage of firewood in this part of Australia. Large branches, even whole trees, lay everywhere on the ground. Sometimes, it appeared, they remained standing for years. He supposed it was because of the climate. In Britain dead wood rotted almost as soon as it hit the ground; here the air was too dry for the mosses and fungi that were the great decomposers at home. On the other hand, in Australia there were termites. As far as William knew, Britain was as bereft of termites as it was of cicadas. Not soon after he had arrived at the camp site he had noticed a large brown extrusion growing high up on a gum tree. When he had asked Donald what it was, he had been told it was a 'niggerhead', an ants' nest. A little more questioning established that it was the nest of 'white' ants — termites. Now, as William began to gather his firewood, he came across the little insects everywhere. Every fallen log and branch concealed hundreds of them.

On one tree, not far from the track, he spotted one of the large nests high up on a broken branch. Though the tree seemed alive and healthy, its trunk was criss-crossed with a network of covered termite ways. Each tunnel looked only wide enough for a single file of insects — perhaps just wide enough for two to squeeze past each other — but dozens of these tunnels could be seen winding down the trunk and disappearing into the ground at the roots of the tree. When he scraped away the roof of one of the tunnels with his fingernail he could see the fat little worker termites within, and because their abdomens were almost transparent he could see that the ones coming down the tree had empty guts and the ones going up the tree had full ones. He was not able to watch them long. Blind though they were, they seemed to sense the breech in the tunnel. Within a few seconds the workers vanished. Strange, pointy-headed soldier termites clustered round the edge of the hole.

He was curious to see how the insects effected the repair: just how did such tiny insects build these yards and yards of tunnels, and that huge nest? Perhaps if he waited long enough he might see. Then he saw the ants. And so it was that William was witness not only to a building project, but to a battle.

nineteen

The supposed portions of egg-shell found by Lieutenant Maule in the nest were probably portions of excrement, coated, as in birds, with the salts of the urine, that secretion and faeces being expelled by the same orifice.
  W.J. Boderip, '*Ornithorhynchus*', *Penny Cyclopaedia*, 1840

'And do tell me, Mr Caldwell, what happened then?'
  Ettie Brown sat sipping tea in her usual chair on the veranda. After spending much of the previous night thinking about the poor girl and her headaches, William had decided to come into town. Perhaps some quinine or laudanum from his medicine chest might be of use. He had been pleased to hear from Mary Brown that Billy Pike's brandy had at least helped her sister to sleep, and though Ettie's head still hurt she was 'on the mend'. Mary was now in the kitchen making more tea while William sat outside with the convalescent. He had already told her how, in trying to see termites build their tunnels, he had removed a piece of the roof.
  'The worker termites soon disappeared and the soldiers arrived. But what I hadn't noticed were the ants. Not two feet away — though I suppose that might be a hundred yards to a termite — was a column of ants, marching up the tree. Single ants were scurrying about on either side — outriders, as it were — and it was one of

these that came across the breach in the tunnel. I saw it pause, wave its antennae around a bit, then hurry back to the column. Within seconds there were twenty ants surrounding the hole.'

'Oh, but why? Were they going to kill them?'

'I had no doubt that was their intention, Miss Ettie. As I understand it more or less anything is food to an ant. They were well armed, too — their jaws can, as I am sure you know, pierce human skin. They would have no difficulty in crushing a termite. But then the soldier termites attacked. I should explain that as far as I could see the soldier termites had no jaws to speak of and are of course quite, er ... blind.'

That pause, that little hesitation. She must have noticed. Oh, damn and blast. He had only thought of it as he was saying it. Why did he have to mention that they were blind? The girl looked at him, and he noticed that she was smiling.

'Bravo, Mr Caldwell.'

'Bravo, Miss Ettie?'

'Mr Caldwell, we have known each other how long now — six weeks, seven? You have known since you first met me that I am blind. We have met and talked together often, and I very much value our talks. But sometimes I feel that there is something missing.'

'You must forgive me, I, er ...'

'Mr Caldwell, it is not good. I noticed you pause then. You tried to avoid saying the word — out of delicacy, out of politeness? I do hope it was not out of pity. There is nothing that I need less than pity, Mr Caldwell, and if I may say so, especially not yours.'

'I only thought —'

'You thought that I did not wish to hear about blind creatures, being a blind creature myself? Did you not think that the reverse might be true, that I might be particularly interested in the challenges and achievements of other blind creatures?'

William looked into her blue eyes. He took a deep breath. 'You do right to chastise me, Miss Ettie. I would certainly never wish that your, er ... blindness ...'

'Try again, Mr Caldwell.'

He took another deep breath. 'That your blindness should come between us.'

The girl smiled again. 'Good. So, pray continue, Mr Caldwell. I am eager to hear the end of your tale.'

'Ah yes, where was I? The ants, yes. The ants began their attack. I had taken out my lens the better to see what was happening but they took no notice of me. And I was amazed to see that the soldier termites were not being crushed and carried off. No, on the contrary, it was the ants that seemed to be in trouble. I watched one of them. It ran towards a soldier termite — ants can see very well, apparently — but as soon as it touched the termite it jerked backward and stopped. It began rubbing its head and antennae with its front legs. But then it couldn't move its front legs. It was as if they were stuck to its head.'

'How strange.'

'Strange indeed, Miss Ettie. I watched another ant and the same thing happened. With my lens I could now see that its legs had indeed been stuck to its head — I could see little strings of glue as it tried to pull its legs away.'

'It was the termites, then, that were behind all this?'

'I am sure of it. I have since examined one of the soldier termites under the microscope. Its head seems to contain a large sac, a sort of reservoir for this remarkable glue that it can squirt from the tip of its strange snout. I thought this most wonderful.'

'So do I. But what happened to them, and what happened to the ants?'

'The ants retreated. Somehow they seemed to get the message of danger and no more tried to attack. Most of the soldier termites went back through the hole and then the repair party arrived. In less than half an hour, the hole was mended.'

'But how, Mr Caldwell? You must tell me how.'

William gave a small cough. 'Well, I suppose that was in itself wonderful in a way. I could see the workers — who are also blind, Miss Brown — trundling up to the hole and feeling around it with their antennae. Then they'd turn around and squirt out a blob of — well, I suppose it's just chewed-up wood really — from the end of their abdomens onto the edge of the hole and then turn around again and sort of mould it with their mouthparts.'

He looked hard for any signs that this coprophagic turn to the conversation was embarrassing the girl. He found none. 'As I say, within thirty minutes the job was done.'

'But tell me, Mr Caldwell, the soldiers. Did they all get back inside before the hole was finally patched?'

'I know that several of them remained outside while the hole was being repaired. Whether they got back later I cannot say, but I rather fear not.'

'Noble creatures,' said the girl. 'I wonder what your Mr Darwin would have to say about that.'

'I confess that I have wondered about it myself. Cooperation and competition do not fit well together — in terms of Darwin's theory, at least.'

'Tell me, Mr Caldwell. Do we fit into Mr Darwin's theory?'

'How do you mean?'

'We humans. Are we, too, subject to the forces of natural selection? Do only the fittest of us survive?'

William paused. 'I think I would have to answer that question with both a yes and a no. Yes, in that we are organisms that have evolved from other organisms, in the same way that all life's forms have evolved. No, in that we seem to have a unique trait, characteristic, call it what you like, that gives us the opportunity to step aside from the path. To choose our own destiny, if you will.'

'The opportunity, but perhaps not the necessity.'

'Indeed so, Miss Ettie.'

'And this trait, this characteristic?'

'Intellect, self-consciousness, free will — I believe they are all aspects of the same underlying attribute.'

'And love, Mr Caldwell?'

'I'm not sure where love fits in.'

The girl smiled and leant back in her chair. At that moment the door opened and her sister appeared. On the tray she was carrying not only a pot of tea but a plate piled high with biscuits.

'Just made them. You'll have one, won't you, Mr Caldwell?'

While she poured the tea he passed the plate to Ettie Brown.

'Perhaps Mr Caldwell would like a few biscuits to take back with him, Mary.'

'I've already thought of that. There's another tray in the oven. I'll just go and see if they're ready.'

'Do you suppose they mind, Mr Caldwell?' said Ettie Brown as her sister went back into the house.

'Mind? Who mind — mind what?'

'The termites. I was thinking of the ones that were left outside the nest. They will surely die. Do you think they mind dying?'

Another of those infuriating questions — so innocent and childlike, yet so complex. But before he could think of an answer the girl continued.

'Would you like to hear what I think is the main difference between us and other animals?'

'Indeed, Miss Ettie.'

'It is simply this. We know that we are going to die. That is the difference. We don't know when we are going to die — surely nothing could be worse than knowing exactly when you were going to die — but we know that we will.'

Wasn't that what Ben Fuller had said, or what his mate Charlie had said to the judge in that story of his? 'I don't mind dying, I just don't want to know when.'

The girl gave him another smile — such a lovely smile — then her face became serious. 'I don't think I will mind dying.'

'You are a young woman, Miss Ettie, for such dark thoughts.'

'But I know death, Mr Caldwell. When I was very sick as a young child I was in a sort of coma, they tell me. I could breathe and I could eat and drink, but I could not hear or speak — or see, of course — and I have no memory of the time. Is that not death? And so it is for all of us, is it not? Each day — or should I say each night — we die, and each morning we are born again.'

'But if you breathed, and you ate and drank, then you were not dead.'

'Not to those looking from the outside, but I was dead inside. I think that is what death means. Death is not an observation, it is a personal experience. No, perhaps I should say that dying is a personal experience. Death is an absence of experience.'

'Do you not believe in the life hereafter, Miss Ettie?'

'I have no reason to. I have reason not to. It is strange, Mr Caldwell, that in all those years with Reverend Bentham he never once asked that question.'

'Not even in the Sunday service?'

The girl thought for a moment. 'Of course, you are quite right — the Creed of the Apostles: "I believe in the Holy Ghost, the Holy Catholic Church, the Communion of Saints, the forgiveness of sins, the resurrection of the body and the life everlasting." Yes, every Sunday the same. But I am not sure that we were really being expected to make a statement. More receive a reassurance.' She turned her eyes towards him. 'And you, Mr Caldwell?'

'Do I believe? I have no reason to, and I have no reason not to. Perhaps I am what Mr Huxley would call an agnostic.'

'I don't know your Mr Huxley.'

'He is a zoologist, a friend of Darwin. I have his books somewhere — perhaps you would like to …'

He was about to say 'perhaps you would like to read them'. How could he keep on forgetting like this?

'You will tell me about them another time, I am sure,' said the girl. 'And if I ask whether you fear death?'

'Perhaps on that I am again an agnostic. I know death is inevitable — in some ways it is indispensable.'

'Indispensable?'

'In the sense that it is the driving force behind evolution. Natural selection is no more than nature's choice of who will live and who will die.'

The girl shook her head. 'No, no, Mr Caldwell. You have already agreed that we all will die.'

'You are right. I should have said, who will reproduce and who will not.'

'That's better. But what is important is not death but birth, don't you think?'

'The opposite, you mean?' said William.

'No, not the opposite. Not the coming from nothing to something. I mean coming from the womb to the world. From a warm, dark, comfortable safety into the cold, bright world. What must that be like — do any of us remember? Why not?'

William was not sure that he could answer this question either. Was it linked with the girl's own experience, of making the other journey — from light to darkness?'

Perhaps sensing his discomfort, she said, 'Marsupials do it so much better, don't you think?'

'Marsupials?'

'Oh, do think Mr Caldwell.' It was the girl who now seemed exasperated. 'You have told me yourself that marsupials develop in the womb just as other mammals. But then what? They are born and they go straight into the pouch. Is this not another womb, a warm, dark, comfortable place?'

The girl hesitated, clasping her hands on her lap. 'When I was a little child — before I was blind — we had a pet kangaroo. Her name was Jinks. She lived around the house — inside and outside, she was free to come and go. And one day we noticed — it was so exciting — that she had a joey in her pouch. We hadn't even known she was pregnant, never mind that she had given birth. When I saw the little head poking from her pouch I was so surprised, so pleased. I spent all my time with Jinks, watching. If her joey didn't like what it saw, or wanted a rest or some milk, it would duck down into the pouch again — back to the warm, dark womb. So you see, Mr Caldwell, for a kangaroo being born is a gradual process, getting used to the world little by little.'

'I must say that I had never thought of it like that before,' said William. 'But what you say is quite right, Miss Ettie. It is a most civilised arrangement.'

'Perhaps that is why we sleep, Mr Caldwell — have you ever thought of that? Perhaps sleep is a "civilised arrangement", as you put it, to get us used, little by little, for death.'

'I must say that the function of sleep has long eluded my comprehension, Miss Ettie. I think I might be getting a little nearer understanding.'

The girl gave a long sigh and unclasped her hands. 'I sometimes wonder just what your professors taught you at Cambridge, Mr Caldwell.'

'So do I, Miss Ettie,' said William. 'So do I.' And he half meant it.

'Thank you so much for telling me your story, Mr Caldwell, about the termites. It was as though I was seeing it for myself.'

'Miss Ettie, I can imagine no higher praise.'

'Now, there is one further thing.' Her blind eyes turned again towards him.

'Yes, Miss Ettie?'

'I would very much appreciate it if you would not call me Miss Ettie.'

'Then what should I call you?'

'Well, let us think.' A pause, and a strange half-smile. 'I think Ettie would be nice, Mr Caldwell. Just Ettie.'

Ben Fuller's disappointment at discovering that William had failed to return from Gayndah with more than two bottles of beer was matched by William's own disappointment at finding no platypuses waiting for him.

'I'm going to need more specimens than this, Ben. Perhaps I should ask Mary Brown to speak to Daraga about it for me.'

'Mary Brown?' said Ben.

William remembered that he had not yet mentioned the two sisters. 'Yes, a woman in town. She speaks their language, you know. She's been most helpful.'

'Oh, I see. How much did you say you pay them, the blacks?'

'We agreed on a shilling for males, two shillings for females. Or the equivalent in stores, of course.'

Ben appeared to think this over. 'Look, Prof,' he said at last. 'Why don't you leave it to me? I'll have a word with them myself — we'll sort something out. I told you I can speak some of their lingo.'

'Why, thank you, Ben,' said William. 'That would be most kind. You certainly seem to have found no problem communicating with Daraga and his family.'

'I've always been able to make myself understood with our ebony brothers, one way or another. And that Daraga and me, we understand each other just fine.'

And so it appeared. Over the next days the supply of specimens rose to such an extent that William once more had little time for anything other than working on his dissections (though Ben usually managed to cajole him into a game of billiards each evening, and usually — though not always — seemed to end up the winner). In the morning Ben would weigh out the flour and sugar for payment, and every afternoon he would return with the day's catch. But while William could just keep up with the scientific work, the culinary challenge of consuming the skinned and eviscerated specimens was proving too much for him. Despite his promise, William could not eat all the platypuses that were now appearing. His companion was no help.

'No food for a white man' had been Ben's comment when William had first suggested he might like to sample some platypus stew. He had refused even to taste the dish, and he clearly could not work out why William ate it so avidly. (William did not mention his promise to Ettie Brown.)

'But look, Prof. I dare say Daraga and his mob could do with some fresh meat.'

Why hadn't he thought of that before?

'Leave it to me,' said Ben with a smile.

Another weight off his mind. Besides his scientific work William had also taken a leaf out of Donald's book. With so many platypuses coming in it seemed wrong to waste the beautiful fur, so before each dissection William removed the skin from each animal and pegged it out just as he had seen Donald doing with his possums. Perhaps he would even have enough to take home a platypus-skin rug. And Miss Ettie — Ettie — would surely approve of his making good use of every part of the specimens.

William was woken in the night by the sound of rain. He lay listening and thinking, his thoughts revolving equally around the danger of another flood, and around Ettie Brown. He very much hoped that she was feeling better. But he had done all he could for her, and he would surely hear if anything was amiss. He lay thinking and listening for what may have been an hour (he could not be bothered to light a match to check his watch), but eventually, lulled by the soft sound of rain falling on canvas, fell back into a deep sleep. When he awoke and pulled back the flap of his tent the sun was already glinting through the trunks of the trees, and its light revealed a most wondrous sight. Raindrops still clung to every leaf and sparkled in the sunlight, while dancing in the air all around were hundreds and hundreds of gauze-winged insects, catching the light like flying jewels.

One tiny fairy creature danced its way into his tent and landed on his bed. It immediately began scurrying in circles and figures of eight, as if searching for something of great importance. It was slender and brown, about half an inch long with four filmy wings now folded flat along its back. The little insect stopped and gave a little shake, and William was surprised to see one of its wings fall off. It shook itself again and another wing fell, then another and another. It seemed to feel no discomfort in losing these appendages — indeed William had the impression it was pleased to be at last disencumbered. The now wingless creature resumed its scurrying around his blanket.

William was not at all sure what kind of insect it was. Though in some ways it resembled an earwig, it had no pincers at the end of its abdomen and its wings were quite different in both number and form from the wonderful folding structures of earwigs (the very ones that had convinced William Paley — and for a short time William Caldwell — of the existence of God). It looked a little like an ant, but had not the narrow waist between thorax and abdomen so distinctive of members of the hymenoptera. If it was not an earwig or an ant, though, what was it? William found his lens and picked the little thing up between finger and thumb. It's body was soft, its legs weak. Holding the insect close to the lens he was able to see its head in some detail. Small jaws, antennae like little strings of beads, a round eye on either side. It reminded William of some other insect he had recently seen — what was it? Of course, the termites. It must be a flying termite.

William rummaged around in the back of his mind for what he could remember about termites. Social insects, probably related to cockroaches rather than ants — though similar communal style of living. These little flying things dancing around outside, they must all be winged reproductives. He put the creature back down on the blanket where it resumed its hurried quest. Another dropped down beside it. The pair paused for only a moment while the second insect shrugged off its wings, then both began scurrying round in tandem, the second insect following the first like a tender to a steam engine. And William remembered that in the heart of every termite colony was not just a queen but a king. Unlike ants and wasps and bees, the female did not store up sperm from her single mating. She lived her whole life with her chosen mate. All around him, all through the bush, kings and queens were finding each other and going off in search of new nest-sites.

A small, grey bird fluttered from a branch, pirouetted in mid-air and returned to its perch. Sticking out from each side of its small beak like a brown moustache were the wings of the termite it had caught. A larger bird — a wattlebird, he thought — swooped through the air and snapped up another with a loud click of its bill. Various other unidentified honeyeaters, warblers and flycatchers were doing much the same. In fact as William walked out of his tent it seemed that every bird in the bush was there. They had arrived for a feast, and the feast was termites.

On the ground a kookaburra and a currawong pecked and pounced on insects that had already landed, ignoring each other in their search for food. The local gang of choughs arrived, ten of them, striding and squawking through the litter, tossing leaves and twigs this way and that with their curved black bills and picking up termites by the dozen. A bird that William had often seen and that Donald was adamant should be called a robin — though its breast was not red but primrose yellow — plucked a termite from the air and returned to its sideways perch on the trunk of a small wattle tree. Then a bird that William had never seen before appeared.

Though not much larger than a thrush, it had a stumpy body and short tail. As it hopped into a patch of sunlight its plumage gleamed like a rainbow. Green wings with flashes of sky blue, yellow breast and a patch of the brightest red beneath its tail. It bobbed its dark head, flicked its tail once and was gone. Then another piece of rainbow detached itself from a branch high above William and glided towards him on sharp triangular wings. As it banked and turned William could see blues, greens, oranges and yellows even brighter than the bird on the ground. The bird snatched a flying termite from the air with a beak like a pair of fine curved forceps and returned to its perch. Now William could see a long tail and a face masked like a dancer at a fancy-dress ball. The bird tossed the insect back into its throat and immediately flew off, upwards this time, to catch another. William could hear the click as the two halves of its beak snapped together. But before it could regain its perch there was a much louder bang. The beautiful bird fell from the air in a tumble of feathers, and William turned to see Ben Fuller lowering his gun.

'Not a bad shot, eh, Prof — though I says it m'self what shouldn't.' Ben Fuller picked up the dead bird from the ground.

'Seen a rainbow bird before? Pretty, ain't they? I'll get two bob for that skin in Bundy.' And seeing the look of incomprehension on William's face, he said, 'They put 'em on women's hats, see? All the fashion in Paris, they say.'

William was finding it difficult to think of the right words to speak. Only moments ago the bird had been a living miracle of light and colour. Now it was a bundle of dead feathers in Ben Fuller's hand. He turned back towards his tent.

'Flying ants — sign of more rain, the darkies say,' said Ben. He looked up at the clear sky. 'Still, they're not always right are they, our sable chums?'

William wetted his shaving brush. There was no reason at all why Ben Fuller should not have shot the bird. He stared at himself in the small mirror. True, Ben had not done it in pursuit of scientific knowledge. Nor had he done it for food.

He took the lid off the soap dish and worked up a lather. But it was not as if Ben killed the bird simply for amusement. He brushed the lather onto his face and picked up the razor. As Ben had said, it was worth two shillings. That its feathers would be used to adorn a woman's hat half a world away from where the bird had lived and died, that was not the point.

He shaved carefully around his moustache, first one side, then the other, and stood back to admire the effect. Two shillings was two shillings. Who was he to deny a man the means of earning a living?

William pulled down the skin of his neck. And who was he to tell Ben what he could and could not do in his own country? He should be grateful — he *was* grateful — that Ben Fuller had offered to help at all.

Upward strokes for neck, downward for cheeks. And a great help he had been, bringing him all the way to Gayndah, and choosing the camp site so well. And especially being able to talk to the Aborigines.

William splashed his face with water and reached for the towel. By the time he had put away his shaving things and dressed, he had managed to put all discomforting thoughts about dead beautiful birds from his mind. All except one. It was only a small one. What — he could not help but wonder as he sat down, newly shaven, to a breakfast of tea and damper with a cheerful Ben Fuller — what would Ettie have said?

twenty

The only chance of success is to get specimens at all seasons, pickle them and send them over: one hundred would not be too many, if we could thereby settle the disputed question, oviparous, ovoviviparous, or viviparous? & how the young suck.
Letter from Doctor Richard Owen to Major Thomas Mitchell, 29 March 1840

The fat, brown fly buzzed past William's nose. It twice circled the table where he was working then dropped down to where the dead platypus lay pinned onto the board, skinned and eviscerated. In another moment the fly was gone.

'Here you are, Ben. A perfect example of ovoviviparity.'

A north wind had brought warmer weather, and with it had come the flies. William had heard and read much about the famous flies of Australia. Had not William Dampier, the first Englishman to set foot on Australian soil, been 'sadly pester'd with the Flies', and it seemed that almost every other visitor since had commented on them. But it was not bush flies that were the problem at the moment so much as the blowflies — these fat brown insects with a loud buzz that, although they did not fly about your face with quite the persistence of their smaller cousins, were most skilful at finding and contaminating any dead thing. They could land

and be away in seconds, leaving behind a mass of tiny squirming maggots.

'Ovo ... what did you say, Prof?'

'Ovoviviparity. We were talking about it yesterday. As I said, most insects are like birds. They are oviparous — they lay eggs out of which the young hatch. These blowflies are ovoviviparous — their eggs hatch inside them and they lay young larvae, just like that one has just done on this platypus. The Paris Professor thinks that platypuses are oviparous, the London Professor thinks that they are ovoviviparous.'

'I see. Well, I think I see. And what do you think, Prof?'

Ben walked over to the table and leant over to inspect the dissection. 'I don't know, Ben, I don't know.' William scooped up the minuscule maggots with the end of his scalpel. 'Platypuses are definitely mammals — they have fur, they're warm-blooded, they have milk glands. But some of their internal anatomy, especially their reproductive system — well, you've seen for yourself. It looks uncommonly like that of a reptile.'

'Anyone here'll tell you that duckbills lay eggs.'

'Yes. But most people round here still seem to think that a baby kangaroo grows from its mother's nipple. That's why we need science, Ben. We need proof. That's why I'm here.'

But before he could solve the problem of platypus reproduction he needed to solve the blowfly problem. It was Ben who came up with the answer, a special tent — perhaps more a gazebo, thought William — made of mosquito netting that they rigged up around the dissection table.

With a steady supply of platypuses coming in the two men had fallen into a daily pattern. After an early breakfast Ben would leave to join the hunt, arriving back at about lunchtime with that day's specimens — usually one platypus, sometimes two. William would immediately begin his dissection, cutting out the reproductive organs and putting them into the first bath of fixative. Each set had to be individually treated through the various stages of fixing and preserving — three baths of ethanol of increasing concentration at two hours each (it was lucky Harry Norton had only sampled the one bottle — now that William had really started his work it was surprising just how much of the stuff he was getting through), then two baths of methanol followed by fifteen minutes in Humbolt's solution and fifteen in his own special stain — three parts bromophenol blue to two parts methyl orange to ten parts methanol — which he now knew from experiment to be the mixture that would best differentiate embryonic from parental tissue. Finally the samples went into a paraffin bath ready for sectioning the following morning. The specimens had to soak in paraffin at least overnight so that they would be ready for the next process, the cutting of each one into the thin sections that were necessary for microscopical examination.

Other than his microscope, the most valuable object William had brought with him to Australia was his Janz automatic microtome. Each morning after breakfast he would set it up on the billiard table (now covered with polished mahogany top and oilcloth) and begin the delicate work of preparing the sections. In Cambridge he had developed a method of coating the hard paraffin in which the prepared specimen was embedded with a layer of softer wax so that the sections would stick one to the other as they were shaved off by the microtome blade. He was pleased to see that despite the increasing heat, the method seemed to work just as well in the Australian bush as in his English laboratory.

'Looks like hard work to me, Prof,' said Ben Fuller as he watched William turning the handle of the microtome with one hand and with the other laying out the strip of sections onto a glass slide.

'All it takes is a bit of practice, Ben — and goodness knows I've had enough of that.'

After smoothing out the batch of freshly cut sections with a camel-hair brush and covering them with a drop of glycerol and a thin glass slip, he wrote out the label and put the slide into a tray. He still had more slides to prepare, but first he should take a look at the specimens Ben had just brought in. Two more females — a good eight hours' work. There would be no billiards tonight. It had been the same the day before, and the day before that. Still, he had not come to Australia to play billiards.

'Well, while you're busy, Prof,' said Ben, picking up his gun, 'I might just wander off and see if I can find a few specimens of my own. And maybe see how our jet-skinned companions are getting on — all right with you?'

There was no doubt that Ben seemed to be getting on well with Daraga and his family. As well as joining them each morning on the hunt for platypuses, after dinner he would often head over towards their distant fires, sometimes not arriving back until after William was abed and asleep. Ben had taken over the job of both collecting the specimens and paying for them. Before he left camp he stuffed a few supplies in his saddlebag for distribution to the hunters.

'See you later, Prof. Don't do nothing I wouldn't do.'

William looked down at the two animals now on the table before him. After another hour at the microtome and a bite to eat, he would be ready to start on the dissecting. There should be time to look at the new slides under the microscope after dinner.

At seven o'clock that night Ben had not returned from the blacks' camp, and by the time William had finished his dissections and preparations and pegged out his skins he was too tired even to boil a billy. After some cold damper and water he went straight to bed. No matter, he thought as he fell asleep, he would look at the slides tomorrow. And Donald would be back soon.

There was no sign of Ben at the camp when William rose the next morning. The fire was out and Belle was tied up alone. William supposed he should feed her. He found a bag of oats then went down to the river to fill her bucket. The river seemed slightly up, though he was sure it had not rained overnight at the camp. He looked towards the west. No, no signs of rain — just a few white clouds on the distant rim of an otherwise clear blue sky. And still no sign of Ben. Well, it was a grand day, perhaps he would go for a little stroll along the riverbank. He had been missing his daily walk. Not far, not for long. And with any luck Ben would be boiling the billy by the time he got back.

He wandered down to the river and along the riverbank as far as a large river red gum. This tree had become one of his favourites. Huge and gnarled, it must have been there for centuries. It was the tree the choughs roosted on at night, as no doubt had countless of their ancestors. It was also where they had built their nest, an enormous mud structure plastered firmly to a branch hanging out over the river. Apparently the whole group of them used this one nest — exactly what were the domestic arrangements that made this possible, Donald had not been able to say and William could not imagine. A little rest, then it would be time to turn back. There was work to be done. No sooner had he sat down in the shade of some tea-trees than a dark bird appeared.

At first William thought it was a chough. But when it passed through a patch of sunlight he saw it was not black but the deepest blue. And it was too small for a chough, or a crow. He stopped, motionless. That the bird had seen him he had no doubt: its movements were wary, it kept its head cocked towards him. But still it came closer and closer until he could see that the eye that was directed at him was not red nor orange nor yellow, but a bright sapphire.

The bird made a quick movement with its head and picked something from the ground. A feather. For a moment William was puzzled — surely no bird eats feathers? He chided himself gently; of course, the bird was collecting for its nest. It took three long hops and put the feather down. It looked up at him, picked up the feather and replaced it in a different position. William noticed other feathers on the ground. The bird took another hop, and vanished.

No, it hadn't vanished; it had gone behind what looked like a miniature fence. The bird hopped out again. It seemed to have forgotten William now, and busied itself rearranging some of the feathers on the ground. He counted two white feathers and seven blue. The blue ones must have come from a parrot — a rosella, probably — the white ones from a cockatoo, perhaps. The bird went back behind the fence, out from the other side and back to the front. It raised its beak towards the trees and began to sing.

Even while he was listening to the song William was trying to describe it in his head — and he was having some difficulty. He had never heard such a strange amalgam of music and noise, soft then loud, sweet then raucous, and with a sprinkling of what sounded to William like the calls of other birds. A snatch of a kookaburra's laugh, a currawong's loud whistle. The singing and mimicry continued for what seemed many minutes.

Though his attention was focused on this extraordinary performer, out of the corner of his eye he noticed another bird appear. It was similar in shape and size but dull green in colour. Its eye was if anything an even brighter blue than the first bird's. For a few moments it sat on a low branch a few feet from the singer, then glided onto the ground and scurried behind the fence. The dark bird stopped its singing. The fence was not solid. Despite the shadows William could dimly see the green bird crouching behind it, wings slightly spread, tail raised. The other bird raced around and behind the fence, and gently climbed onto its back. It was clear that they were mating.

William was familiar with the process of mating. As a child he had observed sticklebacks, newts, dragonflies — and on one memorable occasion through a train window, horses — *in copulo*. At university, he had studied animal and human physiology. He knew all about sex. He had examined microscope sections of both the human male testis and epididymis and could describe the route that spermatozoa must follow in order to reach the ovum — along the vas deferens, past its junction with the seminal vesicle, prostate gland and Cowper's gland, and into the urethra. He knew perfectly well that fertilisation in mammals, including humans, was achieved when the male's penis, in tumescent condition, was inserted into the female's vagina and that stimulation due to friction between that organ and the walls of the vagina caused muscular convulsion of smooth muscles in the accessory glands so that the sperm, now suspended in seminal fluid, was ejaculated onto the cervix. But in all his four and twenty years, he had never yet experienced it for himself.

This circumstance did not exist for his want of trying — or rather, for want of other people trying. Charles Gilbert, his Cambridge friend, had often stated that a firsthand knowledge of sex was a necessary part of every young man's education — why, it was almost as much fun as lying in bed in the morning — and that the world abounded in women only too pleased to act the role of teacher if only you knew where to find them. On one notable and somewhat embarrassing occasion even Uncle Angas had suggested the experiment. It had been William's eighteenth birthday, and after a particularly long lunch at the club, involving two bottles of Krug and an equal number of Château Beychevelle, his uncle had said that he knew of an establishment, 'off Greek Street — just a stroll away', that could always be relied upon to supply an afternoon's entertainment for gentlemen of discernment. William had feigned feeling unwell, but the truth was he was just not interested. Or was it that he found the whole thing slightly distasteful? But human sex was one thing; animal sex was another. This was not embarrassing: it was fascinating.

The two birds behind the fence spent just seconds at their task. The dark bird (which he now knew to be a male) jumped off the female's back. With a ruffle of feathers both hopped out from behind the fence. The female once more shook her feathers and flew off. The male again picked up and dropped one of the blue feathers then also flew off. William stood and looked. The fence: could it have been made by the birds he had just seen?

The first thing he discovered as he walked around the structure was that it was not as he had been imagining it. Because he had been viewing it from the side, he had not noticed that there was not one but two rows of twigs stuck vertically into the ground, one beside the other, forming a short avenue. The avenue was just over a foot long, its walls no higher than the middle of his calf — though the top ends of the sticks curved over almost into a tunnel. The area where he had seen the male bird arranging the feathers looked as though it had first been cleared of debris, then deliberately strewn (decorated?) with not only feathers but sticks and pebbles, and two empty snail shells, bleached white. William got down on hands and knees to examine it more closely.

The avenue was most cleverly constructed, the twigs pushed firmly into the soil and held together with some kind of dark glue. He could not imagine how a bird could accomplish so intricate a task — but Australian animals were full of surprises. Perhaps if he waited he would find out more. There was a fallen log not ten feet from the front of the avenue. It was in the shade and would make a more comfortable seat than the bare ground.

Moments after he had sat down the male bird reappeared. It was carrying something in its beak, a small bunch of blue berries of a type that William had often noticed growing on a grass-like shrub but had not yet put a name to. The bird dropped the berries near one of the white shells. It picked them up and dropped them several times before it seemed satisfied with the arrangement, and in this process one of the berries fell from the bunch. The bird picked it up and tossed it towards the back of its beak as if it were going to swallow it. The berry was then squashed and chewed and squashed and chewed, occasionally being dropped onto the ground where the increasingly glutinous pulp became mixed with the dark dry soil. Taking up the muddy mess in its beak, the bird began smearing it over the inside of one of the rows of twigs.

Once this job was finished the bird resumed its place at the front of the avenue. And once again a female appeared — whether it was the same female William could not be sure. She crept between the two rows of sticks, the male gave a brief burst of song and rushed around the back. But this time he did not mount her. As he was going to the back of avenue she ran, then flew, out of the front. William could not help smiling. Overconfidence, he thought, rising to his feet. The lady needs more wooing than that brief serenade.

When he returned to camp there was still no sign of Ben. Oh well, there was plenty to do. He set up the equipment for his morning work and was soon engrossed in the routine of preparing slides. He would look at these ones under the microscope later, and yesterday's, too. It was important to see what stage of development they had reached. Before he knew it the sun was high up in the sky and he realised that he was hungry. He had had no breakfast. The completed slides were laid out on the table, labelled and ordered. A cup of tea was what he needed. He should start a fire.

True, the wood had been nice and dry, and true, he had no sooner started laying down the twigs on the ashes than the coals buried beneath ignited them. But William couldn't help feel satisfaction at seeing the burst of flame and hearing the crackle of the wood. By feeding on more wood he soon had a fine bed of coals — a real 'cooking fire' as Donald would have said. This bushman business wasn't really so hard after all. He grabbed the billy and went down to the river (yes, it was definitely up a little). Soon the billy was on the fire and the tea-leaves in the pot. Perhaps now, while the water boiled, might be the time to have a look at some of those slides.

By the time he had taken the microscope from its box and adjusted the three mirrors to reflect just the right amount of sunlight up through the stage he thought it might be time to check the billy. It was nowhere near boiling. Perhaps he had filled it a little too full. He fed more wood onto the fire. Now, those slides. But no sooner was the first slide on the microscope than he heard the sound of horse's hoofs. He looked up, expecting to see Ben Fuller. He was surprised to see Mary Brown in the familiar gig. And delighted to see that Ettie was sitting beside her, and looking very much better.

'We find you alone, Mr Caldwell,' said Mary Brown. 'I had expected to meet your visitor.'

She would have heard about Ben Fuller's arrival from Billy Pike.

'Alone no longer, Miss Brown, Miss Ettie. How delightful to see you. I fear Mr Fuller is away from camp at the moment, but as you can see, I'm about to make tea. I trust you will join me for a cup.'

He looked over to the fire. Steam was at last rising from beneath the lid of the billy. Almost as soon as he lifted it from the fire he gave a stifled yelp as his fingers felt the heat. He dropped it. With an embarrassing clang the billy hit a rock and rolled onto its side. The lid fell open and boiling water hissed into the fire.

'Don't tell me, dear sister,' said Ettie Brown. 'I think I can paint the picture in my head.'

William took a deep breath. His blush would soon fade.

'So you were expecting us, Mr Caldwell?'

'I confess I was not, Miss Ettie,' said William, poking at the handle of the billy with a stick in an attempt to rescue it from the ashes of the fire. 'But I have been thinking of you.'

Mary Brown took the stick from William's hand and deftly hooked it under the handle. 'Why don't I fill this,' she said. 'And I think your fire could do with a little more wood, Mr Caldwell.'

He managed eventually to get the fire going again and soon the billy was once more boiling. Mary Brown took charge of making the tea while William showed Ettie to her usual seat.

'You look well, Miss Ettie. May I assume that you are feeling better?'

'Much better, thank you, Mr Caldwell. And all due to your kindness. I'm not sure if it was the quinine or the laudanum, but one of them seems to have effected quite a cure.'

'Perhaps it was the combination.'

'Perhaps it was. But I thought we had agreed that you would call me Ettie. I think we have known each other long enough, and I'm sure my sister will not disapprove.'

'On the contrary, Mr Caldwell,' said Mary Brown. 'And as we two have known each other almost as long, perhaps you would call me Mary.'

'I would be delighted, Miss Brown — Mary. And I hope you will both do me the honour of calling me William.'

'And what have you been discovering since we last saw you, William?' said Ettie Brown.

He knew what would happen if he started talking about copulation, if only between birds. 'Nothing of note, I'm afraid. I seem to have been spending all my time preparing specimens.'

Mary Brown asked him to describe the process, and he went through each step of fixing and staining the delicate tissues of the platypus reproductive system.

'The ethanol removes the water, you see, then the methanol removes the ethanol and is the best solvent for the stains to work in. Then the methanol is displaced by the paraffin, which fixes the tissues ready for sectioning.'

'Ethanol? Methanol? What are these things, William?'

William explained that ethanol was spirits of wine, derived from fermented sugar. 'It's the common alcohol of beer and wine and rum. But methanol is wood spirit, distilled from turpentine.'

'Is it also an intoxicant?'

'I believe so, though it has an unfortunate after-effect.'

'What is that, William?'

William averted his eyes from her sightless stare. 'It makes you blind,' he said.

'Then I shall not drink rum with my hot water and lemon, I shall drink methanol. Perhaps, for me, it will have the reverse effect.' She laughed, and William could not help laughing with her. And when the tea was finally made and poured he decided to describe his recent encounter with the blue-eyed bird.

'Ah, a bowerbird. In the old language its name is Karmi — am I right, Mary? Will you tell William the story?'

'Karmi was an earth spirit. He stole a cloud from Narla the sky spirit, for his bed. As punishment Narla sent down lightning and burned him black, but he didn't learn his lesson. He still tries to steal pieces of white cloud and blue sky from Narla.'

'Mary knows all the old stories, Mr Caldwell — William.'

'It is delightful,' said William. 'And are there stories about the platypus?'

'I know only a little about Dinderi. Dinderi lived in the dreamtime, and his people and the sea snakes were enemies. He chased the sea snakes up the river, but they caught him and turned him into the first platypus. There are stories about all the animals, William. All the animals, all the places. To Aboriginal people, you might say the whole world is one big story.'

'I would very much like to know more.'

'The stories are not for everyone to hear,' said Mary.

William was hoping that the two women would talk more about the old stories but was not sure how — or if — he should ask. He decided to say nothing, and the subject of the conversation turned back to how his own work was progressing.

'I remember you explaining the microscope,' said Ettie, 'but this microtome you talk about. What is it for?'

'It cuts thin sections, for looking at with the microscope.'

'Thin sections of what?'

'Oh, anything from a beetle to a bat's ear. As long as it will fit on the stage, and is properly fixed. You secure your specimen on this stage, you see, and by turning the handle you make it pass across the blade, shaving off a section. The blade must be razor-sharp, of course. Some people even use the edge of a piece of broken glass. And after every turn of the handle the stage moves up just a fraction of a fraction of an inch and it shaves off the next section.'

Ettie took great interest in the operation of the instrument, and William was more than happy to guide her hand around its various parts, making very sure, of course, that her fingers kept well clear of the blade.

twenty-one

> I have received recently such information from the Natives of the interior, as puts beyond doubt the fact that the Platypus is oviparous. Distinct tribes of Aborigines — who cannot be supposed to have physiological prejudices — clearly say the loobra (i.e. female) makes a nest underground communicating with its burrow, the orifice of which is always under water, and there lays a number of soft-skinned eggs.
>
> Letter from Augustus Greeves to Sir Richard Owen, 12 July 1843

By the time the women were ready to leave, Ben Fuller had still not appeared. William thought he should accompany them at least as far as the creek. Though its bed had been dry when he first arrived, ever since the storm it had been flowing strongly.

'You need have no concern for our safety, William,' Mary had assured him. 'The water was well below the wheel axle when we crossed this morning.'

Nonetheless he insisted, and on arriving at the near bank suggested that he go across first on Belle to make sure that it had not risen since. He urged Belle into the current and was relieved when he saw that it came no higher than her hocks. He reached the other side and called for the sisters to come across. It was as Mary had said. Though the current was swift the water was shallow and they should have no difficulty in getting through. Nor would they, had not a tree branch come swirling downstream, half submerged, as their horse was about to make the final pull to land. It swept straight towards the horse's forelegs just as it was taking a pace forward.

William saw the branch entangle itself between the horse's legs, he saw the horse first stumble, then panic. It neighed once, then reared up and twisted in the traces. There was a smart crack as one of the shafts broke. The horse, now even more frantic, tried to free itself, pulling hard on the remaining shaft. A short cry came from one of the passengers — which one, William could not tell — as the gig tipped onto its side. Both women were thrown into the water.

The whole thing took only seconds. Mary had somehow managed to hold on and cried out. Ettie tried to swim towards her but the current and swirling eddies pulled her away and into the centre of the stream. Each moment she was being swept further away, down the creek towards the river, her white pinafore floating like the petals of a flower around her. The gig was sliding into deep water. William leapt from his own horse and ran down to the bank. He waded into the water — careful now, he could not afford to lose his footing — reached the upturned gig and worked his way around it to find Mary being pulled and tugged by the relentless current. She was gasping for breath.

'The reins ...' she said, spluttering.

With one hand she was holding onto the overturned gig but the other seemed to be trapped by something, underwater. The water was up to William's chest. He grabbed hold of the wheel with his left hand and reached out with the right. He could feel the gig slipping along the rocks of the creek bed, pulled both by the current and the horse still tugging and jerking at the shaft. At any moment it might go, taking Mary and him and the horse with it into deeper water. But if he could just reach Mary's hand, if she could just reach his. There, he had her! Now he must pull, pull hard and pull quickly. But still she was being held fast. He would need both hands.

William took an enormous breath, exhaled, took another, and held it. Releasing his grip on the wheel, he dived beneath the muddy water. *Inveramsay, Inveran, Inveraray ... Inverbeg, Inverbervie, Inverboyndie ...* He felt for the girl's arm, then felt his way along it. Yes, the leather strap of the reins was wound round her wrist. *Invercannich, Invercassley, Inverchaolain ...* He eased his fingertips between leather and wrist. *Inveresk, Inveresragan, Inverey ...* He had them through to the knuckles now — if he could just slip that loop off. *Inverkeilor, Inverkeithing, Inverkeithny ...* It was no good — the strap was no looser, and now his own fingers were trapped. *Invernaver, Inverneg, Inverness ...* He strained his fingers and thought he felt the strap giving. *Inversanda, Invershiel, Invershin ...* It was slipping down, it was almost at her fingertips. *Inverugie, Inveruglas, Inveruglass ...* Just one last push. *Kilmichael of Inverlussa.* William clawed for the surface, lungs exploding. Clinging to his arm was Mary Brown. They scrambled to the shore and collapsed to the ground. William turned to see the horse give one last mighty tug at its straps. The second shaft broke and with the reins now free the horse ran up the far bank and off down the track. The gig lurched and twisted and juddered, then could resist the pull of the current no more. It slid into the deeper water and floated away down the creek.

Thank God Mary was safe, but what about Ettie? Getting to his feet William struggled against sudden dizziness. The gig was already twenty yards downstream. As he strained his eyes for Ettie he felt Mary's two hands clutch his arm.

'Where is she? Where is she? Where's Ettie?'

'I can't see her. I can't see anything.'

What should he do? It was no use going back into the water. Even if he didn't drown he would never find her like that. The only thing to do was to try going along the bank. Perhaps she had been carried to the side.

He turned to Mary. 'I'm going to see if I can find her. You stay here.'

'No, no, I'm coming, too. I must.'

Yet as the woman made to push past him she gave a moan and dropped to the ground. She had fainted, but there was no time to help her now. William sat her against a tree, then half ran, half stumbled his way into the scrub.

This was madness. The vegetation was so thick that he could not even manage a walking pace, and all the while Ettie was being swept further and further downstream. Perhaps he should turn around. He should have taken Belle and ridden for help. But that would take an hour, more by the time he got back. What should he do, what was he to do? He stopped; his breath was already coming in gasps, he could feel his heart thumping in his breast. There was a chance she might have been swept to the side, there was still a chance. He plunged again into the scrub, tearing with both hands at branches and thorny creepers. Was that something white in front of him?

'I'm coming, I'm coming,' he shouted.

A minute later he burst through a tangle of vines and bushes to see a white dress snagged by a log at the side of the creek. Ettie Brown was face down in the water. He jumped in but found he could stand — the water up to his waist. Taking the inert body in both arms he struggled ashore.

He lay her on the ground. Her eyes were closed, her lips almost as white as her dress. William shut his eyes tight, and as he did so he saw Uncle Angas standing there in front of him.

Get the water out of the lungs, laddie. Get the water out, then a good thump. Get the water out.

The girl was lying with her feet towards the creek. He rolled her over onto her front, her head on its side and now lower than her body. A small trickle of water ran from her mouth. He put both hands on her back and pushed. A gush of water spurted from her mouth. He pushed again, then raised his fist above his head and brought it down between her shoulders — but he couldn't stop himself pulling back at the last minute.

A good thump, Will. A really good thump.

William raised his fist high and this time struck hard. And another blow, so hard that it caused a grunt. More water trickled out. William raised his fist again and hit hard again. More water. Now she needed air. Almost by instinct he rolled her onto her back, bent over and put his mouth to hers. Ten times he pushed his breath into her lungs, then he rested. Ten more times. Was he imagining it or were her lips losing their pale tinge? He felt in his pocket and pulled out a soaking handkerchief. Wringing from it as much water as he could, he flicked it open and began wiping her mouth and lips.

Above the sound of rushing waters he thought he could hear breathing. Then a cough. And another. When her coughing stopped, he could see that she was breathing deeper now. What should he do? He should get Belle, but he couldn't leave Ettie here. Sliding one arm under her shoulders and the other under her legs, he lifted the limp body and struggled to his feet.

How far he carried her and how long it took him, he had no idea. But when he at last arrived at the track he was surprised to find another figure bending over the still unconscious body of Mary Brown.

'Blimey, you all right, Prof?' Ben stood up. 'I was just going to come looking for you.'

'How's Mary — Miss Brown?'

'She woke up a minute ago but she's gone again. So this is Mary Brown, eh? And who's that you've got there then?'

'Ettie.'

William lay the unconscious girl down, and himself collapsed on the ground. He felt as though he had no more strength left in his body.

'I saw what must have happened, of course,' said Ben, nodding towards the gig that had come to rest against some tree roots thirty yards downstream. 'Something spooked the horse, I suppose.'

'Yes, I was here, I saw it all. Mary — you're sure she's all right?'

Ben leant over her again. 'She's breathing fine, Prof.'

And at that moment the woman gave a small moan and opened her eyes. As they focused on the bearded face above her she gave a small start.

'Don't worry, Mary, don't worry,' said William. 'This is Ben Fuller.'

The woman's shoulders relaxed. She smiled. But as she looked over towards William a sudden panic showed on her face.

'And Ettie is all right, too, Mary. She's alive. Look, here she is.'

Mary struggled to her feet and went to her sister, still lying unconscious on the ground but with at least a trace of colour now.

'William, Mr Fuller. I don't know how we can ever repay you.'

'I've seen it happen myself, a horse getting caught like that.' Ben Fuller was sitting by the kitchen fire in the cottage sipping from a cup of hot water and brandy. Ettie was in bed. How much the worse she was for her ordeal they would only know when she awoke.

'I pray that I shall never see it again,' said Mary Brown. 'But I thank you, Mr Fuller, from the bottom of my heart. And you, William.'

Mary seemed to have no memory of the accident, nor of being trapped and being pulled free by William. Nor had she asked exactly what had happened after William left her beside the crossing. But no matter. The important thing was that they were both alive.

Billy Pike (the hot brandy had been his idea — 'nothing like it to dry out your insides') was pouring himself another from bottle and kettle. No doubt his insides felt a bit wet, too.

'Lucky you two was bloody there, eh, Mr Caldwell?'

'Indeed,' said William. 'But I think that might be enough talk for now. It doesn't do to dwell on these things and I fear that it is tiring Miss Brown.'

Mary smiled, first briefly at William, and then at Ben. 'What I owe to both of you,' she said, 'I will find it difficult to repay.'

And William remembered how as they had ridden into town after the accident — him holding the still unconscious Ettie onto the saddle in front of him and Mary riding on Ben's horse — he had looked behind him. Nothing was to be seen of Mary but her two arms wrapped tight around Ben Fuller's waist.

'You're a dark horse, Prof, and no mistake,' said Ben, as early next morning he and William were heading back to the camp site. They had decided to stay the night at the hotel and now William was eager to get back to camp to resume his work. Yet as he rode along he found his mind was not on platypuses but on pale lips and closed eyes.

'I'm sorry?'

'You haven't been here two months and you've already found yourself two lady friends.'

'No, no,' said William, trying for an offhand laugh (and hoping he carried it off). 'I can assure you that the Misses Brown have been the furthest thing from my mind. Until yesterday, of course. Much too busy, you know, no time for that kind of thing.'

'What kind of thing would that be, then, Prof?'

Ben was curious to find out about the two sisters — one black, one white — and William told him all he knew. They soon reached the creek, innocent now in the fresh morning light but for the wreck of the gig on the far bank.

'Need a bit of fixing, that will,' said Ben.

'You think it can be repaired?'

Ben Fuller pursed his lips. 'Maybe, maybe not. I might have a look at it later. But I'm afraid you won't be having no visits from your lady friends for a while.'

By the time they reached the camp it was almost noon. A whole afternoon then a morning wasted. (Wasted? Saving those two women from drowning? And yet there was so much to do.) And where *had* Ben been yesterday, and what happened to the supply of platypuses?

'So, no specimens yesterday, Ben?'

'I didn't have a chance to tell you, Prof. Bit of a corroboree the other night — I expect you heard. Our charcoal chums, they was feeling a bit tired yesterday morning, I'm afraid. But leave it to me, I'll soon get them moving. I'll go over right now and see what they're up to.'

William's equipment lay where he had left it. Where was he? Ah yes, he had almost finished making the slides from his last dissection. No, he had finished — he had been about to look at them under the microscope. He took the instrument from its case, set up the mirrors and fitted the first of his new sections onto the microscope stage.

He had long been familiar with the development of the ovary in placental mammals — how the separate eggs developed inside it and eventually burst out, leaving behind the distinctive *corpus luteum* or 'yellow body' as proof that ovulation had just taken place. After all the work he had done on possums since arriving here, he was now familiar with the slight differences between their ovaries and those of placental mammals ('giraffes,' he thought with an inward smile). Now he had ovaries from a monotreme, the third group of mammals.

From examination of the animal's anatomy alone, some of the stages of platypus development had already become clear. Just as in other mammals, the ovum developed in its follicle within the ovary. It was shed into the Fallopian tube, where it was presumably fertilised by sperm from the male. Once the ovum was fertilised, though, then what happened? This was one of the things he needed to find: a series of fertilised ova at various stages of development, leading either to the usual mammalian foetus, or to the fabled egg. But first he needed to know that the ova were being shed from the ovaries. He needed to see a *corpus luteum*. He readjusted the mirrors, put his fingers on the focusing wheels, and peered down the eyepieces.

When Ben Fuller returned to camp it was almost dark. He was greeted by a smiling William and the smell of fresh damper.

'I've found it, Ben. I've found it! They've started.'

Ben dismounted and tied up his horse. 'Started what?'

'Ovulating. The *corpus luteum*, I've found it! The females, they're ovulating. Now the real work begins.'

'Very fine I'm sure, Prof. And what's the smell? Have you been cooking?'

'Indeed I have. I thought a celebratory feast was called for — or a celebratory damper at least.'

When first he had seen the mass of cells coloured orange by his stains, William had almost jumped for joy. There was no doubt that it was a *corpus luteum*, and there was no doubt what it meant. But after he had looked at it and looked at it again, what was he to do? There were no more platypuses to dissect, no specimens to prepare. And he was hungry.

The flour had not been hard to find. As he had watched Donald do many times, William put a couple of handfuls into a bowl. What next? Ah yes, the magic ingredient: baking soda. He found an unlabelled tin of the white powder and put in a pinch — no, two pinches — poured in some water and mixed. A little too wet — it was hard to judge these things. But some more flour should do the trick, and if there was more flour he supposed he should use a little more baking powder. When the ball of dough looked about right he tipped it into the camp oven and put it on the fire. That had been an hour ago — and Ben was right, it was smelling good.

'Do you think she's ready yet, Prof? I'm hungry as a bandicoot.'

William hooked a stick round the handle of the oven and swung it from the fire. He slid off the lid and peered inside. It looked good. Using a towel in both hands, William lifted the damper from the oven and carried it over to the table where it landed with a satisfying hollow thump.

'Sounds all right,' said Ben. 'Let's see what it tastes like.'

The damper was a triumph. As light as any that Donald had ever made and a different thing entirely from Ben's solid efforts. Simply spread with butter straight from the tin it was delicious.

'I think something a little savoury might go down well, too,' said William. He rummaged in the store tent and threw Ben a tin of corned beef. 'Here we are, something I brought with me from England.'

'Bully beef, eh, Prof?' He took a heavy clasp knife from his pocket. 'So, which is better: eternal happiness or bully beef?'

'This sounds like another of your conundrums, Ben.'

'No conundrum about it. We all know that nothing is better than eternal happiness, and bully beef is certainly better than nothing. So bully beef's got to be better than eternal happiness every time. I thought you'd know that, Prof, an educated man like you.'

He hacked open the tin and scooped out the contents onto a plate. 'And it's from the old country, you say?' He held up the empty tin to inspect its label.

'Yes. For some reason my aunt thought I might not find corned beef in Australia. She insisted I bring some from her favourite grocers in Piccadilly.'

'Piccadilly, eh? You didn't happen to notice where it came from originally, I suppose?'

'No. Why?' William took back the tin and read out the label. 'ABC Corned Beef. Product of Australian Beef Canning Company, Queensland, Australia.' He burst out laughing. 'As coals to Newcastle, so beef to the Burnett, eh, Ben? But perhaps it's like Madeira wine, tastes better after a long sea voyage. Let's see.'

Whether twice crossing the equator had improved its flavour (and whether or not it was better than eternal happiness), the corned beef seemed to go particularly well with William's damper. And when it had all been eaten and there was still some damper left, William remembered the apricot jam from the previous visit of the Misses Brown. Well, why not? It was a celebration.

'You must try this, Ben. Pure liquid sunshine. From the Misses Brown, don't you know.' William opened the jar and handed it to his companion.

'Ah, the Misses Brown. Fine women, would you not say, Prof? And you'll be pleased to hear young Ettie is much improved.'

'You've been to see them again? I didn't realise.'

'Yes, this afternoon. I went back to the creek to have another look at that gig. It wasn't as bad as it seemed — a couple of broken spokes, and the shafts of course. But me and Blackie here got it out all right and patched it up, so I thought I might as well take it into town. I said I'd fix it for them proper later on.' He got up and fetched over his saddlebag. 'And while I was there, I picked up these from my mate Billy.'

He pulled out two bottles of beer, then another two. 'Come on Prof, clear that billiard table of yours. A pound says I'll beat you.'

William smiled. 'You're on.'

William woke in the middle of the night with a distinctly woolly feeling in his brain, but this was not of immediate concern to him. Nor was the fact that his pocket was a pound the lighter. What was of concern was whether he had enough time. He crawled from his bed and, clenching his buttocks, headed for the latrine in a crouching run. He just made it.

Some minutes later, now covered head to toe in a light sweat, William emerged to hear a groan and see a shadowy figure squatting beneath a tree over near the horses. So, Ben had it too, eh? Damn aunts. Damn Fortum and damn Mason. And damn the Australian Beef Canning Company.

twenty-two

It is to the absence of proof that Doctor Carpenter appears to refer, where he remarks, in his excellent *Principles of Human Physiology* 1842, p.40, 'No *positive* evidence has yet been obtained that its young are born alive.' The minute size of the ovarian ovum and consequently of the vitellus; the presence of small ova with a delicate chorion and without chalazae or shell, in the uterine portion of the oviduct — all are elements of a body of *positive* evidence in favour of the ovo-viviparity of the *Ornithorhynchus*.

> Sir Richard Owen, 'Remarks on the Observations sur l'Ornithorhynque par M. Jules Verreaux,' *Annals and Magazine of Natural History*, 1848

'Feeling better?'

William looked up from the table. 'Much better, thank you, Ben.'

'That's the last time I eat bully beef from Picca-bloody-dilly. Give me eternal happiness any day. But I'm afraid your Ettie Brown is still a bit poorly.'

Despite the unfortunate events of the night before Ben had left early for Gayndah. He had just returned, and from the way he slid from the saddle of his horse William suspected that he might have spent some of his time at the Club Hotel.

'Ettie? What seems to be the matter?'

'I don't know,' said Ben, taking a bottle of beer from his bag. 'Might have caught a chill or something. That's what Mary said.' He swung open the stopper of the bottle. 'Right friendly is that Mary, what with what happened at the creek and me offering to fix up the gig and everything.'

'It was most generous of you, Ben, I'm sure. Will it take long?'

'It's nothing much — thought I might even finish it today but things seemed to take longer than I thought. I dare say you know what I mean, Prof.' He paused and grinned. 'You know, all those cups of tea and chatting and things.'

So, the Misses Brown had been their usual welcoming selves. Well, why not? William had no exclusive claim on their hospitality.

'Yes,' said Ben, taking a long pull at the bottle. 'Very friendly, those two. Very friendly, indeed. 'Specially that Mary, like I said.'

What exactly did he mean? Oh, it didn't matter. William had more important things to do than waste his time on such talk.

'I like to hear a woman laugh, don't you, Prof? They enjoy my little jokes and puzzles, those two. What do you reckon? Think I might be in with a chance? She's not an unattractive woman, that Mary — not for a darkie.'

William's wince did not go unnoticed.

'Come on, Prof.' Ben took another gulp of beer. 'Some like the white meat, some like the brown. And there's plenty to go round, if you know what I mean. Now you, you look like a white meat kind of man to me. I reckon you might be in with a bit of a chance yourself.'

The man was clearly inebriated.

'Don't think I hadn't noticed, Prof.' Ben Fuller climbed back on his horse, still clutching the bottle of beer. 'Like the poet said:

For in this wild uncultured place
Whose maids are rough and few
'Tis sweet indeed to find a face
Like that which shines on you.

Take it while you can, Prof. That's what I say.'

William looked up to receive a broad wink.

'And speaking of our dusky friends,' said Ben, 'I suppose I'd better go and see if they've found another duckbill for you.'

He turned his horse and headed towards the river, leaving an astounded William unsure which he felt more: amazed, angry or embarrassed.

Now, where was he? Ah yes, the slides. But what was it Ben Fuller had said about Ettie? Not all that nonsense — the man was drunk. But hadn't he said she was feeling 'a bit poorly'? Probably just a chill, as Mary said, or perhaps it was one of those headaches again. She still had the medicine, though. She would be all right. Trying to put all thoughts of Ettie Brown out of his mind, William readjusted the specimen in the mount of the microtome and slowly turned the handle.

For the next two days he seemed to be working nonstop. Ben certainly seemed to have roused Daraga and his friends into action and there had been no repeat of the ABC problem. After that first tantalising discovery of the *corpus luteum* he had found two more — though he was still to find a fertilised ovum, either in the Fallopian tube or in the uterus.

The dissections were taking much longer now. Each reproductive tract had to be carefully washed, its contents examined under the microscope for eggs and sperm, and its walls minutely inspected. And there was still the laborious process of preparing slides. There was no time to go into town, though Ben went in there each day as soon as he had come back to camp with the day's specimens.

It was already late afternoon and William had just finished putting an ovary into methanol in preparation for staining when Ben arrived back.

'Looks like you're about ready for a beer, Prof.'

It had been some time now since William had felt like a beer — not since the evening of the corned beef. But he was tired and he was thirsty and it had been a long day's work.

'Do you know, Ben, I think I will.'

'There you are,' said Ben, handing him a glass. 'And I brought back a few things from town. What about some chops with the damper tonight? Oh yes, and Mary gave me some eggs — part payment for fixing up the gig, you might say. Why don't I fry them up, too?'

William took a sip of beer. Should he ask how Ettie was? He took another sip, put down the glass and began tidying up his things from the desk. No, Ben would have told him if anything was wrong. He picked up his scalpel, cleaned it with care and put it into its cloth roll. Yes, this was what he was here for. He had not come to Australia to worry about women, no matter how charming. Winding the tape twice round the roll of instruments he tied it with a firm bow. There was certainly more than enough work to do without worrying about women. He would leave that kind of thing to Ben.

By the time William had cleared away his things the smell of frying meat was already tantalising his tastebuds.

'Sit yourself down, Prof,' said Ben. 'I've cooked us up a special treat tonight.'

He refilled William's glass and passed him a plate. Piled onto it was a large piece of damper, two thick chops and a pair of fried eggs. And nestling next to them, stacked slice upon pale green slice, was a vegetable that William recognised.

'A little something to keep the rot away, eh, Prof?'

Ben pulled up a chair beside him and stabbed several slices of choko onto his fork. But before they reached his mouth he looked over to William and burst into loud laughter. And William could not help but laugh with him. Soon both men had tears rolling down their cheeks. And even when eyes had been wiped and the slices of choko thrown onto the ashes of the fire, small snorts of mirth would still break out from each of them through large mouthfuls of meat, eggs, damper and beer.

Dinner was followed by a game of billiards, after which they sat down by the fire and Ben produced yet another bottle of beer.

'What's the secret, Ben? Whenever I ask Billy Pike to sell me some beer he looks at me as though I'm asking for the blood from his veins.'

'Ah well, you see, Billy and me go back a long way. We had some fine old times, in the old days. There was three pubs in Gayndah then, but his was the best of them, and the biggest. Half the gold that came out of the ground crossed that counter; when there was a big strike it was drinks all round boys. Then one day, Billy ran out of beer. Imagine that, a pub with no beer. Laughing stock of the town, laughing stock of Queensland was poor old Billy Pike. Lucky there was those other pubs or there'd have been a riot. That's not the kind of thing a man forgets.

'But look, Prof, speaking of running out of beer, I reckon my mate Charlie'll just about have drunk that pub in Bundy dry by now. I've been thinking — might be time to head west soon.'

Just as he had the first time that Ben had announced his intention to leave, William felt some surprise. It seemed a hurried departure. He knew that Donald was due back soon and that Ben had said when he arrived that he could only stay a couple of weeks, but nothing had been mentioned since then.

'I couldn't tempt you to stay on? If it's a matter of money ...'

'No, Prof — though I'd like to square things tonight if it's all right with you. I said I'd give Charlie a hand, and mates have got to stick together, remember?'

'I see I can't persuade you, then. But thank you again for all your help. So, we must work out how much I owe you.'

'By my reckoning I'm up seven pounds on the billiards, Prof.'

'Yes, I'm sure you're right. And ten shillings a day again for all your other help?'

'Sounds all right to me.'

'Then we'll make it fifteen pounds.'

'Right-ho. No, wait a minute, I've got a better idea.'

Ben Fuller stood up from beside the fire and walked over to the billiard table. 'What say just one more game, double or quits?'

Just over one hour later William went to the store tent, unlocked the cash box and took out six five-pound notes.

'You're a generous man, Prof,' said Ben, folding the money into his shirt pocket. 'Perhaps I'll see you in Bundy and you'll have a chance to win this back. Another beer?'

Ben poured and William raised his glass.

'Thank you, Ben, and good health.'

Ben Fuller raised his. 'Now, did I ever tell you about the last time Charlie and me and Mac was drinking at the Melbourne Hotel? Serious drinking. I don't remember how long we were there but I remember the bill came to thirty pounds exactly.' He patted his pocket. 'That's what reminded me. Like I said, serious drinking. But then a funny thing happened.'

He sat down beside the fire and turned towards William with an earnest expression. 'We each hand over ten sovereigns to the barman. As he's taking the money to the till he realises he's made a mistake — the bill should have been twenty-five pounds. He can't be bothered trying to work the sums out between the three of us so he thinks a bit and puts two pounds in his pocket. Then he tells us there's been a mistake and gives each of us back one pound. So Charlie, Mac and me, we've each paid nine pounds — that makes twenty-seven pounds all together. The barman, he's got that two pounds in his pocket — that makes twenty-nine. But we originally gave him thirty. So I was wondering if you could tell me, Prof — an educated man like you — where did that other pound go?' Ben got to his feet. 'And while you're thinking that over, I might just wander over and say farewell to our inky pals up the river there.'

There was no sign of Ben in the camp when William awoke. Another corroborree? He lit the fire and soon had enough hot water for tea and a shave. With just one specimen to prepare he might have time to ride into Gayndah later. It was Friday already and Donald would be arriving on the coach. No doubt he would appreciate a lift back to camp. There might even be time to call in to see how Ettie Brown was. He got straight to work. By ten o'clock there was still no sign of Ben, but by half past ten he had saddled Belle and was on the road.

All around him the shrubs and bushes were in flower, from every tree a bird was singing. If there was a sweeter smell — and a lovelier sight — than the cascades of yellow wattle blossoms that lined the road he was now riding down, he did not know of it. And if there was a happier sound than the carolling of the magpies that resounded through the bush, he did not imagine he would hear it this side of heaven. (He hadn't heard his little friend the Weedupwee for a few days — no doubt too busy building a nest to have time for singing.) What were those lines Ben had recited the other day?

Oh gaily sings the bird, and the wattle-boughs are stirred
And rustled by the scented breath of spring

Yes, that was it. Capital. That was it exactly.

Ben Fuller, the bushman with the soul of a poet. As paradoxical as a platypus — or one of his damned conundrums. There was no doubt that William would have found things a lot more difficult without his help. But why had such a man decided to help him in the first place? That was almost a conundrum in itself. There was the money, of course, but Ben Fuller never seemed to have any difficulty making ends meet with his 'bit of this and bit of that'. There was this new-found interest in Mary Brown; but no, he had only just met her. Would he not have been happier back at the hotel in Bundaberg knocking down his cheque with his friend Charlie than hanging round with a naturalist — a 'Prof'?

Ah well, who was William to question Ben Fuller's motives, either with respect to himself or Mary Brown? Ben was his own man, there was no doubt about that, and William respected him for it (even if his attitude to the fair sex, and Aborigines, was a little — how should he put it? — old-fashioned).

But did Mary Brown really find Ben as attractive as he himself seemed to think? William shook his head. Who knew, and who cared? As for Ettie ... He shook his head again and sighed. Women. Ever a mystery and a mystery still. It was a mystery he was still puzzling over when he found himself arrived on the outskirts of the town.

If the bush had seemed beautiful in the spring sunshine, the garden of the Misses Browns' cottage looked almost sublime. Not only was each bed ablaze with colour, the flowers themselves shone like jewels. True, the fresh yellow of the wild wattle was not to be seen, but deeper yellows of rose and hollyhock, reds and pinks of carnations, delphiniums and cornflowers in every shade of blue and countless other flowers besides crowded the cottage garden. William tied Belle to the fence. He was half-expecting to find Ettie sitting on the veranda as first he had seen her, but as he made his way up the path towards the front door he could see that the veranda was empty and the curtains were drawn. He knocked softly. Mary opened it.

'How is Ettie?'

'She is sleeping. I suppose your friend Ben Fuller told you that she was not well?'

'Yes, yesterday when he got back. She is no better?'

'I have been hoping that it is no more than a chill — though she has had one of those dreadful headaches, too. Thank goodness we still had some of your medicine.'

'What can I do?'

'You have already done what you can, William, and I am sure that when Ettie wakes up and hears of your concern it will be better than any medicine.' She smiled, then added: 'There is one thing more though.' Stepping onto the veranda, she closed the door behind her. 'It concerns Ben Fuller.'

So.

Mary Brown gestured for William to be seated and sat down herself, but now she was not smiling. Rather than looking at him directly as she usually did, she stared down into her lap.

'I hope you will forgive me for speaking plainly.'

'What is it you wish to know?'

'Everything. I need to know everything that you know about him.'

Something in her voice suggested that this was not a romantic enquiry. Then what did she want to know, and why?

'I shall tell you all I can. Perhaps I should start at the beginning. As you may know, I met Ben in Bundaberg soon after I arrived. He offered to act as a guide to bring me to Gayndah, and he sold me a fine horse, too — Belle. More recently he returned here, and since Donald has been away he has been a great help to me. It has been a busy time, and Ben has been most useful in negotiating with Daraga and helping with the supply of specimens for my research. As I'm sure you know, he speaks a little of his — your — language.'

'What do you know of his past?'

'Only what he told me. I understand he was orphaned at an early age and has made a living in the bush rather than the city.'

'Has he been to Gayndah before — before he first came here with you, I mean?'

'I believe he was here during the gold strike.'

The woman moved forward on her seat. 'And what do you know about his relations with Daraga, with my family?'

'Only what I have told you. He spends a lot of time at their camp and is out with them during the day. As far as I know he's with them now. Indeed, I seldom see your brother myself these days. Ben brings back the specimens and does all the negotiations.'

'The negotiations?'

'The payments — the flour and so forth. I'm sure you remember.'

'I do remember, William. And do you remember a certain request I made to you?'

William frowned. 'A request?'

'Do you remember, William, that I asked you not to supply alcohol to my brothers?'

'Indeed, Mary. And I can assure you that I have done as you asked.'

Mary Brown turned to look hard into his eyes. 'I believe you, William.'

William was beginning to find the conversation difficult to follow. 'So all is well?'

'No, William, all is not well. My brothers have not been getting just flour as payment for their work. They have been getting alcohol. All is not well.'

Now William was even more puzzled. Did he not see Ben measuring out the flour every day? Did he not see him bringing back the day's specimens?

'But I don't see how …'

'You have told me yourself, William. Ben Fuller. You said he dealt with all the "negotiations", did you not? I fear Ben Fuller has been doing some negotiating on his own behalf.' Again Mary fixed William with her dark eyes. 'Ben Fuller has been giving my brothers alcohol, and he has not only been getting your platypuses in return.

William, how can I put it? In our society — for Tibboora people — the role of men and women is different from what you may be used to. And when a gift of great value is received, a gift of great value must be given. In our society, William, women — the services of women — are a gift of great value.'

William had no reason to doubt Mary Brown, no reason at all. Yet still he could not believe what she was telling him. The services of women? And if Ben had been giving the men alcohol, where had it been coming from? Surely not from his own supplies of laboratory ethanol. Had Ben been stealing from him? This could explain why the supplies had been going down so fast. He had hardly time to digest Mary's disclosure and its uncomfortable implications before she continued.

'There is something else I would like to tell you, William. You will remember that once I told you a little about what happened when I was a girl — how I came to be orphaned. I think now you should know the whole story.'

She shifted her gaze away from his face and stared into space. 'It happened over twenty years ago. I was a girl. My people …' She paused and took a deep breath. 'My people were camping by the river. We had just returned from the Bunya time. Old enmities dealt with, new friendships made. We hadn't seen a white man in many weeks. My family, my blood kin, there were eighteen of us there. It was raining. The white men came suddenly. They came on horses, firing as they rode. They were shooting at us, William. My father and my uncles, they picked up their spears. My mother and my aunties took us children and ran. We ran up the hill, through the rain, up and up. We heard gunshots, we could hear the horses behind us. We ran and ran. The horses came and the men with their guns. My mother, she pushed me down near a rock. "Stay here, Meribu," she said. "Stay still. Stay still as the rock." She ran on with my baby brother. She was carrying my baby brother in her arms. I was behind the rock. I saw one of the men. He had a scarf over his face. He had unhooked one of his stirrups on its strap. He was whirling it round and round. He swung it at my mother, he hit her on the head. She fell. All around I could hear more horses, more guns. The man turned his horse and rode back. My mother was lying still. I thought she was dead. My brother was under her. My brother was not dead, but he was hurt. He was crying. The man picked up my baby brother. He picked him up by the feet. He seemed very light, my brother. The man swung him by his feet, he swung him round so that his head hit a tree. The leaves of the tree shook. He threw him down, onto the ground. I could see the man's eyes above the scarf. He looked around. He didn't see me. I was hiding, still as the rock. He walked around the rock and still he didn't see me, but I could smell him. The smell of him nearly made me sick. But I stayed still, still as the rock. The man, he walked over to my mother. She was lying on the ground, but she moved. She was not dead. When … when he had finished with her, he shot her with his gun, killed her, and he got back on his horse and he rode away.'

twenty-three

Sir, I have great pleasure in being able to inform you of a very interesting discovery in the economy of the *Ornithorhynchus paradoxus*, and one which I have no doubt you will hail with delight. About ten months ago, a female Platypus was captured in the River Goulburn by some workman who gave it to the Gold-Receiver of this district. The next morning, when he came to look at it, he found that it had laid two eggs. They were about the size of a crow's egg, and were white, soft, and compressible, being without anything approaching to a calcareous covering. But I am sorry to say that I never had a chance of examining their contents, as, on inquiring for them a day or two afterwards, I found they had been thrown away, much to my chagrin and disappointment.

Letter from Doctor J. Nicholson to Professor Richard Owen, 1864

It was a sombre and thoughtful William who stood on the veranda of the Club Hotel when the coach from Bundaberg pulled to a halt. As Billy Pike began unharnessing the horses, Donald climbed down from his seat beside the driver.

'Good to see you, Professor.'

He went to open the coach door and from out of it — backwards, slowly — came a passenger. It was a figure William recognised.

'Doctor Bennett, how wonderful to see you. And what a surprise.'

'Surprise?' He indicated Donald, now standing beside the coach. 'Young Master Gordon here told me distinctly that my letter had arrived.'

'But you gave no date.'

'Date? How could I?' The doctor reached inside for his hat. 'How was I meant to know when these infernal contraptions decide to run?'

William chose to ignore this small inconsistency. 'Here, let me show you into the hotel,' he said. 'It is wonderful to see you here in Gayndah. Donald, would you look after the doctor's bags?'

When they were at last seated at a table inside the hotel William tried again. 'I did indeed get your letter, Doctor, as Donald told you, and I'm sorry if there has been any confusion. But did you not say that you would be travelling with your son?'

'Herbert will be here later. He is taking the slow coach, as it were.'

This was something new to William. 'From Bundaberg?'

'Yes, from Bundaberg. I thought you said you'd read my letter? I have come here to look for fossils. I dare say you noticed yourself that those hills between here and the coast are almost certainly Triassic.' Seeing the blank look on William's face, the doctor gave an impatient sigh. 'We met a fellow in Bundaberg who drives a bullock wagon. He said he was bringing up some beer to Gayndah. Now if Herbert is travelling on a bullock wagon he'll have plenty of time to inspect the country and he'll be able to bring along any large fossil specimens he might come across. So I came up on the coach by myself. Now do you understand?'

'Thank you, Doctor, now I think I do.'

'Good. Now tell me, how's the hunt?'

'The platypus hunt? Oh, I have had some success.' He explained how the platypuses were now in breeding condition. 'And I have found ripe ovaries and I have found sperm inside the reproductive tract. But I have not yet found a newly fertilised ovum.'

The doctor's eyes lit up. 'An exciting time indeed, Caldwell. I shall have to come and visit you in your camp. I would very much like to see for myself all these things you have been describing.'

'You will be most welcome, Doctor Bennett. I plan to return there this afternoon. Please feel free to come any time.'

'I'd better wait until Herbert arrives. Then we'll see what we can do, eh? But a *corpus luteum*. This is excellent news. Do you know, Caldwell, I think this calls for a celebration.'

Doctor Bennett turned in his chair and called out to the empty bar room. 'Innkeeper — champagne!'

William was wondering how best to explain to the doctor that he would be lucky to get a glass of beer at the Club Hotel never mind champagne, when Billy Pike's figure appeared at the door.

'All right, all right,' he said, and was on his way towards the cellar door before William could say a word. The sound of footsteps going down the stairs was followed by a minute or two's silence, then by footsteps coming up. He appeared again at the door, in his hand a dusty bottle.

'Don't suppose it'll be any good — been there for bloody years.'

He held out a bottle on which William could see a white label with a red star.

It took the landlord somewhat longer to find and clean two glasses and he had only just finished filling them with the wine when Donald appeared.

'I've given Belle a drink and some oats. She's ready when you are, Professor.'

'Oh, there's no hurry is there, Caldwell? I want to hear more about what you've been getting up to. But first — to success.' The doctor raised his glass. 'Hmm, fine champagne. Thank you, landlord. And a smart lad you've got there, Caldwell. We had quite a chat on the coach, Master Gordon and I.'

'I agree with you, Doctor,' said William, and Doctor Bennett was quite right about the champagne. It was excellent. 'I don't know what I would have done without him. Though I think I've discovered the secret of your damper at last, Donald. Bicarbonate of soda, am I right?'

The boy looked surprised. 'So you found some then, Professor. I thought we'd run out, and I didn't know if they had any at the store here so I brought some back from home. Looks like I won't need it.'

'There was a whole tin of it, Donald, there in the tent.' He turned to Doctor Bennett. 'I have become quite the bushman, Doctor. You must try my damper when you come to visit us. But Donald is the chef par excellence when it comes to baked possum.'

'Thank you, Caldwell. And I hear you have found some help — besides young Master Gordon here, I mean.'

'I have indeed been lucky enough to engage some local Aborigines — as you yourself suggested. They have been invaluable in finding specimens.'

After what he had been hearing from Mary Brown, William was not sure how to explain Ben Fuller's recent part in the operation. It would probably be best to say nothing until he had at least seen him again.

'Splendid,' said Doctor Bennett, pouring more champagne. 'Yes, I remember we discussed the advisability of that when you came to see me in Sydney. But do you think they'll find enough of them?'

'There was a time when I doubted it.' William told the doctor about the flood, and how for several days he had been sure he would have to give up the project.

'What? And leave it to that German chappy?'

'I'm pleased to say that that won't be necessary, Doctor. The flood turned out to be a well-disguised blessing. The animals seem to have survived it, and are now even easier to find than before.'

'You've done well, Caldwell. Very well. But the real work's just beginning, you know.'

'I am well aware of it, Doctor.'

He drained the glass of champagne and got to his feet. 'Well if you're ready, Donald, and Belle is ready, I think we might be on our way. As Doctor Bennett says, there is work to be done.'

'I look forward to seeing you soon, Caldwell. And you, Master Gordon.'

'And I you, Doctor Bennett.'

William was struck by a sudden thought. 'Oh, Doctor, a friend of mine here in town is not well. I wonder, would you have time …?'

The doctor lifted a black bag from beside the chair and patted it. 'Never travel without my medical kit. I'd be pleased to, Caldwell.'

'Capital. Her name is Ettie Brown. I'm sure Mr Pike will show you to the house whenever you are ready. I will let her know that you are coming.'

He and Donald found Mary Brown sitting in the sun on the cottage veranda and he told her of the doctor's arrival.

'Thank you, William, thank you. This is good news. Will you not stay and have some tea? Ettie is still sleeping.'

'I think Donald and I should get back — I have much to do, you understand.'

'I do. And I know it may seem a strange request, but would you please not mention anything to Ben Fuller about the alcohol.'

'I can't see that I can avoid it — if I see him that is. He was planning to leave today for Bundaberg. But if what you say is true, then Ben Fuller is not only a rogue but a thief.'

'Please, William. It is important. Just for a little while. Let us say it is for my sister's sake.'

'For your sister's sake, then.'

When he and Donald arrived back at camp no smoke rose from the fireplace and no black horse was tied to the post. It seemed that Ben Fuller had indeed already left. William had to admit that he was relieved. Lying on the billiard table was a dead platypus. The removable top had not been replaced from the night before and as he picked it up William saw that a patch of blood had seeped out onto the green cloth. Donald saw it, too.

'Leave it to me, Professor,' he said. 'I'll fix that, soon as I've got you a cup of tea.'

William turned the dead animal over in his hand. It was a female.

On the way back from town he had already told Donald how his work had been going. Donald now told him how pleased his mother had been with her birthday present.

'Constable Perry called in a couple of days ago. He liked the rug, too.'

After they had finished their tea William set up his equipment and soon had the new specimen skinned and pinned out onto the dissection board.

The usual procedure — but first, the sharpening of the blade. With Donald watching on, he took the lid off the whetstone, wiped it with the rag and applied a drop of oil. He picked up the scalpel and applied it to the stone as he had done so many times before. Its steel handle warmed quickly to his hand.

'Now, just a couple of wipes on the hide — there, it's ready. Did I ever tell you, Donald, about my professor at Cambridge? Never cracked it myself, but he could put such an edge on a scalpel that it would ... Well, I'll show you what he used to do.'

William took his handkerchief from his pocket, held it for a moment above the scalpel, then let it fall. As the silk square drifted down to settle over his outstretched hand Donald gasped. William was equally amazed to see, poking out of a small slit in centre of the handkerchief, an inch of bright steel.

In at the vent and upwards through the wall of the abdomen. William pushed aside the gut and picking up some small forceps began to cut away at the connective tissue around the reproductive organs, pulling first one, then the other ovary free. After slicing through the urethra and large intestine at their junction with the cloaca then through the distal end of the cloaca itself, he was able to lift the whole reproductive system clear of the abdomen and into the glass dish that was already waiting. If there were a fertilised egg, it would be somewhere in there. He put down his instruments and took a sip from the second cup of tea that Donald had put down on the table beside him. Next, the painstaking job of washing out the reproductive tract and examining its contents and interior surfaces.

Donald had managed to get most of the bloodstain off the table and was now surveying the camp site.

'Looks like there's a bit of work to be done round here, Professor.

And the first job's to get a bit of wood in.'

William looked up from his work. The wood heap was empty again, and he had to admit that the place had a neglected air. Very different from the condition it had been in when Donald left.

'All right if I take Belle to help get the wood, Professor?'

'Please do, Donald. You know, I think she's almost as glad to have you back as I am.'

Boy and horse returned some time later pulling behind them what seemed to be a whole dead tree — trunk, branches and twigs.

'This should keep us going for a while, Professor.'

But Donald had no time to untie the rope before William grabbed him by the arm and pulled him over to the microscope.

'There, Donald, what do you see? Tell me, tell me what you see.'

The boy peered down the eyepiece. 'A pink thing?'

'A pink thing!' William was almost dancing with excitement. 'That's right, Donald, a pink thing. And do you know what that pink thing is?'

The boy shook his head.

'That pink thing, that tiny, little pink thing, Donald Gordon, is almost certainly a platypus ovum, a fertilised ovum. Do you know what this means?'

Donald looked up, bemused.

'It means,' said William, 'that breeding has started. We're close, Donald, we're getting close. Now, I must prepare it for sectioning — immediately, while it's still fresh. We won't be able to see much until it's prepared — fixed and stained and so on. Where's that ethanol?'

'That's wonderful, Professor, it really is. But I've found something else you may want to look at.'

'I'm sorry, Donald, not now. I must get this specimen prepared at once. We don't want it to deteriorate any more than we have to. Now, where is that bottle of ethanol? I'm sure I left it here with the other things. Could you find some for me please, Donald?'

After several minutes rummaging around in the store tent Donald came back empty-handed.

'They're all gone, Professor — but that's what I wanted to show you. Come on, come with me. It's not far.'

He set off back down the track with William following. They turned off near a gully. William could see the marks where the dead tree had been dragged out.

'It's just over here.'

Donald stopped at the edge of the gully. Below them, incongruous in the bush, was what appeared to be a rubbish heap. Empty beer bottles were its main component, but amongst them were a dozen or so larger bottles — of clear glass, not brown. William scrambled down the slope and picked one up. It was one of his ethanol bottles, and it was empty. There could be no doubt what this meant: it was clear evidence of the true currency of Ben's transactions. It was just as Mary Brown had said.

And as William held the empty bottle in his hand a smell began to register. Rot, putrefaction. Further down the gully he saw the wingless bodies of several birds. So, this was also where Ben Fuller had been throwing out the unwanted waste of his plumage hunting. One small body in particular caught his eye. He stepped forward and picked it up. Even with both wings torn off it was clearly recognisable. The black head with the scattering of white spots on the crown and bold white eyebrow, the dappled grey on neck and back, the bright orange throat and orange and red rump. It was the little diamond bird. But it was not the birds that were the main source of the smell. Further down the gully, abuzz with blowflies, was a heap of rotting meat. The platypuses.

William let the small corpse drop and picked up another of the ethanol bottles, then another, then another. Empty, empty, empty. He stood there still, thinking hard. Not about Ben Fuller — that could wait. Without his ethanol what would he do with the fertilised ovum that was even now lying in its dish of water on the table at the camp? His very first ovum, the tiny speck that might hold at least one of the keys to the platypus puzzle. Think. Perhaps if he put the specimen in formalin, that would at least fix and preserve it.

'We won't be beaten, Donald. Give me a hand up, would you?'

He struggled out of the gully and as they headed back to camp he told Donald what Mary Brown had revealed: that Ben had been trading alcohol with the Aborigines.

'But why didn't he say anything to you?'

'It is illegal, Donald, and he knew it.'

The boy paused to think this over. 'Oh well, at least he helped you get your platypuses, eh, Professor?'

Those words came back to William that evening as he sat by the fire mopping his dish with Donald's fine damper. What the boy had said was true. There was no doubt that suspended in preservative in a small jar on his desk sat a fertilised platypus ovum, and there was no doubt that in some ways he had Ben Fuller to thank for it. Ben must have been well aware that if William had known what was going on, he would have forbidden it. But William had not asked. He had left the whole thing to Ben. Did not this make him just as guilty?

The following morning he saw the familiar gig coming down the track, but as it came closer William saw not the slim figure of Ettie Brown sitting in the passenger seat, but Doctor Bennett. And it was not Mary who was driving. He recognised the face and uniform of Constable Jim Perry.

'Doctor Bennett, Constable — it is good to see you both. You have come at a most opportune time, Doctor.'

He helped Doctor Bennett down and led him towards the table.

'Here you are, Doctor: the first fertilised ovum.'

The doctor took the jar from the table and held it to the light. 'This is wonderful news indeed, Caldwell.'

He squinted through the clear liquid at the pink speck within before handing the jar back to William. 'And what, I wonder, is it going to tell us?'

'I am hoping we will soon find out.'

Doctor Bennett surveyed the instruments and glassware spread out over the table.

'You have certainly come well equipped, Mr Caldwell. I am most impressed.'

'At the moment I seem to have everything except the one thing I need. My supplies of ethanol have all been, er … used up. Until I get some more I cannot start the preparation.'

'Ethanol, eh?' said the doctor. 'Well you know I think I may be able to help you there.'

He led William to the back of the gig. 'Strange fellow that publican. I couldn't get him to part with a single bottle of beer but he seemed happy enough to sell me these.'

The doctor lifted the lid of a wooden box and took out one of the three green bottles it contained. He passed it to William. Below the red star on the label was printed 'Brut Imperial, Moet and Chandon, Epernay'.

'A pretty good price, too, I thought — four pence a bottle. He said they'd been in the cellar for years so he couldn't charge me much.'

'If they are as good as the wine we drank yesterday, Doctor, I think you may have got a bargain. But no matter how delicious, I fear your champagne will be of little help. It's pure ethanol I need — to dehydrate the specimens, you understand.'

'Of course you do, Caldwell, of course you do. But you don't mean to say that among all this stuff you don't have something we could use to make a still?'

Doctor Bennett was right — there must be enough tubes and phials and thermometers and goodness knows what else to rig up some kind of distilling apparatus. William led the doctor over to the store tent and by the time Donald had made some tea and handed it round, Doctor Bennett had already found all the parts he thought he needed.

'Now all we have to do is to put the damned thing together, eh, Caldwell? Leave it to me.' He turned to Jim Perry. 'But not a word to the excise men, eh, Constable?'

'All I can see, Doctor, is what looks like a waste of good wine.'

'I haven't asked you yet, Constable,' said William. 'What brings you to see us?'

'Not black grog I can assure you, Mr Caldwell. No, I was hoping I might find Ben Fuller here.'

'I'm afraid Mr Fuller appears to have left us.' William wondered if he should mention the business of the ethanol. 'Have you by any chance been talking to Mary Brown?'

'Yes, I did speak to Miss Brown. She told me all about the

accident, and how Ben Fuller had repaired the gig for them. But I've also been talking to the driver of the mail coach.'

'I don't understand ... the mail coach?'

From their expressions both Donald and the doctor seemed equally in the dark. Jim Perry put down his cup of tea and went over to where William's horse, Belle, was tied to the rail.

'Do you recall where you got this horse from, Mr Caldwell?'

'Indeed, I'm sure I told you — I bought Belle from Ben Fuller.'

'And do you know where Ben Fuller got her from?'

William reflected. 'No. I know that he had her with him when he caught up with Harry Norton and me at the creek. Of course, you'd gone back to Bundaberg by then. But you saw Belle later, when you came to Gayndah, did you not?'

'Oh yes, I saw her then. And the driver of the mail coach saw her yesterday when he arrived in town.'

'I still don't understand,' said William.

'He hadn't seen her for a while, but he recognised her.'

'Now I'm even more confused. He recognised her — is this of some significance?'

The constable went over to Belle and began stroking her nose. 'This white blaze, here on her forehead. And that white fetlock — just the one, front right. And this scar here on her withers, like a horseshoe upside-down. He's pretty sure — no, he's very sure — that Belle was one of the horses stolen when the mail was held up in April.'

'But just a minute, Constable. Didn't you tell me that the horses that were stolen were geldings?'

'Did I, Mr Caldwell? Anyway, me and Sergeant O'Malley happened to be at Gin Gin last night when the coach arrived on its way back to Bundaberg.' (William saw the constable and Donald exchange glances.) 'The driver mentioned that he'd seen this horse in Gayndah and he thought he knew it. So we started off this morning and here I am.'

'Where is the sergeant?'

'Back in Gayndah, having a word with Billy Pike.'

'And you think Ben Fuller might have something to do with all this?'

'Let's say I wouldn't mind having a bit of a chat.'

'I'm sure we all would, Constable. But as I say, when I returned yesterday there was no sign of Mr Fuller. Packed up and left, it seems.'

'That's strange, Mr Caldwell, because he hasn't been back to town, I'm sure of that.'

'Then perhaps he's still over at the native camp.'

'In that case I might wander over there and have a look,' said the constable. 'If that's all right with you.'

'Of course. I'm sure Donald will show you the way.'

The boy gave an enthusiastic nod.

'Right then. If he comes back here, though, perhaps best not to say anything.'

'How is the patient?' said William as soon as Donald and Jim Perry had left.

The doctor turned towards William, and by his grave expression it was clear that he had been expecting the question.

'I have examined Ettie Brown thoroughly and I have questioned her deeply. Please sit down, Caldwell. I'm afraid that the news I have to give is not good.'

William lowered himself onto the stool in front of his microscope.

'I have not told the patient this, nor her sister,' said the doctor, 'but I think perhaps you should know.'

'It is … it is more than a chill, then?'

'Much worse than a chill, I'm afraid. Much worse.' The doctor clasped his hands behind his back. 'Your friend is suffering from a most serious disease. And there is no disease so insidious, so *malicious* — if one may ascribe motive to such a thing. It strikes at men and women, it strikes at old and young. And how does it make its way about the world? Hidden away under the dark cloak of shame.'

Noticing William's frown of puzzlement, the doctor took a deep breath. 'If you have not yet guessed, Caldwell, it is syphilis.'

William's mouth opened, but before he could speak the doctor held up his hand. 'I have seen the symptoms often enough — too often. Syphilis is not an uncommon disease. I have seen primary lesions in a woman of seventy and in a child of six. But your friend does not have the primary lesions. She is beyond even the secondary stage of the disease. I am sorry to have to tell you that Ettie Brown is suffering from the tertiary symptoms. And for the tertiary symptoms of syphilis, there is little I can do.'

twenty-four

The platypus is not oviparous. The gentleman writing from the River Goulburn must have been made a fool of by someone or else he has mistaken a turtle for the *Ornithorhynchus*. The Platypus brings forth his young in the same manner as the cat or dog, the young are born blind and suckled for almost two months. This is opposed by the generality of savants, but it is strictly true nevertheless. All my information on these subjects I have from the aborigines, and they never lie in matters pertaining to the animal life in their respective districts. Therefore you can place implicit reliance in what I have said herein.

Letter from Peter Beveridge to Sir Richard Owen, 9 August 1864

Questions unbidden crashed into William's mind. Syphilis: surely that could only be caught in one way? Tertiary symptoms, the doctor had said: how long had Ettie had the disease? And most hateful of all: did this mean that all this time she had been deceiving him? The doctor seemed to see his thoughts.

'Shame, Caldwell, and ignorance.'

William averted his eyes. 'You say she doesn't know.'

'No, but it is possible that she may suspect. Your friend is an intelligent woman, is she not? My examination and my questions were bound to take such a direction that she may well have made certain connections. But before we go any further ...' The doctor stepped towards the chair where William was still seated. 'Can I talk to you man to man?' he said, an eyebrow raised in enquiry.

William nodded.

'I have to ask you then, Caldwell, if there is any chance that you may yourself have this disease.'

William felt himself flush, whether from anger or embarrassment he did not know. His reply started as a shout and ended as a whisper. 'No. No, Doctor Bennett, there is no chance.'

The doctor looked into William's eyes for perhaps a count of five, then walked back towards the fire. He gazed at the flames for several more seconds without speaking.

'How much do you know about syphilis, Caldwell?' he said, at last.

'I confess that my fields are anatomy and embryology, Doctor Bennett. I know little medicine.'

'You are familiar with Pasteur's work on the germ theory of disease?'

'Certainly, I have read of his experiments and find his conclusions convincing, though I confess I do not understand all the details.'

'Never mind the details of the experiments; I, too, am convinced by them. These are exciting times for medical men, Caldwell, and just because we may live in Australia, far from the centres of research, does not mean we cannot share them. No more miasmas or vapours or humours, at last we can see the enemy, see the whites of his eyes. We have a target to aim for. And the target in this particular case appears to be a bacterium — a spirochaete to be more exact. But ...'

The enthusiasm that had been rising in Doctor Bennett's voice halted. 'But, Caldwell, I fear that knowing the enemy is sometimes not enough. We may have identified him but we have not yet found his weak spot, and treatment is far from sure. Oh, you can find any number of pox-doctors who will claim to cure the disease — things are little different now from how they were when I began my medical training in the '30s.'

He went to the table and picked up the dusty green bottle that he just placed there. 'Are you familiar with the trick of keeping the bubbles in an opened bottle of champagne?'

William's puzzled look led the doctor to continue.

'It is a trick I learned years ago, when I was a student in London. If you suspend a silver teaspoon in the mouth of an opened bottle of champagne, it will still be quite fizzy and drinkable the next day. I tested it many times in my youth, and I assure you that it works.'

William continued to stare with blank incomprehension.

'But being a man of science — like yourself, Caldwell — I thought I might try a little test. I opened two bottles of champagne and drank a glass from each — a pleasant enough experiment you will agree. In one bottle I then suspended the silver teaspoon, the other I left as it was. The following day the wine in both bottles was equally fizzy and drinkable. So, should we say that the silver spoon had no effect? Or should we say that the absence of the silver spoon was equally as effective as its presence?'

The doctor gave a slight smile. 'Medicine is often like that, Caldwell. I fear that, even today, for many conditions lack of treatment is often as effective as treatment. The real cure is time alone.'

'I think I see what you are getting at, Doctor Bennett. You are perhaps implying that some of your pox-doctors might be like sellers of silver spoons.'

The doctor put down the champagne bottle. 'The facts of syphilis are these. There are two ways to catch the disease. The commonest by far is the one with which you are no doubt familiar. The disease is contagious, the germ is passed on from one person to another by contact and this usually happens during the act of sex. And what happens when you catch the disease? A few days or a few weeks later you get a chancre, a sore, at the site of infection. This is most often on the penis of a man, or in a woman the external pudenda or vagina — though it may be on any part that has been in contact with an infected person. It is usually at this stage that the doctor is consulted, and the symptom — the hard Hunterian chancre — is easily recognisable.

'As I say, Caldwell, we can treat the symptoms. There are several tried and trusted formulations — or several silver spoons, perhaps.

Simple topical application of cinnabar ointment or an aqueous solution of potassium iodide are the commonest, and will result in the sores quickly disappearing. But the sores will usually disappear whether treated or untreated. And in perhaps two out of three cases, treated or untreated, the patient has no further symptoms.

'But a third will not be cured, the germs will not be vanquished. After a year or two of apparent good health — or it might be five years or ten — the secondary symptoms appear. Not chancres this time, but a rash. It may be mild or severe, it may just appear on the palms of the hands and the soles of the feet or it may cover the whole body, it may last for weeks or for months. In this second stage, syphilis can mimic all the different skin diseases under the sun, from smallpox to measles to impetigo.

'Again, treated or untreated, it will eventually disappear. Well, not quite disappear. It often leaves its mark behind on the palms of the hands, pale brown scars, about the size of a penny piece. Sailors' pennies, some people call them — perhaps you have seen them somewhere yourself. They are a sure mark of the disease.'

William dropped his head and slowly shook it. The circular brown marks on Ettie's palms. He had thought they were burns. 'And then what happens? Blindness, is that what you are going to tell me?'

'The tertiary symptoms are the most to be feared, Caldwell, and though again they do not strike everyone who has had the disease they can attack almost anywhere. I know of no organ or part of the body that is safe from their ravages. Blindness, lameness, madness, heart disease, bone disease, skin disease. The third stage of syphilis is a most terrible thing to see, Caldwell. It eats away at the very body in which it lives, though again it may take years until the final stage is reached. And there is no cure.'

'But you said ....'

'I have given your friend something to help the pain. I can relieve the symptoms, that is all I can do.'

'She will die?'

'It has reached her brain. She will die, Caldwell.'

Death. Universal, inevitable. The fate of every organism, the fuel of evolution. But ... Ettie Brown? William slumped in his chair.

Only when he felt a gentle hand on his shoulder did he realise that the doctor had come closer.

'You may remember me saying, my dear Caldwell, that there are two ways that this dread disease can be contracted. I described the most common. But it is also possible for a child to be born with the disease, passed on from its mother while it is in the womb, or during birth. Hereditary syphilis, it is called. It is possible that Ettie Brown, er ...'

The look William gave him put a sudden end to the doctor's sentence. What did it matter how she acquired the disease, by what pathway the deadly bacteria had entered her body to begin their monstrous work? Perhaps the same disease had infected her mother and been the cause of the madness Billy Pike had told him about. Perhaps the girl had acquired the disease from her, perhaps she had acquired it ... later. Either way, it was hardly to be borne.

The drop of clear liquid swelled at the end of the glass tube until, pulled down by its own weight, it fell into the waiting jar.

'Hah! Here you are, Caldwell — pure spirits of champagne.'

From a flask immersed in a boiling billy an array of glass and india-rubber tubes led upwards to the table. It was at the end of this apparatus that the drop had appeared. William found it difficult to share Doctor Bennett's enthusiasm.

'You are sure,' he said, for at least the fifth time, 'that she is not in pain?'

'I have found codeine most effective in these cases,' the doctor once more assured him. 'It is a new compound — derived from morphine, you know — with all of that drug's benefits and few of its problems. I made sure to leave Miss Brown with an adequate supply.'

Should he go in and visit her? No, he must stay here and do his work. There would soon be enough ethanol to start the preparation. And what had happened to Ben Fuller? It had been two hours since Donald and Jim Perry left to visit the native camp. If they were not back soon, the constable and the doctor would be returning to Gayndah in the dark.

Drop by drop the jar filled, but by the time Donald and Jim Perry did arrive back at the camp the sun was already sinking towards the trees on the far side of the river.

'No luck then, Constable?'

'Oh, Ben Fuller had been there all right, but he left before we arrived and he must have taken another route. Seems he's good at that, doesn't it? How's your work been going?'

William pointed to the jar with its clear liquid. 'The doctor has succeeded admirably.'

'First bottle of champagne almost gone,' said the doctor, pointing to the flask in the billy. 'I think that will be enough to start with. Look, Caldwell, I have an idea. Why don't you leave me to put your specimen in the ethanol — thirty per cent did you say? — and you ride into town. I have a feeling — a professional feeling — that a visit from you might do our patient a lot of good.'

'That's all right with me, Mr Caldwell,' said Jim Perry. 'If you leave now you should get there before dark. I'll bring the doctor as soon as he's finished. The moon'll be enough to get us back.'

William felt a burst of relief and gratitude. 'Thank you, Doctor. And thank you, Constable. Donald, saddle up Belle for me, would you?'

By the time he and Belle were on their way the sun was almost setting. Wattle blossoms blazed in the last light of evening, while all around the forest resounded with a late chorus of songbirds. But the colours had lost their lustre and the songs their sweetness. William urged his horse into a trot.

Belle had made the journey into Gayndah often enough that William had no qualms about riding in the twilight. She picked her way with care and confidence until just as they reached the outskirts of town she shied and came to a sudden stop. This was unlike Belle. William urged her forward. She took two reluctant paces and stopped again. It couldn't be a snake, not so late in the day. It was only when William heard a clink and saw the glint of metal that he realised that tied to a fencepost, just off the road, was another horse. Even in the shadows he could see that it was a black horse. Taking a wide circle, he urged Belle on towards the town.

A lamp shone in the window of the cottage, but beyond the reach of its feeble light even the flowers in the garden looked black. William dismounted, tied Belle to the rail and pushed open the gate. He had almost reached the door when he heard through the half-open window a voice, a man's voice.

'Why don't you have one yourselves, ladies? Might do you good.'

From the way he spoke William could tell that Ben Fuller had been drinking. But what was he doing here?

'Thank you, but no, Mr Fuller.' Surely that was Ettie's voice? She must be feeling better, then. Thank goodness for the doctor. 'But please help yourself. After all you have done for us, a little rum is the least we can offer you.'

'What, fixing that gig? Always pleased to help the ladies — if you know what I mean.'

'Indeed I do, Ben.' This time it was Mary speaking. 'And now, let me help you.'

William heard the sound of liquid being poured. Mary Brown, giving rum to the very man she had accused of supplying grog to her family? Perhaps this was not the best time to call. But how long had Ben been here, and how was it that Jim Perry had not passed him on the road?

'Thank you. Very generous of you. Now, where was I?'

'You were going to tell us another of your conundrums.'

'Oh yes, please do, Ben.'

William heard the familiar musical laugh. Ettie was clearly much recovered, and Mary too seemed in good humour. There was nothing for him to do here. But still he stayed.

'All right, ladies, all right. I will if one of you answers me this question — honest now, yes or no.' William could hear the sounds of a glass being lifted and the smacking of lips. 'Will the next word you say to me be no?'

There was a brief silence.

'Yes,' said Ettie, 'I mean no, I mean …'

Ben Fuller laughed and William could hear the two women laugh with him.

'You liked that one, did you?' said Ben. 'Then here's another for you. Did I ever tell you about my old mate, Fred Darby? I didn't? Well' — the sound of more drinking — 'a good friend of mine was Fred but he had the miner's lung since I don't know when and a couple of years ago he died. Like I said, he was a miner but he was a farm boy at heart and he always liked horses, did Fred. When he died he had eleven of them. Eleven horses and three sons. In his will he said that Adam, his eldest, was to get half of the horses, his middle son Bill was to get a quarter of the horses, and his youngest, Charlie, was to get a sixth.'

'Why, that's impossible' — Ettie's voice again, light and laughing — 'you cannot have half a horse.'

'What say you, Mary? Impossible? Then you haven't been reckoning on your man Ben Fuller here. Soon as I hears about this I thinks a bit, then I rides up to his place and ties up my horse in the stable. Now there's twelve horses there, see? Right, I says to Adam, you gets half of them — that's six. Bill, you gets a quarter — that's three. And Charlie, you gets a sixth of them — that's two. Six and three and two, that's eleven altogether, the very same eleven horses that was there to start with. I takes back my horse out of the stable and off I goes, job done.'

'And I see you're nearly done drinking that rum,' said Mary. 'Can I pour you another?'

'I will have another glass,' said Ben.

There was a silence, during which William could hear the splash of a glass being filled. From the sound that followed Ben had not left it long on the table.

'Fine grog. But you know, there's another thing on my mind right now, Mary Brown.'

'What would that be, Ben? Something to eat, perhaps? A little more rum?'

'I'll have the rum, and I wouldn't mind a bite of something. But I was thinking about something else besides.'

'What could that be?'

'Something that you might like, too, Mary Brown.'

William heard a small scuffle, then Ettie's voice again, light and slow and measured.

'Ben, please let go of my sister.'

'Don't you worry, Miss Ettie. A little kiss from Ben Fuller never hurt a girl.'

Mary spoke. 'Please, Ben. Let go of my wrist.'

'What, just when we're getting friendly? Just a little thank you for old Ben, eh? Just a kiss, just a little one.' William heard a small grunt of exertion. 'Here, come back. What is it — not good enough for you, am I? Good enough to mend your gig, not good enough for a little kiss? Oh, come on. Well how about you then, Miss Ettie — you'll give me a little kiss, won't you?'

By her voice, Ettie seemed not at all alarmed. 'No, thank you, Ben.'

'Oh yes, Miss Ettie.' Now there was anger in Ben's voice and William heard a chair being scraped back from the table. 'I want you, Ettie Brown, and I mean to have you.'

'I think not, Ben.' Ettie's voice again, light and measured.

'You think not, do you? I think so, Ettie Brown. I had your mother and you'll see if I don't have you.'

What was this? William moved nearer the window. Ettie was sitting down on the far side of the table, one side of her face lit by a single oil lamp. Ben Fuller was sitting with his back to the window and William could see a bottle and glass on the table in front of him. The bottle was almost empty. Mary was standing by the door into the passage. Ben got to his feet. Three steps would take him round to where Ettie still sat quietly. As he began to move the girl spoke again.

'Please stay where you are, Ben.' She raised her hands from her lap. In one of them was a pistol, small and shining in the lamplight. 'Stay where you are,' she said again. 'I don't want to have to shoot you.'

The girl's words and the sight of the gun had caused Ben Fuller to stop short, but then William saw him relax. He began to move, very slowly, to his right.

'I asked you not to move, Ben. It really would be best if you didn't. I know what you're thinking. How can a blind girl shoot me? Ben, do you see that lamp on the mantelpiece, the unlit one?'

Ben Fuller turned his head and with one movement the girl pointed the gun at the fireplace, fired one shot, and was aiming again at Ben Fuller's chest before he could do a thing. The glass from the broken oil-lamp tinkled to the ground.

'As you can see, Ben, I can use this gun, and I can hear every move you make. And do you know what else I can do?' The girl moved her other hand to the lamp in front of her. With a flick of her finger and thumb the room was plunged into darkness. 'There, that's better. We can all see the same. Now, Ben, please sit down. And what was that you said about my mother? Would you like to tell me more about it?'

William could hear Ben Fuller sit down.

'There's nothing to tell,' he said.

'Oh, I think there is. Hands on the table, please, Ben. Thank you. And keep them there. Let me tell you something, Ben. Blind people, people like me, we may not be able to see but, as you know, we can hear well — very well. And our other senses become heightened, concentrated. I don't think I've shown you round my garden, Ben, but it is full of the most beautiful flowers. I'm sure I get just as much pleasure from smelling a rose as anyone does from seeing one. I can smell things that you wouldn't believe, Ben. A few minutes ago I could smell your desire. Now I can smell your fear.'

'Listen, just let me go. You can't blame a man for ...'

'Stay where you are, Ben. I haven't finished yet. People like me, you see, blind people, not only do we hear and smell at far higher levels than you could imagine, we use sounds and smells for memories, just as you use sights. I can remember the smell of a rose just as you might remember its colour. I can even remember the smell of my mother. Do you remember, Ben — you mentioned my mother? But even sighted people remember smells.'

'Look, what's this got to do with me?' said Ben Fuller. 'You invited me here. For a drink, you said.'

'Did you enjoy your rum, Ben?' It was Mary speaking now. 'We got it especially for you. But as my sister was saying, sometimes a smell can trigger a memory in a way that a sight or sound never can. Sometimes even a memory from childhood. Has that ever happened to you?'

Ben Fuller grunted some words that William did not pick up.

'Yes, Ben, when you took me on your horse, when I held you

close, I remembered. I remembered the smell of a man whom I had met long ago, a man on a horse. I was hiding, Ben, and it was raining, but I saw this man. I was a child. I saw him kill my brother. I saw him defile my mother, I saw him kill her. I saw this man and I smelled him. I smelled the animal in him. It was you, Ben. It was your smell, I remember it. It was you.'

William stood transfixed. This was no dream. It must be true, it must be. Now everything made sense, all that Mary and Billy Pike and Jim Perry had told him. But what was he to do? He had no gun, no weapon. Should he go for help? There was no time. He looked around him. There was a chair over by the stairs, the one where Ettie so often sat. He could use it to break the window, then he could jump through and then — then what exactly?

Before he could answer his own question he heard a mighty roar. Ben Fuller had risen from his seat, tipping and pushing the table towards the girl. He heard a crack of a pistol shot and the crash of breaking furniture. He grabbed the chair and swung it at the window. Before the glass had even had time to reach the floor he was inside the house. But where was Ben Fuller? Where was Ettie? He heard a low groan from the floor in front of him, then a voice.

'Ah, there you are, William.'

Someone lit a match and he saw Mary standing by the door with a candle. Ettie was by the dresser. The pistol was still in her hand. She seemed very calm and quite unharmed. She turned to him.

'I was beginning to think you were going to stay out on the veranda all night.'

From the floor came another groan, softer this time.

'I'm sure I only shot him in the shoulder, but could you just see?'

'Here,' said Mary, handing him the candle, 'take this. I'll light another.'

William took the candle from the woman's hand. Ben Fuller was lying face down on the floor. One sleeve of his shirt was wet and red. William managed to roll him over. His eyes were open but unfocused.

'I think he'll live,' said William. 'Not that he deserves it. Ettie, I heard everything.'

'Yes, and I heard you arrive, of course — did you think I had not? Oh dear, William. Was it very wrong of me to shoot him?'

'Had I been you I would have shot him long before, and not in the shoulder.'

'But he has already suffered enough. He drank nearly the whole bottle, you know.'

'A sore shoulder and a sore head is hardly punishment enough for what he has done to you — to you both.'

'Oh dear,' said Mary Brown, looking down at the crumpled figure on the floor. 'You didn't tell us about the sore head, William. You just said that drinking methanol would make you blind.'

twenty-five

The natives in various parts of the country have exhibited their ignorance of natural history by asserting that the young are produced from eggs. It is not difficult to see how this error may have arisen. In the ordinary condition of the male, the testes are quite insignificant bodies, no larger than a pea, but as the time of sexual intercourse draws near they become enlarged, and are then about the size of a pigeon's egg. In this condition the male has probably been mistaken by the natives for a female ready to deposit her eggs, particularly as the number of young is never more than two. I have passed many nights in native camps, but I never heard the heavy breathing which characterises the larger-brained European.

    Arthur Nicols, *Zoological Notes*, 1883

'William, is that you?'

    The clock on the mantelpiece said four minutes past noon but Ettie Brown was still in bed. Though the curtains were drawn against the bright Queensland sunshine in proper sick-room fashion, William could see as he entered the room that Ettie was sitting up and wearing a fresh nightgown. Her dark hair, newly brushed, fell over each shoulder almost to the top of the sheet. Mary indicated the chair beside the bed and quietly left the room.

'Ettie, I, er ...'

'William, it *is* you. Mary tells me you have some exciting news.'

William sat down. 'I suppose I have. But I didn't come here to talk about what I have been doing, I came to see how you were.'

'William, dear William.' She was smiling at him now, a most tender smile. 'You know how I am as well as I do — or should that be I know as well as you do? I am dying, William. Now, tell me your news. I am sure it is much more important.'

'Dying? Why I, er ...'

'William, did you think I did not know? Come now, I may have very little time left, and if you do not tell me your news soon it will be too late. You have found a platypus's egg?'

'Yes, Ettie, I have found an egg.'

So much had happened since the previous night it seemed that time itself had changed. What a night it had been. Though the sound of Ettie's shooting had brought Billy Pike and Sergeant O'Malley and half the rest of the town rushing over to the cottage, by the time they arrived there was little to be done. Ben Fuller was still lying on the floor, drunk and bleeding. Ettie had collapsed into a faint and been carried to bed by William and her sister. When, soon afterwards, Constable Perry and Doctor Bennett arrived in the gig, the doctor immediately got to work, first dressing Ben Fuller's wound then seeing to Ettie. The sergeant listened to William's account of what he had seen and heard, and, after questioning Mary Brown, had taken Ben Fuller into custody. William had already decided he would tell the truth and nothing but the truth — whether he would tell the whole truth, he was not yet sure. As far as he knew neither Pat O'Malley nor Jim Perry knew about the methanol. Perhaps it would be better left that way.

Doctor Bennett had shown no signs of suspicion. 'There's nothing you can do here now, Caldwell,' he had told William. 'Your time will be better spent back at your camp.'

William had ridden back to camp by moonlight and worked through the night to prepare the specimen the doctor had left soaking in his newly distilled ethanol. He was still at his work when Daraga and his two companions arrived the next morning. They brought with them another platypus, a fine glossy female. It was only as William accepted the specimen that he noticed another of the men was carrying something else.

The bunch of dead brown leaves and twigs looked like the kind of thing he had seen them use to carry smouldering fire around in, ready to blow into flames whenever they needed it. But the leaves were not smoking. The man held the bundle out to William. He took it and put it down on the table in front of him. Now he could see that it had an opening in one side. It appeared to be a nest. Very gently, he teased it open. And when he was holding between finger and thumb the small, brown, soft-skinned sphere that lay within, he knew that at last he had found what he had been searching for.

'Tell me more,' said Ettie, sitting up in bed. 'Tell me all about it.'

'I have found an egg — or should I say Daraga has found an egg. And I have also found a fertilised ovum, and made a preparation.'

'With all your solvents and stains, you mean, and then you looked at it with your microscope?'

'Exactly.'

After seeing the egg in the nest William had immediately begun dissecting the dead platypus. In her urogenital sinus he found a second egg, fully formed. There was no doubt now, no doubt at all. As for the fertilised ovum that he had spent the night preparing, it revealed after careful sectioning that the original single cell had already divided into four. Two large and two small blastomeres were sitting on the yolk. Stopping only to embrace a startled Donald and give a wave to the mystified Aborigines, William saddled Belle and rode straight into town. He must send a telegram — but not before he had called in at the cottage.

'So not only are we now sure that platypuses are oviparous, it is clear that the cleavage of the ovum is meroblastic rather than holoblastic — that is to say, it more resembles that of a reptile than a mammal.'

'William, dear William, this is wonderful news, quite wonderful. You realise what this means?'

'It means the puzzle is solved at last.'

'Yes, and …'

'It means that, well, perhaps it means I shall be famous.'

'Yes, and …'

'It means that, well …?'

'It means, dear William, that in your whole life you will never have to eat another platypus.'

It was only when the two of them had stopped laughing that Ettie reached towards his hand, now resting on the white counterpane. She seemed to know exactly where it was.

'And have you anything else to tell me, William?'

'Yes, Ettie, I have.'

William took her hand between his own. He sat a little more upright, though still holding her hand, and looked into the sightless blue eyes. 'I have made another discovery, which I think may be even more important.' Even in the dimness he could see those eyes shining.

She spoke. 'You have discovered that you love me?'

'Yes,' said William. 'But … how did …?' He felt the familiar blush creep from neck to cheek. The girl gave a deep sigh, but he knew it was not an unhappy sigh.

'Oh, William. I have been wondering how long it would take you.'

'You already knew?'

'Really, William, what *did* you learn at your university? Yes, I have long known that platypuses lay eggs. And yes, I have long known that I am dying. And yes, I have long known — for seven weeks and one day to be precise — that you loved me. Which is exactly as long as I have known that I loved you.'

And she moved her hand to his face, and gently touched his moustache, and then his lips. And when Mary Brown returned to the room with a pot of tea, a milk jug, three cups and saucers and a plate of buttered scones still warm from the oven, she found William still holding her sister's hand. And across their faces were two of the largest, most foolish-looking smiles she could ever remember seeing.

It took the telegraph operator several attempts to read the words on the form.

'MONOTREMES OVIPAROUS OVUM MEROBLASTIC.'

When he had read them back to William correctly for the third time, and the address — Professor Moseley, Cambridge University, England — William watched him tap out the message. What a stir those words would cause. As soon as the confirmation signal came back down the line William handed over his six shillings and stepped out of the telegraph office into the hot afternoon sun.

Billy Pike hailed him from the veranda of the hotel. 'How's it going, Professor? Ready for a beer — or will it be champagne?'

'A glass of water, thank you, Mr Pike. I'm not sure I feel like celebrating — not yet.' He followed Billy Pike into the hotel.

'I heard about your egg,' said the landlord, pulling William's glass from below the counter. 'So you bloody believe us now, eh?'

The bush telegraph, thought William. Almost as fast as the wires. 'Yes, Mr Pike, I bloody believe you.' He drank the water and handed back the glass. 'How's Ben Fuller this afternoon?'

'That constable's with him now. Doctor Bennett saw him first thing, thinks he'll live. Have you seen Ettie?'

How much did Billy Pike know about what had happened at the cottage last night, or about Ettie's illness? William was relieved to see the back door open and Doctor Bennett enter the bar.

'Ah, Doctor Bennett. Mr Pike was just asking me about Miss Ettie.'

'Much improved — in spirit at least,' said the doctor. He glanced across at William, then turned to the landlord. 'I have already explained to Mr Caldwell that Ettie Brown has a tumour of the brain, Mr Pike. I'm afraid it's a bad one.' He paused to let his words sink in. 'A very bad one.'

Seeing the expression on Billy Pike's face William thought he should say something. 'If it is any consolation, Mr Pike, she knows.'

'I suspected as much,' said the doctor, shaking his head. 'An intelligent woman.'

The publican was silent. His head had fallen to his chest.

'But, Caldwell, speaking of spirits. I saw Mr Fuller again this morning. He was complaining that something seems to be wrong

331

with his eyes — in fact he can't seem to see at all.'

'Really, Doctor?' Before William could think what else to say the doctor continued.

'You may remember that I examined him last night. I observed then that his pupils were fixed and dilated, and I couldn't help noticing that the rum he had been drinking smelled a little unusual. Of course I saw immediately what must have happened.'

Doctor Bennett gave William a look of knowing innocence. 'Yes, Donald told me that Mr Fuller had been stealing ethanol from you. He must have taken some methanol, too, by mistake — probably watered it down a bit and added some molasses to make it drinkable.'

'Ah. Yes, I, er ...'

'Quite. It's not uncommon. I talked to Mary Brown this morning about it, of course, and she thought my explanation a most excellent one.' The doctor looked at Billy Pike, then back at William. 'You never know, Caldwell, sometimes the police ask questions about these things.'

'I see.'

'Good man.' The doctor clapped him on the shoulder. 'I thought you would.'

'But Doctor, is there anything you can do for him — for his eyes, I mean?'

'Nothing, I'm afraid. Methanol poisoning is quick and irreversible. He will be blind for the rest of his life — how ever long that is. But thank God Ettie Brown had the gun, and knew how to use it.'

'As you told me yourself, Doctor,' said William, 'she is a remarkable woman.'

'Well, well, well,' said Billy Pike, as the doctor left the room. 'I don't think he's going to get out of this. Not this bloody time.'

'Ben Fuller? What do you mean?'

'I know what happened last night, Mr Caldwell. Mary told me about it — or as much as she thought I ought to know. But I can put two and bloody two together.'

'But you said, not *this* time.'

The landlord stared hard at him, then seemed to make up his

mind. 'I suppose there's no harm telling you now, Professor. You remember that business with Joe Brown I told you about — you know, my partner.'

'Ettie's father?'

'Yes. You remember what I told you?'

William nodded. The murder, the rape, the massacre.

'Well the bloke who found them, the bloke that raised the alarm, that was Ben Fuller.'

William frowned. 'I didn't realise.'

'No, well you wouldn't have. But it's not just that.' Billy Pike seemed to be having some difficulty knowing what to say next. 'There's no proof, of course, but there were some who said Ben Fuller wasn't telling the whole story.'

'How do you mean?'

'There were some who said that it wasn't the blackfellows at all.'

William grasped for the meaning behind Billy Pike's words. 'Do you mean that it wasn't Aborigines who attacked Ettie's parents?'

'Well, it was all a bit strange, when you look at it. They'd always been friendly enough, and they didn't run off, see — they was just down there by the bloody river, peaceful as you like. They didn't start running till we started firing.'

'You, Mr Pike? You were there, you were one of the men?'

'Oh yes, Mr Caldwell, I was there. Look, I'd just heard that my partner had been killed, that Betsy had been raped, right in their own house. I ain't proud of it now, but I was bloody there all right.'

William did not know what to say.

'But like I said,' continued Billy Pike, 'at the time I believed it — we all did. Ben Fuller comes rushing into this very pub, telling us to come quick, that Joe and Betsy's place is being attacked by blacks. I grabbed my gun and ran to the cottage. When I gets there, I sees Joe with his throat cut wide open, sees Betsy crying and bloody — and it wasn't just Joe's blood. How would you have felt? There wasn't a black to be seen but Ben says follow him, he knows where they've gone. So we gets on our horses and we follows him and we finds them. They're down by the river, just like Ben says they'll be. Then — well as I say, I ain't bloody proud of it.'

'But now you're saying something else might have happened?'

'Well like I said, looking back on it, those blackfellows was acting strange bloody calm for people who've just killed a white man. And Ben Fuller, he was the only one to see them do it.'

'But why? Why would Ben Fuller say it was the blacks?'

'Why indeed, Mr Caldwell? Why indeed?' And speaking more softly, he said, 'There was the gold, of course.'

'The gold?'

'The strong box had been forced open — did you not hear about that?'

'I remember something about a robbery.'

'Well, nobody ever found that gold, and anyhow — what use does your blackfellow have for bloody gold? You know that for yourself.'

The landlord opened a bottle of beer, filled a glass and pushed it towards him. William did not stop him, but neither did he drink. He just sat there, thinking.

It must have been some minutes later that he heard a sharp crack of a stockwhip and a shout from the street.

'Stop, you bounders. Pull up there I say.'

The whip sounded familiar, the voice did not. William hurried out onto the veranda to see a bullock wagon rolling down the street towards him. Harry Norton was in the driver's seat, slumped forward, apparently asleep. Next to him, reins in one hand and stockwhip in the other, was a long thin figure whose face William thought he recognised. But it was a face so far out of context that he took a while to remember where he had last seen it. In Sydney, in the office of Doctor George Bennett. It was Herbert.

Despite — or perhaps because of — Herbert Bennett's impressive use of the stockwhip, the bullocks showed no sign of stopping. It wasn't until Billy Pike stepped out in front of them and grabbed the traces of the leading animal that they came to a halt. In the comparative silence that followed William could hear a familiar sound, the sound of Harry Norton snoring. Still clutched in his hand was a bottle. An empty bottle. Herbert Bennett climbed down from the wagon, covered from hat to boot in finest Queensland dust.

'Mr Bennett, you are here at last. Welcome to Gayndah.' As William shook his hand he once again had the strange feeling of a small dead fish being slipped into his palm. 'Your father told us that you were coming, of course, and would be travelling with my old friend Harry Norton. The journey seems to have quite tired him out.'

'Tired, Mr Caldwell? That man's not tired, he's drunk, inebriated. Tight as a hat-band, oiled as a Frenchman, drunk as a fiddler's bitch.' Herbert Bennett took a deep breath. 'And so, Mr Caldwell, so am I.'

With this spontaneous oration — by far the longest William had ever heard him utter — Herbert Bennett slumped against the wheel. He tried in vain to grasp the dashboard of the wagon, then slid slowly to the ground.

Billy Pike appeared on the veranda of the hotel. 'Better leave this to me.'

He disappeared round to the back of the hotel and came back carrying two full buckets, the ones he used for watering horses. He walked straight past the thirsty bullocks to where Herbert Bennett was still propped against the wheel. Putting one bucket down on the ground beside him, he hurled the contents of the other towards the still sleeping bullocky. The effect was immediate.

Harry Norton sat bolt upright, spluttered and shook his head. He looked first at William, then over to where Billy Pike was still standing, the empty bucket in his hands. He looked up into the air, up into the cloudless blue sky. 'Scupper me scarplins,' he said in his familiar toothless mumble, pipe still clenched in gums. 'Wet for the time of year, ain't it?' He looked again at the landlord. 'Ah, there you are, Billy. I brought your beer.'

'About bloody time,' said Billy Pike.

While landlord and bullocky unfastened the tarpaulin that covered the load, William looked down at the second bucket, still full. Should he try the same treatment on Herbert Bennett? He was spared the decision by the appearance of Herbert's father.

'Good God,' said the doctor, seeing the figure still slumped against the wagon wheel. 'Herbert?'

'Your son appears to be a little tired,' said William. 'He must have had an exhausting trip.'

Doctor Bennett leant over him, then straightened up, frowning slightly. He took the empty bottle from the seat where Harry Norton had left it, sniffed it once, and carefully replaced it. He walked around to where the other two men had already rolled back enough of the tarpaulin to expose a jumble of rocks, picked up one of the smaller ones and examined it closely. The same with another, then another.

'Caldwell, you know a little geology? Come over here a moment, would you?'

He passed William one of the rocks.

'Would you say, Caldwell, that this was from a sedimentary formation?'

William turned the rock over in his hand, noting the coarse crystals that covered its surface.

'From the structure, I would say this was an igneous production.'

'Hmmm.' The doctor handed him another. 'This one?'

'Again igneous, though slightly metamorphosed.'

Doctor Bennett nodded. 'And you know something of fossils? In your experience, are igneous rocks, as a rule, fossiliferous?'

'No indeed, Doctor. I would look for fossils only in sedimentary formations.'

The doctor nodded again. He replaced the rock and looked down at his son. It took him only six steps to reach the second bucket, still standing beside the wagon, still brimming full.

'So, tell me, Sergeant, how did you find out it was Ben Fuller?'

Pat O'Malley was standing at the bar, a bottle of beer beside him. 'Well, Mr Caldwell, shall we say a little bird told me? No, I'll be straight with you, but I'd appreciate it if you'd keep this under your hat. It was Maggie.'

'The landlady at the hotel in Bundaberg?'

The sergeant nodded. 'She heard about it last week from Charlie Boyd while he was knocking down his cheque at the pub — don't suppose he'll be remembering much about that week. Of course, Ben Fuller told him all about it when they was droving. Couldn't help himself — they never can.'

'The Pat O'Malley theory of the criminal mind, eh, Sergeant? So was Belle really stolen?'

Sergeant O'Malley smiled, and nodded again.

'But I still haven't worked the whole thing out. If, as you say, Sergeant, Ben Fuller robbed the coach and stole the horses, what did he do with them, and why did he offer to come with me?'

'The horses, he had them tucked away in a bush paddock near Ten Mile Creek. He planned to wait until things had quietened down, then move them on and sell them — which he did.'

'When?'

'He picked them up just after he met up again with Charlie Boyd. The cattle, they helped hide the tracks, see? And no one's going to notice three extra horses in a droving gang.'

'And it worked, too,' said Jim Perry. 'Fooled me, he did.'

'But I'm sure you told me that the horses were all geldings,' said William. 'Belle isn't a gelding.'

Sergeant O'Malley and Constable Perry exchanged a glance.

'I have to say that was my idea,' said the sergeant. 'I'd already had a little inkling about Ben Fuller, see. But if you'd suspected he was the thief, you might have given the game away.'

William thought over the sergeant's words, and Ben's. Mates should stick together.

'All right, I can see that, but I'm still not sure I understand. Why did he offer to come with me in the first place?'

'He'd heard we were coming to town. It was a good excuse for him to get away for a while.'

'So, in a way, I helped him. He really did *long for woodland and grove*, though not for the reasons I imagined.'

'What's that?'

'Oh, nothing, Sergeant, just a line from a poem. And now I see why he asked me to swap horses a little while ago. If he had got Belle back, he would have been able to make sure no one saw her who wasn't meant to.'

'You mean the coach driver?' said Jim Perry.

William nodded.

'But tell me, Mr Caldwell, what did you say when he asked you to swap?'

'I said no. That black gelding is a fine horse but I have grown fond of Belle.'

'Only I was thinking, Mr Caldwell. I'm going to have to take that horse of yours back to Bundaberg, I'm afraid. If you *had* agreed to swap horses, then you'd still have one — if you see what I mean.'

'I think I see what you're getting at, Constable,' said William. 'And it is most thoughtful of you, I'm sure. But as I say, I made no agreement with Ben Fuller.'

'Mr Caldwell is quite right, Jim,' said Sergeant O'Malley. 'But I've been thinking, too. The doctor says Ben Fuller should be all right to travel tomorrow. We two are going to have our work cut out just looking after our one prisoner without having an extra horse as well. Now we have to take your Belle of course — she's evidence, and she can carry Ben Fuller. But if Mr Caldwell was to agree to look after that black horse — just for a while — it would save us a powerful lot of aggravation.'

'What do you say, Mr Caldwell?' said the constable. 'Would you be willing to help two officers of the Queensland Colonial Police Service in the execution of their duties?'

'If you put it like that, Constable, I can hardly refuse.' William took a sip from his glass of water. 'But what'll happen to him — Ben Fuller, I mean.'

'It'll be the rope, for sure. The courts don't take kindly to robbing the mail — not to mention what happened in the cottage.'

And not to mention the murder of Ettie's father, thought William, and the rape of her mother, and of Mary's. But there was no use bringing that up. Nothing more was to be gained, and it would do neither Ettie nor Mary nor Billy Pike any good. Ben Fuller would hang. And would it be better or worse for him if his blind eyes could not see the steps up to the gallows, or the noose before it was put around his neck? There would be no Judge Barwick for Ben Fuller. He would know for sure the day and hour of his death.

William got to his feet. 'Thank you, gentlemen. Now, if you will excuse me, I have a visit to make.'

'Of course you do, Mr Caldwell,' said Pat O'Malley, giving him his broadest smile. 'And please, give the lady our very best regards.'

The next two days were spent packing up the camp site. There seemed little point in further research. He had the eggs, he had slides of the fertilised ovum. The full embryonic sequence? Well, perhaps the German fellow would come up with that; it didn't seem so important now. Harry Norton loaded up the wagon with his familiar grunts and grumbles, though now there were fewer stores it was a much lighter load than the one that had arrived eleven weeks before. William had thought to give Daraga and his family most of the camping equipment — surely they would appreciate sleeping on beds rather than the bare earth, under canvas rather than the sky? But no. All that he could persuade them to take, apart from food, were some ropes and knives. As for the billiard table — well, perhaps he might set it up in the Club Hotel, at least for a while.

When he arrived at the cottage the doctor was just leaving.

'I've done all I can, Caldwell. As I've said before, she is in no pain, nor will she be.'

'I thank you, Doctor Bennett. That is a great reassurance.'

Doctor Bennett put his hand briefly on William's shoulder then turned to go. 'Oh, Caldwell, there was one other thing that I noticed when I examined Mr Fuller.'

'The marks on his hands, the sailor's pennies?'

The doctor looked surprised. 'You saw them yourself?'

'Some time ago — though they meant nothing to me at the time.'

'You see what I mean, then, about how common they are. But I'm sure that in this case there is no ... connection.'

William paused. Should he tell the doctor what Billy Pike had recounted of the murder and rape and massacre? That it was Ben Fuller who raped Ettie Brown's mother — and that this might explain how Ettie had been born with the terrible disease? He looked back towards the cottage. 'Who knows where the truth lies, Doctor?'

The doctor smiled and shook his head. 'But at least we now know the truth about the platypus, eh, Caldwell? Fine work, damned fine work.'

'I haven't fully thanked you for your own contribution, Doctor Bennett.'

'My contribution? Oh, that was nothing. A bottle of champagne, no more — and a damned cheap one at that. I'm glad you got there first though, Caldwell. Couldn't have some continental fellow beating us. What would Sir Richard have said, eh?'

It was William's turn to smile.

'You leave these to me, Professor.' Donald swung the bundle of platypus skins onto the wagon. 'That rug'll be ready for you when you come through.'

The wagon was packed and ready and now Donald was heading back home.

'As I say, Donald, I don't know exactly when I'll be leaving here. But I'll pick up the rug on my way through to Bundaberg. You're sure I can't pay for your labour?'

The boy shook his head. 'Like I said, Professor, I'd like it to be a sort of going-away present. Oh, and here's another one.'

The boy took something from his pocket. 'Baking soda. That tin you found, that wasn't baking soda, you know. That was Epsom Salts. I never knew you could make damper with Epsom Salts, but I still reckon this is better.'

As he took the small packet William couldn't help smiling. So, it hadn't been the corned beef after all. Sorry, Aunt Agnes.

'I'm sure you're right, Donald, I'm sure you're right. And I'd like you to take these.' William took from his own pocket a small wooden box, a tin of oil and a rolled cloth. 'A sort of going-away present, too, you know. For future possums.'

Donald took the dissecting equipment from him with half-reluctant hands. 'Bloody oath, Professor.'

'Well, Caldwell, good luck,' said the doctor, putting down his bags beside the wagon. 'I'll write to you from Bundaberg and let you know what's been happening. Apparently we should get there in three days — if that bullock driver and my intemperate son don't get their hands on more rum.'

'Mr Norton will need to take a very long detour to find a bottle between here and Bundaberg, Doctor.'

'Humph,' said Doctor Bennett. 'But speaking of bottles, I might just have time to see if our landlord could provide something for my own journey. Master Gordon, would you mind seeing to my bags?'

'Right-ho, Doctor,' said Donald. 'Now, Professor, you're sure you're going to be all right?'

'Don't you worry, Donald, I'll be perfectly comfortable. I have my bed here at the hotel, and you know what a wonderful cook Mary is. She has promised to feed me just as well as you did.'

When the doctor returned moments later he was looking far from happy. 'Can't spare me any beer, he says, not now he's got a guest staying, and there's no champagne left. Can't sell me any beer: what kind of hotel is the man running?'

'An unusual one,' said William. 'A most unusual one.'

The doctor was still shaking his head as he climbed aboard the wagon and settled into his chair. The Army and Navy Store collapsible armchair had at last been unpacked from its crate and was lashed to the wagon just behind the driver's seat

'Now look, Caldwell, don't forget — if you need any more codeine, or anything else, let me know.'

'I shall, Doctor Bennett.'

'As I've said: it could be days, it could be weeks. May I say though, Caldwell, that I think it's a fine thing you're doing. Her sister is an excellent nurse, but with you here, too, Ettie Brown couldn't wish for better care.'

Harry Norton cracked the whip. As the wagon lumbered off into the dust, William walked slowly from the hotel and down the main street. He stopped at the little cottage gate. The jonquils were finished now, but the woodbine was still blooming, and the stocks. Their sweet scent would be wafting through the open windows into the bedroom where Ettie lay. He pushed open the gate and walked up the steps of the veranda to the front door. Without knocking, he turned the handle and went inside.

Historical Note

William Hay Caldwell was born at Portobello in Scotland in 1859. After gaining a first-class degree in natural science at Cambridge he worked briefly with Professor Francis Balfour. In 1883, this 'attractive young man, on the tall side of middle height and well made, with finely cut features and carefully twisted little fair moustache' travelled to Australia on the inaugural Balfour fellowship to investigate the reproductive biology of monotremes and lungfish. His telegram on 29 August 1884, 'MONOTREMES OVIPAROUS OVUM MEROBLASTIC', caused a scientific sensation.

William left Australia early in 1887, taking with him an Australian wife. On 17 March he presented his paper 'The Embryology of Monotremata and Marsupialia — Part I' to a meeting of the Royal Society in London. The Caldwells returned briefly to Cambridge before settling near Inverness, where William had inherited a paper mill from an uncle. 'Part II' of the paper was never completed. Their only son was killed in the First World War.

William Caldwell died at home in Scotland in 1941.